JAMES HARPER

DO UNTO OTHERS

This is a work of fiction. Names, characters, organizations, places, events and incidents are either products of the author's imagination or are used fictitiously. Any resemblance to actual persons, living or dead, or actual events is purely coincidental.

Copyright © 2023 James Harper

All rights reserved

No part of this publication may be reproduced, or stored in a retrieval system, or transmitted, in any form or by any means, electronic, mechanical, photocopying, recording, or otherwise, without express written permission of the publisher.

www.jamesharperbooks.com

ISBN: 9798856868790

PROLOGUE

5 YEARS AGO

Atchafalaya National Wildlife Refuge, Louisiana

'Sweet Jesus, it's going to crash.'

They stared in disbelieving horror, feeling like gawking tourists at the top of the Empire State Building watching helplessly as an American Airlines Boeing 767 plowed into the side of the north tower of the World Trade Center in New York City. Except there was no explosion as twenty thousand gallons of jet fuel ignited, no billowing black smoke and licking flames. Just an eerie silent glide into the canopy of trees, the outward calm belying the panic and fear inside.

They stood for what felt like forever on the wooden bridge spanning Alabama Bayou where only a moment ago he'd rattled the flimsy guard rail joking how one false step and they'd be lunch for the hungry 'gators waiting in the swirling brown water below.

Then he was on the move, years of training kicking in.

'C'mon.'

'Are you out of your mind? What do you think you can do?'

He stopped as if he'd run headlong into a tree, his brow as lined as its bark.

'Huh? Have you forgotten what we do for a living?'

The truth behind the accusation in his voice stinging more than the hordes of airborne biting insects could ever do.

Then he was racing away down the dusty trail, only his disappointment left behind.

Nothing to do but go after him, fight through the fear and growing dread.

He stopped again before diving into the mass of trees, his breath coming in heaving gasps, not so fit as he liked to think and brag about.

'You go back to the car. See if you've got a signal there. Call it in. Or drive to where you've got one.' The compassion in his voice as he offered an easy face-saving way out harder to bear than any accusation.

Screw that!

Fighting their way side by side through the dense undergrowth in the relentless strength-sapping heat, tripping and stumbling as gnarly roots and creeping vines snared their feet and branches clawed and scratched at their eyes, startled birds and unseen critters scattering ahead of them in their crazy flight towards God knows what.

Then stopping in their tracks at the sight of the carnage that greeted them, the light aircraft like a broken toy discarded by a spoiled child. Front end caved-in, one wing ripped off and half of the horizontal stabilizer missing, a gaping rent in the fuselage like an open knife wound. Twisted, snapped trees and flattened brush on all sides, a drifting cloud of white smoke lending the scene an ethereal otherworldly feel, the oily smell of gasoline fouling the forest air.

Like a private preview of hell itself.

'I'm going in.' Sounding like some comic-book superhero, the rousing music running through his head spurring him on banishing fear and thoughts of personal safety. 'They might still be alive.'

'Are you crazy? Can't you smell that? It might explode any minute.'

'We'll just stand here and watch them burn instead, shall we?'

Already fighting his way towards the wreckage. Turning to yell, *stay there*, like he was talking to a disobedient dog.

The plane creaked and shifted as he approached, twisted metal complaining. The rear passenger door had burst open on impact. He stuck his head inside. Told himself it was just another Saturday night call-out in downtown Lafayette. Blood and broken bones are the same anywhere whatever their cause.

Two men inside.

The pilot slumped forward onto the control wheel yoke, blood streaming down his face. Sunlight filtering through the shattered windshield drawing crazy patterns intermingling with the blood.

And a passenger. In the back, not up front with the pilot.

Also slumped forward, his arm stretched behind him as if he'd tried to hold onto his chair as they plowed into the trees.

Jesus Christ! He was handcuffed to it!

The cuffed man moaned as his rescuer scrambled up and leaned halfway in.

'Help me. Please.'

He recoiled at the sight of him. Not at the blood on his face, he was used to that. At the man himself. The sort of man honest citizens cross the street to avoid. The sort of man he strapped to a gurney every Saturday night. The loser in a knife fight. Or the man world-weary police officers bundled into the back of a cruiser for putting the loser in a condition to need that gurney.

The cuffed man moaned again.

'*Please*. The pilot has the key.'

He climbed all the way in, worked his way to the pilot. Still alive but unconscious, a ragged gash splitting his forehead, the white-gray of bone visible through the glistening sea of blood.

He dug frantically in the pilot's pockets, blood mingling with sweat making his fingers slick, the choking smell of aircraft fuel thick in the air.

'Hurry,' the man behind called, his voice growing weaker, more desperate.

At last, he found a ring of keys in the pilot's vest. The pilot moaned softly as he pulled them out, words barely distinguishable.

'*Por favor.*'

He hesitated, vital seconds lost, a flame of anger igniting in his belly.

They should both be in here helping.

He hurried back to the cuffed man. The guy pointed with his free hand at the keys.

'That one.'

He didn't have time to think how he knew. Slipped the key into the lock and set him free. The man slumped heavily, crying out in pain as his arm settled at an angle nature never intended.

Dislocated shoulder at the very least.

The freed man coughed at the smoke now filling the interior, mumbled through his pain.

'Help me up. I can't feel my left leg.'

Getting him to his feet wasn't easy, the injured man swaying unsteadily as the plane settled into the soft ground. Looking as if he might pass out any second.

'The pilot,' he said, starting towards him all the same.

'I'll get him. You get out.' Taking hold of his good arm, stopping him as he said it.

The guy laughed, an unhinged pain-wracked sound.

'What are you? A Good Samaritan?'

Aftermath of a plane crash or not, the man was deceptively strong for his size. He went to the pilot as if nothing heavier than a small child was hanging onto his arm trying to prevent him. And although he was neither big nor broad across the shoulders, his body blocked any line of sight as he ran his hands over the pilot's unresisting body.

What the hell was he doing? Stealing the pilot's wallet?

Suddenly there was a black Glock 43 pistol in the man's hand, not looking so shell-shocked now.

He watched open-mouthed, frozen by fear and revulsion at the unfolding nightmare, as the guy placed the barrel against the pilot's temple and pulled the trigger with as much emotion as if he was putting a dog that had been run over in the street out of its misery.

Then the guy turned, all trace of the grateful released man long gone, and now the gun was facing straight at his rescuer's chest.

And in his last moments before he went to meet his maker, the Good Samaritan understood the cynical wisdom in the old saying that no good deed goes unpunished.

1

Present day.

Evan Buckley groaned inwardly as he pushed through the door of the Jerusalem Tavern, his heart sinking at the realization that his evening had just changed. And not in a good way.

It wasn't because they'd strung a big banner over the bar —*No Beer*—or even that an escapee from the local lunatic asylum had snuck in and put Abba's *Dancing Queen* on the jukebox. It was because payback time had come earlier than he'd anticipated.

Or prayed.

Stan Fraser was sitting on his, Evan's, stool up at the bar. Looking like he owned the place and lowering the tone at the same time. He was watching Evan intently in the backbar mirror as he made his way across the room. As if he wanted to be ready to move quickly should Evan do what any right-minded person would, turned tail and ran.

Fraser was almost as wide as he was tall, as much flab on him as a bull rhinoceros in training for the mating season. Like that rhino, he'd have a surprising turn of speed for such an unathletic-looking man, one that would catch a lot of men unawares.

Evan put some bounce into his step, worked a look of pleasant surprise onto his face. As if his day had been completed by a chance encounter with an old friend. A deception that fooled Fraser for as long as it would take him to break a man's fingers.

Fraser had a world of experience in that field. A lifelong criminal, an old-school dinosaur who had yet to encounter a problem on his eventful and often-harsh journey through life that couldn't be resolved with violence. A palpable aura of menace exuded from his pores that triggered hard-wired primeval defense mechanisms in other men, caused them to look away. Or better still, get themselves someplace else.

Except Fraser had risen to a level in his chosen profession that meant he didn't need to dirty his own hands these days. Not unless he wanted to, and even the satisfaction from that was waning as he grew older. It was the job of his minders-cum-leg-breakers, one of whom was sitting to Fraser's left. In Kate Guillory's seat. A provocative choice, as was Fraser's, sitting in Evan's chair. He too was watching Evan approach in the backbar mirror.

Evan had come across Fraser's minders before. They were large and aggressive caricature thugs with shaved heads and pervasive tattoos that advertised a toxic mix of bigotry and ignorance and a penchant for hurting people for no reason other than being able to do so.

This man was different.

He almost looked normal, a worrying trait in a man who clearly isn't.

Aged around forty, he was dressed in a crumpled blue suit over an open-necked white shirt, his salt-and-pepper hair cut short in a 1950s-style flattop. He could've been Fraser's attorney, if it hadn't been for the soul patch—the gray tuft of hair under his bottom lip—that he sported. If people were the weather, he made Evan think of a wet winter's day with a biting wind that made you wish you'd worn a thicker coat. Or better still, not gone out at all.

He was drinking water. Evan got the impression nobody had called him a pussy for it. He figured a lot of overly-confident young bucks too full of themselves had learned the hard, aka painful, way that appearances are often deceptive.

The seating arrangements at the bar were proof of it. The seat to Fraser's right was empty. Evan took it, as he was meant to, glancing to his right as he did so. All the seats along the bar were occupied. Beside him were two college-football types, gym-toned pumped-up muscles straining their matching black T-shirts. A third clone was standing between them. Maybe they hadn't wanted to sit in a line along the bar like three wise monkeys. Conversation would be easier in the tighter group. Except Evan didn't think so. Not from the way the man without a seat glared at him as he sat down on the stool he clearly believed should be his own.

Unless it was the smell. Evan worked hard at not wrinkling his nose as he became aware of it. Eau de stale ashtray. It was coming from the man on the other side of Fraser. Now that he looked closer, Evan saw that the man's suit was flecked with ash.

He did his best to ignore it. Wondered how Fraser—these days a committed non-smoker—put up with it. Except all smells had their work cut out navigating the bends in Fraser's nose.

'Ban you from The Backroom for good behavior, did they?' Evan said.

Fraser chuckled in acknowledgement of the joke. The Backroom was a dive bar from where he ran his illegal operations—of which Evan knew nothing and was happy to keep that way. The last time Evan had come looking for him there, Fraser had made a similar crack about Evan being banned from the Jerusalem.

Fraser glanced to his left. The man seated beside him was still watching Evan in the backbar mirror as he sipped at his water.

'Landry here wanted to sit on Detective Guillory's stool. He's heard a lot about her.'

Evan was accustomed to Fraser's voice. Deep and croaky, the rasping aftermath of a partial laryngectomy rather than the electronic distortion of a full removal. The result of a two-pack-a-day habit, of too many nights spent in smoky bars before the interfering, overprotective do-gooders took away half the fun. He guessed the unnerving sound of it had further encouraged the three young men to leave a seat free for him at the bar.

'All good, I hope,' he said in response to what Landry might or might not have heard about Guillory.

Fraser shrugged, answered as if a different question had been asked.

'You do know her association with you isn't doing her career any good, don't you?'

'I'm worth it.'

'That's not what I hear.'

Fraser was clearly enjoying himself killing two birds with one stone. Insulting Evan in a good-natured way, while at the same time demonstrating the depth of his inside knowledge of the local police department.

It went to the core of why Fraser was here, in Evan's bar, sitting on Evan's stool. They'd traded favors back and forth in the past. The last occasion had been when Evan asked him to make discreet enquiries of those police contacts of whom he was so proud about whether a detective called Tony Giordano was on the take. Fraser had reported back that the guy was so clean his shit sparkled. Evan had been in his debt ever since.

That chicken had now arrived firmly home.

There were no prizes for guessing what he'd soon be doing for Fraser.

'Arlo,' he said.

Fraser nodded, sipped at his drink. Whiskey, as always.

'Yeah.'

'Why now?'

'I'm getting old.'

'You've been doing that for years. Why now?'

Fraser laughed out loud, slapped him on the back. A lot like a grizzly bear would. Ribs flexing, lungs compacting.

'That's what I like about you, Buckley. You don't care what you say to anybody.'

Evan smiled self-consciously as if Fraser had paid him a compliment.

'It just sort of slips out.'

'I've heard that's what Detective Guillory says, too.'

Evan chose to ignore the smutty innuendo, asked his question a third time.

'Why now?'

Fraser swiveled on his stool to look directly at him, a crease in his brow. The young guy standing up who had been staring at Fraser as he talked, turned quickly away.

'Does it matter?'

'Maybe. You might have received a postcard from him.'

'Then I wouldn't need you.'

Wouldn't that be nice, Evan thought and had the sense not to say—even if Landry was looking at him as if he'd read Evan's mind.

Arlo was Fraser's son. Evan had come across the girl he'd run away with—Eleanor Fields—in the course of one of his investigations. That knowledge had filtered back to Fraser through his connections in the police department and caused Fraser to come looking for him. Evan's confirmation through Eleanor that Arlo was alive and hadn't been abused, killed and buried in a shallow grave by an itinerant child molester as Fraser had always believed, put Fraser in his debt.

Except it hadn't been good news all the way.

Evan had been obliged to tell Fraser that his son had run away not only to be with the girl he believed he loved at the time, but to escape from his father's influence. So as not to slip into a life of crime, allow himself to be groomed to take over the reins from the old man when the time came. Luckily, that disclosure—*you're a shit dad*—had been mitigated by a surprising degree of self-awareness on Fraser's part.

Trouble was, the bad news hadn't ended there.

Arlo and Eleanor had gone their separate ways as they entered adulthood, an amicable split as they grew apart. As a result, she hadn't known anything of Arlo's current whereabouts. Or even if he was still alive, for that matter.

Evan hoped he was.

Not only because nobody wants to see a young life cut short, but because Fraser was eminently capable of shooting the messenger if he wasn't.

Hence the weight that had settled on him when he saw Fraser at the bar.

Fraser sipped his drink and it seemed to Evan that he was very ill at ease, very unlike his usual self. If Fraser hadn't been Fraser, Evan would've teased out more details. Because something was lurking in the background.

But Fraser *was* Fraser, so that was the end of that—remarks about saying anything to anybody notwithstanding. Then it came to him. Fraser was embarrassed about what he was about to say.

It took a while, until eventually he came out with it.

'I didn't get a postcard. I got a call.' He immediately backtracked. 'I don't know for sure that it was from Arlo. The phone rang. An unidentified number. As soon as I answered, they hung up. I tried calling back. No answer. The next time I tried, it was dead. People say don't fix it if it ain't broken. I say don't waste your time trying to fix something that *is* broken. The relationship with Arlo was broken so I let it go for all these years. It's when suddenly I think it isn't too late after all that I want to do something about it.'

Now Evan understood the reason for Fraser's embarrassment. Here he was, the big bad criminal, the man honest citizens crossed the road to avoid, reduced by his personal loss to clutching at straws. A single call from an unknown number—very likely a wrong number—was all it took to turn him into a worried father like any other. Just another man with his own personal cross to bear, no heavier nor lighter than anybody else's.

'What makes you think it was Arlo?'

'You got kids?'

Fraser knew that he didn't. It was simply the way he chose to phrase his inability to provide an adequate explanation. And to remind Evan that as a man without them, he hadn't earned the right to question another man about his children.

Evan shook his head.

'Then I can't tell you,' Fraser said. 'I know, is all.'

Evan didn't argue or press him. He certainly didn't point out that wanting something so badly that you ached was not a guaranteed means of achieving it. He also knew the spiteful tricks Fraser's own mind played on him in the small hours of the morning. The questions that would pop unbidden into his consciousness as he lay wide awake staring at the ceiling.

Was it Arlo and my voice was sufficient to make him hang up?

Or has the man who killed him found his phone and is now calling numbers at random?

Evan got out his own phone.

'Send me the number.'

Fraser's phone was out in a heartbeat. Evan's pinged a moment later. He dialed the number Fraser had sent him.

Fraser mouthed *Dead?* as Evan put the phone to his ear. Evan nodded.

'Have you got a picture you can send me?'

Fraser looked at the phone lost in the expanse of his large hand and laughed, a self-deprecating sound at his lack of technical savvy.

'Not on this thing, I haven't.'

He got out his wallet and fished out an old photograph. Studied it a long while before handing it over.

It showed a dark-haired teenager already more a man than a boy, tall and starting to fill out. He was standing in the back of a boat holding a good-sized largemouth bass, a proud smile on his face.

'He gets his looks from his mother,' Fraser said, 'before you start blowing smoke up my ass saying what a good-looking kid he is.'

It was true, even if Evan hadn't been about to rub Fraser's ego and say so. He took a picture of it, then made notes as Fraser gave him his son's basic details, as well as telling him all the things Evan could see with his own two eyes from the photograph.

Then it was time to waste his breath.

'What can you tell me that might give me somewhere to start?'

It was vague to the point of being less than worthless. Besides, he was only going through the motions. He knew exactly where he was going to start. But Fraser would expect more than a quick, *leave it to me*. It was also pointless by definition. A man whose son runs away because he's scared of turning out like his father is not going to have access to the boy's heart and mind.

Fraser shook his head to confirm it. Eyes down, his words damning all fathers, not only himself.

'We didn't talk.'

'What about his mother?'

Again, the headshake.

'Is it okay for me to talk to her?'

That made Fraser smile, a sadness in his eyes behind the amusement.

'I'd like to see you try.' He pointed upwards, eyes also raised to the ceiling. 'She died a month before Arlo ran away.'

Evan nodded without saying anything. No meaningless insincere platitude about being sorry a decade after the event. But it made sense. The future for the boy looked bleak with his mother gone, his only ally against his overbearing father. More difficult for him to resist his father's efforts to push him into a life that scared and appalled him.

Evan glanced at Landry in the backbar mirror as a random irreverent thought went through his mind.

Did you have anything to do with it?

The guy stared back at him as if he'd read his mind. Then it was as if he passed it on to Fraser, by osmosis, perhaps. Whatever it was, Fraser felt the need to unburden himself. He swallowed thickly, took a sip of whiskey to ease the words.

'Janet had pancreatic cancer. It tore me apart watching her suffer. I've done some terrible things in my life and I'll burn in hell for them. At times I thought the monster, the so-called loving God up there'—pointing again at the ceiling—'made her suffer for my sins. At the end, all she wanted was for me to put her out of her misery.' He lifted his hands, held them flat side-by-side and pushed down into the bar top. 'A pillow over her face and it's done. She didn't need to say the words. I knew. And I couldn't do it. So I watched her die slowly and in pain instead.'

It seemed to Evan that the whole bar had fallen silent. A mark of respect in the face of Fraser's own pain. Or dumbstruck at the revelation of human weakness in a man people crossed the street to avoid.

In reality it was only Evan reluctantly invited into a private place with Fraser while his unnerving companion, Landry, watched over them.

In the silence that followed he waved at the Jerusalem's manager, Kieran, for another round. He didn't know if Fraser had more to say, but he sure as hell looked as if what he'd already said had left him needing the emotional support that lives in alcohol.

The arrival of the drinks a minute later followed by Kieran's hasty retreat to the far end of the bar snapped Fraser out of his reverie. Less of the maudlin in his voice, too.

'I told you last time about that bartender. He needs to work on being more friendly.'

'He's worried you'll offer him a job at The Backroom if he is.'

Fraser coughed out a wry laugh.

'Always got an answer. I think I told you that last time, too. Your mouth will get you in trouble one day.'

Guillory's astonished face popped into Evan's mind, her incredulous squeak in his ears.

What's with the future tense?

He was thinking how and whether to ask the question that was in his head when Fraser turned away from him towards Landry. Something passed hands. Then Fraser gave him his attention again.

'Don't think I don't know how unfair this is. All I did for you was ask a couple people some questions. Now here I am sending you running around all over the country looking for Arlo. So I'm paying you.' He held up a large callused hand before Evan could object. 'Don't worry, we're square as far as owing favors goes. Accepting the job takes care of that. But I'm paying you, too.'

Evan hadn't been aware that the option to decline had been available. It was academic now, as a fat manila envelope landed in his lap.

'That'll keep you going for a while,' Fraser said.

Evan didn't inquire how much the envelope contained. That would be rude. Nor did he ask whether the IRS had already taken their share. That would be stupid.

And to turn Fraser's money down would be stupider still. An insult. He worked the envelope into his pocket, then avoided the question in his head once again, asking another instead.

'Why did you bring Landry with you?' He patted his bulging pocket. 'Getting old or not, you don't need a minder just because you're carrying a wad of cash around.'

Fraser smiled broadly at the compliment.

'No, I don't. I wanted you to meet each other.'

Meet didn't seem an appropriate word for sitting three feet away from a man who did nothing but stare impassively at your reflection in the mirror. However, it wasn't his place to lecture Fraser on his choice of words. Instead, he leaned forwards, nodded at Landry. *How-do.* Landry nodded back. Evan got the impression that in Landry's world it was now as if they'd known each other since elementary school.

'Why?' he said to Fraser.

'In case you need any assistance.'

Evan looked at Landry again. The point of the exercise being to demonstrate that he was aware of the nature of the assistance a man like Landry might provide.

'Do you have any reason to think I'll be needing any?'

Fraser shook his head firmly.

'No.'

It had the ring of absolute truth about it. The subtext of what he said next revealed another undeniable truth.

'I want you to keep in touch just in case.'

Evan translated: *He's keeping tabs on you.*

'I gave him your number,' Fraser said. Then to Landry, 'Send him your number, Landry.'

Evan's phone beeped and he couldn't help wondering if another of Fraser's associates wasn't grubbing around under his car at this very moment fixing a tracker to it.

Fraser downed the last of his drink in preparation for leaving. It was Evan's last chance to ask the question on his mind.

'What if I find Arlo and he doesn't want to be found?'

Fraser didn't even have to think about it. He prodded Evan with a thick finger where the fat envelope sat in his pocket.

'I'm paying you to find my boy. Not to play at being some crackpot shrink telling me I can't see my boy because I didn't hug him enough when he was a kid. You find him, you let me know, or you and me are going to have a big problem.'

It wasn't necessary to say that the problem would come in the guise of Landry.

2

Evan shouldn't have asked the question.

He'd wanted to get a feel for how far Fraser's supposed slide into mellow middle age, his desire to put right old wrongs, extended. Whether he would've given a dismissive wave, his voice resigned as he told Evan that if that was the way his son wanted it, to never see or hear from his father again, he'd respect his decision.

Obviously not.

It had been stupid to ask, nonetheless. Worse, had he not delayed Fraser and his dour sidekick for an extra minute or two, they'd have been gone by the time Guillory turned up.

As it was, they almost bumped into each other, Guillory's fault as she made her way across the room, head-down, concentrating on her phone.

Except from where Evan sat, it looked as if Fraser deliberately stepped in front of her. He beamed at her as she recoiled.

'Detective Guillory! We were just talking about you.'

Guillory scowled at him as if she'd stepped in a giant talking dog turd while she wasn't paying attention to where she was going. Fraser carried happily on before she recovered her composure, extending his hand towards his companion.

'This is Landry. He's been keeping your seat warm for you.'

Guillory gave Landry the same icy glare she'd been using on Fraser, her voice like a cold wind blowing through the crowded bar.

'That's very kind. I'll be sure to return the favor and keep a cell warm for you.' Then to Fraser, 'Yours is always available, Mr. Fraser. Any time you feel like dropping in. Now, don't let me keep you.'

She stepped to the side, staring at the two men's backs as they shouldered their way through the throng.

Evan took the opportunity to lean over the bar and grab a damp cloth that Kieran used to wipe the bar top. He was busy scrubbing Guillory's seat with it when she turned up.

'I hope that's got bleach on it. In fact, don't waste your time. I'll fetch a Hazmat suit from the car.'

The game over, he swapped the seats around so that they both had a dry stool to sit on. He considered offering the still-wet one to the young man standing with his friends, thought better of it.

Guillory sniffed a couple times as she climbed onto the stool. 'What's that smell?'

'You mean the one like someone pissed in a full ashtray?'

'Yeah. Exactly like that.' Still sniffing.

'It's Fraser's minder.'

'*Jesus*. I'd rather break down the door of an apartment with a month-old dead body in it. What did he want? Fraser, I mean.'

Evan had come across situations like this before. Cases in which the unvarnished truth really was the only option—even though a predictable and negative response was guaranteed.

'He wants me to find his son.'

Despite asking the question, she hadn't yet moved past her

annoyance at almost colliding with Fraser. It lent a sharp edge to her tone.

'He said you'd been talking about me.'

This was most definitely not another of those truth-called-for moments. Tell her how Fraser claimed their relationship was jeopardizing her career. She was irritated enough by the quick exchange with Fraser as it was. Besides, in her heart, she knew it anyway. He wasn't sure she always agreed he was worth the sacrifice. Glossing over it was the way to go.

'It was nothing. Joking about sitting on your stool, that sort of thing. I wish it had been all about you, and not about finding his son.'

She was well aware of Evan and Fraser's history, both the favor trading, as well as the background events leading up to it.

'He's the one who ran away with . . .' She scrunched her face, then shook her head. 'I can't remember her name.'

'Eleanor Fields. And his son's called Arlo.'

Unfortunately for him, her memory was a whole lot better when it came to remembering exactly what Fraser had recently done for him. Her brow creased at the injustice of it, a note of indignation entering her voice.

'That sounds very unfair. All he did for you was ask his dirty contacts a few questions. Now he wants you to traipse around the country looking for his son. Who, if he's got any sense, has changed his name six times and spent every penny he's earned or stolen on plastic surgery to disguise himself.'

She was seconds away from putting it all together when Kieran arrived with their beers, a brief stay of execution but a welcome one, nonetheless. This time Kieran hung around, fixing Evan with a disapproving scowl.

'I'm going to have to ban you, Evan, if you keep bringing that criminal and his thugs in here.'

Guillory joined in, pointing at the stool Evan had wiped down.

'You're going to have to buy a new stool, as well. Two of them, in fact.'

It wasn't worth pointing out that Fraser had been there first. And good luck to anyone who tried to tell him he wasn't welcome. Evan slipped off his seat and left them to it. At the jukebox he spent a couple of minutes browsing, settled on Ry Cooder's *My Girl Josephine*.

Kieran was busy serving other customers when he got back. Guillory was equally busy eyeing him up as if she'd caught a known pervert loitering outside the ladies' bathroom.

He took his stool nodding along to the music as he waited dutifully for the axe to fall. Her tone when it did was similar to the one she'd used on Fraser and Landry.

Frosty.

'How much, Evan?'

'How much what?'

Stupid, but *hey-ho*.

'How much is he paying you to even the favors up?'

He held up a finger to quiet her, his ear cocked towards the music.

'Listen to that slide guitar—'

'*Evan!* How much?'

'I haven't looked. I thought it would be rude to count it in front of him.'

She nodded approvingly as if she was responsible for his good manners.

'You didn't want to hurt Mr. Fraser's delicate feelings. Embarrass him in front of the help.'

'Exactly.'

'Or he'd have asked his creepy friend to break your legs.'

'Very possibly. Arms too, if he'd seen any disappointment on my face.'

She made a *gimme here* gesture with her fingers. He extracted the envelope from his pocket, handed it over. She tipped forward as if he'd dropped a bowling ball into her hands, then opened it, flicked through the sheaf of notes. Let out a low whistle.

'I'm in the wrong job.'

'Funny, I feel the same way. But for different reasons.'

'At least you're getting paid well.'

'I need to. The price of failure will be a lot worse than a slight hiccup in my promotion prospects.'

She handed the envelope back. Made a point of rubbing her fingers together as if they were coated with sticky grime.

'I feel like I should go to the bathroom, scrub my hands for an hour. You think Kieran's got any of that bleach left?'

'And here I was about to offer to buy you dinner with it at *EWE*.'

It was her favorite restaurant, not a female sheep. He couldn't remember what it was actually called, but *Eye-Wateringly-Expensive* fit the bill better than whatever fancy French name was written above the door.

'Actually no, thank you. I'd rather lick the men's room floor clean.'

He had the good sense not to extend his hand in that direction, *be my guest*. They lapsed briefly into silence, Evan wondering if the job that had been foisted on him was going to cause a problem between them.

'Are you going to talk to me while I'm working for—'

'The enemy?'

'Don't you mean Satan?'

She shook her head firmly, a look on her face that Satan would've given his right arm to perfect.

'No, that's—'

It was as if the heavens had parted, the clear radiance of enlightenment shining down upon her. It put a nasty glint of suspicion in her narrowed eyes to accompany the note of barely-suppressed disbelief in her voice.

'When you say *talk to you*, what you really mean is do all the legwork for you.'

He consulted with his beer for a long moment, there not being much he could say to counter the accusation.

Business as usual, while true, wasn't recommended at this juncture. Then an idea came to him. A means to deflect the focus away from himself prompted by her exchange with Fraser and his sidekick.

'I bet you're going to look up Landry whether I ask you to or not.'

She nodded, good point.

'He *was* kind of creepy. Not one of Fraser's normal knuckle-draggers. Why'd he bring him along? Apart from helping to carry all that dirty cash, of course.'

'He's my minder. Fraser wanted us to get to know each other.'

She tried the words out in her mouth, an attempt to bridge the gap between that concept and a man like Landry.

'Uh-huh. And how did that go?'

'He didn't say a word. Staring at me in the mirror the whole time. Giving me the evil eye. Too much of it and you'd want to break your own legs, save him the trouble.'

He saw her thinking through her own brief encounter with the man before she proved him right.

'I'm going to look into him, after all.' He was smiling *told you so* to himself when a rigid digit appeared quivering an inch off the end of his nose. 'But don't think I'm searching every available database for Stan Fraser's son for you.'

He shrugged like it was no skin off his nose. He'd achieved what he set out to do. A foot in the door. The kindling of her curiosity. Just as she knew him, he knew her too well. She wouldn't be able to help herself

She turned to face him, elbow resting on the bar, a small furrow in her brow. It was a pose he knew well, one that signified that the flame of curiosity had already caught.

'Okay, what's the plan?'

'First thing, talk to Eleanor Fields.'

'Makes sense. And after she tells you, sorry, she hasn't heard from him in six years?'

'Don't be so negative.'

'*Realistic* is the word you're looking for. What else?'

'He got a phone call from an unknown number he thinks might have been Arlo. The caller hung up as soon as he answered.'

Her response was swift and to the point, made him feel like he'd dialed *D for Derision*.

'A wrong number. Okay. Next?'

He thought back to the conversation with Fraser, the strange turn it had taken and the surprising personal admissions he'd shared.

'There's something not right about the mother, Janet.'

'Being married to him would do that to a person.'

He shook his head, pointed upwards as Fraser had.

'She's dead.'

'Okay.'

'Getting more interested?'

'All I said was *okay*.'

'Yeah, but it's a different *okay* to when I say I want another beer.'

She worked hard at not saying *okay* again, asked a difficult question instead.

'What's not right about the mother? You mean her death was suspicious?'

'I'm not sure . . .' He recounted what Fraser had told him about his wife's illness. How she'd supposedly wanted him to put her out of her misery, an act of mercy that he'd been unable to perform for her.

Guillory interrupted before he could finish.

'No, I'm not having it. You're trying to make it sound like he's actually human, with feelings.'

'He's not so bad.'

She pulled a face. Mainly pity. As if he'd invited a cockroach onto his dinner plate because it had a bad leg and looked hungry.

'Arlo ran away shortly after his mother died,' he said. 'I can understand why he didn't want to be left alone with his old man. A criminal. I still got the feeling there was more to it.'

She held up her hands in surrender, her voice weary.

'Tell you what. I'll check if there's anything in the system about it first thing in the morning. Happy now?'

'Uh-huh.' He patted his bulging pocket provocatively. 'You've definitely earned yourself dinner.'

'Not funny, Evan. I already feel like I'm working for Stan Fraser.'

He put his hand on her arm, felt her stiffen at the patronizing gesture.

'Look on the bright side. If there is something suspicious, it could come back to bite Fraser on the ass. You'll get all the credit.'

Now it was her turn to be condescending, her tone rather than a physical gesture. As if she was explaining the bad news about Santa Claus and the Tooth Fairy to a small child.

'Things like that only happen in Buckley La-la Land, Evan, not the real world. Since we're talking about fairy stories, what are you going to do if you actually find him? What if the kid wants to remain lost? Are you going to turn his life back ten years and undo everything he's done to distance himself from his old man? If he'd wanted to build bridges, he'd have made contact himself. A wrong number who hangs up doesn't count.' She tapped his pocket where the envelope sat, more gently than Fraser had. 'I'd want a lot more than what's in there to make a decision like that.'

'I asked him the same thing.'

She rolled her hand, keep it coming.

'He reminded me who I'm working for. He didn't need to remind me it's the real reason Landry will be keeping tabs on me.'

She sucked air in through her teeth, the sharp hiss beloved of motor mechanics the world over.

'Rather you than me, although that's true most of the time. Maybe you better spend his money while you still can. Let's get dinner after all.'

'Sure? You might die of indigestion.'

She jabbed her finger at the floor, diametrically opposed to where Janet Fraser now supposedly rested in peace.

'Then I'll see you downstairs after you've given Stan the bad news.'

3

Eleanor Fields wasn't pleased to hear from him.

It was unfair, if understandable, and it had nothing to do with the early hour at which he called her the next morning. People are eager to distance themselves from any reminder of their own faults and failings—and in Eleanor's case, mistakes with grave legal consequences should they come to light, not least of which being the loss of her liberty.

Because Eleanor had shot and killed a man she believed had murdered her younger brother and planned to kill her to protect himself. Evan had helped her evade justice for that killing for reasons that he wasn't sure he fully understood—beyond the fact that the guy had it coming and Eleanor's young life had been blighted by the death of her brother.

As an added twist, one of fate's little quirks, the unregistered Sig Sauer pistol that Evan had used to make it appear that Eleanor had acted in self-defense had been supplied by none other than his new best friend and unwelcome client, Stan Fraser.

So, Eleanor owed him.

She just didn't want to be reminded of it. She wanted to meet him even less. Reluctantly, she agreed to meet for breakfast at the Rusty Spoon diner.

She was already there when he turned up. A situation that had less to do with her being closer to the diner when he called than a desire to get it over with as quickly as possible. She was sitting at a table in the window picking at her fingernails and looking very ill at ease, a cup of coffee untouched on the table in front of her.

With anyone else he'd have asked how she'd been since he last saw her, how things were at home. That would only have increased her unease. Like Arlo, she'd run away from home primarily to escape from the claustrophobic influence of her father. Unlike Arlo, her father, Wesley Fields, was an old-school fire-and-brimstone preacher who'd have been viewed as having a broomstick up his ass even back in the Victorian era. Evan knew exactly which one of them he'd have taken his chances with. As a result, a casual, *how's your dad?* wasn't going to help any.

She shook her head at the waitress when she came to take their orders. Evan over-compensated and ordered enough for both of them. Eggs, bacon, link sausages, home fries and anything else that was lying around unwanted in the kitchen, plus toast and juice. Working for a known criminal had given him an appetite. He only hoped it wasn't the first of a rapidly-diminishing number of last suppers.

In line with passing on breakfast and making it clear she wasn't in the market for pleasantries, inane or otherwise, she got straight to it.

'I'm guessing this is about Arlo.'
'Uh-huh.'
'I suppose his father hired you to find him?'

The way her mouth twisted downwards when she said *his father* wasn't an encouraging start. Although it did mean there might be a wealth of insightful anecdotes, albeit negative, waiting to be unleashed.

'For my sins, yeah.'

'Why?'

'Why what? Why does he want to find him, or why me?'

'Both.'

His coffee turned up as he thought about the best way to answer. Once more the truth seemed to fit the bill—or an edited version of it.

'He wasn't able to put his finger on it. He's getting old, that sort of thing.'

She looked at him as if he'd spat in her coffee.

'What? He wants to make his peace with him before he dies? What a load of crap. Why you?'

'Because I owe him.'

It wasn't what she was expecting. She took a sip of her coffee for the first time, studied him over the rim of the cup. He chose not to volunteer anything, waited for her to ask.

'What for?'

That one was easy.

'You don't want to know.'

'That sounds bad.'

He shrugged, thinking, *not as bad as what I did for you.*

Her mouth twitched. Then she took another sip of coffee to stop herself from pushing him harder. She'd seen the determination in his eyes to not tell her. And he saw the connection made in hers. The reluctant acceptance that a man who'd broken the law for her out of little more than pity and a perhaps-misplaced sense of fairness was allowed his privacy.

His breakfast arrived at that point, a convenient means of moving them on from the brief awkward silence that ensued. He dug in, waited to see if she volunteered anything. Which she did soon enough and nothing he wasn't expecting.

'I haven't heard from Arlo, if that's what you wanted to know. Not for years. Certainly not since...'

He nodded as he chewed. An acknowledgement that he understood she was referring to their short history, their shared shame. It wasn't to be taken as an indicator that he believed her. He figured she'd only ever heard negative complaints and whining from Arlo about the problems of growing up with his father. As a result, she would go to great lengths to protect him from his old man. She might owe Evan for what he'd done for her, but it didn't outweigh the feelings, residual or otherwise, she had for the young man with whom she'd run away to make a new life.

He speared a link sausage with his fork, then took the conversation in a direction she couldn't have anticipated.

'Tell me about Arlo's mom. She died right before he ran away with you, didn't she?'

It did the trick as far as surprising her went. She stared at him as if he'd pulled off a Halloween mask to reveal Janet Fraser herself underneath come back from the dead.

'What about her?'

'Did you know her?'

'Not really.'

'Did Arlo talk about her?'

'Some.'

Although the question had surprised her, it hadn't shocked her into a fit of volubility.

'What was his relationship with her like?'

Eleanor thought about it a moment, toying with her cup as she did so.

'Normal.'

'So it wasn't like his relationship with his father?'

She shook her head, still concentrating on her cup, her tone mocking.

'Obviously he wasn't scared of turning into his mom.'

'Was he upset when she died?'

Stupid question, but the aim hadn't been to get an answer. He wanted a reaction. Which he got, the first he'd provoked in her. She came right back at him.

'What do you think?'

He shrugged, talked through a mouthful of food to be deliberately dismissive.

'No idea. You've told me nothing to allow me to form an opinion. You've said their relationship was *normal,* whatever that's supposed to mean. Just because he had a better relationship with her than he did with his old man, it doesn't mean it was good. *Normal* might mean she was always on his case because he was a typical, sullen, pain-in-the-ass teenager for all I know.'

She did a pretty good impersonation of sullen herself. Staring at the table top, saying nothing. Not meeting his eyes.

He got more personal, pointing at her with his fork.

'You think I'm a pain in the ass that you have to humor because I kept you out of jail for killing a man. Maybe you're only here because you're worried that if you'd said no, I'd threaten to tell the cops what really happened. And you're pissed off because you were hoping you'd never hear from me again and suddenly I've gone and ruined your day.' He reached across the table, tapped her cup with his fork. *Ding.* 'But guess what? If I hadn't lied for you and planted that gun for you, every day of your life would be a whole lot worse than having to sit here and listen to me asking questions you don't want to answer. I don't suppose there'd be many questions from the bull dykes in the shower block. Maybe you'd prefer that.'

The outburst took him by surprise as much as it did her. Too many food additives in the link sausages, perhaps. He pushed his plate away, dialed it down with an equal softening of his tone.

'I'm in a difficult situation, as well. You know what Arlo's old man is like?' He waited until she nodded before continuing. 'What would you have done in my place when he asked me to find his son? Tell him, sorry Stan, I've got a busy day lined up. I've gotta pick my nose and scratch my ass. Or maybe I tell him, you find your own son, you criminal piece-of-shit. I hope he's dead when you do.'

Her head came up, all signs of sullen long gone. Looking like she wanted to yell at him but didn't know where to start. He stopped her with a raised hand before she could.

'Let's assume he didn't shoot me on the spot or get one of his minders to break my arms and legs. I've caught him on a good day. He's feeling mellow. So he says to me, uh-uh, not so fast you douchebag PI, because he might be mellow but that doesn't mean he's cleaned up his language. Then he says, you're forgetting that you owe me. I pretend that I've forgotten like you're trying to pretend you can't remember owing me.' He slapped the table hard, the sudden blow rattling their cups. 'And he slaps the table like that. Sticks his face in mine and asks me, are you forgetting I gave you that unregistered gun? The one you used to make it look like Eleanor Butter-Wouldn't-Melt Fields shot that guy in self-defense, didn't straight out murder him because she was having a bad day.'

He threw himself back in his seat, drained, mouth dry from all the talking. Took a sip of now-cold coffee. Then summed it up in a lot less words since Eleanor had been struck dumb with her mouth hanging open like she was catching flies.

'So, yeah, I'm in a tight spot with Arlo's old man because of what I did for you. And it doesn't stop there. Because if I find him, I have to decide if I'm going to tell Stan. My problem is I'm not a heartless monster who's happy to turn Arlo's world upside-down and send him back to what he's spent half his life running away from. Any bright ideas about how to tell Stan Fraser *no* would be much appreciated at this point, by the way.'

Her phone rang during the silence that followed. She ignored it, let it ring out, which was a good thing. For her. She wouldn't have to waste more time and money buying a new one after he snatched it out of her hands and stomped it.

Trouble was, she still wasn't talking. He waved to the waitress for a refill, tried again after she'd topped them up and cleared away his plate.

'This isn't a threat, Eleanor, even if it sounds like one. Stan Fraser is determined to find Arlo. Now that he's decided it's time, he's not going to give up. If I fail, he'll try himself. Where do you think he's going to start?'

A little mouse answered for her.

'With me.'

'Yep. And he'll do more than tell you a few unpalatable home truths if he thinks you're holding back on him.'

'But I'm *not*.'

He shied away, held up his hands at the force of the word *not*.

'*Hey!* It's not me you have to convince. Trouble is, people like Stan never look at themselves when things go tits up. I never asked him, but maybe he blames you for encouraging Arlo to run away in the first place. Anyway, all this coffee's getting to me. I've gotta go to the men's room. If you decide to leave while I'm in there, you don't have to worry. I won't come after you or call you again. But it means I'm more likely to fail. At the moment you're all I've got. No pressure.'

He felt her eyes on him all the way to the men's room like he was the last lifeboat from a sinking ship disappearing into the distance.

It was both good and bad when he got back from pretending to take a leak.

The good was that she was still sitting at the table.

But if he was hoping that she'd look like a different person, the tortured look on her face of someone who can't wait to unburden themselves of the terrible secrets they've carried around for far too long, he was disappointed.

If she looked anything at all, it was resigned. And a little scared that she wasn't going to be able to help him.

Despite that, he was confident she'd be more responsive to direct questions.

'Did he change his name at all?'

'Not while we were together. Why go to the trouble and the expense when you've got a name like Fraser? There must be millions of them in the country. Besides, he didn't think his old man would actually come looking for him. Or spend any of his dirty money getting someone else to do it.'

The remark echoed Guillory's reaction of the previous evening—although it hadn't stopped her from eating her expensive dinner. It went with the territory when you worked for a man like Fraser. That wasn't to say it didn't rankle, the implication that by accepting it, he was as dirty as the money itself.

'Has he got a middle name he might be going by?'

He thought it was a reasonable question, but it made her laugh—in a very dismissive, scornful way.

'Yeah. You want to guess what it is?'

After her reaction, it was a no brainer.

'Stanley?'

'Yeah. He hated it. If he'd changed any of his names, that would've been the first to go. He'd ask people to call him *shithead* before he used it.'

'Where were you right before you went your separate ways?'

'Brownsville, Texas.' She shook her head immediately before he even made a note of it. 'We'd moved around so much before that. There's no reason to think he wouldn't have continued doing the same. I did. Brownsville sure as hell wasn't anywhere either of us wanted to stay.'

'Can you remember the address?'

He got another solid headshake.

'It wouldn't matter if I could. We'd fallen behind on the rent. We snuck out one night without paying. No way were we leaving a forwarding address.'

'Was there anywhere in particular he used to talk about, places he'd always wanted to go?'

She shook her head yet again. Not only a negative response but to underline what she said next.

'He won't come back even if you find him.'

'I realize that's a possibility.'

'It's more than a possibility. It's a fact.'

The forcefulness of the assertion was at odds with the resigned apologetic delivery of the previous negative answers. For now, he resisted the urge to press her. She'd only clam up again.

They spent a while longer with him asking questions and her failing to supply adequate answers until he was as bored of it as she was. At one point she admitted that although the split had been by mutual agreement, it hadn't been one hundred percent amicable. The result was an unspoken pact between them that there wouldn't be any contact in the future, no catching up and reminiscing about their wild times on the road together.

His last question was more of a statement, a confirmation of what he already knew or had guessed.

'It was his mom's death that finally made him take the plunge and go.'

He was expecting a quick nod, which he got. He wasn't expecting the look on her face as if he'd produced Stan Fraser and two of his evil-looking henchmen out of a hat. He almost turned to look behind him.

'What?'

He wanted to shake her as she stared back at him without answering. Once more he forced himself to give her time, hard as it was as the knowledge of what she was about to say grew in his own mind.

'It had nothing to do with not wanting to be left alone with his dad without his mom,' she said. 'He told me his dad killed her.'

4

EVAN DIDN'T THINK HE WAS ANY MORE PARANOID THAN THE NEXT man. Despite that, he felt that he was being punished as he said goodbye to Eleanor outside the Rusty Spoon diner.

He was feeling guilty for being harder on her than either of them would have expected. Bullying, and in the process frightening her. Sometimes it was necessary in order to move forward. A small sacrifice in the interests of the greater good. The government knew all about things like that. As did the citizens called upon to make those sacrifices without their prior consent.

Except, as is often the case with governments on a much grander scale, it hadn't worked out the way it was meant to. It was hard to comprehend that from a starting position of no information or leads whatsoever, he'd actually gone backwards. It had to be a record of some kind. *Ergo*, he was being punished for giving Eleanor a hard time.

Her revelation that Arlo believed his father had killed his mother made his job a hundred times more difficult. It didn't matter if it was true or not—if Arlo believed it to be so, he'd never agree to come home.

He wasn't so consumed with his guilt as he left Eleanor that he didn't notice the nondescript silver Hyundai parked at the curb on the other side of the street. Even with the windows up and the sun reflecting off the glass, he knew who was inside. Landry. He'd been aware of the car following him as he drove to the Rusty Spoon. The guy had made no attempt to hide the fact that he was tailing him.

Evan was tempted to cross the street, rap on the window. Suggest that they take one car to save on gas. Except Landry stayed parked at the curb when Evan drove past. Watching Eleanor as she leaned against the wall outside the diner, phone in hand.

His own words came back to him.

This isn't a threat, Eleanor, even if it sounds like one. Stan Fraser is determined to find Arlo. Now that he's decided it's time, he's not going to give up. If I fail, he might try himself.

He just hadn't expected it to be so literal. That Landry planned to re-interview everyone he talked to immediately afterwards.

There was nothing he could do about it. A phone call to Fraser asking him to call his man off would achieve nothing other than put questions in Fraser's mind about why Evan didn't want to be followed around. Whether he was indeed planning to filter and edit what he reported back.

Hence his somewhat troubled demeanor as he stood on Elwood Crow's front step waiting for the old buzzard to get his aged bones to the front door.

Crow had been an investigator himself back in the day, his methods and morals dubious even by the lax standards of those far-off times. Worse, his perception of his own importance in the way in which the universe unfolded had been somewhat skewed. At times, the line between the pursuit of wrong-doers and the swift administering of Old Testament-style justice hadn't so much blurred as become a wide dirty smudge lacking distinct boundaries. Now that he was well into his second century—according to Evan—and too wrinkly for the rough and tumble of the job out on the streets, he increasingly viewed Evan as his protégé.

As such, he furnished Evan with often-disturbing insights into the darker, seamier side of life that otherwise Evan could only have imagined, making use of internet skills for which no Microsoft certifications exist, in order to stick his beak of a nose into places it had no business to be, from the dark recesses of the Victorian pile he called home.

It would be unfair to say that Crow enjoyed other people's misfortunes—perhaps not—but his home sure as hell wasn't the place to go looking for a sympathetic ear.

Here we go again would've been an apt way to describe his expression when he pulled open the heavy front door and ushered Evan in.

'Left or right?' Evan said as he headed down the hall, Crow trailing behind him.

'Left.'

At least that was something.

Left meant through the kitchen and out onto the back porch. Right implied the back room. A place of secrets and things best left unsaid, the cradle of many an ill-advised and often ill-fated plan. Guillory hated it. After his unsatisfactory meeting with Eleanor, Evan wouldn't miss it, either.

'I'll be outside while you get the coffee on,' Crow said.

Evan hopped to it, his mind wandering as he busied himself. At times he wished he could be more like Crow. Not old and wrinkly, of course, but with a conscience that was a stunted, withered thing if it existed at all. If Crow had taken Fraser's money, he'd have brought the boy home without a second thought had he found him. Wriggling under his arm if necessary.

Evan could also rely on Crow to make some pertinent, if insensitive, remark on any occasion. Which he did, as soon as Evan carried the coffee outside.

'If I had a dog that walked around with a look on its face like the one on yours, I'd either teach it to walk backwards or have it put down.'

It was a bit rich given that Crow resembled nothing more closely than an underfed and ageing vulture, but Evan was happy to respond in kind.

'And if I was your dog, I'd drive myself to the vet's clinic and shave my leg in preparation.'

That got the pleasantries out of the way. It was one of the things Evan liked about Crow. No need to feel obliged to make small talk. They'd get down to business soon enough, but in the meantime they were both content to sit quietly awhile, enjoying the sun on their faces—even if the sound of Crow slurping noisily took some of the shine off the moment.

'What's up?' Crow said eventually.

'Stan Fraser.'

Crow nodded sagely, enough said.

'Payback time already?'

'Yep. He wants me to find his son. All the evidence points to him not wanting to be found. As well as having a very good reason why not.'

He took Crow through it, mentioning the minder that Fraser had sicced on him as he did so and ending with Eleanor's revelation.

'I don't think I'd want to come home,' Crow said, which, while true, wasn't particularly helpful. 'Did she give any reason why he thought his father killed her?'

'She got a bit vague at that point. I'd already pointed out how

Fraser might ask her the same questions if I couldn't get any answers, so I don't think she was holding back.'

Crow echoed Evan's own unhelpful thoughts.

'It doesn't matter. If the boy believes it, he won't agree to come home.' He paused a moment as a thought struck him, peering at Evan as if his head were turning into a potato—a transformation Guillory said would be difficult to spot. 'You're not thinking of trying to find out if it's true, are you? That Fraser killed his wife. With his money already in your pocket.'

'Uh-uh. But Kate's intrigued. She's looking into it.'

Crow smiled a wrinkly smile, his face resembling a plowed field.

'*Intrigued* as in you badgered her into agreeing to do your legwork for you.'

'*Some* of it,' Evan corrected.

Crow understood what was being said. He was aware that Evan was a firm believer in the maxim, why keep a dog and bark yourself. He didn't mind. It stopped his brain from atrophying, kept the steadily-cooling juices flowing for a little longer.

'What is it you want me to do?'

'See if you can find Arlo Stanley Fraser anywhere in the system.'

Crow gave him a knowing look.

'Didn't manage to *intrigue* Kate that much, eh? Got a date of birth?'

Evan got out his phone, found the note he'd made. He recited it to Crow, along with the rest of the sparse personal details Fraser had shared with him. Finished on an optimistic note.

'Eleanor didn't think he would change his name.'

Crow snorted.

'I would say that's something, except degrees of impossible don't make much difference to anything.'

'You could also check out Fraser's man Landry, first name unknown.'

Crow mulled it over for a long moment. Not so much the daunting prospect of trying to find a man with only a surname to go on, more the implications.

'Fraser doesn't trust you. Landry will step in the minute you locate his son in case you decide to side with the boy.'

'Looks like it.'

'Should I speak to Caleb?'

Caleb was Crow's son. Physically, he was the spitting image of his father. Tall and angular with a shiny bald dome of a head, lacking only the wrinkles. In terms of personality, he was one of life's great nature–nurture debates, his morose demeanor making Crow's curmudgeonly outlook seem endearing. Evan couldn't blame him, having Crow for a father and guiding light. That didn't mean their relationship had been anything other than strained ever since they'd first met. Caleb had always resented Evan, the fact that he felt Crow favored Evan over himself, his own flesh and blood.

Much as he hated to admit it, it was the main reason for Evan's visit. He didn't expect Crow to find Arlo in a publicly-available, or even a not-so-publicly-available, database. Nor did he expect anything useful back relating to Landry. But Stan Fraser was right to not trust him. Already, he was aware that he couldn't rule out the possibility of going against Fraser's wishes. And Caleb was a man with a very particular skill set.

'It can't hurt.'

The words were out before their stupidity had registered.

Because Crow's son had shot and killed Evan's wife, Sarah.

Through a cruel twist of fate, Sarah had ended up incarcerated against her will in an asylum by a man called Newcomb. Evan had come up with a misbegotten plan to break her out. He'd turned to Caleb with his particular skill set for the ill-fated attempt that ended in disaster. Left Sarah lying dead in the street, her death on his conscience, her blood on his hands. But it had been Caleb's finger on the trigger. Caleb who accidentally shot and killed her with a high-powered rifle, a stray round hitting Sarah in the confusion and pandemonium of the ambush.

So actually, yes, it could hurt a lot.

And they both knew it.

'You could ask him about Landry,' Evan said in an attempt to recover. 'He probably knows the guy.'

A normal father might have taken umbrage at the slur on his own flesh and blood. Not Crow. He was far from a normal anything, his son the same as a result—but good to have at your back when there were difficult things to be done without the tiresome whine of a troubled conscience distracting you.

So long as you weren't Sarah Buckley, that is.

5

EVAN NEEDN'T HAVE WORRIED ABOUT WHAT MIGHT HAVE BEEN happening to Eleanor at Landry's hands while he was closeted with Crow.

The guy was waiting for him as he came out of Crow's house. Leaning his butt against the fender of Evan's car and smoking a cigarette.

Evan worked a look of disappointment onto his face as he approached, his voice full of regret at a missed opportunity.

'You should've let me know. I'd have fetched a bucket and sponge and you could've cleaned it while I was inside.' He glanced at Landry's Hyundai parked immediately in front of his own car. It looked like it had been used to transport troops in Iraq. 'Although looking at that, you haven't got a lot of experience.'

Needless to say, it washed over Landry.

Evan didn't waste any more breath asking if the guy was interested in carpooling to save gas, got in instead. Except he wasn't going anywhere. Landry had boxed him in. He couldn't have driven away with Landry's butt still on the fender if he'd wanted to—which he did.

Too late he realized his mistake. He'd feel like an idiot getting out again. He was forced to wait while Landry came around and climbed into the passenger seat, bringing his half-finished cigarette with him.

'Leave the door open,' Evan said.

Landry gave a twitch of his shoulders as if he'd been planning on doing exactly that, didn't need to be asked. He left one leg outside stretched across the sidewalk.

'That was the girl Arlo ran away with at the diner, was it?'

Evan got the impression he knew already, answered all the same.

'Yep.'

'Did she have anything useful to tell you?'

'Nope. The last time she heard from Arlo was when they split up in Brownsville ten years ago.' He was careful to make it sound like a fact, that there was no room for doubt. Prefacing the answer with *she says* or, worse, *she claims,* would only increase the likelihood of Landry taking things into his own hands.

'And that's the old fart who does all your legwork for you in there, is it?' Pointing at Crow's house with his cigarette as he said it.

Again, he was simply looking for confirmation of what he already knew.

'Uh-huh. How did you know I'd be here?'

He wasn't expecting Landry to admit they'd put a tracker on his car, nor did he. What he did say was further proof that Fraser believed in background research. It implied he'd had Evan followed in the past, that he'd gained a feel for his modus operandi. The dismissive way Landry chose to phrase it made Evan want to ask him why Fraser had even bothered with hiring him when he already had Landry.

'You're a creature of habit, like everyone. You meet with

someone, you come running to that old fool to ask what to do next. You'd have been better keeping eyes on the girl.'

Evan didn't point out that he lacked the advantage of anonymity that Landry enjoyed. That he couldn't have observed her without Eleanor knowing.

'Why? What did she do?'

Landry took a deliberately long drag on his cigarette. Made a point of leaning out of the car to exhale. It didn't make a lot of difference. Evan still got a blast of second-hand smoke when he replied.

'Made a phone call—'

'I saw that.'

'—then went back inside. A young guy turned up five minutes later.'

Evan saw the opportunity to say something stupid and grabbed it.

'Not Arlo?'

Landry almost smiled. Evan figured it was as close as he ever got.

'No.'

'You recognize him?'

'No.'

'You break his fingers afterwards to find out what he wanted?'

He didn't say that, but it was close.

'What happened?' he said instead.

'They had an argument.'

'You went inside? Did you hear what it was about?'

'No, I stayed in the car. The girl sat in the window seat like she did with you. It was obvious they were arguing but I don't know what it was about. Specifically.'

They both knew what it was about in general terms.

Eleanor had either flat out lied to Evan, or she'd withheld

something from him. Something important enough to make her immediately call someone else to convene an emergency meeting.

'I'm surprised you came looking for me to pass it on,' Evan said. 'I'd have expected you to follow one of them, ask them yourself.'

Landry shook his head, ignored the pointed emphasis Evan had put on the word *ask*.

'Mr. Fraser wants to get this done amicably.'

He didn't need to add what was taken as read.

If possible.

'I followed the guy,' Landry went on, parking his cigarette between his lips and pulling out his phone. 'He works a couple of blocks away from the diner. I'll send you the address and a picture of him.'

Evan's phone pinged. He opened the message. The image showed Eleanor and the unknown young man embracing on the sidewalk outside the Rusty Spoon despite the argument Landry had observed. They both looked very uncomfortable with it.

'They know each other,' Landry said, as if Fraser had told him Evan was slow on the uptake and needed things spelled out.

Evan responded by being deliberately disingenuous.

'Maybe he's her latest boyfriend.'

Landry acted like he hadn't spoken.

'They were arguing about Arlo.'

Evan couldn't disagree. The question was, what about? There was only one way to find out. And he planned to get right on it as soon as Landry was out of the car. Except he needed to get something out of the way first.

'What do you do now? Report back to Fraser immediately? Tell him it looks as if Eleanor lied to me? Then talk to her yourself?'

Again, Landry ignored the mocking emphasis Evan put on the word *talk*.

'No. Mr. Fraser allows me to exercise my own judgment up to a certain point.'

But you have to ask before you kill someone, Evan thought and didn't say.

Landry turned his head to look out the open door as if some sixth sense had alerted him to danger nearby. The way his lip curled and his derisive tone suggested not.

'That old fool's watching us through the window. What's he going to do? Come and attack me with his walking stick?'

He took a final drag on his cigarette. Balanced the butt on the pad of his thumb, his middle finger poised ready to flick it away, send it sailing into Crow's front yard. Evan slapped it away, a quick backhand strike. It took Landry by surprise, unsettled his studied composure as the butt landed in the gutter.

'*Hey!*'

They played eyeball chicken for a long moment. By default, Evan was always going to win. Landry had to get out of the car at some point, a de facto climb-down.

Evan helped him on his way.

'Run along now, back to Stan. Tell *mommy* how the naughty new boy's getting uppity, won't play nicely. And tell him if he wants a step-by-step account of everything I do, just ask. You don't have to follow me around.'

It was a mistake. Not the attempt to bait Landry. The opportunity it delivered him on a plate.

He unfolded himself from the front seat, stuck his head back in the car. Gave Evan another blast of second-hand cigarette smoke in case the words themselves weren't offensive enough.

'You ask me, it's lucky I followed you to the diner today. Otherwise you'd still be sitting around in a week's time with your finger up your ass.'

. . .

Evan took a picture of Landry's license plate as he drove away, sent it to Crow. Then he drove to the address Landry had sent him—a multi-tenanted office block half a mile from the Rusty Spoon diner, as Landry had said. Evan ran his eyes down the list of companies on the sign beside the front door. None of them meant anything to him, nor did he expect them to. He guessed Landry had done the same.

Half a block away on the opposite side of the street there was a coffee shop with three brightly-colored metal bistro tables on the sidewalk outside, each with two chairs. Five out of the six seats were occupied, all by women. He went inside, got himself a bucket of Americano, then asked the single young woman at the third table if the empty chair opposite her was free.

She looked him up and down, considering her options. Deciding whether to say she was expecting a friend, real or imagined. In the end she gave him a quick nervous smile, told him to go ahead, then went back to her phone.

He did the same, getting out his own phone to refresh his memory of the young man he was waiting for. The woman relaxed visibly, a palpable release of tension. Not a serial killer stalking his next victim, after all. Serial killers don't waste their lives playing with their phones. They sit staring malevolently. Everybody knows that. It meant that in this modern day and age he never had to worry about appearing conspicuous. A man reading a newspaper was conspicuous. People have watched too many old spy movies. But a person with their phone in their hand immediately becomes invisible.

That didn't mean he couldn't spoil things with a little conversation to pass the time.

'Anyone would think we're on a date, the way we're both

sitting here playing with our phones and not talking to each other.'

The woman looked up briefly, the small nervous smile flitting quickly across her face again. Hoping that was the end of it.

Guillory could've told her—dream on.

'Sometimes I want to ask them, why did you come out together instead of each going out with the person you're texting? I don't, of course. It's strange, though. Presumably it would be unacceptable to both sit there talking to someone else on the phone, but for some reason it's okay to ignore each other and text non-stop.'

Seemed the woman didn't have an answer for him, or even an opinion. What she did have was a hastily remembered appointment she was late for.

A moment later he had the table to himself.

Although it hadn't necessarily been his aim, it did mean he was able to change seats, from where he had a better view of the entrance to the office block.

He scanned the street thoroughly and regularly as he waited, saw no sign of Landry or his shitty Hyundai. People came and went while he waited, some sharing his table allowing him to nip inside and get a refill without losing his seat.

Then, at a little after midday, the young man who'd met with Eleanor emerged from the door Evan was watching, closely followed by a rail-thin young woman who fell into step beside him.

Evan jumped up and followed them down the street, loitering on the sidewalk as they went into a Subway restaurant to buy a sandwich and coffee each, before making their way to a small park.

He perched on the end of the bench nearest to the one they took, then buried his nose in his phone again. Wondering as his stomach growled whether he had time to get back to Subway to get himself something to eat. He decided against it, did his best to listen in on their conversation instead.

It soon became clear that it was dull, work-related stuff and not a secret discussion about Arlo Fraser's whereabouts, at which point he tuned them out, although not before overhearing the woman call her colleague Aiden.

After twenty minutes they were still on the bench, eating and talking. Aiden had long-since finished his lunch, the woman whose name he hadn't caught still working on it with the appetite of a sparrow. Nibbling at the edges of the sandwich that was the best part of fifty percent of her body weight. Evan's stomach growled again as he pictured it going in the trash can at the end of the bench at any minute.

Fifteen minutes later and there was still no sign of them making a move, going their separate ways to get some chore done before heading back.

He couldn't wait any longer.

He got up, cleared his throat as he stood in front of them. Sparrow Appetite glared at him as if he was wearing a park warden's uniform and was there to move them along, having exceeded their allocated time. Evan gave her a quick dismissive smile, then turned to Aiden.

'Sorry to interrupt. You're a friend of Eleanor Fields, aren't you?'

It took Aiden by surprise, understandably, suspicion coloring his voice.

'I know her, yes.'

Sparrow Appetite immediately stood up as she sensed the wariness in Aiden's tone.

'It's okay, Aiden, I've got stuff to do. See you later.'

She glanced briefly at the left-over sandwich in her hand as if deciding whether to save it for later, then dumped it in the trash can before Evan had a chance to say that he'd have it.

Evan dropped onto the empty seat beside Aiden as soon as she'd walked off, repeated his apology.

'Sorry to interrupt like that. But I do need to talk to you.'

'Who are you?'

'How well do you know Eleanor?'

On the face of it he'd completely ignored Aiden's question. But he needed to understand the dynamic in order to better answer. Whether he knew of Eleanor's past, and might have heard of him as a result—which would make him a very good friend indeed.

It wasn't to be.

'I don't, really. I'm more of a friend . . . of a mutual friend.'

Evan immediately cut to the chase given such a perfect lead-in.

'Arlo Fraser.'

Aiden pointed at him as the penny dropped.

'You're the investigator Arlo's old man employed to find him.'

'Yeah. I met with Eleanor right before she called you. She told me she hadn't heard from Arlo since they split up. The fact that she called you the minute my back was turned suggests that might not be true. Either that or she wanted to know if you had.'

Evan felt encouraged that Aiden didn't immediately jump to his feet at the mention of Arlo's name and, more so, his father's. He had a ready-made excuse, after all. By Evan's reckoning he only had five minutes left before his lunch hour was up.

His continued presence said something about the argument Landry witnessed. That Eleanor tried to persuade Aiden to agree not to tell anyone what he might know about Arlo's whereabouts—and that Aiden hadn't been happy with doing so.

'Were you good friends with Arlo?' Evan said.

Aiden smiled as the years rolled back.

'Yeah. At school everybody sucked up to him. When you're a kid it's cool to have a friend whose old man's a criminal. Mine works in a bank. All the other kids read him wrong. They thought the thing to do was to pretend their dads were into illegal stuff too, even if they had regular jobs. Except that was the last thing Arlo wanted to hear. I never tried to pretend my old man was anything other than what he is. I think that's why we became friends. Arlo hated what his old man was.'

'I know. That's why he ran away with Eleanor. To get away from him.'

'Yeah.'

'I realize that's why Eleanor's acting the way she is. She's protecting him. Stop his old man from finding him. I get the feeling you don't agree. That's what you were arguing about in the Rusty Spoon diner.'

Aiden had taken Evan's appearance at his bench without batting an eyelid. Similarly, there was no reaction to the mention of the argument. He didn't question how Evan knew about it. A man employed by a criminal like Stan Fraser would have resources, would be able to achieve such things without raising a sweat. Too much TV and too many hours wasted playing video games would only reinforce that view. Evan would've felt like a comic-book superhero if it hadn't been for Landry's assistance.

He capitalized on his newly-acquired status as the man who already knew everything, who could find out what he didn't with a click of his fingers.

'Was there more to him running away than not wanting to grow up like his old man, get pushed into a life of crime?' He paused, then when nothing was forthcoming, 'Eleanor told me Arlo thought his old man killed his mother. Did he ever say anything like that to you?'

A look of horror mingled with surprise passed across Aiden's face. It was the first he'd heard of it. Seemed Eleanor was selective about what she told to whom. Aiden shook his head, leaning away. Distancing himself as if Stan had sent Evan to do the same to him.

'He never said that to me. He was upset when his mom died, leaving him with his dad, but he never said anything like that. But I wasn't his girlfriend. He's not going to tell just anybody. But if that's what he believes, he's never going to come back. You might as well give up now.'

Something passed behind his eyes as the words rolled out of his mouth. Evan knew what it was. Enlightenment. And fear. Eleanor had told him what Evan had said about the consequences of him failing—how Fraser would send more physically persuasive men. Sooner or later, those men would find their way to Aiden's door.

Aiden confirmed it, a hint of accusation edging into his voice.

'Eleanor said you threatened her.'

'I didn't threaten her. I told her the facts, is all. You know what Stan Fraser is like. You can figure out what he'll do if I get nowhere. It's a fact, not a threat. I've got no say in it.'

None of which was any comfort to Aiden. If Fraser's thugs turned up on his doorstep, it didn't make a lot of difference how they got there. Bones would get broken regardless, a journey into a world of pain set forth upon.

Aiden was quiet a while as the implications sank in. The fact that it was already too late. Evan went back to his original question.

'What were you arguing with Eleanor about? I get the impression she wouldn't help me to help Stan Fraser even if she could. You obviously disagree with her or you wouldn't have been arguing.'

Aiden glanced at his watch, a spasm of irritation crossing his face. He stood up.

'I'm late getting back from lunch. Can we walk as we talk?'

Evan was already on his feet, his hand extended back the way they'd come.

'You don't work for Fraser full time, do you?' Aiden said as they set off, Evan doing his best to slow the pace.

'No way. I owe him a favor. If what you're asking is where my loyalties lie, the honest answer is, I don't know. If I go against Stan Fraser's wishes, there'll be a price to pay. But I wouldn't drag Arlo home come what may just to keep on the right side of him.'

Aiden seemed somewhat satisfied with the answer. Evan, in turn, felt somewhat slimy for not mentioning Landry. How his role was to step in should Evan have any such second thoughts.

'I want to make one thing very clear,' Aiden said. 'I wouldn't piss on Fraser if he was on fire. And I wouldn't lift a finger to help you to find Arlo to bring him home to ease his father's conscience, make him feel like he isn't the monster he is. The only reason I'm talking to you is because I'm worried something bad has happened to Arlo.'

6

Jack Bray looked up from the memo he'd been struggling with for the past hour as the internal phone rang, thankful for any interruption, however brief. The demands of political correctness and diversity and using this week's correct pronouns so as not to offend the clouds in the sky outside made his head spin. Turned what should've been a two-paragraph communication into a thousand-word essay.

The relief didn't last long.

A nauseous sinking sensation settled in the pit of his stomach the moment he heard his secretary's voice.

Very little rattled Theresa. He worked her like a dog for a pittance of a salary that no right-minded person would get out of bed for. She put up with his unreasonable demands on a daily basis without complaint, maintaining an unfailingly cheery frame of mind in the face of his random mood swings and legendary bouts of bad temper. He had no illusions. He was a nightmare to work for. Theresa was a saint. It was lucky her reward awaited her in heaven because all her colleagues were of the mind that she'd done her time in hell, and some.

Just not today.

And since he hadn't heard the commotion that would accompany armed terrorists storming the building, he knew exactly what was wrong.

'The Grim Reaper is here to see you, Mr. Bray.'

Except she pronounced the visitor's name as *Mr. Ritter*. Sounding as she'd been forced to speak the name of the Antichrist and knew she would surely burn in hell for it, the Inquisition already at her door.

'Shall I send him in?'

What he heard behind the desperation: *get him out of my sight.*

'No. Tell him I'll be out in a minute.'

He kicked back from his captain-of-industry-sized desk, pushed himself up wearily from his real-leather executive chair, a look of something close to longing on his face for the half-finished, bullshit memo on his desk.

Oh, to be bored stupid.

He went to stand at the window as he prepared himself for what he knew was coming. Leaned his forehead against the coolness of the glass as he took a moment to compose himself, a single thought racing through his frantic mind.

Why now?

If it had been possible to open the window more than six inches, and had his office been on a lower, less prestigious floor, he'd have climbed out, run for the hills and to hell with it all.

Theresa was busy typing at her computer as he came out of his office, her fingers a blur above the keyboard. It looked to him like a random string of meaningless text. Anything to maintain the appearance of having things to do, having no time to stop and engage with Ritter in conversation.

He'd heard through the office grapevine that Ritter had

propositioned her one time. She'd immediately gone to the ladies' bathroom where she vomited copiously in the toilet and refused to come out again until he'd gone.

Ritter was currently lounging on the big sofa opposite Theresa's desk. Long legs spread provocatively and wearing his trademark khaki safari jacket. A look on his face that Bray had hoped he'd never see again. Barely-contained glee at his role as the bearer of bad tidings coupled with an atavistic animal excitement at what would surely follow from that news.

The two men walked in silence to the elevator, Ritter trailing unease behind him like a smoker trails the stink and smoke of cigarettes. Bray laughed to himself, a dry mirthless sound more like a sob, as they walked side by side. Like prisoner and sad-eyed padre, the words *dead man walking* competing with the incessant clamor in his mind. The silence stretched out until it was a silent scream as they rode the endless elevator down.

Outside, Bray drew the air deep into his lungs. Couldn't help but wonder for how much longer he'd have the liberty to do so. Only then did Ritter spoil what would otherwise have been a beautiful day like the black cloud on humanity that he was.

'The file's been pulled.'

What Bray heard: *you're going to hell, head of the line.*

A lot of the time the anticipation is worse than the event. Not today. This confirmation of what Bray had dreaded was as bad when it arrived as he'd always expected it to be.

Five years of hearing nothing since that first hateful email—*we'll be in touch*—with its damning career-ending attachment and he'd started to believe that he never would, that he was home free. Now it felt like five minutes.

'When?' he said as they made their way down the steps and headed across the crowded plaza.

'A week ago.'

Bray stopped dead. A man behind him carrying a cup of coffee shunted him. The cup went flying, an explosion of hot brown liquid as it hit the ground spattering both men's shoes. The guy cursed, looked as if he was about to remonstrate. Then he recognized Bray. He mumbled an apology as if it had been his fault, and went on his way.

Bray dried his shoe on the back of his five-thousand-dollar suit leg, then rounded on Ritter, indignation melding with panic in his voice.

'How come I'm only hearing about it now?'

Ritter shrugged, the carefree nonchalance of a man whose career and personal life isn't about to go down the shitter in the gesture.

'No idea. People are lazy. Sloppy. They've got their head stuck up their ass most of the time. I only heard about it myself today.'

Bray leaned in, hissed at Ritter.

'I don't pay people good money to be lazy and sloppy.'

Again, Ritter responded with a dismissive shrug. After all, what could he do or say? *You know now,* wasn't going to calm the egotistical asshole any.

Bray resumed walking. Nothing would be achieved by dwelling on the delay, other than to work himself into more of a gibbering nervous wreck than he already was. Besides, he was more concerned about the answer to his next question.

'Who pulled it? Not Internal Affairs, I hope?'

Ritter shook his head. Bray wanted to punch him for not immediately volunteering who actually had pulled the file. Except he knew how badly that would end—for him.

'What, then? Some cold case unit?'

Set up to persecute me, he thought and kept to his paranoid self.

'No. A semi-retired sheriff's deputy called Mercer nosing around.'

Bray searched his memory. The name meant nothing to him. Not even a vague feeling that he ought to recognize it. He was good with names, rarely forgot one. It was important in order to do his job properly. The fact that it meant nothing, and, by implication, signaled the introduction of an unknown element, lent an added sharpness to his tone.

'What's his interest?'

'No idea. I told you, I only found out myself today. You ask me, he's finding stuff to do so they don't retire him completely. Doesn't want to end up going crazy watching daytime TV or looking after the grandkids.'

Bray was right on it, his fear pushing aside what little remained of his conscience.

'Has he got grandkids?'

Ritter gave him a look that made Bray shudder.

And I'm supposed to be the evil bastard?

He fell back on his favorite phrase.

'No idea. It's what retired people do, is all. Is that the approach you want me to take if he has?' There was the shortest of pauses, its purpose nothing more than to emphasize what followed. 'I thought you liked kids.'

Had they not been in a busy public place, had their relative physical prowess been reversed—and Bray also had an axe handy—he'd have happily buried it in the top of Ritter's head. Wiped the impertinent smirk off his face for good.

In the absence of all of those factors, Jack Bray had no choice but to suck it up.

But he would remember.

'What do you want me to do?' Ritter said, looking like nothing so much as an excited attack dog straining at the leash as it waited for its master's command.

The answer was hanging in the air between them.

What you do best. Make the problem go away.

Except Bray's reply hissed under his breath made it clearer still.

'Whatever it takes.'

7

'Let's back up,' Evan said. 'The fact that you're worried about Arlo tells me you've been in contact with him.'

Aiden dropped his eyes as if he'd been called out by the teacher for jerking off under the table in class.

'Yeah.'

'How long for? Ever since he ran away?'

Aiden shook his head. He glanced at his watch and quickened his pace as he did so.

'I didn't hear anything for a couple of years at least. Not until he split with Eleanor. That's when he got in contact again. It was like he'd only been gone a week. We've kept in touch by phone and email ever since. He doesn't do social media. He's a bit paranoid, you know? Actually, he's a lot paranoid. Conspiracy theories and all that shit. It must have been growing up in the environment he did, made him that way. He thinks everybody's tracking you, and his old man might find him somehow. Like Facebook's got a *find a runaway son* service that he could get a monthly subscription for.'

It wasn't what Evan wanted to hear. The kid did not want to be found. End of.

It also made him think about the phone call Stan Fraser had received. Arlo's paranoia and his desire to stay lost suggested it had been a wrong number after all. Back in the day, when good manners held some sway in the world, a person dialing a wrong number would apologize. These days, the ignorant bastards simply hung up. Aside from making the world a slightly less pleasant place in which to live, it meant it was impossible to tell.

For now, he moved on.

'What about Eleanor? Has she kept in touch with Arlo despite what she told me?'

It was a difficult, perhaps impossible, question to answer. Eleanor wasn't obliged to keep Aiden updated on the status of her relationship with Arlo. But that wasn't what made Aiden hesitate before answering.

'I don't think so. The split with Arlo wasn't as amicable as she likes to make out. I don't know what happened but Arlo asked me not to tell her that we were still in contact. Like he was scared she might stalk him.'

They were almost back to Aiden's building by now. Aiden himself had slowed, saving Evan from having to do so. He cleared his throat, a nervous tic as he prepared to move away from facts and into the realm of speculation.

'I don't think it's got anything to do with protecting him from his dad. I think it's to do with how they split up. But I might be wrong.'

'Does she know you've been in contact?'

'She does now.'

The emphasis on the word *now* told Evan everything he needed to know.

'That's what some of the argument was about?'

Aiden smiled nervously at the memory of it.

'Yeah. She went apeshit. She only called me because I was his best friend before they ran away. She was expecting me to say, no, I haven't heard from him, either. Instead, she got a nasty wake-up call. He hasn't shriveled up and died of a broken heart, after all. I had to tell her. I've never been good at lying. Especially when someone asks me a direct question.'

'Did anything come of it?'

'Like what?'

'I don't know. You've just told her how you're still in contact. She wants to go one better. Says, you think you're such big buddies, think again. I know about this great big secret, whatever.'

'No, nothing like that.'

Evan had sidetracked himself for long enough. The petty jealousies of the three-way dynamic between Arlo, Eleanor and Aiden wasn't of any immediate interest to him—beyond proving that Eleanor had lied to him about how the relationship had ended.

'Have you got an address for him?'

Aiden laughed, more at Evan and his funny old ways than any intrinsic humor in the question.

'I never asked. He's living in Lafayette. Louisiana, not Indiana. I don't have an address. It's not like I need it to send an actual letter to him in the mail. I've got an email address and his phone number.'

Evan went to get out his phone, stopped himself. Turned it into a quick scratch of his armpit. He'd wait for Aiden to send him the details, then check the phone number against the one that had called Stan Fraser without Aiden looking over his shoulder.

'Send them to me.'

'It won't do you any good. I haven't heard from him for a week now.'

Coming from the point of view of a man, it didn't seem so unusual to Evan. Guillory couldn't understand it, but he knew plenty of people he didn't contact from one month to the next. Some of them, one year to the next.

'Is that unusual?'

'Not normally, no. This is different. He's spent the last however many years drifting aimlessly. Picking fruit, working in bars, anything he could get, basically. Living hand to mouth. One time when he was feeling really down he told me he'd even thought about coming home. Not following in his old man's footsteps, but at least he'd have a roof over his head.'

'Then something changed?'

The door behind Aiden suddenly opened, made him startle. A middle-aged woman in an expensive tailored gray suit came out. She saw Aiden standing in front of her and frowned, her thin lips pursing. She extended her arm, made a point of looking at her watch. Tapped the face a couple times, tut-tutted and went on her way.

'Your boss?' Evan said.

Aiden stopped showing the departing woman's back his middle finger, coughed out a sour laugh.

'The Ayatollah. I'll get it in the neck now...'

He looked as if he was about to launch into a litany of the myriad ways in which the woman made his life a misery. Evan cut him short.

'You were saying how Arlo's situation changed?'

Aiden watched his boss disappearing into the mass of people on the sidewalk for a moment longer. He appeared more relaxed now that his lateness had already been registered. May as well be hung for a sheep as a lamb.

'Yeah. He landed a proper job when he got to Lafayette. He'd always wanted to be a reporter—'

'Anything other than turn out like his father is what I heard.'

Aiden nodded enthusiastically, a wide grin spreading across

his face. An overreaction to Evan's remark on the face of it until he explained—or at least made Evan work for it.

'That's actually not true. What do you think he really wanted to be?'

It was a no-brainer. Take Stan Fraser's line of work—if work was in any way the right word—add the amusement on Aiden's face and fate's penchant for sticking its finger in your eye, and there was only one thing it could be.

'A cop.'

'Got it in one.'

Evan smiled with him. Wishing that Aiden hadn't already made it clear that it hadn't turned out that way. He'd have given his right arm to go back to Fraser, tell him the good news. Sitting at Stan's table in The Backroom, making sure the minders were all huddled around, his voice loud enough for everyone to hear.

Your boy's a cop. Stick that in your pipe and smoke it.

Aiden soon brought him back to earth.

'The thing is, he's not stupid. He knew it wasn't ever going to happen. He'd spent all his adult life as a bum, basically. It's not what the police are looking for. And he knew that even if they let that slide, everything would go to shit as soon as they ran background checks. He lowered his expectations, settled for being a crime reporter. *Wanting* to be one, that is.'

'That's not so easy for ex-bums to walk into, either.'

'I know. Has his old man given you a picture of him?'

A strange way to answer. Evan got out his phone, nonetheless, found the picture he'd taken of the photograph Fraser had shown him. Aiden leaned in, glanced at it.

'That's so old. I'll send you a more recent one.' He took the phone from Evan, studied it more closely. 'You can still see that he wasn't a bad looking kid. He just got better looking as he got older. Like God crapped on his head by giving him a criminal for a father, so he evened the score by giving him movie-star good looks.'

Evan couldn't fault the logic. Thinking he'd put it to Guillory the next time he spoke to her that on the basis of looks being inversely proportional to parental criminality, her partner, Ryder, must have been the result of a quick liaison between Mother Teresa and Mahatma Gandhi.

He made an easy guess at Aiden's point.

'He used his looks to get the job?'

'Yeah. He never had any problem picking up women. Reading between the lines, that was the problem with him and Eleanor. She's okay looking, but it's not like she makes heads turn in the street. And she's jealous as hell.'

'Arlo shacked up with an older woman?' Thinking, someone like your boss, the Ayatollah.

Aiden looked horrified at the suggestion, clearly thinking the same thing.

'No way. He met a girl whose dad is the editor of a local paper. She persuaded him to give Arlo a chance. It's not exactly star reporter for the New York Times, but it's a start. I've never known Arlo so excited. It actually got really boring. But I was pleased for him. And then, *bang!*' He chopped his open palm with the edge of his other hand like a guillotine coming down. 'Nothing. I emailed him, called him, texted him. Nothing. Like he's disappeared off the face of the planet. Okay, he's really busy. I get that. But a week? He could send a text to update me while he's taking a dump, if he's that busy.' His face clouded as his own words made his concerns clearer in his mind, sounding as if he'd already received the bad news. 'I wouldn't be worried if they'd got him covering the local Little League. But the crime desk...'

'Do you know if he was working on anything in particular?'

Aiden smiled guiltily as if Evan had just brought him, and by extension Arlo, down to earth.

'He got a bit vague about that. Like they hadn't actually given him anything to do yet other than photocopying and he doesn't want to admit it.'

Evan could've suggested a number of alternative reasons for that vagueness.

That he'd stumbled on something big and wanted to play it close to his chest. Even to the extent of excluding his friend twelve hundred miles away.

Or, at the opposite end of the scale, that he'd uncovered something that had scared him, and he wanted to forget all about it.

Pressing the point would only invite further speculation. He steered them back towards facts.

'Do you know the girl's name?'

'I can't remember. I know he told me. I'll find it and text it to you.'

'What paper was he working for?'

Aiden shook his head before the question was all the way out.

'He never told me. Maybe he didn't want me calling them, asking to speak to the new ace reporter—'

He did a small double-take as he watched the street over Evan's shoulder. Evan turned to look, saw Aiden's boss striding purposefully towards them, weaving her way through the pedestrians.

'Shit. She's coming back already. I've gotta go.'

With that, he was gone. Not another word, the door banging shut behind him. Evan stepped backwards out of the way as the Ayatollah swept past without giving him a second look.

He made his way back towards the park where he'd first accosted Aiden, stopping on the way to pick up a sandwich from a deli that was popular with flies, judging by the number of dried-up corpses in the window. Two bites in and his phone pinged.

He pulled it out expecting it to be Aiden.

Wrong.

It was Landry.

He couldn't stop himself from glancing around. See if the guy was watching him from a bench on the far side of the park. It was only ten minutes since he'd left Aiden. Landry had either followed him and he hadn't spotted him, or it was a damn good guess.

The message was short and to the point.

Anything useful?

Plenty, Evan thought. *None of which you're getting until I'm ready to give.*

He started to compose an equally terse and completely unhelpful reply. Then stopped, backspaced all the way.

Thought about what he was doing here. Already he was aware of kicking back against Fraser's constant surveillance through Landry. What he couldn't say was whether he was subconsciously keeping open the option to not tell Fraser what he discovered, or whether it was simply him objecting to being monitored or supervised in any way.

Guillory would have no trouble answering that one.

Ornery and pig-headed it is.

He tapped out a lesson in vagueness, instead.

Too early to say. Waiting for more information.

Perfect. A polite way to say, *fuck off and mind your own business*. Guillory would be proud of him.

If he hadn't been expecting a text from Aiden he'd have switched off the phone. Stop any chance of a pointless dialogue back and forth between them. Instead, he sat there feeling like a man watching a two-horse race he'd bet his house on, willing Aiden's text to come through first.

Which it did, five minutes later.

As promised, Aiden had sent him an email address and a phone number, as well as a girl's name—Elise—and a note saying, *that's her in the photo with Arlo.* He opened it, spent a minute studying it as he finished his sandwich.

Arlo Fraser was a good-looking young man, no doubt about it. Better still, not a trace of his father in his features—to the extent that it wouldn't be unreasonable to question whether Stan Fraser was actually his father at all. Not question Stan directly, of course. As Aiden had also implied, the girl with him, Elise, put Eleanor in the shade. To be fair, she'd do the same to most women, her face radiant, long blond hair blowing in the wind as they stood on a beach together somewhere, sunlight sparkling on the azure sea behind them.

All that remained was to check the phone numbers.

They matched.

Something came alive in the pit of his stomach at the discovery. Everything Aiden had told him pointed to the fact that Arlo would not have called his father. Somebody else was in possession of his phone. And it wasn't some helpful soul who happened to find it lying on the street.

8

Evan and Guillory were in Ted's Bar and Grill. Given the choice, they'd have been in their usual seats up at the bar in the Jerusalem.

Except the Jerusalem wasn't two minutes from Charlotte's house. Nor was the choice theirs.

Charlotte was Evan's baby sister. A couple of years younger than him, she was married with two kids. A situation she believed ought to be law, and strictly enforced.

Guillory's biological clock had long been of grave concern to her.

And tonight, they'd been invited to dinner. Guillory had muttered something under her breath about roasted fertility hormones in a pheromone sauce when he'd told her.

In her desperation, she'd spotted Ted's as they were driving past five minutes earlier. She'd grabbed the steering wheel as she saw it, forcing Evan to brake hard and the car behind to almost tailgate them, the angry blare of its horn as it swerved around them not unjustified.

'Pull over. *Now!* I need a drink.'

'We'll be late.'

'Don't worry. I'll blame work. I'll say I got delayed at a particularly gruesome murder scene. Mitch loves all that shit.'

Evan pulled to the curb, kept his thoughts to himself. That there was a good chance there'd be a real-life gruesome murder if they stayed in Ted's too long—with him in the starring role.

So here they were, sitting at a table in a pleasant neighborhood bar, even if it wasn't the Jerusalem, Jolie Holland's *Damn Shame* playing on the jukebox. Despite the mellow ambience, Guillory couldn't relax.

'You think I don't know. I've seen the way she mouths *tick, tock* at you when she thinks I'm not looking. There'll probably be an hourglass on the table while we're having dinner. I can hear her now. Evan, be a sweetie and turn Kate's hourglass over, will you? My, doesn't it slip through fast. And Mitch will be sitting there smirking and winking at you. Do all of us a favor and knock her up, will you?'

Wise man that he could be when pushed, he concentrated on his beer, let her work through her angst. There was no stopping her now. She looked at her watch.

'Why do you think they invited us so early?'

It took him a moment to realize that a reply was required. Luckily, he'd been paying attention with one ear and was able to oblige.

'Something good on the TV they want to watch later on?'

He was surprised when she nodded enthusiastically.

'You got it. *The Handmaiden's Tale*. After dinner we're all going upstairs where Charlotte and Mitch will hold me down on the bed while you do your duty to God and Country and Charlotte's opinion of how other people should live their lives.'

It didn't sound so bad to Evan, apart from having his baby sister watch. This thought remained firmly unspoken. In this way, the integrity of his facial bone structure was maintained. For now, at least.

Sadly, it still wasn't over.

She pushed up her sleeve, thrust her bare arm at him.

'Go on, take a big bite. No? Too pale and unappetizing? Don't worry, you can wait until Charlotte's finished grilling me.'

This time he felt comfortable speaking his mind.

'There are other parts I'd rather bite.'

She gave him a look, one that he had no trouble interpreting.

After your sister has finished with me, I'm sewing myself into my panties.

He needed to distract her.

If she continued to monopolize the conversation, her drink would still be as full in an hour's time as it was now. While women are able to multi-task, drinking and talking at the same time is still a challenge.

'I thought you'd never ask,' he said.

Confusion stopped her from resuming her rant.

'What?'

'My day. More productive than I'd hoped.'

He ignored the muttered, *or than anyone expected*, and took her through it. Meeting with Aiden, the information he'd been able to provide—that Arlo was living in Lafayette, his girlfriend Elise, the contact details and his new job. He saved the best until last.

'Guess what he really wanted to be.'

It was as easy for her as it had been for him, helped by her knowing how he enjoyed fate's little games as much as fate did itself.

'A cop.'

'Yep.'

A wave of mock regret washed over her face, at odds with the malicious spark in her eyes every bit as bright as the one in his.

'If only I had some influence with the Commissioner. I'd do anything to get him into the job.'

'He could be your new partner.'

'If he worked hard for three years and made detective, yes he could. I realize that misses your point, which was to annoy me and insult Ryder at the same time.'

Detective Ryder, aka Donut, was her long-term partner, his long-term bête noir. Their relationship amounted to nothing more than a war of attrition. Evan felt that Ryder typified the systemic apathy and laziness that he'd encountered when his wife went missing and he was told that they couldn't waste public resources chasing after every woman who woke up one morning and decided the grass was greener some place else. On the flip side, Ryder believed that Evan led Guillory astray, dragged her, willingly or otherwise, into situations that could get her fired or even killed.

'How is the fat tub of lard?'

'He's very well, and don't be so disrespectful. Even he would be impressed by what you've achieved so far. I know I speak for him when I say we can't wait to see what happens next.'

'Well, for one, you were wrong about the phone call Fraser received. It wasn't a wrong number at all.' He pointed at her glass. 'C'mon, drink up. We're late already.'

She waved it off, made no move to touch her drink.

'The call was from Arlo's phone?'

'Uh-huh. Either Arlo had a massive change of heart and called dear old dad, then backed down when he heard his voice and all the bad memories came flooding back . . .'

'Or someone else has it.'

'And it won't be a little old lady who found it on the street.'

He told her what Aiden had said about the abrupt end to the regular contact that had preceded it, how Arlo hadn't responded since.

'Something's happened to him,' she said. 'What are you

going to do now? Give Stan the bad news as it comes in, or save it and dump it all on him at the end?'

'His guy Landry is doing his best to ensure he gets a minute-by-minute account. He's practically stalking me. He texted me the minute I'd finished with Aiden.' He glanced around the bar. 'I'm surprised he isn't in here now watching me.'

'What did you tell him?'

'I kept it vague.'

That got him an affectionate smile and a leg squeeze to go with it.

'*Attaboy*. Your specialty.'

'Speaking of Landry, did you get a chance to look into him?'

She rocked her hand, her voice equally ambivalent.

'I took a quick look. There's nothing. Most of Fraser's guys have got a rap sheet as long as your arm. Not this guy. It's like he doesn't exist. Maybe if I dug deeper there'd be something. But there's only so much time I can waste looking for someone just because they're a creep and stink of stale cigarette smoke.'

His phone pinged at that point as a text arrived. He pulled it out, saw the name on the screen. Guillory raised an eyebrow at him.

'Charlotte?'

'Yep.'

'Tell her we won't be long. We're busy making a baby.'

He pocketed the phone without reading or replying to the text, got to his feet.

'C'mon, let's go.'

She half stood up herself, a light in her eyes he'd seen before. Mischief, and not completely without malice.

'You sure? I was about to tell you what I heard about Stan Fraser's wife.'

'You're lying.'

She stood up all the way, smoothed the creases out of her pants. Like it made no difference to her if he believed her or not.

'Okay, I'm lying.'

'That's not fair.'

'Who said life is?'

Needless to say, they both sat down again, him without anything to drink, too. She noticed his empty glass.

'Are you going to get another drink?'

'Just get on with it.'

All trace of humor slipped off her face, the joking of a moment ago a distant memory.

'The file's missing. But I spoke to the lead detective who worked the case. The word on the street is that Arlo killed his mother to put her out of her misery. Stan took the blame. He didn't get prosecuted because he paid off the Commissioner and the lead detective. Did I say that the guy lives on a luxury yacht moored in the Bahamas?'

Evan got to his feet, trying hard not to laugh, even if he was the butt of her joke.

'*Ha, ha.* Very funny. C'mon. Don't make me drag you.'

'What? That's the sort of thing you were expecting to hear.'

He couldn't argue, although he wasn't about to admit it. The problem was, she still hadn't made a move to get up. She wasn't calling his bluff. See if he'd be stupid enough to try to manhandle her out of the bar.

She had something for real.

He lowered himself back onto his chair, hoping that nobody in the bar was paying them too much attention. *Up, down, up, down, up down.*

'Tell me,' he said.

'There is no file. Not on his wife's death, anyway. There was no suspicion of foul play. But there is a rumor. His wife left him six months before she died for a guy called Tony Christensen.

Then she got ill and her new man promptly dumped her. Not what he signed up for. Saint Stan took her back and looked after her until the end. You want to finish the story for me?'

He pretended to think about it, a deep furrow in his brow.

'Not sure. Either the other guy hasn't been seen since, or he was found floating face-down in the river.'

She nodded approvingly, as if spending time with her was finally rubbing off on his detective skills.

'What's it gonna be?'

'I'm going with the river.'

'Yep. Except he didn't drown. He'd been beaten to death.'

'Like a lesson? So that he could understand what it feels like to die in pain, like Fraser's wife did.'

'Exactly. But without the intravenous morphine.'

Finally, she pushed herself to her feet and they headed out. They didn't talk on the short journey from Ted's to Charlotte and Mitch's house. It had nothing to do with Guillory's upcoming ordeal striking her mute, either.

It was the message behind the parable of the heartless criminal who took pity on his cheating wife and took her back and cared for her in her final days. A parable from the gospel according to Guillory just for him.

That's the sort of man you're working for.

A FEW MILES AWAY ON THE OTHER SIDE OF TOWN, SAINT STAN WAS at his usual table in The Backroom. Landry was with him.

The atmosphere was far from good.

'He's holding back,' Landry said. He pulled out his phone, showed Fraser the text Evan had sent him.

Too early to say. Waiting for more information.

'He was with the guy for a quarter hour or more. Then he went and sat in the park. He got a message. Looked like he'd won the lottery. I'm telling you, it was from the kid he met with. A kid he wouldn't have known existed if I hadn't told him in the first place. The guy's incompetent, as well as holding back.'

Fraser concentrated on his whiskey glass as Landry vented his irritation, making a looping figure of eight with it on the table top.

Had he been wrong to trust Buckley with the job?

Except there was a connection between them beyond the trading of favors back and forth.

Unlike Landry who had all the compassion of a scorpion, Buckley understood what he was going through. Understood his pain and frustration.

When Buckley's wife had gone missing all those years ago and the lazy, incompetent cops had given him the bum's rush, told him they didn't have time to chase after every woman who decided she wanted someone with a bigger bank balance or a bigger johnson, the guy had gone to the station house and punched the captain, for Christ's sake.

His kind of guy.

Stan's situation wasn't so different.

He'd been treated like a piece of shit because of how he made his living. As far as the cops had been concerned, his son going missing meant one less potential criminal to worry about. A low-life taken off the board before he could get started. It was a positive thing, a cause for celebration. Less work for them in the future, which, as Buckley knew, is how they liked it.

Lazy, incompetent assholes.

Not Guillory. But that was a different story.

The thing was, Buckley knew what it was like to not know. To be tormented by the *what ifs* in the small hours of the morning when sleep is an alien concept, a luxury reserved for others more deserving of its temporary respite.

It suddenly struck Stan that Landry's news made him sad more than it made him angry.

Not only that, it made him realize that it's not possible to control everything in life. That everything comes with a price. He believed Buckley's empathy would work in his favor. And he had to accept that the guy's conscience might work against him.

The alternative was Landry, a man not troubled by the burdens of conscience.

Thankfully Landry had lapsed into silence. At least he had the sense to realize that saying, *Buckley's holding back* for the sixth time in the space of five minutes would achieve nothing other than to annoy him.

'What do you suggest?' Stan said.

'I'll talk to the kid.' He waved his phone angrily in Stan's face. 'I went back to where he works after Buckley sent this bullshit text and waited for him. Followed him home.'

Stan knew what Landry *talking* to someone entailed. He'd *talked* to people on Stan's behalf many times. You didn't tend to see those guys around much afterwards. He'd had a particularly intense *talk* with Tony Christensen after Janet died. It had actually been a three-way conversation. Stan's fist clenched just thinking about it.

Whoever this kid was didn't deserve that. It might come to it if Buckley didn't come through, but not yet.

'No. Let's see what Buckley does next.'

Guillory could've told him, it was a question never far from her mind.

If he'd been paying more attention to his face, Stan would've seen exactly what Landry thought about it, too.

9

Twelve hundred miles away, Theresa Thibodeaux stood outside The Bulldog sports bar on Perkins Road in Baton Rouge. She was sucking hard on a cigarette like her life depended on it, feeling slightly light-headed, the thundering of her heart in her chest making her nauseous. She took a long last drag, dropped the butt and ground it to dust under the sturdy sensibleness of her heel. Already she wanted another one. Instead, she took a deep breath, held it, then let it out slowly—as if that had ever made a difference to anything or anyone.

About as much use as getting down on her knees and praying to a stone-deaf God. Something she felt she'd been doing a lot of recently.

At least Innocent Lejeune's money provided where the Good Lord manifestly failed to do so—which was at the end of pretty much every month, thanks to the miserly salary Jackass Bray paid her.

But while the money was nice, doing something for it, not so much. Although it wasn't a fortune, she'd come to rely on it. And until today, she'd never had to lift a finger to earn it.

She almost felt disloyal. *Almost.* Briefly closing her eyes in order for an unwelcome picture of the Jackass to appear in her mind's eye soon put an end to that nonsense.

She couldn't put it off any longer.

She pushed through the door, the smell of beer and fried food and too many noisy excited people packed into too small a space greeting her. The sound of D.L. Menard's *The Back Door* struggled to be heard above the clamor making her head spin.

On the far side of the room Innocent Lejeune was seated at a table looking like he owned the place. He probably did, for all she knew.

Had Theresa not been a devout church-going woman and, instead, prone to cussing, she'd have thought to herself, *innocent my ass*. He was the most inappropriately-named man she'd ever come across. On the planet, for that matter. She was aware that he was a criminal of some kind. She'd asked around when he first approached her. One of her sister's husband's less savory drinking buddies had known the name, the reputation more so. Fortunately, he'd been short on details—or he'd chosen to withhold them. That suited Theresa just fine. Avoided difficult decisions of conscience and too much time on her ageing knees in the confessional.

Lejeune was also the scariest man she knew. Given that her time was split between the office and the Sacred Heart Catholic Church on Main Street, that wasn't necessarily much of a feat in itself. That caveat didn't stop the leaden feeling in her legs as she made her way across the room, the queasy churning in her stomach.

That's not to say Lejeune was the most immoral man she'd ever known. A hard-fought contest it might be in the godless place the modern world had turned into, but it would be a cold day in hell before Jackass Bray was knocked off that particular pedestal.

Innocent rose from his seat as Theresa approached, pulled

out a chair for her. All smiles as he pushed it under her butt like a fawning waiter in a fancy restaurant—not that Theresa spent a lot of time in up-market restaurants.

He raised a hand that Theresa suspected had killed more than one man, and immediately a waitress appeared at the table with a glass of chilled Sauvignon Blanc for her, the condensation beading on the glass as she liked it. Theresa didn't want to know how he knew what she'd have chosen.

Had she been a braver—and more stupid—woman, she might have said to him, if you know so much, what do you need me for?

Seemed the omnipotent Lejeune could see through walls, too. Or at least he smelled the lingering cigarette on her breath. He inhaled deeply, a gesture that seemed vaguely obscene to Theresa, as if he was taking a part of her into himself, then smiled broadly.

'I'd have joined you if I'd known you were outside smoking. I miss the old days when you were allowed to smoke inside.'

Theresa missed the old days when she wasn't beholden to a man like Innocent Lejeune. She raised her glass in response to him raising his, nonetheless, clinked glasses.

'I was surprised to hear from you,' Lejeune carried on. 'I was beginning to think I never would.'

It wasn't a criticism, she knew that. He wouldn't have wanted her to invent something simply to appear to be earning her money. She still wasn't a hundred percent sure that her call had been warranted. Nevertheless, here she was, sharing a table with a known criminal in a busy bar for everyone to see. She glanced nervously around the room. Hoped Father Ignatius hadn't snuck in for a quick one after the altar boys guzzled all the altar wine.

She looked at Lejeune, didn't know where to start. Or whether to start at all. He'd been so vague about what he was interested in when he first approached her.

Any unusual behavior. Anything that appears to be worrying Bray.

Theresa had been tempted to tell him to keep his money. The old bastard was so ill-tempered the whole time, how was she supposed to spot the difference?

Except Ritter was bad news.

She felt it in her bones. A man who believed that by bringing misery into the lives of others, he could fill the emptiness inside himself. To be in his presence was to feel dirty and defiled for reasons that she could never identify. All she knew was that she did not want him near her. And if he were ever to touch her . . .

Off to the side, the door to the kitchen opened. A waiter carrying two plates loaded with fish tacos bustled out, billowing steam and the smell of hot cooking oil coming with him. Mercifully, the food wasn't destined for them, an unasked-for, unwanted meal courtesy of Lejeune. The waiter brushed the back of her chair as he swept past.

It jolted her into action. She took a sip of wine, told him what she thought she might have of interest.

'Bray had a visitor today. A man called Ritter.'

She shuddered at the mention of his name. Tried to wash away the taste of it with another mouthful, thinking it would take half a vineyard to do so. Lejeune didn't miss the sour twist of her mouth, the loathing in her voice.

'You don't like him?'

'He gives me the creeps.'

'Does he work for Bray?'

'Not officially, no. He's not on the payroll. He does occasional jobs for him.'

Lejeune nodded and smiled again to indicate that he knew what Theresa was telling him. It wouldn't be to lend a hand when Theresa was snowed under and needed help with the filing and correspondence.

'How did Bray react to Ritter turning up?' Lejeune said.

Theresa couldn't stop herself smiling at the memory of it.

'Like he'd seen a preview of what's waiting for him in hell. I've never seen a person turn so deathly pale. Even the blood in the broken veins in his cheeks drained away.'

'Did you catch what they talked about?'

Theresa dropped her eyes. Shook her head.

Lejeune leaned across the table, put his hand on her arm. It was unpleasantly hot and moist. Theresa prayed that he hadn't felt her recoil at his touch.

'It's okay. I don't expect you to be able to hear through walls. And I wouldn't want you to do anything that made him suspicious. I don't want to cause you any trouble.'

Theresa would've believed a rattlesnake telling her it didn't mean to poison her before she believed that. She felt the need to explain herself, all the same.

'They went out immediately.'

Lejeune let go of her arm, opened his hands like the Pope at Easter. Say no more.

'How was he when he got back?'

Theresa stifled a laugh. It came out as a wine-infused snort. There was more than a hint of spiteful pleasure, of schadenfreude, behind it that she'd have to do extra time in the confessional for.

'In a foul mood. And don't ask me how I can tell the difference.'

Lejeune smiled with her, a gold eye tooth flashing. Rocking gently back and forth on his chair.

'So Ritter had bad news for him. I wonder what it was.'

Theresa knew that in the next moment or two Lejeune would become even more charming in advance of asking her to do her best—no pressure—to find out what that bad news might be. Except she suddenly got the feeling that he already knew.

That when he first approached her, he wasn't interested in just anything out of the ordinary concerning Jack Bray. He was waiting and paying to hear about something in particular.

A moment later he proved her right, but not before noticing that her glass was empty. Up shot his hand and before she knew it a second chilled glass had materialized. She didn't even have time to pretend to object.

Lejeune leaned back in his chair, a faraway look in his normally lifeless eyes. She was aware that the music had changed. Something mellower, as if the management matched the music to the changes in his mood. After a minute she recognized Cajun L'Angelus' cover of *Lac Bijou*. For one heart-stopping moment she thought he was about to offer her his hand and ask her to dance. He was only reaching for his drink.

'I never told you what lies behind my interest in Bray, did I?'

Theresa shook her head and took a gulp of wine. Hoping this wasn't one of those *I'll have to kill you afterwards* situations.

'I don't think so.'

She didn't want to know, but knew better than to say *no* to a man like Innocent Lejeune. She cocked her head as if she couldn't wait to hear a tale of greed and corruption and wanton violence.

Except she was wrong.

'My younger brother, Thibaud, was involved in a plane crash five years ago . . .'

10

If the kid didn't stop crying soon, Landry was going to give him something to cry about.

First Stan going soft. And now this.

He didn't know what the world was coming to. He was glad he wouldn't be around in fifty years' time because God knows how fucked up things would be by then, the way young people were.

Jesus. You'd have thought he'd broken both the kid's legs, not his little finger.

He leaned down, stuck his face in Aiden's. Close enough for their noses to touch.

'Stop sniveling. I can't hear what you're saying through all the snot.'

'I *told* you. I don't have an address.'

Whine, whine, whine. It made Landry want to spit.

He kicked the chair over onto its side in disgust, the sniveling kid with it. The pussy howled again as the side of his head hit the tiled floor.

Landry thought about giving it a good stomp. Could not be

bothered. It'd be like kicking a kitten into a wall so hard its internal organs burst. Too easy.

He smiled to himself. Maybe he needed to change his technique. Move with the times. How about if he promised to buy an electric car and never eat red meat again? And call everyone *they*.

He couldn't help wondering what Stan's son Arlo would be like if they ever found him. If he was anything like his friend Aiden tied to the chair, Landry wouldn't have wanted him back. Maybe he'd have a word with Buckley. Tell him if he finds Arlo and he's turned into a faggot from turning too many tricks in public urinals, it's okay by him if he tells Stan that he couldn't find him.

That was for the future.

Right now, he had to decide if the kid was telling the truth.

He knew these days it was all email and Instagram and all that online shit, but why wouldn't you give a friend your address, too?

I've moved to Lafayette but I'm not gonna tell you where.

What kind of friend is that?

Landry didn't have any friends so he couldn't say for sure, but it didn't sound right. If he did have a friend who said, *I'm not giving you my address*, he'd be thinking, *well fuck you, pal, get yourself a new friend*.

He took a minute to look around the kitchen. It was a nice place the kid had here. Except for the lock on the front door, that is. Cheap piece of shit. Might as well have left the door wide open, tacked a note to it: *come on in and make yourself at home*.

Which is what Landry had done. The kid almost soiled himself when he jerked awake, saw Landry sitting on a pile of discarded clothes on the chair in the corner of his bedroom at five o'clock in the morning.

He stepped over the upended chair to get to where the

saucepans were hanging on a rack above the kitchen counter. Selected a big one and filled it with water from the faucet. Put it on the stove and got the gas going. Couldn't see where the saucepan lids were. No matter, he wasn't in a hurry. The kid's whiny voice drifted up from the floor behind him.

'What are you doing?'

Landry closed his eyes. Counted to ten.

'What's it look like I'm doing? Boiling some water. *Jesus Christ.*'

'I don't have an address.'

Whine, whine, whine, again. Much more of this and Landry was going to lose his temper.

'I don't believe you. Where's the sugar?'

That shut the kid up. Then a stupid question, his voice breaking.

'What for?'

Landry squatted down beside him. Pretended he was talking to a puppy. The runt of the litter, at that.

'It's not because I'm going to make you a nice sugary cup of coffee. You young people waste your whole damn lives on the internet but you still don't know jack shit about anything. Sugar makes the boiling water stick to the skin, dummy. So it doesn't run off.'

Landry stood up again. Saw that a different sticky liquid was running out of the bottom of the kid's pajama pants leg. You wouldn't want that thrown in your face, either.

Seemed he'd asked for more whining. The kid obliged, bubbling snot nearly as fast as the water on the stove.

'*Please.* You've looked on my phone. You've looked on my computer. I haven't got a fucking address for him. You think I keep all my friend's addresses in my head?'

Landry looked at him in a different light.

This was more like it. Ignoring that he'd just pissed himself, that is. A little spark of something that wasn't more whining.

And he had a point.

It gelled with a theory Landry had. In the future, wars wouldn't be fought with guns and missiles or even chemical weapons. The weapons of the future would be designed to immobilize all of the enemy's cell phones. Then the whole army would be left standing there like spare pricks at a wedding not knowing what to do because their phones weren't telling them to breathe, to walk, to take a dump, whatever. They'd literally fill up with shit until they burst. Someone had pointed out to him one time that if the phones weren't telling them how to eat, how would they fill up with shit? That was the last time that guy asked a stupid question.

Reluctantly, Landry turned off the gas.

Whatever people thought about him, he didn't hurt people for the sake of it. Punishment, to get information, but not for fun like some sick bastards.

He gave the kid a gentle kick.

'It's your lucky day.'

Funny how the kid didn't look as if he believed him. Whatever. He pulled out a knife, flicked it open. *Snick*. One of his favorite sounds. Pointed at the kid with it, who was looking like he was about to shit himself.

'Relax.'

One-handed he pulled the chair upright with the kid on it, then sliced the tape securing his ankles and wrists. The kid immediately slipped off the chair onto the floor like he wanted to lie in a pool of his own piss.

Landry let out a weary sigh, felt like rubbing his face in it.

Sometimes he despaired for the future of the human race.

11

Six hours after Aiden had woken up in the middle of a living nightmare, Evan landed at Lafayette Regional Airport. It had necessitated a stupidly early start to his day and he'd been relieved when he didn't see any sign of Landry tailing him on the way to the airport. Or hear from him, by text or phone call, demanding to know what was on today's agenda.

He'd relaxed. Enjoyed the flight as much as anyone can enjoy being squeezed into a too-small seat in goat class next to a nervous sweaty fat woman who should've booked two seats and who talked incessantly for five hours.

That all ended the minute he switched his phone back on.

His heart sank when he saw three missed calls from Aiden. He called him back immediately. Feeling like he was dialing *G for Guilt*, his text to Landry in his mind.

Too early to say. Waiting for more information.

Whatever had happened to Aiden—and it wouldn't be good—it was likely as a result of him not telling Landry the truth about what Aiden had told him. So much for the crap Landry came out with about Stan Fraser wanting to get things done amicably.

Aiden's opening words confirmed it. A torrent of panic and fear and accusation pouring out of him like a single rising-pitch scream.

'I'm in the hospital. One of Fraser's psychopaths broke into my apartment this morning and broke my finger then threatened to throw boiling water in my face because I couldn't tell him Arlo's address...'

Evan held the phone away from his ear as he waited for Aiden to exhaust himself. Feeling his own pulse quicken in a primeval response to Aiden's fear. Finally, Aiden ran out of steam, a deep shuddering breath coming down the line. Evan felt drained with him.

The worst had already happened and there was nothing he could do to change it. But there was something he needed to say before they moved on.

'I didn't tell him about you. He followed me when I met Eleanor. He was watching the argument you had with her. He's the one who told me about you, not the other way around.'

If silences can be disbelieving, that's what he heard now. He waited for Aiden to say something.

'Which means Fraser didn't believe you when you told him I don't have an address for Arlo. That's why he sent that animal.'

Landry might be an animal, but Evan was currently feeling like a much lower life form. Something that lived at the bottom of a pond, perhaps, or under a flat rock. Something without a backbone, anyway, that nature had decided wasn't going to evolve.

Honest Evan—not present at this juncture—would've told the truth. That he'd deliberately chosen not to tell Stan anything, which is why he'd sent Landry.

Mea culpa.

Grateful Evan went with the flow, let Aiden believe it was all Evil Stan's fault.

Mea douchebag.

'So Landry knows Arlo's here in Lafayette?' Evan said.

He did his best to keep any hint of accusation out of his voice. Trouble was, Aiden was listening for it. Heard it whether it was there or not, an irritating whine in his voice that Landry would've recognized.

'I didn't have any choice. He broke my finger. I can't type, can't do my job, with all my fingers broken...'

Again, Evan waited. This time as Aiden worked through his own guilt. Evan knew what was hurting him more than the throbbing ache of a broken finger. A bone-deep hurt that the doctors can't prescribe a little colored pill to soothe, that no mommy can kiss away as she folds you into the comfort of her welcoming bosom.

I should've fought back.

I should've been braver, tougher, not a snot-bubbling pussy lying in my own piss.

And I shouldn't have set a monster on my friend so that my own pain stops.

There was nothing else to say. On either side. A great big guilt trip all round. They ended the call quietly, as if someone had died and their conversation was intruding. No empty promise to keep Aiden updated from Evan, no encouraging *Good Luck!* from Aiden.

Evan stood for a long while with his phone in his hand, passengers flowing around him on either side, the occasional muttered complaint about what the hell was he doing standing there blocking the way washing over him.

One question in his mind.

To call Stan, or not to call him?

What would he say?

What the hell do you think you're doing?

Call your attack dog off.

I quit.

Shove your dirty money up your illegal ass.

In the end, good sense prevailed. Cue applause from Guillory, and not a little surprise. No good would come from it. Not with him in the mood he was in at the moment. Fraser was not a man anybody wanted as an enemy. Besides, something Landry had said had come to him as he listened to the story of Aiden's ordeal.

Mr. Fraser allows me to exercise my own judgment up to a certain point.

There was a chance Landry was acting on his own initiative —if that was the right word for breaking a person's finger. Stan might know nothing about it.

He pocketed the phone and took from the situation what he needed.

Landry would soon be in Lafayette shadowing him. Re-interviewing the people he felt Evan had failed to elicit sufficient information from. Bringing his own brand of happy sunshine into their unsuspecting lives.

And only a stupid man would believe that Landry drew the line at breaking fingers.

It put an unwelcome additional pressure on him. An unpalatable choice to be made. Keep Stan updated real-time, or accept that more innocent people would get hurt.

He rented a car and drove from the airport to his bed and breakfast accommodation feeling somewhat conflicted. The amount of cash Fraser had pressed on him had made him forgo the nastiness of the cheap airport motels he would normally stay in. Instead, he'd booked himself a suite on the second floor of an 1820s restored Creole house nestled on a quiet street in the Sterling Grove Historic District.

After the disturbing conversation with Aiden and its

implications for the rest of his investigation, that luxury now seemed even more indulgent and inappropriate.

In his room, he took a minute to update Crow by text. Advise him that he had sufficient leads to work with and certainly more than anything Crow might find in any online database. Then he set about making inroads into those leads.

He'd spent some of the time while he waited for his flight researching the local papers in the Lafayette area. It hadn't taken long—there were only two of them.

The switchboard operator at the first one, *The Lafayette Daily Advertiser*, took the inquiry seriously when he asked to be put through to Arlo Fraser, who he believed was a new hire on the crime desk. She checked the system and informed him that they had no record of an employee by that name, past or present.

The second one was different. The woman who answered the phone at *The Daily Acadian* laughed out loud as if he'd asked to be put through to General Robert E. Lee, then said she'd never heard of him. Ignoring for now that she'd have heard of General Lee.

Evan couldn't see what was so funny.

'Why did you laugh?'

He pictured her shaking her head, the laughter still in her voice as she asked a question of her own rather than answer his.

'Are you sure it was the crime desk? Not the travel desk or the fashion desk or the sports desk . . .?' Trailing off and chuckling to herself as she ran out of desks to suggest.

'You're telling me you're not very big?'

'You got it. Used to be bigger, in the good ol' days. *The Daily Acadian* was a good place to work back then. Not the graveyard it is now. Mr. Broussard, he's the owner, he's about a hundred and ten and he's not interested anymore. Going ga-ga too, by all accounts. He was upset when they forced him to employ women to do anything other than clean and make the coffee. He certainly didn't want to spend the money producing an online version.' She let out a heavy sigh that made her sound old enough to have been at school with old Mr. Broussard herself. 'I figure we'll be gone by Christmas. I don't mind. I only came back part-time and I was thinking of quitting anyway. It's hard on the youngsters...'

He got the impression she'd be happy to explain exactly how hard it would be on each member of staff and the reasons why, if he stayed on the line long enough. He headed her off.

'Who's the editor?'

The direct question put a pause in her stride. She answered nonetheless.

'Ralph Fontenot. He's nearly as old as I am. He'll most likely retire, same as me.'

'The name sounds familiar.'

The woman laughed again. A good-natured sound that suggested she'd known Fontenot for a long time, that she was laughing with him, not at him.

'Yeah? It's not because he's won the Pulitzer Prize, that's for sure.'

'No, I used to know a girl called Elise Fontenot.'

'You don't say. She's his daughter.'

Evan played his part, said *small world*. He felt a time-filling anecdote looming. How the woman on the other end had been to Europe one time and met another woman she'd known in high school in the ladies' bathroom of the restaurant her husband had taken her to for their anniversary, or something similar and equally uninteresting. He cut in before the first, *I remember one time...*

'Can you put me through to Ralph?'

'He's not in the office at the moment. I can let you have his cell phone number if you like. He'll be glad to get a call on it. It doesn't ring that much these days.'

He'll wish it had stayed that way, Evan thought as he took the number down and they ended the call.

It was quiet in his room, the low hiss of the air conditioning and the background traffic hum outside the only sounds. A situation that had suited his purpose so far. Allowed him to concentrate on the voices of the people he'd called. Perhaps identify any hesitation or wariness when he asked to speak to Arlo.

Now he turned on the TV, surfed the channels until he found a noisy kid's program that did more for birth control than any known contraceptive ever had. Cranked up the volume. Dialed the number he'd been given for Fontenot. It was answered immediately. The curt professional bark of a man who wants to make it clear that it was business as usual at *The Daily Acadian* despite all the unfounded and malicious rumors flying around.

'Fontenot.'

Evan moved the microphone away from his mouth, maximizing the background noise going down the line. Took a flyer on how he guessed Arlo would've addressed his girlfriend's father and worked a breathless urgency into his voice.

'Ralph? It's Arlo.'

Relief mixed with exasperation came back at him.

'*Jesus*, kid. Where've you been? You've had me worried sick.'

Evan hit the red button on the TV remote, plunged the room back into a welcome silence once again.

'Don't hang up Mr. Fontenot, but it's not Arlo.'

There was a momentary pause where it could've gone either way. Then Fontenot's voice, suspicion pushing aside the relief.

'Who are you? You're not from around here.'

'No, I'm not. And I'd rather not have this conversation over the phone. I'm sorry I tricked you. Your reaction tells me you're worried about Arlo. So am I. We can meet in a coffee shop or a diner if you don't want me coming to the house or the office.'

As is often the case, suggesting an alternative that is totally unacceptable—a stranger coming to his house—as well as one that could be construed as a threat—coming to a person's place of work—makes the other options more palatable, reduces the chances of a direct refusal. How about not at all?

'You know the Magpie Café on Garfield Street?' Fontenot said.

'I can find it.'

'I'll be there in half an hour.'

EVAN HAD TIME TO KILL BEFORE MEETING WITH FONTENOT. He passed some of it by calling a person who at times wanted to kill him—Guillory.

He started with what he would later learn was a prescient greeting.

'You'll be sorry to hear my plane didn't crash on the way down.'

Things hadn't gone particularly well the previous evening. Charlotte hadn't actually dinged her wine glass with her fork to get everyone's attention and then demanded to know when Evan and Guillory were going to do their duty to the future of the human race, but it had been close. She'd steered the conversation towards the joys and achievements of hers and other people's children whenever possible until Guillory's eyes glazed over and he felt an unpleasant wilting sensation below the belt line.

Then, on the way home, he reminded her that he was flying to Lafayette the next morning. She claimed he hadn't told her. He foolishly said she'd forgotten because she was so annoyed at Charlotte.

Worse, it was her day off the following day. She was looking forward to a lie-in. So, no, she wouldn't be driving him to the airport at five o'clock in the morning, aka the middle of the night.

Now, he was planning on telling her that the parable she'd told about Saint Stan and the man who'd been found floating in the river, Tony Christensen, had already been proved true.

It took her a moment to get over the unorthodox greeting before she responded in kind.

'Doesn't matter. Running Stan Fraser's errands guarantees you'll get caught up in something bad before too long. You won't make it to the end of the week. Done anything to earn your dirty money, yet?'

He was standing at the French doors looking out across his balcony to the lush gardens beyond. Ancient oak trees dotted the well-kept lawn, dappled sunlight filtering through their branches. A circular ornamental fountain took pride of place in the path leading to the vine-covered front gate. Now he turned away, took in the room with its fancy carved wooden bed and crisp linen, the Persian rug on the floor with its air of faded grandeur, the antique table and chair against the wall. From here it looked as if crime paid very nicely, thank you. He kept the thought to himself, soon chased away by the memory of his conversation with Aiden.

'Did you look any further into Landry?'

'On my day off? Actually, no. I've been too busy washing your car.'

'Really?'

'Of course not. But I'll keep it a lot cleaner than you do after you get killed on Stan's behalf and it comes to me. You have left it to me in your will, haven't you?'

Had they not been to Charlotte's for dinner the previous

evening with all that it entailed, he might have said, *no, Charlotte's son Kyle wants it.*

Not today.

Besides, she'd already moved on. Or back.

'Why are you so concerned about Landry? Is he down there with you?'

'Not yet.'

Two little words. That's all it took to condemn him.

It took her a moment to catch on, all trace of the joking that had been in her voice as they discussed the future ownership of his car gone.

'You said you kept things vague about what Aiden told you. You didn't tell him Arlo's in Lafayette, did you?'

He thought about letting silence answer for him, silences being obliging that way, came out with it himself instead.

'Landry asked Aiden himself. At five o'clock this morning.'

'When I wouldn't get out of bed and take you to the airport?'

'Exactly. Although I don't think the two are connected.'

'I'm assuming Aiden was happy to supply Landry with the information he wanted?'

'After Landry broke his finger, yeah.'

A sharp hiss came down the line at him. She stopped short of wasting her breath, stating the obvious.

Your fault because you kept the information to yourself.

'You think Aiden would be prepared to press charges?' she said.

It didn't take a lot of cerebral activity to answer that one, the memory of the fear and panic in Aiden's voice still fresh in his mind.

'I doubt it. Landry scared the shit out of him. But it's worth asking.'

'Handy for you if he agreed. Keep Landry out of your hair.'

'That's what I was hoping.'

They left the words that were pulsing on the airwaves between them unspoken.

Ask Aiden to antagonize Landry, put himself at risk of reprisal, in order to make your life less complicated.

Not what anyone would call a fair deal. Even if it was one that she understood and was all too familiar with as a law enforcement professional. The perennial problem of persuading innocent witnesses and victims to put themselves in a violent criminal's crosshairs for the good of society as an undeserving ungrateful whole.

She chose to end the call on a lighter note. One that highlighted the fact that she'd be spending at least part of her day wasting her time and breath after all.

'Stranger things have happened in Buckley La-la Land.'

12

The mid-afternoon lull had set in at the Magpie Café, the place virtually empty when Evan arrived ten minutes later. The sole waitress on duty was eating her lunch at a table beside the kitchen door when he walked in. He waved at her to finish her meal but she came across all the same, wiping her fingers on her pants and finishing a mouthful of food.

He ordered coffee and got a free *is that all?* look thrown in, and Fontenot had turned up by the time she brought it over. Evan waved at him as he stood in the doorway, looking exactly as he'd expected. Somewhat disheveled in a white shirt and a striped tie at half-mast, the only thing missing being the stereotypical green visor beloved of Hollywood newspaper editors, or a permanent indentation in his forehead where one habitually sat.

Fontenot started with the same question Evan had avoided on the phone.

'Who are you?'

Evan pushed a business card across the table to him, gave him a moment to digest it.

'I'm working for Arlo's father. He's hired me to find him.'

He left it at that. He had no idea what Arlo might have told Elise. Less idea about what she might have told her father. If you're trying to persuade your dad to take a chance on your boyfriend, you might not mention that he's the son of a career criminal.

In this instance, a complete lack of knowledge on the part of the Fontenots, a clean slate, would be the best situation, leaving Evan untarnished by his client's reputation.

It wasn't to be.

Fontenot toyed with Evan's card a moment longer, then put it in his own wallet. An encouraging sign at odds with what he then said.

'I know something about Arlo's family history. I know he ran away from home when he was a teenager and he's been drifting ever since. That suggests to me that he doesn't want to go home. And until you turned up today, his father wasn't particularly concerned that he's not there, either. Unless you've been looking unsuccessfully for the past ten years.'

Had the last line been delivered with a smile, mocking or otherwise, Evan would've capitalized on the chance to create a bond with humor. *Only ten years? I'm just getting started.* As it was, he shook his head. Like everyone before him, Fontenot wanted to know, why now?

An abridged version of the truth was called for since it gelled so well with Fontenot's own experience.

'When I tricked you, you said, *You've had me worried sick.* Not just plain worried. Worried sick. And all you are is his girlfriend's dad.'

The truth hit him as the words rolled out of his mouth. Fontenot hadn't known Arlo well, or for long—no more than a few months at most. There was something else at play. Something that caused him to be more worried than he should have been over the safety of a young man he barely knew.

Guilt.

Whatever might have befallen Arlo, Ralph Fontenot believed he was to blame.

All the more reason to tell the truth, to leverage that guilt.

'Arlo's old man got a call from Arlo's phone. Not necessarily from Arlo. His phone. The caller hung up without saying anything. That's why he hired me. That's why he's looking now, after all these years. Whatever it is, it's the same thing that's making you worried sick. You want to take me through it from the beginning?'

Everything about Fontenot screamed, *not if I can help it*. He waved at the waitress who'd disappeared completely for the past five minutes, then waited until she'd brought a cup of coffee for him and refilled Evan's before launching into it.

'Elise met Arlo six months ago. I didn't like him to start with. I thought he was a waste of space. It was clear from what Elise said about him that he'd spent his whole life drifting from place to place. That was the last thing I wanted for her. To get attached to him and then one day he's gone. Either without her, which would break her heart, or with her, and that'd do the same to mine. But he hung around and he was an okay kid. He got a job tending bar and I grew to like him.

'Then Elise started working on me. How Arlo really wanted to be a reporter and couldn't I give him a chance? A break.' He paused, took a sip of coffee, a faraway look in his eyes to go with the soft smile on his face. 'My wife died a couple of years ago. I could never say no to Elise before, and after her mom passed, it got ten times worse. I was thinking about myself, too. If I got him a real job here in Lafayette, he'd be less likely to move on. I told her I'd see what I could do. I don't suppose you're aware of the situation at the paper—'

'Gone by Christmas because you haven't got an online edition is what the woman on the switchboard said.'

Fontenot looked like he wanted to spit, anger tempered by resignation in his voice.

'Bernadette ought to keep her mouth shut. If she says it to the advertisers as easily as she said it to you, it'll be more like Labor Day. Anyway, I suppose what I was thinking was, how much harm can he do if the paper's going down the toilet come what may? And he'd have a bit of experience under his belt when we shut down that would help him get a job elsewhere. The thing is, old man Broussard isn't looking to take on new hires right before we go belly-up. It couldn't be official. I paid him out of petty cash. He was still tending bar and didn't want much. It was the opportunity to prove himself he was after. To have something published to show future employers. Except, like I couldn't put him on the payroll, I couldn't send him out there as our new crime reporter on the breaking stories.'

'You put him on a cold case?'

'Yeah. See if he could string two words together without using any of that shorthand shit they use to text these days. But more than that, find out what his instincts were like.'

'And now you're worried sick they were too sharp for his own good.'

Fontenot nodded, looking like he'd taken a mouthful of cold coffee dregs.

'I should never have put him on that story.'

Evan didn't waste his breath saying that he couldn't have known. That hindsight is a wonderful thing, so don't give yourself a hard time. Fontenot didn't have the look of a man who'd made an honest mistake. Evan had a premonition growing inside him that the guy had known exactly where things would lead. Instead, he asked a question he already knew the answer to.

'Have you reported him missing?'

Fontenot gave him a look. *Are you serious?*

'I might have if I thought they'd take it seriously. You'd like to report a drifter who ran away from home when he was sixteen as missing, would you, sir? This is the same drifter you paid a few bucks and told him to go research a story that's been dead five years? And now you're surprised you haven't heard from him?' He shook his head, no thank you. 'I don't need to make an official report to have people laugh at me. They'd accuse me of making it up to try to boost sales of the *Acadian*. Charge me with wasting police time.'

Evan couldn't disagree. It still didn't feel right.

'Have you heard from him at all since you gave him the job?'

'No. I didn't expect to.'

He didn't need to spell out why not. Arlo had spent the past ten years living on his wits. Looking out for himself. His pride meant he wasn't going to call Fontenot every two minutes for guidance or a pat on the back. He wanted to walk into Fontenot's office, slap a front-page-ready article on his desk, *bet you're glad you took a chance on me now*.

'Has Elise heard from him?'

'She hadn't the last time I spoke to her. She's not talking to me at the moment.'

'She blames you?'

Fontenot opened his hands wide, what can I say? Then laughed, a nervous reaction to the memory of his own stupidity, which he now explained.

'I mentioned that she was the one who wanted me to give him a job in the first place.'

Evan winced in sympathy. Didn't need to state the obvious. That pertinent facts have no place in a heated argument with a woman.

'She said I should never have put him on that story,' Fontenot said. 'That I knew it would end badly.'

Evan felt like grabbing his tie, hauling him over the table. Yelling at him.

Tell me what the damn story is.

Instead, he made a stab at the second mistake written all over Fontenot's face.

'I hope you didn't point out that Arlo was the sort of ambitious young man who wouldn't have accepted anything less than a serious story to get his teeth into.'

Fontenot nodded unhappily.

'I'm afraid so. As a result, I'm the monster who won't accept responsibility for my bad judgment and wants to blame Elise and Arlo himself. She hasn't spoken to me since.'

Evan had planned on talking to Elise. That conversation now became more pressing. Fontenot's feeling of guilt had been obvious from the start. His daughter's accusation that he recklessly put Arlo on a story he knew could end badly suggested that guilt was well-founded.

For now, he needed to get the facts from Fontenot.

'Tell me what you put him to work on.'

13

Jack Bray's factotum Ritter got to St. Martinville about the same time as Evan met with Ralph Fontenot in downtown Lafayette. He drove directly to the Long Branch Cafe on South Main Street. A black sheriff's office SUV with the biggest bull bars Ritter had ever seen and *Serving Since 1813* painted in gold lettering on the front fender, was parked on the shoulder immediately outside.

Dixon was already inside waiting for him. Filling his time and his doughy face with a piece of pecan pie the size of a brick and washing it down with gulps of coffee before he'd finished chewing. Ritter ordered coffee and gave the pie a miss. Thinking the table didn't look substantial enough to take the weight of another piece. Besides, if he felt hungry, there were more than enough crumbs on Dixon's khaki sheriff's deputy uniform to satisfy any normal person's hunger.

He got straight to it as soon as his coffee arrived and the girl had gone back behind the counter.

'Tell me about the guy who pulled the file, Mercer.'

'Semi-retired deputy. He retired six months ago, got fed up

with being a full-time carer for his two grandkids, came back part time. Can't say I blame him.'

Ritter had seen the file. The name Mercer meant nothing to him.

'He wasn't involved with the original investigation, was he?'

Dixon had just shoveled another piece of pie into his mouth. Ritter was forced to wait while he chewed enough of it to allow him to talk through the remainder. Spray through it.

'Uh-uh. That was a detective called Lou Bordelon.'

Ritter smiled to himself. He remembered the name *Bordelon*. Remembered the guy's dog, too. Yappy little thing. Especially at the end. Bordelon had never known Ritter's name, but Ritter was sure he wouldn't have forgotten his visit. Forgotten the warning. He asked anyway. Memories were short. You never knew.

'Is Bordelon taking an interest?'

Dixon swallowed the last of his mouthful, took a big noisy slurp of coffee. Belched.

'Uh-uh. He quit.'

Sensible guy, Ritter thought. *Unlike this new pain in the ass, Mercer.*

'What's Mercer's interest?'

Dixon shrugged.

'No idea. Could be he wants to go out on a high. Crack a big unsolved case before he retires for good.'

It made Ritter want to take him outside, teach him a lesson. Dixon hadn't even asked. It was the same lazy attitude which meant they were only hearing about it now. There was nothing lazy about the way the guy took Bray's money.

Ritter put his anger to one side. Thought about the half-assed explanation Dixon had come out with.

It didn't ring true to him.

It hadn't been Mercer's case. There was no professional pride attached to it. He'd come back part-time and he was seriously expecting to waltz in five years after the event and solve in two or three days a week what they couldn't do at the time?

Get real.

So. Somebody else asked him to pull the file.

Somebody with a genuine interest in the case.

Sad sack of shit Lou Bordelon with his tail between his legs?

Ritter didn't think so. He had a motive for sure. Except the fact that he'd quit suggested he'd learned his lesson. Paid the price for not stopping when he'd been told to the first time around. Was he that stupid to take another run at it? Ritter seemed to remember that the problem had been the opposite. He was too bright, too conscientious, for everybody's good. Particularly his own. And his yappy dog's. He made a mental note to talk to him, just in case.

Who else had an interest?

Not-So-Innocent Lejeune?

Definitely. But why now? How would he even know who Mercer was? Even if he did, Mercer would never help a man like Lejeune. Not willingly, anyway.

Same went for Esteban Aguilar.

Or somebody else entirely?

But who?

There was only one way to find out.

'You got an address for Mercer?'

He was expecting a sorry headshake back. Dixon surprised him. Got out his wallet, extracted one of his own business cards.

Ritter groaned inwardly even before the guy turned it over to reveal a hand-written address.

Dixon pushed it across the table. Closer up, Ritter saw that it was actually two addresses. Dixon tapped the card with his stubby index finger.

'Top one is Mercer's address. The other one is his son's. Luke. Like I say, Mercer spends a lot of time there, looking after the grandkids. Him and his wife most of the time. They do it together if they can. Some days it's only her if he's working.'

Ritter nodded. *Good to know.* A doting old lady looking after two young children close to her heart. He couldn't think of a better way to apply pressure.

'What about today? Is Mercer working?'

Dixon consulted his watch as if he couldn't remember what day it was and needed to check in the little window in the watch's face.

'Not as far as I know.'

Ritter pulled out his phone, took a photograph of the addresses on the back of Dixon's card. Pushed the card back across the table at him like it was contaminated.

'I suggest you burn that. If you hadn't eaten so much pie and I wasn't worried you'd be sick all over me, I'd make you eat it now so that I could be sure you're not going to put it back in your wallet, then give it out to the first member of the public you come across.'

He got up, dropped a five-spot on the table and left Dixon staring at his back all the way to the door like he couldn't figure out what he'd done wrong. Outside, he glanced at the motto on Dixon's vehicle thinking that if he had a pot of gold paint he'd change the wording.

Being a dickhead since 1813.

Back in his car, he put Mercer's address into Google maps. He'd take a drive past, have a look around if the place was empty. Then he'd head over to the son's house. See if he couldn't catch some kiddies having fun in a swimming pool while proud Grandma and Grandpa watched over their charges, unaware that their perfect lives had already started to circle the drain.

14

'Let's go for a drive,' Fontenot said. 'You turning up has unsettled me. I won't be able to sit still. Besides, it'll help give you a feel for the situation.'

From downtown Lafayette they took I-10 heading east. They passed Breaux Bridge and Henderson, then immediately after crossing the Louisiana Airborne Memorial Bridge, they came off at exit 127. From there they took State Highway 975, also known as Whiskey Bay Highway, heading north and following the Atchafalaya River into the Atchafalaya National Wildlife Refuge. After only a couple hundred yards, the so-called highway turned into a poorly-maintained gravel road. They followed it for three miles or so, then made a right onto Bayou Manuel Road. A couple miles later Fontenot pulled off the road, immediately before it crossed Alabama Bayou.

He stopped Evan from getting out straight away, took a can of DEET spray from the glove compartment.

'Little bastards will eat you alive,' he said.

They sprayed every patch of exposed skin—no doubt at the cost of some kind of long-term damage to brain cells—rolled down their sleeves and buttoned the cuffs, did the same with their collars. Then they got out and walked to the middle of the narrow wooden bridge. The dirty brown water of the bayou ran dead straight in both directions, cutting through the unbroken mass of cypress trees lining its banks.

They were five miles from the Interstate as the crow flies and twenty-five miles from Evan's hotel. It could've been five hundred to the nearest road or human habitation.

Evan had waited this long for Fontenot to begin his story and he was forced to wait another couple of minutes as they both stood, hands grasping the flimsy metal mesh barrier that lined the bridge, staring down the bayou. He couldn't help wondering if Arlo was somewhere down in all that water, a concrete block chained to his ankle.

'I'm going to tell you exactly what I told Arlo,' Fontenot said eventually. 'What we printed in the paper at the time, basically.' He pointed in a north-westerly direction. 'Five years ago, on May twentieth, two thousand eighteen, a Piper Cherokee 6 light aircraft crashed in the middle of the trees somewhere over there. NTSB investigators subsequently identified a problem with the fuel switch. Seemed it got stuck in the middle or something so that it wasn't supplying fuel from any of the tanks.' He waved it off, an unimportant detail compared to what would follow. 'They'd filed a flight plan that showed them departing from Baton Rouge Metropolitan Airport with a final destination of Aeropuerto del Norte in Monterrey, Mexico. If they'd made it that far, a refueling stop was planned at Aransas County Airport, thirty miles north east of Corpus Christi. Park rangers found the plane twelve hours later.'

'Nobody saw it come down?'

Fontenot pointed south.

'I-10 is five miles due south. It wouldn't have been visible from there.' He made a broad sweep with his arm, took in the wilderness all around them. 'There's nothing else in any direction for miles. Except that misses the point. Inside the aircraft they found the pilot dead. No surprises there, you'd think. You hit a bunch of cypress trees in a small aircraft, you're gonna come off second best. Except he'd been shot.' He tapped his temple a couple times.

'Like an execution?'

Fontenot nodded. Exactly like that.

'They also found a second dead body. A man called Justin Sanders. He'd also been shot with the same gun that was used to kill the pilot. The gun was never found.'

'So pilot and passenger were both shot...'

Fontenot shook his head like it was an easy mistake to make.

'Come with me.'

They carried on across the bridge heading west. Fifty yards past it, Fontenot stopped at the junction of the gravel road and a smaller trail on the right heading north and running parallel to the bayou.

'That's Big Alabama trail. It came to light later that Sanders had been hiking in the area. Investigators figured he was on this trail when he saw the plane go down.'

He paused, let Evan feel his way towards an explanation.

'He saw it crash, went to investigate. See if he could help. The dead pilot and Sanders ending up the same way suggests there was a third person at the scene.'

'Yep. The APIS manifest—'

'The what?'

'APIS. Advanced passenger information system. It lists the details of everyone on board. It's mandatory for flights into Mexico. The manifest for this flight listed two people on board. The pilot and a passenger. Clearly, Sanders wasn't that passenger.'

'Who was?'

A small curl appeared at the corners of Fontenot's mouth at Evan's impatience.

'I'm telling it to you exactly as Arlo heard it so you can retrace his steps.'

Evan didn't like it, couldn't do much about it. He shrugged fair enough. Waited for Fontenot to stretch his story out a bit longer.

'They also found something unusual in the plane.'

If the flight had been the other way around departing from Mexico into the US, Evan would've been thinking drugs—ignoring how difficult it was to fly drugs into the US these days, what with the government's Tethered Aerostat Radar System and Customs and Border Protection Black Hawk helicopters and F-16 jet fighters patrolling the border.

Fontenot wagged his finger as he saw the thought go through Evan's mind.

'Not drugs. They found a set of handcuffs still attached to the frame of one of the back seats. Justin Sanders' fingerprints were all over them.'

Again, he let Evan make a stab at putting it together.

'Sanders saw the plane go down, went to investigate. He found an injured pilot and a passenger handcuffed in the back. He freed the passenger, who somehow shot him and the pilot . . . hang on . . . if you came across a situation as obviously suspect as this one, you'd call it in. Not set the guy free. He was handcuffed for a reason.'

'Unless you thought the plane was about to go up in flames.'

'I suppose.'

'Get your phone out.'

Evan did so, anticipating Fontenot's point. No signal.

'You go further in,' Fontenot said, 'it gets even worse. Besides, he didn't have a phone on him. Not when they found him, anyway.' He opened his hands wide. Here endeth the lesson. 'Now you know everything I told Arlo. Plane crash, two men shot to death, handcuffs, evidence of a third man who was never seen again.'

Evan could see why Fontenot might be feeling guilty. He asked a question, the answer to which only confirmed it.

'Who owned the plane?'

'A man called Esteban Aguilar. A Mexican national with business interests'—making quotes in the air as he said it—'here and in Mexico.'

'Drugs sort of business interests?'

'Drugs, arms, human trafficking. If it makes money and it's illegal, Aguilar's got his greasy finger in the pie.'

They turned back towards the bridge and Fontenot's car parked beyond it. Evan stopped again in the middle of the bridge, gazing down at the muddy waters of the bayou swirling around the bridge supports below them. It was as good a place as any to state the blindingly obvious.

'I get the impression there's a lot more to this that you're not telling me.'

Fontenot laughed, a nervous, guilty sound.

'Oh, yes. There wouldn't have been any point in giving it to Arlo if all he was likely to do was confirm what I'd already told him. What we'd already printed five years ago. There were a number of loose ends. Inconsistencies. I sent him to talk to someone who was better placed to answer his questions. Point him in the right direction.' He paused, cleared his throat as if the word *right* had stuck in his craw. Evan wasn't surprised. *Wrong* was the word he was looking for. 'He's an old friend of mine. Ed Mercer. He was a sheriff's deputy at the time. He's semi-retired now. I thought we'd go see him now. Like I said, re-tracing Arlo's footsteps.'

Shifting some of the blame and guilt for potentially sending Arlo down the road to an early grave from yourself onto Mercer, too, Evan thought and kept to himself. *Stan Fraser would have the pair of you at the bottom of the bayou in five minutes flat if he ever found out.*

Fontenot called Mercer's cell phone as soon as he had a signal, bumping and bouncing their way back towards the Interstate. He got put through to voicemail, left a message.

Hey, Ed, it's Ralph. I'm bringing somebody to talk to you. Let me know where you're at if you're not at home.

Back on I-10 Fontenot pretended to be too busy concentrating on driving to make conversation or explain further. Evan was happy enough to play along. What he'd been told so far was sufficient to whet his appetite, as it would have done Arlo's. Except it was nothing more than what thousands of people would have read in the paper and seen on the local news five years previously. By implication, whatever Mercer had to add would be information not in the public domain. Details that had been the catalyst for sending Arlo down a very dangerous road.

He got the feeling that even if he were to ask, Fontenot would claim that he didn't know exactly what Mercer had told Arlo.

They'd been on the Interstate for a little under ten minutes when Fontenot slowed, flicked on the indicator. Evan looked up, saw the Henderson exit approaching. A moment later Fontenot canceled the indicator, put his foot back on the gas.

Evan glanced at him. Fontenot gave him an apologetic smile back.

'Wrong exit. I must be getting old.'

Evan didn't comment. But it seemed off.

He thought about the message Fontenot had left, the way he started it.

Hey, Ed, it's Ralph.

Just Ralph. Not Ralph Fontenot. They were good friends. If he was John or Steve he might need to add his surname to clarify things however good friends they were. Not if you were Ralph. No last name required meant they knew each other well. And he couldn't remember what exit to take to get to his house?

No way.

There was something about the Henderson exit or somewhere close to it that Fontenot had been about to share with Evan and had then changed his mind at the last minute.

Hopefully the answer was waiting for them at Ed Mercer's house.

Something else sure as hell was.

15

Ritter had been watching Mercer's house for the past hour. Pale gray clapboard and with a corrugated metal roof, it sat on a quiet street running down to Bayou Teche. A dusty Ram pickup was parked in the driveway behind a Toyota Camry. It suggested both Mercer and his wife were at home. There'd been no sign of any children running in and out of the house or playing in the yard for the whole time Ritter had been watching. Ritter didn't have children, nor did he want any, but even he knew that no right-minded person would keep two young children cooped up in the house on a sunny afternoon when there was a perfectly good yard outside.

Ideally, he'd wanted to take a look around, get a feel for the lay of the land. Check for the presence or otherwise of security cameras and so on, for when he came back later. Then head over to the son's place to get some photographs or video footage of the grandchildren to help concentrate Grandpa's mind.

He'd waited to see if they went out, which they hadn't. It was looking less and less likely that they would do so as dinner time approached. He was thinking about driving to the son's house, maybe catch the kiddies having fun with a rubber duck and bubbles at bath time, when a Jeep Grand Cherokee pulled up outside the house.

Ritter came alert as two men got out. An older guy who looked as if life had beaten him down with a big stick for fifty years and another, younger man. Bigger, too. He looked to Ritter as if he could take care of himself.

As always, Ritter's camera was ready to go on the passenger seat, telephoto lens already attached. He took a number of fast shots of both men as they left their car and made their way towards the house. The younger man lagged behind, looking around him as if he'd beamed down from an alien spaceship and was assessing Breaux Bridge for a possible future invasion.

He also got a couple of good shots of Mercer himself as he opened the door. He gave it five minutes after they'd all gone inside, then crossed the road and took one of the Jeep's license plate.

Then he called Deputy Dixon. A man he was already thinking of as about as much use as Deputy Dawg. Asked him to run the plate. Managed to bite his tongue, stop himself from adding *today* to the request.

He took his laptop from the glove compartment while he waited for Dixon to call him back, transferred the shots he'd taken onto it.

Five minutes later, his phone vibrated on the passenger seat, Deputy Dawg's name on the screen.

'It's registered to Ralph Fontenot. He's the editor of a small newspaper in Lafayette called *The Daily Acadian*. Word on the street is that it's about to go under any day.'

Ritter typed Fontenot's name and *Daily Acadian, Lafayette* into Google as Dixon talked, hit return. Then clicked on the images tab.

The same older man he'd just photographed going into

Mercer's house stared back at him. At least running a DMV check hadn't been beyond Dixon's abilities.

'Give me your personal email address. I'm going to send you a picture of another guy. Let me know if you recognize him.'

He typed it in as Dixon recited the address, relieved that it was a Gmail account. At least the guy would be able to check it immediately.

Then he thought about what he had.

Mercer had pulled the file for a man who worked for a newspaper—it was too much of a coincidence otherwise.

Why? Because he was hoping to revive a failing newspaper's flagging sales with a big story? One story couldn't do that, however big Jack Bray's downfall might be.

It didn't matter. What mattered was that somebody was digging.

Mercer had pulled it a week ago, so why was Fontenot back again? Mercer hadn't worked the case. It wasn't as if he could supply clarification on what was in—or missing from—the file.

Mercer and Fontenot had both been around for the past five years since the plane crash. Suddenly questions were being asked. *Ergo*, the unidentified bigger guy had to be the catalyst. So why was he only meeting Mercer now?

Then it came to him, a minor epiphany.

Fontenot asked Mercer to pull the file. He couldn't get anywhere with it, so he called the new guy to help. He wasn't a cop. Ritter didn't think he'd ever seen anyone who looked less like a cop. An investigator of some kind, then.

He did an image search on Google, uploaded one of the pictures he'd taken of the guy.

Nothing.

It had been a long shot. It wasn't as if the guy was a celebrity.

Dixon called him back a couple minutes later.

'Never seen the guy.'

Ritter wasn't surprised. The only way Dixon would've recognized him was if his face was painted on the top of a piece of pie. He thought about asking him to show the picture around the sheriff's office, make up some bullshit story about a complaint being made about the guy acting suspiciously. He decided against it. He had a feeling that the more he minimized Dixon's input, the smoother things would go.

'I'll call you if there's anything else.' Then, in order to head off any misguided show of initiative, 'Keep it to yourself for now.'

He thought about his next move after he ended the call, the images of Fontenot and the unknown investigator open on the laptop in front of him.

Fontenot didn't have the look of a man who'd do the digging himself. Sure, he would've started his career that way. Now, he looked worn down and worn out. Happy to sit behind a desk waiting out his time until the crappy paper he worked for went *whoosh* down the toilet.

Had he spent the last week doing what he'd left behind twenty or thirty years ago? Or had he put someone else on it who got nowhere, hence the call to the new guy? A big shot of some kind presumably—even if he wasn't big enough for Google to recognize him.

Reluctantly, Ritter was forced to accept that it was no longer necessary to speak to Mercer. Whoever Fontenot had put on the case before he brought in the big shot had failed to get anywhere and was therefore not a threat.

The new guy was the problem.

And while Ritter would have enjoyed showing Mercer the photos he'd taken of the kiddies having fun, then showed him another photo from five years ago—of the detective Lou Bordelon's yappy little dog—before letting Mercer's own mind make an unpleasant comparison, he was above all else a practical man.

There were easier ways to find out who the interfering newcomer was.

Mercer would never know how narrowly he'd avoided the worst day of his life.

16

INSIDE THE HOUSE, THINGS WERE MUCH AS RITTER HAD IMAGINED. Mercer was at home alone with his wife, Margaret, the two grandchildren with their parents. Margaret was busy in the kitchen preparing dinner and shooed the three men out of her way and into the back yard.

Mercer grabbed three bottles of a local IPA from the Parish Brewing Company from the fridge and they all got themselves settled on molded plastic chairs on the small deck at the back of the house.

So far, Fontenot had simply introduced Evan as *Evan*, no explanation for his presence given. Whether he'd deliberately held off from saying more while they were in Mrs. Mercer's earshot Evan couldn't say. He got straight to it as soon as they were outside.

'Evan's a private investigator. He's working for Arlo Fraser's old man.'

Mercer kept his face emotionless.

'Okay.'

Evan didn't miss the fact that a fuller explanation wasn't

required. How its absence only served to emphasize what wasn't said.

Who's gone missing because of what we gave him to do.

Evan would've been hard pushed to say which one of the two men looked more uncomfortable. If pressed, he'd have said Mercer. If only because it was obvious that their presence here in his back yard was to enable Fontenot to shift the blame onto him.

'I took Evan to the crash site,' Fontenot said.

Mercer said *okay* again. Took a long swallow of beer.

'Gave him the details that we printed at the time and told him how I pointed Arlo in your direction. I thought you could take it from there.'

It seemed to Evan that Fontenot demonstrated a superhuman degree of self-control as he forced himself to remain sitting in his chair. Didn't immediately leap up and run for his car, the buck successfully passed.

The scowl on Mercer's face suggested the same thought had crossed his mind.

But if Evan thought that meant there was some kind of bond developing between them—beyond both having eyes in their head—he was mistaken. He'd already noticed the way Mercer was looking at him. The sort of barely-concealed contempt he was used to getting from the badge-carrying professionals when the words private investigator were spoken and they heard *interfering pain in the ass.*

Except this time, it was worse.

Mercer glanced at Fontenot.

'I didn't tell you this, Ralph, because of Elise.' He then turned his attention to Evan who knew exactly what was coming, even if Fontenot didn't. 'Ralph told me what he knew about Arlo's background. Where he was from, running away from home and all the rest of it.' He glanced again at Fontenot who was looking like he was wishing he'd made that dash for the car after all. 'After Arlo went missing, I made a few inquiries about the original missing person report.'

'What for?' This from Fontenot.

'Can't really put my finger on it. He went missing before and now he's gone missing again.' He held up a hand to stop Fontenot from saying that it wasn't the same circumstances. 'I thought it was worth asking. As it turned out, it wasn't. Not in terms of what happened here. But I talked to a guy who told me all about Arlo's old man.' He extended his hand towards Evan, his voice filled with disgust. 'Seems our investigator friend here is working for the sort of man I've spent my life trying to put behind bars.'

Fontenot stared open-mouthed at Mercer as if he'd said Evan ate a small child for breakfast each morning. Then looked at Evan for a response to the accusation. Mercer carried on before either of them could say anything. He held up a placatory hand towards Fontenot.

'I'm not saying that reflects badly on Arlo. But it says something about . . .' Inclining his head towards Evan rather than speak his name out loud.

Evan took a gulp of beer while he thought about what to say.

Bet you wish you hadn't given me this beer wasn't going to do anything to help.

At least I didn't send a young man to stick his nose into the business of a man who traffics drugs and arms and people was also out.

And an explanation of how he came to be working for Fraser would only sound like he was making half-assed excuses.

In the end, he kept it simple. Gave Mercer some of his steely-eyed look back as he did so.

'Is it a problem?'

It would've been so easy to say more. Remind Mercer that it wasn't more than two minutes since he'd said Arlo's father being a criminal didn't reflect badly on Arlo. Ask him whether choosing a life of crime meant you automatically waived your rights as a parent.

Or best of all, ask him if it had worked. Whether painting Evan as a bottom-feeder at the beck and call of violent criminals had shifted any of his own guilt about what he'd helped get Arlo into.

Tell him to justify his self-appointed position on the moral high ground, basically, or back off.

Instead, they played eyeball chicken while Fontenot looked back and forth between them not knowing what to say.

'I hope not,' Mercer said eventually. 'I thought it was important everybody knows what's what, is all.'

For reasons unknown, beyond the fact that fate likes to poke its finger in your eye, a picture went through Evan's mind of Landry visiting Mercer as he'd done Arlo's friend, Aiden. It made him want to say, *you think I'm bad, wait until you see what comes after.*

The thought put a smile on his face—which naturally annoyed the hell out of Mercer.

'What's so damn funny?'

'I hope for your sake you don't find out.'

Mercer bristled, chin jutting and eyes narrowed.

'Are you threatening me?'

'Yep. Tell me what I want to know or I'll make a call and my criminal buddies will come and break your legs while your wife watches.'

It was out before he could bite it back.

But he was sick of it all. Felt like getting up and walking out. Literally, seeing as he didn't have a car.

Mercer was struck speechless, his face as red as if his wife had boiled it along with whatever she was cooking for dinner—dinner that smelled pretty damn good, but which Evan didn't think he'd be invited to stay for.

'That's what you expect me to say, isn't it? I understand Ralph feels guilty and he's dumped it on you. Now you're trying to make yourself feel better somehow by blaming me for working for a criminal, although I can't get my head around that one. Assuming it worked and you feel we're all equally guilty of something, how about we start over?' He turned to Fontenot now looking like he wished he'd brought his notebook. 'Hey, Ralph. Why don't you reintroduce me? Tell Mercer that I'm actually working for the Pope. Then we'll see if it makes any difference to anything.'

Margaret Mercer stuck her head out the back door at that point, the smell of dinner intensifying, of fried onions and piment doux and andouille sausage.

'Everything okay out here?'

'Three more beers would be good,' Evan said.

Mercer nodded at her as she looked to him for confirmation.

Fontenot was busy inspecting some interesting dirt on his shoes from their earlier visit to the crash site.

Nobody said a word until she'd brought the beers out. Evan gave her his empty bottle to take inside, went back to her husband as soon as she'd closed the door.

'What's for dinner? I'm starving.'

He didn't say that, of course.

'So. Shall we start over?'

Mercer made a point of finishing his first beer, then carefully placed the bottle on the ground beside his chair leg. Sat cradling the fresh bottle between both hands. Evan could've told him it was going to make it warm up twice as fast.

Finally, Mercer kicked off with the first of many caveats.

'I wasn't involved in the original investigation. But Ralph sent Arlo to talk to me—'

'Ed's the only person I know in the sheriff's office,' Fontenot cut in.

Mercer nodded, looking like he wished it wasn't true.

'There wasn't really anything I could tell him. That's when he asked if I could pull the original file for him. I didn't want to do it.'

'Why not?' Evan said.

'Because we don't give anyone who walks in the door the key to the filing cabinet and say, knock yourself out.'

Or because you knew where it was going to lead, Evan thought and kept to himself, having already come out with enough home truths for one short meeting.

'You've never met him, have you?' Mercer said. 'Arlo, I mean.'

Evan shook his head.

'He ran away before my time.'

Mercer glanced at Fontenot before continuing.

'Ralph will back me up on this, but I got the feeling the kid's stubborn as hell.'

'As a mule,' Fontenot echoed.

'I knew that if I didn't let him see the file, he was going to start digging anyway.'

The implication was like a flash of heat lightning in the evening air illuminating the truth.

That would have been worse.

Evan bit his tongue for now, let Mercer continue.

'I pulled the file, then snuck him in the back after most people had gone home. Put him in an interview room with the file and left him to it. I knew he'd take photographs on his phone. I'd already decided to let him read it, so I didn't waste my breath telling him not to. The length of time he took, I figure he simply photographed everything to read later. Then I sent him home and put the file back.'

'Does anyone know you pulled it?'

Mercer hesitated. Not for long, but it was there.

'I don't think so. Like I said, most people had gone home.'

Evan heard something different.

I hope not.

Mercer's obvious discomfort, his repeated ass-covering use of *most people* rather than *everyone*, made Evan wonder if he hadn't bumped into another deputy, dropped the file and together they'd picked up all the loose papers. Arlo's disappearance reinforced the likelihood that his hopes had been misplaced.

Mercer couldn't miss the skepticism on Evan's face. Evan justified it with a different question rather than straight out accuse him, risk bringing the interview to an early end.

'Did you look at the file yourself?'

Mercer gave a solemn headshake. Holding Evan's eyes the whole time.

'Nope.'

'You weren't interested?'

Mercer looked away, at his wife visible through the kitchen window.

'I retired once, came back part-time and I get the feeling I'll be quitting for good before long. Your presence here makes me think it's gonna be sooner rather than later. I'm not looking for any excitement. Not interested in solving a big one before I go. The Sheriff asked me to go back part-time because they were having staffing issues. It's not because I've got a fire in my belly that I can't ever put out. I'm too old for all that.'

What Evan wanted to say was simple and to the point.

Bullshit.

Ever mindful of how the first half of the conversation had gone, he bit his tongue and changed direction—for the moment.

'Do you know what Arlo did next?'

He got another solid headshake back.

'No idea. I didn't discuss it with him. I got him out of the building pronto. I didn't expect to hear from him again, either. I wasn't on the case. There was nothing more I could help him with. There would've been better leads, if you want to call five-year-old dead ends leads, in the file.'

'You want to make a guess?'

Mercer blew the air from his cheeks. His face said, *what I want is for you to go now*. Again, he looked away at his wife in the kitchen before answering.

'The lead detective on the case would be the obvious move. Lou Bordelon.'

'Is he still working?'

'Nope.'

Mercer was looking increasingly uncomfortable. Evan got the impression he was feeling as if he was being pushed further into a corner. As if his repeated glances at his wife in the kitchen were an attempt to force her out by willpower alone. Have her appear at the door and announce that supper, aka Mercer's salvation, was served.

And since he wasn't going to be offered any of that supper, Evan pushed harder, jamming Mercer right into that corner.

'Retired? Or quit?'

For one four-letter word it took Mercer a long time to get it out.

'Quit.'

The bullshit accusation moment had arrived. Even if Mercer's responses weren't so much bullshit now as incomplete, the most important facts being those missing.

'You said a minute ago that you let Arlo see the file because he'd have kept digging on his own if you didn't. The implication is that would have been worse. Now you're telling me the lead detective quit. What aren't you telling me that links those two things?'

This time Mercer looked at Fontenot. He was too busy looking at his shoes again to be of any help. But it jogged Evan's memory, Fontenot's words coming back to him.

There were a number of loose ends. Inconsistencies.

And he thought, why not spread the discomfort around?

'Ralph told me there were inconsistencies. What sort of inconsistencies? Something to do with the Henderson exit on I-10?'

Fontenot's head shot up at that, Mercer's going down at the same time as if their noses were roped together through a ring set into the deck.

'Nothing to do with getting old and forgetting how to get here, was it?' Evan said.

Fontenot gave him a guilty smile.

'No.' He glanced at Mercer, didn't wait to get a confirmation back. 'You remember the hiker who was found shot dead in the plane? Sanders. They found his car parked in a Texaco gas station just off the Henderson exit. I checked the odometer when we were driving back. It's thirteen miles down I-10 to exit 127 where we came off. Who wants to walk all that way—'

'Ralph,' Mercer cut in.

Fontenot looked at him, irritation on his face at being interrupted.

'What?'

'You're getting into too much detail. That can wait.' Then, to Evan, 'The reason I didn't want Arlo poking around on his own is the same reason Lou Bordelon quit, like you implied. There were rumors flying around at the time about a cover-up.'

. . .

Ritter thought they must be staying for supper, the length of time Fontenot and the investigator were in the house. Eventually, they came out again. Mercer didn't come down the path to their car with them or even wait at the door to wave goodbye as they drove away. He almost clipped the investigator's heel with the door, he closed it on them so fast.

The investigator looked around him as he had before. As if he was thinking maybe it wasn't such a great place for an invasion after all. Ritter got the impression he thought somebody might be watching them. It couldn't be him. The guy didn't know of him any more than Ritter knew who he was.

Even so, he waited to the last moment before pulling away to follow their car, then tailed them back to Lafayette and the Sterling Grove Historic District. There, Fontenot stopped outside a big old Creole house that had been converted to bed and breakfast accommodation.

Ritter carried on for another block before pulling to the curb. He glanced sideways at them as he drove past.

The conversation in their car looked heated. The investigator had turned in his seat to face Fontenot. Fontenot had his arms up, his hands clasped behind the back of his head as he stared up at the car roof. Like the investigator had asked him a difficult question and Fontenot was trying hard to find a way to say, *no*, thought maybe the answer was written on the roof lining.

Ritter got the impression Fontenot was being dragged deeper into the situation than he wanted.

He couldn't blame the guy for that.

A couple minutes later, the investigator climbed out. Fontenot burned rubber driving away like the more distance he could put between them, and the faster, the better.

Once more the investigator took a minute to look up and down the street. Seemed to Ritter that something had spooked him. The fact that it wasn't him added a new dimension to things. He watched as the guy pulled out his phone and made a call, pacing up and down the street as he waited for it to be answered. He then dialed again almost immediately. Didn't get an answer to that call, either, gave up and went inside.

Ritter settled in to wait.

As his momma used to say, good things come to those who wait. It just happened that in Ritter's case, those good things tended to be bad for somebody else.

17

Kate Guillory's phone rang in her pocket. A spasm of irritation rippled across her face as she pulled it out, checked the display.

Evan.

She dropped it back in her pocket, let it go to voicemail. *Bad timing, Evan.* Except he had no way of knowing.

Then she pushed through the door into The Backroom. It seemed to her that the place fell silent, all eyes on her as she stepped inside. As if she had a pulsing neon sign on her head.

Cop Alert!

She'd swear she felt crosshairs lining up on her back as she threaded her way towards Stan Fraser's table on the far side of the room, all her senses heightened. Feeling the sticky pull of spilled beer on the soles of her shoes. The myriad odors of collected humanity assaulting her from all sides. A sweaty armpit here, too much sickly-sweet perfume there.

Fraser had his nose buried in the newspaper when she arrived at his table. He was alone, a glass of whiskey on the table in front of him.

If he was surprised at her presence in his domain, he didn't show it.

'Kate Guillory, what a pleasant surprise.'

She didn't miss the use of her first name. The lack of her title. Detective. Even if she felt as if her profession was known to everyone in the room, he clearly did not. Nor did he want to advertise it.

'Want something to drink?' he said. 'Are you on or off duty?'

'I'll have a beer. And it's my day off.'

He smiled at her as if she'd made his day.

'I'm honored that you choose to spend it with me.'

She gave him an equally insincere smile back.

I'm hoping to change that before long.

'Don't be.'

He waved at the bartender, mouthed *beer* at him. Neither of them said anything until it arrived. Then they clinked bottle against glass and took a drink.

She made a point of looking around the room. Didn't say anything fast enough to prevent him from making a facetious remark.

'Nice place, huh? You should come here instead of the Jerusalem Tavern.'

'If the Jerusalem ever burns to the ground, maybe I will.'

'I can make that happen.'

'I'm sure you can. Where's Landry? Down in Lafayette?'

The mocking smile that had accompanied the previous exchange slipped off his face. Genuine confusion replaced it. It made her think she'd missed something.

'No, he'll be here soon. Why would he be in Lafayette?' He immediately answered his own question. Criminal or otherwise, he wasn't stupid. 'That's where Buckley's traced Arlo to?'

'You know it is.' Feeling as if it were a lie as the words came out of her mouth.

His face hardened, anger at being the last to know in his eyes.

'It's the first I've heard of it.'

She bit back her initial response—*don't give me that crap*—as she heard the clear ring of truth in his voice. Saw it on his face. Then felt her way cautiously forward, the realization that she'd jumped to an understandable, but incorrect, conclusion throwing her off balance. It made the outright aggression of the line she'd planned to take somewhat inappropriate.

'You know Evan talked to a friend of your son—'

'His name's Arlo.'

'—called Aiden?'

'Uh-huh. Landry told him about him. You mentioning Lafayette tells me Buckley lied to Landry when he said he didn't get any information out of him.'

'You're saying you didn't send him to see Aiden at five o'clock this morning to break his finger?'

Fraser shook his head. Looking like he wanted to break some of Landry's bones. Evan's, too, while he was at it.

'No. Is that why you're here? To warn me off? Tell me to keep Landry on a leash?'

'Sounds to me like he should be in a cage, not on a leash.'

He extended his hand towards her, that's your job.

They stared at each other for a long moment, then Fraser's mouth turned down in disgust.

'Did Buckley ask you to come here?'

'No way. He'd kill me if he knew.'

Fraser nodded to himself, the scowl on his face melting away as quickly as it had appeared.

'You're right. It's not his style. This is your bright idea.'

'Uh-huh. You don't need me to tell you that I'm not happy about Evan working for you.'

'Has he bought you a little something nice with the money I paid him?'

She ignored the attempt to get a rise out of her—for about a heartbeat. Pointed at him with her beer bottle.

'You'd know if he had. It'd be halfway down your throat by now.'

His eyes went wide, his mouth becoming a perfect O.

'*Oooh*. I can see why he likes you. I'd offer you a job if you didn't already have one.'

She took a long swallow of beer. To stop herself from hitting him over his smug head with the bottle as much as to quench her thirst.

Told herself to take a step back.

Because at the moment he was winning. And she did not like it. Not. One. Bit. Worse, he knew it.

'I was saying, I don't like him working for you. Not on a professional or a personal basis.'

'But you're not his keeper.'

'Exactly. I have to accept it. But I draw the line at your psychopathic sidekick following him around and interrogating anyone Evan talks to. The young man whose finger Landry broke is too scared to press charges, which is the way you and he like it. There's nothing I can do about it. But if it happens again, with or without your knowledge, you'll both wish you'd never been born—'

She clamped her mouth shut hard enough to rattle her teeth, the words that had been halfway out bitten back.

Just like your son.

Except he already knew, the mocking laughter in his eyes of a moment ago when he tried to bait her, a thing of the past.

He leaned back, folded his arms over his chest.

'Message delivered. Now let me give you one to give to

Buckley. Don't lie to me. Whatever Landry did is because Buckley didn't tell him the truth. He shares the blame.'

You think he doesn't know that? she thought. Although, once again she might as well have come out and said it. The knowledge was in Fraser's eyes.

In her anger, the bar and the people in it had receded into the background. A noisy mass of humanity lacking definition. Now individual sounds came to her. Voices and laughter that made her think of grown men snickering at a dirty joke.

She twisted around, saw Landry standing with another of Fraser's thugs. Watching her. Leering at her. Arrogant grins on their faces that she wanted to wipe off with a nightstick or better still her fist, feel teeth break and lips split against her knuckles.

She pushed to her feet. Ignored them.

The meeting had not gone as she'd hoped. She'd delivered the warning. But she still felt as if Fraser had come out on top.

She gave him a curt nod.

'Thanks for the drink.'

He tapped his index finger to his temple in a one-fingered salute.

'Any time.'

She hadn't taken more than two paces towards the door when she heard Landry's voice behind her.

'*Mmm hmm.* Still warm.'

She hated herself for her weakness, for her lack of self-control and professionalism, but there was nothing she could do to stop herself from turning around.

He had the flat of his palm pressed against the seat she'd been sitting on. Then he lifted his hand to his face. Keeping his eyes on hers. Sniffed his fingers. Three times. Deep long breaths sucking right down into the bottom of his lungs. Shuddering as if he'd just taken a hit of cocaine.

Fraser was standing by now.

Yelling at Landry to stop, to shut up, to get the hell out.

Too little, too late.

She thought about her job, her partner, how she was letting them all down.

She thought about Evan, his gleeful face, his words filled with encouragement.

Attagirl.

The red mist that he knew so well had already enveloped her. Made her feel closer to him than she'd ever known as she embraced the catharsis that unbridled violence promises.

She kicked Landry hard in the balls. Harder than she'd ever kicked anything or anyone. As good as put them through the top of his head. Eyes bulging, breath punching out of him as he doubled over.

She placed her hands one over the other on the top of his head, lovingly almost, ready to power her knee up into his face which wasn't laughing quite so fucking hard now, smear his sniffing nose across it like a bloody red paste, see if she couldn't knock his squashed balls back down his throat again. Then changed her mind. Threw him sideways to the floor like the trash he was. Dropped onto his chest with both knees as he struggled to breathe. Spitting words of vitriol into his pain-wracked face.

'Sniff your fingers now, you misogynistic piece of shit.'

Grabbing his hand by the fingers, thrusting them into his face. Bending them backwards until he hissed in pain.

'I said sniff them, you—'

Her phone rang in her pocket, the insistent noise snapping her out of it. A picture of Evan's grinning face in her mind once again.

You're every bit as bad as me.

She threw Landry's hand away. Pushed herself up off him.

Disgusted with him. More so with herself.

Looking at Fraser as her phone kept on ringing. See if there was any hint of a smile on his face. He showed her his palms, pointed at her pocket.

'Aren't you going to answer that? Tell Buckley what you've been getting up to while he's running around in Lafayette?'

She pointed right back at him. Thankful the adrenalin rush was still coursing in her blood, her finger as steady as her voice.

'Remember what I said. This is my day off. If this piece of shit'—kicking Landry not-so-gently with her toe—'wants to do anything about what happened here today, he doesn't have to worry about me hiding behind my badge.'

Fraser's eyes crinkled, a spiteful light in them.

'I don't think he's got the balls for it.'

She didn't know how she kept the smile off her face. Turned on her heel. Shouldered past the man who'd been laughing at her with Landry. *Cocksucker* muttered under her breath because there was no getting away from the fact that it felt better in the mouth than *misogynist* or any other fancy word. Striding through the mass of gawking onlookers parting in front of her towards the door.

And behind her the sound of clapping. A solitary pair of hands to begin with—she figured Fraser—then a second pair, and pretty soon the whole bar was applauding.

That didn't stop her from hearing Fraser's voice above it all.

'They're made for each other.'

18

Ritter didn't have to wait for long before the investigator went out again. No more than the time it takes for a quick shower and to throw on a change of clothes. He watched him in his side mirror as he came out of the bed and breakfast, then stopped on the sidewalk to do his meercat impersonation glancing up and down the street, before he set off on foot in Ritter's direction.

Ritter waited until he'd gone past, let him get a good long way ahead, then got out and followed him. The guy didn't go far. After half a mile he went into a diner, took a table in the window and immediately pulled out his phone.

Ritter doubled back. Went past his car and into the bed and breakfast. Gave the bell on the empty reception desk a brisk ding.

A young woman appeared from a door off to the right a minute later, regret on her face at the prospect of having to turn someone away.

Ritter beat her to it. He already had his ID out. It identified him as Detective John Rawlings of the Baton Rouge PD. He thrust it towards her. Gave her a chance to take a good long look at it if she wanted to, not a quick flash to arouse suspicion. She only glanced at it, satisfied that it was genuine. Which it was, apart from the bogus name. It helped that people said he had the look of a grubby big-city detective about him, a lifetime spent in the gutter of society permanently rubbing off on him.

'I'd like to have a quick word, Miss . . .'

'DuBois. *Mrs*. DuBois.'

Ritter smiled like it was the name he'd have chosen if he'd had any say in who his parents were.

'I don't want to alarm you, Mrs. DuBois, but we have reason to believe that a man we've had under surveillance for some time is currently staying here.' He raised a placatory hand. 'As I said, there's no reason to be alarmed. He's not violent. He's not going to steal anything. I'm sure you can appreciate that I'm not at liberty to discuss the details of the case with you . . .' He waited, let her nod that she understood, then continued. 'His name is Oakes. That won't be the name he's checked in with. Can I show you a photograph?'

She told him to go ahead.

He got out his phone, showed her the best shot of the investigator outside Mercer's house.

'Do you recognize him?'

She was torn between the excitement of being involved in a real live police investigation and the potential hit her business would take if it became known that her establishment was the go-to choice of criminals.

'He checked in earlier today.'

Ritter smiled as if it was all coming together nicely now.

'And what name is he using?'

'Buckley. Evan Buckley.'

Ritter scrunched his face. Like his life had suddenly gotten a whole lot more complicated, his voice reflecting a never-ending succession of obstacles.

'That's a new one. It's almost impossible to keep track of all the names he goes by.'

'He seems like such a nice man.'

'That's what makes him so good at what he does. People see a friendly face and they trust him.'

He gave her a minute to tut-tut, then asked a bunch of questions that he had no interest in the answers to. The length of Buckley's stay, whether he'd had any visitors, and so on. The only thing he was interested in was when he asked her to come outside and point out Buckley's car. Finally, he worked a serious whole-case-up-in-smoke note into his voice.

'I can't stress too highly how important it is that you keep this to yourself. It's vital that you treat him exactly as you have so far. If he suspects that something has changed in your attitude towards him, he'll be off. It could take us months to track him down again.'

Mrs. DuBois nodded as if the future of the entire human race had been placed in her hands.

'I'll do my best.'

Ritter gave her a big shit-eating grin to let her know that he couldn't have wished for more.

'It's lucky for us he chose to stay here, Mrs. DuBois. I know we can rely on you. We'll set up a number of observation posts in the vicinity, but you won't see us.' He smiled again, a smaller self-deprecating one this time. 'We wouldn't be very good at our jobs if you did.'

He left her standing in her hallway looking at the rooms around her in a different light. Deciding whether she should mention it on her Trip Advisor listing for all he knew.

Five minutes later he was parked outside the diner. Buckley

was still inside, drinking his after-dinner coffee. Ritter took his laptop from the glove compartment, opened the web browser and did a search for *Evan Buckley private investigator*. See what he could find out about the man he was up against.

The man whose last case this might very well be.

19

Kate Guillory couldn't get Fraser's words out of her mind as she made her way back to her car parked half a block away from The Backroom.

They're made for each other.

On today's performance she couldn't disagree. It'd sure as hell make his sister, Charlotte, coo and fuss—although not if she knew what Fraser meant.

She called Evan back as soon as she was settled in the car. Slumped in the seat, head against the rest, eyes closed. Feeling drained as the adrenaline rush subsided and her pulse leveled out, the door halfway open to let in some much-needed air.

'Found Arlo yet?' she said before he had a chance to say, *hello*. Not because she gave a flying shit about whether he found Fraser's son or not. It gave her a moment's breathing space before he asked her how her day had been.

'I'm surprised you're interested enough to ask.'

'I'm not.'

'I know. The sooner I'm done down here, the quicker I'll be back.'

She smiled with him, feeling the tension ebb away, her shoulders relaxing.

'Yeah. Then we can get back to the assignment Charlotte set us.'

'Is that what it is?'

'Feels like it sometimes.' Then, before he had a chance to object, 'I don't mean that.'

'I know. Rough day?'

She blew the air from her cheeks thinking, *you have no idea.*

'I'll tell you about it in a minute. How's it going on your end?'

'Warming up...'

She'd opened her eyes by now. Sitting up straight as she listened to Evan tell her about what sounded like a very long day. How he'd traced and met with Fontenot, the drive out to the crash site, the acrimonious conversation with Mercer giving rise to the revelations about inconsistencies in the evidence and rumors of a cover-up. And how they'd sent Arlo on a wish and a prayer into the midst of it all.

'And Mercer had the nerve to give me a hard time about working for Fraser,' he said.

'The guy can't be all bad.'

Half a block away, the door to The Backroom opened. Two men came out and lit up. Landry and the other thug he'd been laughing at her with. Suddenly her pulse was throbbing in her neck again, her breath quickening. The second man blew smoke directly up into the air then looked her way. Nudged Landry with his elbow and pointed, leaning in to say something. Landry looked where he was indicating, his face hardening. He stared malevolently at her for a long moment. Spat on the ground.

She realized she'd missed what Evan had said.

'What was that?'

'Did you speak to Aiden about pressing charges against Landry?'

'He's not interested. Can't say I'm surprised.'

'That's what I thought. I think Landry's here in Lafayette already.'

She couldn't help smiling to herself as she looked out through the windshield at Landry staring back at her not more than fifty yards away.

'Yeah? Why's that?'

'I'm being followed. I've seen the same car a couple of times today. It's parked across the street from me now.'

'I'm impressed that you even noticed.'

'It must be all the time I spend with you.'

She smiled to herself. The boy was learning.

'Right answer. But I can tell you for free that it's not Landry.'

'Why's that? A woman's intuition?'

'Close. I'm looking at him now.'

He was at a loss for words momentarily. Not something that often happened. She waited, let him grope his way towards an incorrect assumption.

'How come? You haven't arrested him, have you?'

He probably wishes I had, she thought and didn't say.

'Not yet, no. But I'm thinking I might charge him with assaulting a police officer. I've just been to have a chat with your new best friend, Stan.'

'What for?'

'To give him a piece of my mind.'

He groaned on the other end of the line, his voice beyond resignation.

'Now Fraser thinks I asked you to tell him to call Landry off. Like running to teacher.'

'Don't worry. I told him it was my idea.'

He didn't waste his breath asking whether Fraser had believed her. The damage was already done. He moved on.

'And Landry assaulted you?'

'Yep. He attacked my right foot with his balls. I don't think he'll be flying anywhere for a while. Not unless he can book a double-wide seat so he can keep his legs apart.'

She heard the smile in his voice, pictured the gleam in his eye as he invited her to take him through it.

'What happened?'

She leaned forward in her seat, forearms resting on the wheel. Still eyeball to eyeball with Landry, the blood coursing in her veins. Feeling again the hot mean worm of excitement turning over in her belly at the memory of it. That exquisite moment as she wiped every last trace of amusement off his leering, cocksucking face.

He couldn't fail to hear the throatiness in her voice, share the pleasure as her answer condemned them both.

'Let's just say I had a Buckley moment.'

There was only one thing to say to that. And he was the man to say it.

'Was it good for you?'

'The best.'

Neither of them mentioned Charlotte's assignment. But they'd have been lying if they'd tried to say it wasn't on both their minds.

'Where are you now?' he said.

'In my car. Still outside The Backshithole. Landry's doing his best to melt the windshield staring at me. Like he thinks I'm gonna piss myself.'

He asked a question then that he wasn't sure he wanted to hear the answer to. It was the strangest of situations, their roles reversed.

'Is round two imminent?'

'That's his call.'

'You sound as if you wish it wasn't.'

'You must be rubbing off on me, too. Hang on, something's

happening...'

She watched as Landry flicked away his cigarette butt, then made a pistol with his hand. Index finger rigid and pointing at her, thumb up cocked backwards, his whole hand kicking up with the recoil.

She pushed the door all the way open in the space of a heartbeat. Halfway out of the car before the two men had time to go back inside the bar.

'Any time, asswipe.'

She heard Evan laughing on the other end of the line as she dropped back into the seat. Expected him to ask her if she was feeling better now, the words, *you bet* already forming on her tongue.

Except she was wrong. He had a different assignment for her.

'Define the word *professional* for me.'

20

EVAN THOUGHT ABOUT HIS OPTIONS AFTER THEY ENDED THE CALL.

Taking a leaf out of her book sounded good. Confront the man sitting in the car opposite watching him. Because if it wasn't Landry, who the hell was it?

Trouble was, unless he could sneak up on him—hard to do when you're sitting in the well-lit window of a diner—the guy would drive off as he approached.

He'd get the license plate, but that would be all. That wasn't nearly enough. He needed to get the guy out of the way, not simply identify him.

The conversation with Fontenot when he dropped him off at his bed and breakfast earlier had been less than amicable. Paraphrased, it went as follows:

You put Arlo in danger by giving him this case to work on. Now I want you to do the same with your daughter, Elise.

He needed to speak to her. If Arlo had confided in anyone, it would've been Elise. Fontenot didn't want her dragged into it, understandably. In the end he'd come to the same conclusion that Mercer had when deciding whether to let Arlo see the case file. If he didn't help Evan, Evan would find another way. And that might be worse. He'd reluctantly given him her number and address, something he'd never have done if Evan had mentioned that he thought they were being followed.

The first step was to get rid of the guy watching from across the street.

In an ideal world, aka Buckley La-la Land, he'd lose the guy without him realizing he'd been made. That wasn't going to happen here.

He stretched, made a big deal of it. Movement in the window to catch the guy's eye in case he wasn't paying attention. Then he got out his phone again. Called his voicemail to be told that he had no new messages which he already knew. With the phone still pressed to his ear he waved the waitress over, asked for the check. Then stood up, asked her where the men's room was. She pointed towards the back. He nodded, dropped the phone on the table and went to find it.

It wasn't much of a deception, but it was better than nothing.

The fire exit was at the end of the corridor that led to the washrooms, bags of trash piled up in front of it blocking the way. He stepped over them, pushed through the door into a small yard with a service road at the back running behind all the store fronts. He went right, then right again into an alley that brought him out onto the street thirty yards behind the car with the mystery man inside.

It was on the other side of the road facing away from him.

He made a mental note of the license plate, then had to make a quick decision. Walk down the middle of the road to approach on the passenger side hoping to keep in the blind spot. Or cross the road, creep up on the driver's side keeping to the shadows while the guy concentrated on the diner, waiting for his supposed return from the men's room.

He went with the driver's side. Waited for a car to pass and crossed the road behind it.

The guy was already suspicious.

He glanced in his rearview mirror at the sudden movement behind him. The engine coughed into life, a puff of exhaust gases, and he was gone, pulling into the traffic without indicating as Evan quickened his pace half-heartedly behind him.

Back inside the diner the waitress was standing at his table, his phone in one hand, the unpaid check in the other.

He pulled his head down into his shoulders, tortoise-style, gave her the *aw-shucks* grin that made Guillory gag.

'First time I try leaving without paying and I forget my phone.'

She shook her head at him. Pointed through the window.

'Uh-uh. I saw you chase after the car that was parked over there. What's going on?'

He leaned in close, dropped his voice.

'He's a private investigator my wife hired to follow me. She thinks I'm cheating on her.'

'Are you?'

He gave her a sly grin, one that would also make Guillory heave.

'What time do you get off?'

She slapped him on the arm. Rolled her eyes at him.

'I'm old enough to be your mother. C'mon, pay the check and get outta here.' She shook her head, mock scolding in her voice hiding the evident pleasure behind it. 'Propositioning a woman of my age, I ask you.'

Outside, he put the address of a much younger woman he'd have been happy to proposition any day of the week into Google maps. Fontenot's daughter, Elise. Then he called her.

Seemed overly-protective Pops had already primed her.

'My dad told me you wanted to speak to me,' she said, wariness in her voice at anything connected to her father.

He made it worse.

'I thought you weren't talking to him.'

A weary note entered her voice, at odds with the picture he had in his mind of the good-looking young woman with Arlo that Aiden had sent him.

'He told you about that, did he?'

'He mentioned it in passing.'

'Yeah, right. I'm surprised he hasn't put it on the front page of the paper. What do you want to know?'

'I'd rather come to your apartment.'

'I'm sure you would. Why should I let you?'

He was hoping she had access to the copies of the file that Mercer said Arlo had made. The problem was, if she was as determined to be kept out of it as her father was to protect her, that wasn't going to encourage her to help him.

He went with vague, what Guillory referred to as his signature approach.

'Because I don't like doing business over the phone. It's too impersonal.'

'Impersonal? You mean it's harder to tell if I'm lying?'

If he didn't still have the conversation with Guillory in his mind, hadn't just chased off a man up to no good who'd been tailing him, he might have smiled with her and continued in the same vein. Said how it was also harder to beat a confession out of her. In the circumstances, it wasn't the way to go. The thought of it brought an unwelcome image to mind. Of Aiden's broken finger sticking out at an angle a basic knowledge of anatomy deemed impossible after Landry snapped it.

'You got me,' he said instead. 'I can be there in ten minutes.'

'Meaning you'll come anyway, even if I say no.'

He let his silence answer for him, the same resigned note as before in her voice.

'See you in ten.'

He could easily have done it in half that. She lived four hundred yards as the crow flies from where he'd eaten dinner. But after the incident with the guy watching him, he took a circuitous route, stretching the short journey out and cutting through Parc Sans Souci to get to her apartment block on East Main Street.

She buzzed him up and was waiting for him at the gray-painted door of her apartment on the top floor of the modern new block, hair still wet from the shower, a preparation he didn't think was as a result of his visit. Although still strikingly attractive, there was none of the carefree joie de vivre he'd glimpsed in the picture of her on a beach with Arlo. The advantages that fate and genes had bestowed on her were no match for the unrelenting strain of constant worry.

She led him through and offered him a chair in front of the floor-to-ceiling windows overlooking the communal pool below. The newspaper her old man worked for might be going down the tubes any day, but Elise was doing okay. It was easy to see why Arlo might have decided Lafayette was a good place to end his drifting days. She took a seat on the sofa opposite, tucked her bare feet up under her butt—sadly not equally bare.

It was time to test the water. See what kind of resistance he might be up against. The last thing he wanted was for the conversation to go the same way it had with Mercer.

'I'm assuming your dad told you I'm working for Arlo's father.' Watching her closely to see if there was any reaction.

Which there was. She laughed in his face.

'I can see you watching my expression for tell-tale signs.' She narrowed her eyes at him, leaning forwards and scrutinizing his face back. 'You shouldn't make it so obvious. Arlo told me all about his dad. I'm not shocked. I don't hold it against him. He ran away from home to get away from him, after all.'

'But I bet you want to know why I'm working for a man like him.'

She shrugged, not really. Pulled her legs further up underneath her butt, an uncomfortable way to sit as far as any man is concerned.

'I'm sure you've got your reasons. You don't look like the sort of man who'd work for a man like him, if that makes you feel better.'

What it made him feel was sorry for her if Landry got his balls under control and his ass down to Lafayette. He didn't look like a caricature thug, either.

The thought of Landry and what he'd done to Aiden, and from there his thoughts segueing to Stan Fraser, made him say something now that he hadn't put into words before. He was hoping she'd open up to him, so it was only fair that he be honest with her—even if it wasn't the sort of thing anyone wants to hear from a stranger turning up out of the blue one evening. He started with the good, what little there was.

'I'm not going to force Arlo to go back to his father if I find him.'

'Okay.' Making it sound like, I'd like to see you or anyone else try.

'But there's another man following me who will. He's already broken the finger of one of Arlo's old friends back home to get the information he wants. I'm not saying this to scare you or threaten you to make you talk to me. I say it so that you understand how serious things are.' He paused, then stated what had been obvious from the moment she opened the door. 'Except I think you already know that.'

She nodded unhappily, all trace long gone of the young woman who'd made fun of him a minute ago for watching her so closely and obviously for a reaction.

'Your dad told me he hasn't reported Arlo missing,' he said.

'He claims he didn't think the police would take him seriously. I think you haven't done so for a different reason.'

She nodded again, biting her bottom lip. It made him want to offer to do it for her.

'Arlo told me not to.' She smiled briefly at the apparent nonsense. More like a facial tic that was over in the blink of an eye. 'Not after he disappeared, of course. He said if anything happened to him, I shouldn't get involved. It would only bring me to the attention of these people, whoever they are.'

'And that includes not notifying the police?'

'He said there'd been a cover-up. I might identify myself to whoever did the covering up. Turn myself into a loose end.' She leaned towards him, elbows resting on her knees, the anguish in her voice cutting through him. 'How long did he expect me to sit here and do nothing? I'm going crazy with worry. I can't sleep at night.' She waved her hand in the direction of a half-empty bottle of wine on the side table, an empty wine glass beside it. 'I'm drinking too much to help me get to sleep and I'm worrying at the same time that I won't wake up if someone breaks in to attack me in the middle of the night.'

He wanted to tell her not to worry, not to be so silly. Except the words wouldn't come. They'd only insult her intelligence even if he managed to spit them out.

He needed to move her on. Get her past obsessing on the worst-case, scorched-earth scenario.

'I was told Arlo took photographs of the original case file. Did he make copies? Do you have access to them if he did?'

She unfolded her legs from under her and jumped up. Relieved to be doing something, anything, other than focus on the unthinkable. He followed her into the kitchen where her phone sat on the counter on a wireless charger.

'Arlo was totally OCD about backing stuff up. A legacy from all the time he spent traveling light while he was drifting around the country, I suppose. If they're anywhere, they'll be in his Dropbox account. I've got access to it on my phone.'

He leaned against the counter, watched her while her slim fingers flew over the keyboard tapping in the login details. Again, he thought of Landry following in his footsteps. Pictured her delicate fingers held in his, then a quick snap and a piercing scream.

The curse of an over-active imagination—or having been around the block a time or two, recognizing the world for the uncaring place it was.

'Got it,' she said, the triumph in her voice reflected in her face.

She held the phone towards him. He took it, saw a list of folders. The one she'd scrolled down to was named *original police file copies*. He opened it, the list of files extending all the way down the screen. As Mercer had said, he'd copied every document in the original case file.

'Can you send them to me?'

'Have you got a Dropbox account?'

'Uh-huh.'

'It'll be easier if I transfer them across.'

He gave her the details, waited as she set up a shared folder and ran through the steps to transfer the files and give him access.

'All done.'

He pointed at her phone.

'You mind if I check to see if he uploaded anything else?'

'Like what?'

Guillory would've said it was his face that gave him away. That, like all men, it had a built-in lascivious leer ready to pop up at a moment's notice. It would appear this was one of those moments. She narrowed her eyes at him.

'I hope you're not thinking what I think you're thinking.'

He gave a guilty shrug.

'Gotta be some benefits to the job. What I was actually thinking of is any notes he might have made. What he was planning on following up on. His thoughts about any conversations he had, stuff like that. Unless he already told you?'

She shook her head.

'No. I remember he was really excited when he got home. Stayed up half the night reading it all. But he didn't say anything to me about what he planned to do first. Sorry.'

He didn't miss the fact that the phone was still firmly in her hand, not on the way to his.

'I understand if you don't want me digging through all of yours and Arlo's private stuff...'

'I can do it for you, if you like. It'll give me something to concentrate on. Feel like I'm helping.'

'You've got my number. Any time you're having trouble sleeping...'

He didn't say that, of course.

Not even in Buckley La-la Land.

21

He called Guillory as he walked the streets back to his bed and breakfast from Elise's apartment.

'How did round two with the asswipe go? That was the word you used, wasn't it?'

'It was. And it didn't happen. One Buckley moment per day is enough for anyone. Except you, of course.'

He had a good idea where she was from the background noises on her end. The sound of conversation and laughter, Steve Earle's *Someday* on the jukebox. He asked nonetheless—in a roundabout sort of way.

'Sounds like you've gone back inside The Backroom.'

She snorted, unpleasantly loud in his ear.

'Don't be ridiculous. I'm in the JT.'

'What? Without me? It won't be the same.'

He didn't like the way the answer came back so fast. Or the heartfelt emotion behind it.

'It isn't.'

He decided against asking for clarification.

'Long story short, I felt like I'd earned a beer,' she said.

He couldn't argue with that either. Violence tends to give a person a thirst.

'Right foot okay?'

'Couldn't be better.'

He stopped walking, slipped into the shadows of the trees lining the street. He didn't expect to see the car that had been parked outside the diner following him, but it paid to be careful. He'd been equally cautious on his way to Elise's apartment, hadn't seen anything suspicious then, either.

Seemed Guillory was in tune with his thoughts.

'Did you find out who's following you? The guy who isn't Landry?'

'Not yet...'

This time, his face wasn't to blame for giving him away. It was simply that he was who he was. A gentle laugh came down the line at him. One that spoke of a resigned acceptance that there are some things in life that cannot be changed, that the fastest route to a padded cell in a secure wing is to try to fight against it.

'Let me get this straight,' she said, the laughter still in her voice. 'I've just been in a fight because of your case—'

'Sorry, I missed who you said started it.'

'He did when he sniffed his fingers. Anyway, after—'

'Enjoying yourself more than you can remember doing in living memory?'

'Certainly more than having dinner at Charlotte's, yes. So, after fighting your battles for you—'

He sucked air in through his teeth at that one, didn't need to put his hurt into words.

'—now you want me to run a license plate to identify the man—'

'Who isn't the man you kicked in the balls.'

'Exactly.'

There was a short pause while they both made sure they understood who and what they were talking about. He set off walking again. Still paying attention to the cars going past, any that were driving more slowly than you'd expect or stopping too frequently.

'Text it to me,' she said. 'I've only got proper police work to do tomorrow, after all. Why wouldn't I want to put that to one side to help find Stan Fraser's son, the most sensible kid in the world if you ask me. What will you be doing while I'm busy with that?'

He ran through his meeting with Elise, told her about getting hold of copies of the original file. He didn't invite further ridicule into his life by saying that he'd asked to have a nose through Arlo's private files. Like Elise herself, she'd only think the worst.

'I haven't read it yet,' he said, 'so I don't know where I'll be starting.'

'Be sure to let me know if it throws up any more errands for me to run for Stan.' A long pause ensued, made him picture her trying hard not to laugh. 'I mean you. I'm getting confused about who's who.'

'Sounds like you need another beer.'

'Funny you should say that. Hang on.'

He heard her calling to Kieran, the Jerusalem's manager, in the background. Felt his mouth water as he imagined a cold one sliding down his throat. He'd arrived back at the bed and breakfast by now, didn't immediately go in. Parked his butt against the low picket fence that surrounded the property's extensive grounds, instead, invisible in the shade of a mature oak on the other side of the fence. Not so much concerned about being followed now, but simply to enjoy the freshness of the night air.

He had a question for her when she came back on the line.

'I heard you order two beers.' Trying his best to keep any accusatory note out of his voice. Not sure that he succeeded.

'You've got good hearing when you need to.'

'Is the second one in advance of going back for round two with Landry?'

'I told you, one Buckley moment is enough for anyone. I thought I'd have a beer for you, too, is all.'

'*Aw*. That's so thoughtful. I can almost taste it.'

'I know. And Evan?'

'What?'

'It's not the same without you.'

22

Laura Hunt hated herself at times. Most of the time, in fact. She was going to hell, head of the line.

'You want another glass?' Fleur Sanders said, sounding as if she'd already had one too many. She held up her hand, finger and thumb pinched together. Closing one eye as she squinted at the non-existent gap between them. 'An eensy-weensy little one.'

Laura bit back the opening words to her reply—*for Christ's sake, Fleur*—and softened it. Worked a smile onto her face, God knows where she dragged it up from.

'You really want to see a headline about me in the paper? *Prominent local doctor pulled over for DUI.*'

Fleur giggled, joined in with a suggestion of her own.

'How about, doctor caught self-meditating? Medicating, I mean.'

Laura laughed with her. Thinking, *it's not your damn career on the line*.

But there was no putting Fleur off. She put a hand on the arm of the sofa that Laura thought was the most tasteless, hideous piece of furniture she'd ever seen—she could only think that Fleur had chosen it so that when she drank too much red wine and vomited all over it, the stains wouldn't be too noticeable—and pushed herself unsteadily to her feet.

'I'm having another one.' She pointed her finger at Laura's face. Hiccupped. 'You can be as boring as you like.'

She stood in front of Laura, weaving gently from side to side. A challenge on her face. For reasons unknown, Laura felt the need to justify herself to her intoxicated friend. She thrust her stomach out, pinched a lot more than an inch of flab around her midriff.

'It's okay for you, you never put on an ounce of fat. I don't get the time to do any exercise these days. I'm not as fit as I used to be.'

Fleur threw her eyes and shook her head, her voice dismissive as if they'd been over this too many times before.

'You're not quite Mrs. Blobby yet. Besides, it's not as if you've got anyone who's going to notice.'

She stared at Laura a moment longer to give her a chance to change her mind. Tottered off towards the kitchen when she didn't, a mumbled, *sooo boring* trailing behind her.

Laura almost laughed out loud.

Fleur's idea of self-control was leaving the bottle on the kitchen counter, not bringing it into the sitting room. As if the short walk to the kitchen and back made any difference to the amount she drank. She also suspected Fleur took a big gulp straight out of the bottle while she was in there out of Laura's disapproving sight. And the minute Fleur closed the door after she left, she'd open another one. Guaranteed.

Laura couldn't blame her, not really.

But the unkind crack about not having anyone to share her life with hurt—even if she'd never let Fleur see it. And Fleur herself wouldn't remember in the morning.

Besides, she knew what people thought, the puerile whispers and tittle-tattle.

It used to be said that a man and a woman couldn't ever be friends. That at least one of them would harbor some sexual interest. These days, nobody accepted that two people of the same sex could be friends. Two lonely women—her an overworked doctor and Fleur a still-grieving widow—finding comfort and companionship in one another's company. People thought they were lesbians. Or at least she was. Her stature didn't help any—five-eleven in her stockinged feet and with broader shoulders than a lot of men. An amazon. A bull dyke if you wanted to be offensive. The opposite of diminutive, bird-like Fleur with her delicate bone structure. She batted for both sides, given that she'd been married—and to a man, no less. QED. Simple, easily-applied rules for simple bigoted folk.

She got up out of the matching hideous armchair, drifted across to what she thought of as *the shrine* on the other side of the room. She picked up one of the photographs. The frame it was in was the second-most-tasteless item Laura had ever seen. And God knows there was no shortage of stiff competition for that dubious honor in this room alone.

Despite the garish frame, she couldn't deny that Justin Sanders had been a good-looking guy. No wonder Fleur missed him so badly. Her hand went involuntarily to the small gold cross she wore around her neck under the crisp white and tastefully-professional blouse she always buttoned all the way to the top.

There but for the grace of God go I.

She knew that at times, in her darkest moments when sleep evaded her and her mind would give her no peace, Fleur wished she had been with him when it happened. That they were together now on the other side for all eternity.

What a load of horseshit.

Laura could never understand how some members of her profession—a number of them known to her personally—

managed to reconcile their medical training with a superstitious belief in the afterlife.

Fleur could tell them a thing or two about the existence or not of a merciful God.

Blind desperate hope in the face of all the facts.

She couldn't help laughing to herself. At herself. She might not believe in heaven and the angels, but there was sure as hell a hell—*ha, ha*—presided over by one evil son of a bitch.

She heard Fleur behind her, turned towards her, the photograph still clasped in her hands. In Fleur's hands were two glasses of red wine, not one, despite Laura's protestations.

There was no point in arguing. Fleur was stubborn at the best of times. Alcohol only made it worse.

They did a swap. The photograph for one of the glasses of wine. Laura pretended to take a small sip, the glass that could do with a proper clean barely kissing her lips as Fleur gazed at her dead husband's smiling face. Her voice was a sorry sad whisper filled with endless pain.

'I still miss him.'

Laura put her hand on her friend's arm, squeezed gently.

'I know you do. It's only natural.'

Thinking, *after five years you should've pulled yourself together by now*, two-faced bitch that she was.

Fleur cleared her throat, her voice apologetic more than sad now.

'Did you bring me any . . .'

Shit, Laura thought.

'I'm so sorry, Fleur, I forgot them. I'll come by again tomorrow.'

She was resigned to the fact of her complicity in helping a thirty-five-year-old woman become addicted to the prescription sleeping pill, Zolpidem. What she didn't need was Fleur looking at her as if she'd deliberately forgotten them, *how could you?* in her accusing eyes.

She'd been happy to prescribe them after it first happened. Ease the horror of losing her husband before their life together had gotten properly started. Gradually she'd weaned her off them, the pair of them self-medicating with Pinot Noir as their relationship transitioned from doctor-patient to close friends.

Now Fleur was in a hell of a state again. Right back at square one. Forget the pills, Laura felt like banging her head against the wall at times.

It had been that damned reporter—who wasn't even a real reporter—turning up a week ago asking questions that had set it all off. Dragging back into the unforgiving light of the present what they'd both hoped had slipped quietly into the all-consuming darkness of the past.

Laura understood that it was the not knowing that eats away at you. How you gradually learn to live with it. Time, the great healer. Better than any prescription medication.

And now, the last thing Fleur needed in her delicate state of mind. False hope. The promise of answers.

Laura could've told her not to delude herself. It wasn't going to happen. Period.

They'd adopted a two-pronged approach between them. She'd prescribed more Zolpidem and Fleur had doubled her alcohol intake overnight. Voilà, the problem had receded. The inborn imperative to go on living life dictated that each iteration of grief should be less intense, shorter-lived than the last one.

Then today, a hysterical call on her private cell phone. Shouting down the line while she was closeted with an elderly patient who, thankfully, was deaf as a post.

Somebody's watching the house.

Hence her presence here tonight, the Zolpidem unfortunately forgotten in the never-ending rush that passed for her life. At least she could still dispense a sensible matter-of-fact approach to banish the bogeyman.

Except there was a chance Fleur had been right. Perhaps it was simply that Fleur had put the idea into her head. The fact that she was actively looking for a shady character spying on her friend's house made her notice a car parked in the shade of a tree, the dark silhouette of a man inside.

Not that she was about to admit that to Fleur any time soon.

So here they were a number of glasses of Pinot later, mission accomplished—for now. Fleur was more concerned about where her next drink was coming from than worrying about cold-blooded killers lurking in the shrubbery.

Good for her, Laura thought sourly, fingering the cross beneath her blouse once more.

Because while Fleur snored the night away in an alcohol-induced stupor, she herself had the horror of her recurring nightmare to look forward to.

INNOCENT LEJEUNE REACHED UP AND TURNED THE INTERIOR DOME light to permanently *off*, then quietly got out of the car once the woman had disappeared into the house following a brief hug on the front step. He crept across the road and made a note of the Subaru Forester's license plate before returning to the safety of his own car. There, he texted it to a contact who would run it through the DMV database for him.

It was probably nothing.

He'd spent some time thinking about how to proceed after Theresa Thibodeaux had told him that something had spooked Bray.

That something had to be somebody digging up the past.

She'd mentioned Bray's man, Ritter, the man tasked with cleaning up after Bray—a full-time job if Innocent had ever heard of one. The best bet would've been to shadow him, benefit from his legwork and inside knowledge. Trouble was, Innocent didn't know him from Adam, or where to find him.

He'd needed another way.

Unfortunately, his influence within the world of law enforcement was limited to his DMV contact. He didn't have the luxury of access to the original case file.

That had left him with the article published in the newspaper at the time. The details had been sparse, at best. He'd had a simple choice. The lead detective named in the article, Lou Bordelon, or the dead hiker's wife, Fleur Sanders. There'd been a picture of her with her husband in happier times in the paper.

Innocent wasn't stupid. The chances of Bordelon giving him the time of day were precisely squat. That left the widow Sanders.

She hadn't been difficult to find. The paper had reported that she'd been a teacher before the bottom dropped out of her world. Luckily for him, she'd found comfort in the turbulent mass of youthful humanity that was a school and had remained one. It hadn't taken long to identify which school, then follow her home.

The woman in the Subaru had been the first visitor she'd had in all the time he'd been watching the house.

He hated that he had so little information. He felt like a bat with broken radar flying around in a cave, hitting the wall over and over.

The only thing he knew for sure was that his brother, Thibaud, was dead. His body hadn't been found in the wreckage, but neither had Innocent heard from him. It was inconceivable that he'd survived the crash and had disappeared with the money—there'd been no mention of that, either. Or of the video. Bray would be behind bars if they'd found that.

There were only two possibilities as far as he could see.

Thibaud had been injured in the crash, concussed or worse. He'd stumbled out and fallen in the bayou then drowned or had been eaten by a hungry 'gator.

Or somebody else had been involved.

He wished his presence here outside the widow's house made him feel more confident that he was making progress towards the truth. Sadly, it didn't. He felt as if he was wasting his time, his life.

His phone pinged five minutes later. He might only have one contact, but at least the guy got his finger out when necessary.

The message was short and to the point. A name.

Laura Hunt.

He put the name into Google, added *Lafayette* and hit *return*. Then smiled at his own good fortune, the warm glow of a man with God on his side in his belly when a match popped up.

Dr. Laura Hunt MD, a partner in a local doctors' practice.

He tapped the images tab. The first item was from a local newspaper dated a couple of years ago. It showed the woman he'd seen go into the widow's house shaking the hand of a man in a dinner suit as she accepted an award of some kind. The most pills prescribed that year or something similar. Like him, she was smiling at the camera. All dolled-up in a low-cut evening dress, looking pretty damn good to Innocent. He wished his doctor looked like she did. And made house calls late at night to rub better whatever needed rubbing. He could make good money out of her, too, doctor's uniform and all that kinky business.

It all made sense. And it made him very pleased he'd continued to pay Theresa Thibodeaux all these years. Her judgment couldn't be faulted, either.

Whatever had spooked Bray had also unsettled the widow. Hence her sudden requirement for sleeping pills, anti-depressants, whatever. The fact that they'd hugged on the doorstep suggested there was also a personal relationship. It didn't mean anything. Doctors have friends like anyone else.

He slipped down further into his seat now that it looked as if the good doctor was on more than a regular house call, reflecting on how only a minute ago he'd felt as if he was wasting his time.

Now, the cracks were starting to appear in what he'd known had been a cover-up from the beginning. The thought tightened his jaw and hardened his resolve.

He'd see his brother avenged yet.

23

BACK IN HIS ROOM, EVAN OPENED THE FRENCH DOORS LEADING out onto the balcony, then pulled up a chair in front of them and got himself comfortable with his laptop. He sat for a while thinking and enjoying the night air on his face, then logged into his Dropbox account and dived in.

On May 20, 2018 a Piper Cherokee 6 light aircraft crashed in the Atchafalaya National Wildlife Refuge a mile and a half west of the dividing line between St Martin and Iberville parishes, putting the subsequent unholy mess firmly in the lap of the St Martin Parish Sheriff's Office.

NTSB investigators subsequently attributed the crash to fuel starvation. The fuel selector switch had jammed in a position where the engine was not feeding from any of the aircraft's four fuel tanks. The underlying cause was a combination of inadequate maintenance and sloppy pre-flight checks. In layman's terms, shit happens. In this case, nobody dealt with it.

It was noted that no mayday call had been made.

The aircraft was owned by Esteban Aguilar, a Mexican national with links to the Mexican cartels. Señor Aguilar—who was not on board the plane for its fateful flight—was known to be involved in narcotics, arms and human trafficking with a reputation for sadistic violence above and beyond what passes for the norm in those circles.

Despite that, all the paperwork appeared to be in order. This wasn't a quick hop across the border hoping to sneak in under the radar. A flight plan had been filed. The aircraft had departed from Baton Rouge Metropolitan Airport, the final destination Aeropuerto del Norte in Monterrey, Mexico, with a refueling stop planned at Aransas County Airport, thirty miles north east of Corpus Christi.

The APIS manifest required for all flights into Mexico had been duly filed and listed two persons on board. José Hernández and Juan Pérez.

So far, so good. Everything appeared to be above board, ignoring the reputation of the owner of the plane and the lack of a mayday call—and the fact that whoever was responsible for maintaining the aircraft deserved to be shot.

As were the two dead men found in the wreckage by park rangers.

That's when all the fun and games started.

Both names listed on the APIS manifest subsequently proved to be false. With the benefit of hindsight, the fact that the names José and Juan and the surnames Hernández and Pérez all featured in the top half-dozen Mexican first and last names respectively made this unsurprising.

The pilot was later identified as Oscar de La Cruz, aged forty-seven, an ex-Aeroméxico commercial pilot who'd spent fifteen years flying sun-seeking Brits back and forth between London Heathrow and Puerto Vallarta until he was fired when he tested positive for cocaine in a routine mandatory drug test. He subsequently flew anything with wings for anyone with the money to pay him to places most people didn't want to go in order to feed his drug habit. The cartels were his employer of choice given their willingness to pay in cash and product. His toxicology report had shown high levels of methamphetamine in his system at the time of the crash. That finding supported the view that the pre-flight checks had been perfunctory, at best.

His injuries were consistent with flying a light aircraft into a dense mass of healthy trees. They included, but were not limited to broken ribs, collar bone, radius and ulna in both arms, as well as multiple cuts and contusions and damage to a number of internal organs. In addition, a basilar skull fracture would very likely have resulted in traumatic brain injury had the cause of death—a single 9mm gunshot wound to the left temple—not made that worry somewhat academic.

The second man found dead at the scene was Justin Sanders, aged thirty-one, a paramedic from Whittington Oaks, Lafayette, who worked out of Our Lady of Lourdes Regional Medical Center. He'd been shot twice in the chest at close range with the same gun that had been used to kill de La Cruz. The gun was never recovered. Ballistics failed to match the slugs recovered from Sanders and de La Cruz's bodies with anything in the system. It was noted that the Mexican authorities' helpfulness left a lot to be desired. The gun could've been used to kill half the population of Mexico City and they'd never have known about it for all the information that came back.

Sanders had not been on the flight. He was not the second man listed on the APIS manifest as Juan Pérez. There was no sign of that man at the scene, despite the fact that evidence suggested he'd been handcuffed to his seat in the back during the flight. The handcuffs were found still attached to the seat.

Investigators put it together as follows:

Sanders, a keen sportsman, fitness fanatic and ornithologist, had been hiking in the area when he saw the plane go down. He'd gone to investigate and provide assistance if anyone was still alive using his skills as an experienced paramedic. He'd found Pérez cuffed to his seat, presumably badly injured from the crash. The key to the handcuffs had been found on the floor underneath the seat. Sanders' fingerprints as well as those of the pilot were found on it, as well as fibers matching the lining of the pilot's jacket pocket. The assumption was that Sanders entered the aircraft, fished the key out of the pilot's pocket and released the cuffed man, Pérez. In doing so, he assumed the role of the Good Samaritan who paid the ultimate price for risking his own life to help save an agent of the Antichrist. The man only identified as Juan Pérez then shot Sanders and the pilot to death. How this happened could only be surmised. The most likely scenario was that the gun had belonged to the pilot. He may have left it on the co-pilot's seat for ease of access and it ended up in the back of the plane after the crash. Or Pérez might have pretended to check to see if the pilot was still alive, taken the gun from his pocket and quickly remedied that situation before shooting the hapless hiker.

Whatever it was, two men ended up dead and Pérez made good his escape.

Evan put his laptop down on the floor, went to get a glass of water. So far all he'd read was what Fontenot and Mercer had already told him but with a few added details—none of which moved him forwards. He thought about hitting the sack, continuing in the morning. Except sleep wasn't an option. He'd lie in bed staring at the ceiling for five, ten, thirty minutes—his choice—before getting up again to work his way through the rest of it.

He saved himself the bother of undressing and got settled in the chair, dived back in. The next document he came across was the transcript of the original interview between Justin Sander's wife, now widow, and the sheriff's office detectives, Lou Bordelon and Frank Crowell.

Bordelon: Thank you for speaking to us, today, Mrs. Sanders. I realize this is a very difficult time.

Already Evan liked Bordelon. He hadn't wasted anybody's time with insincere platitudes about being very sorry for her loss.

Sanders: I just want to help find the man who killed my husband.

Bordelon: We all do, Mrs. Sanders.

Crowell: Absolutely.

Evan wasn't so impressed with Crowell. What was that supposed to add?

Bordelon: If you could take us through your husband's movements on the day he died insofar as you're aware of them.

Sanders: Can I get you something to drink? Coffee? Water?

Bordelon: We're fine, thank you.

Crowell: Not for me, Mrs. Sanders.

Bordelon: Your husband's movements?

Sanders: Sorry. There isn't a lot I can tell you.

Crowell: The smallest details can be important even if you don't realize it at the time.

Seemed to Evan that Frank Crowell was your man if you needed somebody to state the blindingly obvious.

Sanders: I suppose. Justin has, sorry, had a long-standing arrangement with his friend, Kevin. They'd arranged to go hiking together in the Atchafalaya—

Bordelon: If I could stop you there, Mrs. Sanders. You're saying that your husband wasn't hiking by himself? He was with his friend, Kevin?

Sanders: As far as I know, yes. They've been doing it for years. Who'd want to go for a walk in the woods on their own?

Evan stopped reading for a moment. It explained the inconsistency that Fontenot had referred to. That Justin Sanders' car had been found in a gas station thirteen miles away. The two friends had arrived in their own cars separately, grabbed a coffee and a Danish and something for the trip, then continued on their way in one car—Kevin's. Against that, it was clear this was the first Bordelon had heard of it. He went back to the transcript.

Bordelon: You're sure about that, Mrs. Sanders?

Sanders: That's what he told me as he was leaving. Are you saying he wasn't with Kevin?

Bordelon: At this point it looks as if he was alone when he saw the plane go down.

Evan imagined the look Bordelon and Crowell had exchanged. They'd be having a word with Kevin, last name currently unknown, in the very near future. A conversation Kevin might not enjoy.

Bordelon: Is there anything else you can tell us about this particular trip, Mrs. Sanders? Anything out of the ordinary?

Sanders: Like what?

Bordelon: Was he his normal self on the day or in the days leading up to it? Was he depressed? Problems at work? Anything that might have made him think he wanted a long walk in the woods on his own to get his head right?

Sanders: We hadn't had an argument if that's what you're implying.

Bordelon: Not at all, Mrs. Sanders. I apologize if I gave that impression. But as my colleague said, the smallest thing could be important.

Evan smiled to himself. Felt sorry for Bordelon, having to dance around her delicate feelings. He knew what Bordelon had really wanted to say. *Funny you should bring that up. Do you argue with your husband a lot?* He could hear the already-taken offense in her voice when she answered, picture the set of her mouth.

Sanders: There's nothing I can think of.

Crowell: That's okay. You're in shock. This is a very stressful time for you. Maybe something will come to you over the next few days.

Sanders: I can't think what.

Bordelon: Did your husband take his cell phone with him when he went hiking?

Evan gave Bordelon a retrospective thumbs-up for moving them swiftly on.

Sanders: Of course he did. In case of emergencies. And to let me know what time to expect him. Sometimes they went for a beer on the way home. Why?

Bordelon: He didn't have it on him, and it wasn't in his car. Perhaps he forgot it. You haven't seen it lying around the house, have you?

Sanders: Definitely not. I tried calling him when I didn't hear from him. It went to voicemail. I'd have heard it if he left it on the kitchen counter or in the bedroom.

Crowell: Did you call Kevin?

Sanders: I tried. That went to voicemail, too. I thought it was a bad signal in the middle of all those trees. That's why I couldn't get either of them.

Bordelon: I think that's all for now, Mrs. Sanders.

Sanders: Do I have to identify the body?

Bordelon: One of his parents could do it if you don't feel up to it.

Sanders: No. It's not fair on them.

Bordelon: Someone will be in touch to make arrangements.

Sanders: What about his personal effects?

Bordelon: Was there anything in particular?

Sanders: Yes. No. It doesn't matter.

Bordelon: You'll get everything back in due course, Mrs. Sanders.

Evan felt his eyes fluttering at that point. His ability to focus, to concentrate, waning. It had been a long day. He knew exactly what was needed to revive him—get into bed and try to get to sleep. He plowed on, searching for the transcript of the detectives' interview with Justin Sanders' hiking buddy, Kevin.

Expecting it to be an interesting read. In the Chinese curse sense of the word—*may you live in interesting times*.

It wasn't. It was short and dull.

Kevin Clark claimed that he had injured his right knee the previous weekend and had been unable to accompany his friend on their planned trip. He wasn't able to provide proof of the injury, having not seen a doctor or physiotherapist about it. The detectives had naturally wanted to know why he hadn't told his friend in advance.

Turned out it had been a minor injury and he had hoped it would clear up before their scheduled trip. As a result, he hadn't said anything to Justin in advance, knowing that Justin the never-off-duty paramedic would have given him the third degree over it all week long. Was he doing this exercise and applying that cold compress and so on? Kevin was, as it happened, and the injury had duly cleared up. Then he got out of bed too quickly on the day, slipped on the bedside rug and twisted it again. Justin was already on his way to the agreed rendezvous when he called to let him know.

While he was unable to provide the detectives with proof of the injury, he had no problem supplying the name of a colleague at work who could—and subsequently did when questioned—vouch for his presence in the office all day long. If he couldn't hike in the woods, he sure as hell wasn't going to waste a day off sitting on his butt at home.

At the end of reading the transcript, Evan had more questions than he did at the beginning. But the biggest anomaly didn't relate to anything he'd read in the file. It was to do with what wasn't there.

A man handcuffed to a seat in the back of an aircraft that crashed would be thrown violently forward. The handcuff around his wrist would, at the very least, cut into his flesh, if not break his wrist. His blood and tissue would be all over it. His DNA.

So where was the report from the lab?

Mercer's remark about a cover-up now made a lot more sense. It was about all that did in the face of the mounting questions.

Who was the passenger handcuffed in the back?

Why was he handcuffed?

How did he manage to kill two men and escape?

And why was his identity covered up?

Because Evan was convinced that was what had happened. If his DNA had not been in the system, there'd be a report in the file stating exactly that. *No match.*

The fact that the DNA report was missing implied that he was in the system, but that somebody—with an implied degree of influence—wanted his presence on the plane to remain a secret.

He couldn't help thinking about the unknown man following him as he finally climbed into bed and tried to grab a few hours' fitful sleep.

24

Ritter was thinking about weak links and loose ends as he dug into his breakfast in a greasy spoon diner off Highway 90, the air thick with the smell of bacon fat and freshly-brewed coffee.

Innocent Lejeune clearly didn't have the video in his possession or he'd have used it years ago. Followed up on the initial threat that had almost—but unfortunately not quite—given Bray a cardiac arrest. A man like Lejeune couldn't spell *long game*, let alone play it. He was a walking premature ejaculation.

But he was aware of the video's existence. He'd made the damn thing, after all. Him or his brother, at any rate.

He'd laid low for the past five years and said nothing. A truce of sorts. *We don't hear from you and you won't hear from us.* That didn't mean he wouldn't roll over if he was hauled in and asked a direct question as a result of the current renewed interest in the matter.

Best to take him off the board just in case.

He pulled out his phone and called a guy they'd used a couple times before. Marvin Fleck. Not the sharpest knife in the drawer, but he knew how to pull a trigger and, more importantly, how to keep his mouth shut if things went sideways and he was caught.

'Yeah?'

'It's Ritter.'

'You sound funny.'

'That's because I've got a mouthful of breakfast.' He finished chewing. Ran his tongue around his teeth thinking, *at least I don't sound like a moron.* 'Better?'

'Whatever.'

'I need Innocent Lejeune taken care of.'

'No problem. How do you want it done?'

Ritter sighed. He might as well do it himself. Looked out the window at the people going about their daily business. Should he ask one of them to do it? That woman over there, perhaps, the one with the stupid hat? He didn't make any effort to keep the sharpness out of his voice.

'I don't care. Burn him to death in his own goddamn whorehouse while one of his diseased whores sits on his face for all I care.'

A strained silence came down the line as if he'd used too many long words or put short ones in the wrong order. He wasn't sure he liked Fleck's attitude when he eventually came back at him. Like he was talking to a puppy.

'What I meant was, do you want him to simply disappear, or do you want the manner of his passing to send a message?'

Maybe the guy wasn't so stupid, after all.

'Got you. No message. Quiet as a mouse. Here today, gone—'

He guessed from the dial tone in his ear that the guy had gotten the message. That, or he'd listened to enough cheesy clichés for one day already.

He went back to his breakfast, took a slurp of too-warm OJ,

then chased egg yolk around the plate with a slice of buttered toast as he thought some more about loose ends.

Ex-sheriff's office detective Lou Bordelon sprang instantly to mind.

Yap, yap, Ritter thought to himself as he speared a link sausage and stuffed it into his mouth along with the eggy toast.

No, the guy had been well and truly scared off. Besides, what would he do? Stamp his big flat foot and demand the DNA report be mailed to him? And even if it was? He'd know Lejeune's brother was on the plane. So what? The call he'd just made to Fleck had already tied off that loose end.

What about the widow Sanders? What threat did she present, if any? She could point someone—the investigator Buckley, most likely—at Bordelon. No problem. Refer to the above.

So, a two-pronged approach. Sayonara Innocent Lejeune, asap. And keep on keepin' on shadowing the investigator, Buckley. Which might well lead in turn to *adios, Señor investigador.*

He could always make that happen right now. Hit redial and give Fleck a second target. Maybe even get a reduction on the price. Buy one, get the second one half-price. A scorched-earth policy has its uses at times. Except the damn video was still out there somewhere. It needed to be found. Preferably by his good self.

His mouth twisted in a sour parody of a laugh. At times, he got so incredibly bored playing nursemaid to Bray he might even post the damn thing on YouTube if they ever did find it, and to hell with the egotistical jackass and his perverted fantasies.

He checked his watch. Wondering if Buckley was an early-morning sort of guy, already out and about. Then he got out his phone, opened the tracker app.

Nope, the guy's car was still parked where it had been last night when he snuck in and fixed the tracker to it.

Three miles away, Evan was sitting at a table in the window of the bright airy dining room of his B&B. Pouring ice-cold milk onto a big bowl of Cheerios and gazing out over the front lawn, the subdued early-morning conversations of the other guests all around him, classical music playing softly in the background.

A very civilized way to start one's day.

But not for long.

His phone vibrated in his pocket, the ringer set to silent, not wanting to be the anti-social guest to spoil the relaxed atmosphere in the room for everyone. He pulled it out, immediately getting to his feet, the caller's name on the screen guaranteeing a conversation best conducted outdoors.

Stan Fraser.

At least he'd only eaten a couple of mouthfuls of Cheerios, not sufficient to give him serious indigestion.

Stan got right to it, not big on early-morning pleasantries.

'We need to get some things straight.'

'That's easy. Put Landry back in his cage and don't let him out again until I'm done.'

'Landry didn't walk into the Jerusalem Tavern and kick Guillory in the pink taco.'

'Guillory didn't sniff her fingers like they'd just been holding his shriveled dick. Besides, what do you expect me to do about it? Tell him to make a complaint to Internal Affairs.'

Despite a residual mental fuzziness caused by reading so late into the night, he'd been bang-on about it being an outdoors sort of discussion. If it kept going the same way he'd have to think about making his way to the middle of the Mojave Desert.

They needed to dial it down. Seemed Stan felt the same way.

'You're right. He was out of order. But she shouldn't have walked into my bar and tried to tell me what to do and then threaten me.'

'You shouldn't have sent Landry to break Aiden's finger.'

'I didn't. The blame's on you for Landry taking things into his own hands. It wouldn't have happened if you'd told him the truth.'

Evan didn't bother arguing. Point out that Landry's presence was the root of the problem. And it was too early for a philosophical conversation about whether one person doing something gave a second person carte blanche to do whatever the hell they liked in response.

He'd started across the front lawn as they talked, heading for the front gate set into the picket fence that surrounded the property. He didn't expect to see the guy who'd followed him the previous day sitting in his car eating a breakfast roll watching the property, nor did he.

He was only going through the motions. Because something else had come to him. After a quick glance up and down the street, he headed towards where his car was parked. He went back to Stan as he walked.

'You know I'm in Lafayette?'

'Yeah. You found anything down there yet?'

As he had the previous day when talking to Elise, Evan got a mental picture of Landry getting ahold of her slim finger, casually snapping it at the joint as he had Aiden's. Or doing the same to Fontenot. Or even semi-retired going-to-seed Mercer.

'I'm scared to tell you. Perhaps if they paid commission on referrals to the broken-bones unit at the hospital...'

'I've told him. No more of that.'

Evan thought about saying, *but did he listen?* Decided against it, the conversation having leveled out somewhat after the initial escalating accusations and counter-accusations.

But there was something in the way Fraser had said it made him ask the question he did now.

'Where is Landry?'

'On his way to you.'

'Here in Lafayette?'

'Yeah. There in Lafayette. You got a problem with that?'

Evan had arrived at his car by now. He made a quick lap of it, feeling under the wheel arches. He found it on the front passenger side. A black molded plastic box measuring five by three by two inches. The sort of GPS tracking device you can buy on Amazon for a hundred and fifty bucks, next-day delivery included.

He pulled it off, considered his options. Put it on one of the other guest's cars? Let the guy spend a day following them around Lafayette's tourist attractions. Go out onto the street and find a plumber or an electrician's van, stick it on that? Drop it in a bucket of water or stomp it to pieces?

In the end, he re-affixed it to his own car.

Fraser's voice had more of its usual hard edge to it with an added undercurrent of impatience when he repeated his question.

'I said, is that going to be a problem?'

Two minutes ago, and the answer would've been a big fat *yes*. You bet your criminal ass it is. In the light of his recent discovery, that answer had just changed.

It didn't mean he was going to let Fraser think he'd accepted the situation without complaint.

'That depends on Landry. What he's planning on doing. Either what you've told him to do, or another bright idea of his own. Why'd you send him, anyway, if you've told him he's not allowed to hurt anybody?'

Fraser laughed, the last thing Evan would've expected—even if there wasn't a lot of humor in it.

'To get him out the way. Stop him from sitting around obsessing about what he's gonna do to Guillory.'

Evan couldn't stop himself from smiling with him. More at the thought of what Guillory would say when he told her that Stan Fraser was looking out for her.

'Great. You decided to transfer her problem onto me.'

It was said tongue-in-cheek. That didn't change the fact that he should've kept the thought to himself. Not given Stan an easy comeback riding out on the back of genuine amusement.

'Way I hear it, that'll make a pleasant change. I'm sure she'll appreciate it. Landry will be in touch as soon as he gets in.'

25

Evan was having a problem with the w-word.

Not worrying or walking or wriggling, but waiting.

He had to wait for Guillory to get back to him with details about the guy following him, which would probably be a dead end anyway. If the guy was part of the cover-up—and it was too much of a coincidence to think that he wasn't—a simple DMV check wasn't going to identify him.

He also had to wait for Landry to arrive. So that they could do something about the guy Guillory would hit a brick wall trying to identify.

Trouble was, he was no good at it. He'd tried it once before and it hadn't worked out.

He decided to shake things up. Make himself into a person of interest to the people Arlo had gotten worried. He already was, but he might as well make sure, belt and suspenders—and hope they didn't simply shoot him the first chance they got.

Whoever was worried by the renewed interest must have been alerted somehow. Seemed to him the St. Martinville sheriff's office was a good place to start. The place where the investigation began and then prematurely ended.

He took a leisurely drive there, heading east to pick up the smaller Highway 353 rather than hack directly south down US-90. Give the guy tailing him time to get his act together, his ass in gear. Stopped at a gas station on the way for some gas he didn't need for the same reason. Managed to stretch a fifteen-mile, twenty-minute journey out to thirty-five minutes. It was probably unnecessary. The leak was likely already in the sheriff's office.

He went inside, asked if Deputy Mercer was on duty that day. The guy on reception took his name, made a call. Turning away from Evan to do it to give Mercer the opportunity to not be there. A couple minutes later Mercer came out, surprise and curiosity battling it out on his face.

'I was wondering if we could have a word,' Evan said far too loudly. He hooked his thumb at the door before Mercer had a chance to reply. 'Can we talk outside?'

Already halfway there before the words were out of his mouth. Mercer followed him, didn't really have a choice, the crease in his brow deepening.

'I want to apologize for the way things started yesterday,' Evan said. 'I overreacted. I know we got past it, but I wanted to clear the air.'

Mercer waved it off.

'I shouldn't have dropped it on you like that.'

Evan followed Mercer's lead, batted the remark away thinking it was turning into a regular apology fest.

'I also want to make it clear that I'm not clearing the air just so that I can ask you a favor.'

Mercer said absolutely not.

'But I do want to explain,' Evan said.

A car went past on the street behind Evan at that point, tooted its horn. Evan twisted at the waist, saw a red Chevy

Silverado with a middle-aged guy driving it, his suntanned arm out the window in a wave.

Mercer waved back, told Evan to go ahead.

Evan couldn't help thinking how difficult it must be to get anything done in a small town where everybody knew everybody else. Except today it was helping. Everybody would know that a stranger had been in town talking to Deputy Mercer about something that was best said outside.

'I don't normally work for men like Arlo's old man. That's not strictly true. I *never* work for men like him...'

He then took Mercer through the Eleanor Fields case. Explained how it had connected to Arlo in an indirect way, confirming to Stan Fraser that his son was alive, not dead as he'd always feared.

'I'd never heard of Stan Fraser before that. Then he came to me and asked me to try to find his son. What was I going to do?'

One thing he was definitely going to do was say nothing about the favor trading back and forth between him and Stan that followed. Need to know, and Mercer didn't.

'The thing is, it struck a raw nerve with me. My wife disappeared some years ago.'

He paused. Let Mercer—who had no qualms about coming out with insincere platitudes years after the event—say how sorry he was to hear it. Evan was about to continue, then changed his mind. Dropped his eyes, looking down at the ground between his feet. It was always better when you made someone ask.

Mercer played his allotted role.

'Did you ever find her?'

'Not alive, no.'

Once again Mercer said how sorry he was to hear it. At least he didn't say *for his loss* like he was talking about his phone or wallet.

Evan cleared his throat, met Mercer's gaze. The guy was looking as if his own wife had died in the night after Evan and Fontenot's visit. Anyone observing them would conclude they were talking about some serious shit.

'It's my opinion,' Evan said, 'that if I'd looked harder and earlier, she'd still be alive today.'

Mercer shook his head as if he'd rolled his dead wife over and found one of the grandchildren suffocated underneath her.

'That's gotta weigh on your conscience.'

'Believe me, it does. So when Stan Fraser came to me and asked me to find Arlo who he thought was in trouble, there was no way I could say no. The first thing that came to mind was that I couldn't stand it if he came back a few weeks later and told me Arlo had been shipped home to him in a body bag. Then he accuses me, says I could've prevented it if I'd gone looking for him like he'd asked me three weeks earlier.'

Mercer was looking as if—had he not been a sheriff's deputy standing in the middle of the sidewalk in the town he was sworn to serve—he'd be wiping away a tear by now. His voice was a little more gravelly, too.

'I see what you mean about a raw nerve.'

'Yeah.'

'I'm sorry I jumped to the wrong conclusion.'

'Don't worry about it. Let me show you something.'

He pulled out his phone. Opened the photo gallery and scrolled back, the months and years flying past as he flicked the screen with his middle finger. Finally, he found one of Sarah. Showed it to Mercer.

'That's her.'

He got a sudden premonition that Mercer was about to say something superficial again. About what a good-looking woman she'd been, accompanying it with an encouraging smile.

Evan didn't want any smiling. Nosir.

'I don't want to go into details, but she was gunned down in the street. I was there at the time.'

Mercer's face darkened as if his remaining grandchild had been out with Sarah at the time and had taken a stray round. Anyone watching was going to be asking themselves what kind of serious shit can they be talking about now, for Christ's sake?

Evan felt a little slimy for manipulating Mercer and using his own personal tragedy in such a barefaced, shameless way, but needs must when the devil drives.

He worked a solemn expression onto his face, stuck out his hand.

'Sorry to dump all that on you. Sometimes it just comes out.'

Mercer took his hand. Gave it a brisk man-to-man pump.

'Not a problem. I'm glad we cleared the air.'

He turned on his heel, marched back into the office.

And Evan thought to himself, *make of that what you will, whoever you are watching.*

He still had time to kill.

He got back in the car, put the Texaco gas station where Justin Sanders had parked on the day he died into Google maps, then headed across country taking twenty-five minutes to get there. Whoever was following him and was involved in the cover-up would also be familiar with the original investigation. They'd know the significance of the gas station.

They might wonder what he thought he was going to achieve five years after the event, but at least they'd believe him to be thorough, a worrying trait in a man you were already worried about.

After a quick look around, he went inside to get himself something to eat, not having gone back to his breakfast after Stan Fraser's call interrupted it so rudely. He bought himself a sandwich and coffee, and was carrying them back to the car when Guillory called him.

26

'How's your head?' he said.

'It's fine. Any reason why it shouldn't be?'

'How about all those beers you drank for both of us last night?'

She snorted like he'd insulted her. He imagined the dismissive look on her face as she waved it away. *You call that a lot to drink?* He gave her something else to be dismissive about.

'You don't have to worry about Landry.'

'I'm not.'

Echoing her response in his head as she said it, two minds as one.

Dismissive in her reaction or not, the remark had intrigued her.

'Why would I no longer need to worry, had I been worried in the first place?'

'Stan's sent him to keep me company down here.'

'Lucky you.'

'And to keep him away from you. He's worried you'll go back to The Backroom tonight for round two. Word on the street is that you've got a nasty temper and a mean streak.'

'Is that so?'

'Uh-huh.'

'You wouldn't have anything to do with starting that particular rumor, would you?'

He decided it was a question best treated as rhetorical, asked one of his own.

'Any luck with the license plate?'

'That's why I'm calling. I've got a name for you. Thomas Nieves. And an address in Baton Rouge if you want it.'

Something wasn't right. Apart from the fact that it was too easy. It was her voice. That best-until-last ring to it. He played along.

'I get the feeling you've got something else for me as well as a name and address.'

'No flies on you, huh? Nieves' age. You want to guess?'

He pretended to think about it as the words *dead end* went through his mind.

'Ninety?'

'Close. He's eighty-four. Does that sound like your guy?'

'So the car's stolen.'

'That, or the plate's been cloned. Probably find old Tommy has been in a wheelchair for the last ten years or he's gone ga-ga and the car's been on bricks in his front yard ever since.'

He wasn't surprised. At least Landry wasn't going to have a wasted trip. He almost felt sorry for the guy tailing him. After suffering the physical pain of a kick in the balls and the longer-lasting loss of face at having his ass whupped in front of his peers, Landry was going to have a lot of pent-up anger to work out. And if that wasn't enough, he had five hours in a cramped seat in goat class with Delta to put him in the mood for hitting somebody.

'What's the plan now?' she said. 'Or shouldn't I ask, given who's about to join you?'

'At the moment I'm busy painting a target onto my back.'

She laughed, more of an incredulous disbelieving sound than humorous, one that he knew well.

'Is there any room? Why can't whoever it is aim at one of the existing ones? Maybe I should start calling you speed-dial again.'

He laughed with her, even if it wasn't that funny if you were on the receiving end. She'd gone through a phase of calling him speed-dial in recognition of the fact that he appeared to go out of his way to put himself in every maniac's crosshairs—hence the Grim Reaper had him on speed-dial. It was only a matter of time before he got through.

That's when the penny dropped for her. She made the connection between her not-unexpected failure to identify the man tailing him, Landry's imminent arrival and him using himself as bait.

'I'm going to stop asking questions now before I hear something I'll regret hearing. Ignoring for now that covers a lot of our conversations. Speak to you later.'

If she heard his parting remark—*it's your fault for kicking him in the balls*—she chose to ignore it.

He was wary of not wanting to sit still in any one place for too long. Potentially arouse suspicion in the mind of the man following and watching that he was simply killing time while he waited for backup. He did a search on Google for nearby backpacking and outdoor gear stores, then headed off to pick up what he needed.

EVAN WASN'T THE ONLY ONE TO TAKE A DISAPPOINTING PHONE CALL that morning.

Following Buckley from St. Martinville, it had become

obvious to Ritter as he took LA-347 that he was headed towards the Texaco gas station where Justin Sanders' car had been found. Ritter was now sitting in the McDonald's parking lot off Grand Point Highway, a hundred yards as the crow flies from where Evan was parked in the gas station.

It made sense to Ritter. Buckley would most likely head over to the Atchafalaya National Wildlife Refuge where the plane had gone down at some point. Not because he expected to find anything useful either there or at the gas station after five years —he was an idiot if he did. He was getting a feel for the case, is all, before digging deeper.

It was a strange game they were playing.

Buckley clearly knew he'd been followed the previous day. Hence his attempt to sneak up on him as he, Ritter, sat watching the diner where Buckley was eating his dinner. He would expect to be followed again today. It made changing cars or license plates a pointless exercise. He'd be made again in no time at all, even given the advantage the tracker gave him, allowing him to hang back further.

At some point he could expect Buckley to attempt to give him the slip.

Until then, Ritter was happy to tag along as the guy familiarized himself with the case. He would've liked to know what he discussed with Mercer outside the St. Martinville sheriff's office, but hey-ho, you can't always get what you want.

That's when Ritter took the call from Marvin Fleck, the man he'd tasked with getting rid of Innocent Lejeune, only to be told that nobody had seen Lejeune around for a couple of days.

The news, while disappointing, was informative. It told Ritter that Lejeune had also been alerted to the renewed interest in the case somehow. He was nosing around Lafayette and the surrounding area himself.

Perhaps they'd both end up following Buckley around. It would make his life easier, if they did.

And save him Fleck's fee.

27

Landry was as good as Stan Fraser's word. Evan was sitting in his car in the parking lot of Atchafalaya Camping & Hiking in Henderson, his purchases on the seat beside him, when Landry called at a couple of minutes past eleven. Evan took a moment to decide how to start the conversation when he saw Landry's name on the screen.

How are your balls?

I'm not rubbing them better however much you offer me.

Kate Guillory says, hi.

In the end, he kept it simple, not so provocative.

'Welcome to Lafayette, Landry.'

Landry grunted something in response. It sounded a lot like a complaint about the early start the trip had necessitated. Then he got down to business, the background sounds confirming that he was still in the airport.

'Where are you?'

'About fifteen miles away.'

'Okay. I've gotta take a piss, then I'll grab a cup of coffee, see you outside in what? Twenty minutes?'

Evan had no idea whether Landry's assumption that they'd

be driving around together was his own idea, or what he'd been told to do by Stan Fraser. Didn't matter. It wasn't going to happen. It wasn't ever going to happen, but certainly not now that the tail Guillory had failed to identify had to be dealt with.

'Change of plan. You need to rent a car—'

'Stan said—'

'I don't care what Stan said—'

'You wouldn't say that to his face.'

'Yeah, well, he's not here, is he? Besides, I'm not trying to avoid driving around with you. There's something we need to do that requires two cars ...'

He took Landry through the situation and what they needed to do about it, then gave him directions—the same route he'd driven the previous day with Ralph Fontenot. I-10 heading east to exit 127, then north on Whiskey Bay Highway as far as Bayou Manuel Road.

'Go past the turning, turn around and pull off the road where you can't be seen. Then wait for us to go right onto Bayou Manuel Road.'

'It won't work. The guy's not stupid. You nearly caught him last night. He's not gonna follow you down a dirt road in the middle of nowhere.'

Evan had originally thought the same thing. Then he'd taken a more detailed look at the map. From the bridge over Alabama Bayou where he stopped with Fontenot it was possible to continue on and rejoin Whiskey Bay Highway further north. From there it was a straight run all the way up to where it joined Highway 190 at Krotz Springs. The guy tailing him knew he'd been made. He couldn't take the risk that when Evan headed north on Whiskey Bay Highway and then made a right onto Bayou Manuel Road supposedly going to the crash site—a pointless exercise and everybody knew it—he was actually trying to give him the slip. For it to work Evan would also have needed to find the tracker so that he could ditch it in the middle of the Atchafalaya wildlife refuge—and the guy couldn't afford to assume he hadn't.

He wasn't about to explain all that to Landry.

'Believe me, he will. The alternative is that I call Stan, tell him how I can't find his son because you won't help me get rid of the guy tailing me.'

Landry was quiet a long moment. As if he was considering it before making his own mind up, rather than hopping to it on Evan's say so.

'Give me an hour and a half. I'll be in position by then.'

'It's a thirty-minute drive.'

'I've got to rent a car. There'll be a line.'

'There wasn't yesterday.'

Evan pictured Landry's face. The frustration and irritation on it, as he deliberately argued for the sake of it. Not because he was willfully perverse—although plenty of people said that he was—but because he wanted Landry to confirm what he suspected. Which he did soon enough.

'I need to stop off in Lafayette.'

He didn't need to say any more and they both knew it. He hadn't been able to bring a gun with him on the plane. Stan had arranged for one to be made available locally.

'Okay. Text me as soon as you come off I-10. I don't know how long after that you'll have a signal.'

EVAN HAD JUST CROSSED THE ATCHAFALAYA RIVER WHEN THE TEXT arrived. He'd kept an eye on the rearview mirror the whole time, hadn't identified a tail. To be fair, he'd been driving for less than ten minutes since leaving the camping store and thanks to the tracker the guy could afford to hang well back. He'd have to trust that he was behind him somewhere.

There was no sign of Landry's car when he turned right onto Bayou Manuel Road twenty minutes later. And he was looking for it. The guy following had no chance.

A little over a mile later, he went around a sharp right-hand bend three-quarters of the way between the junction and the bridge over the bayou Fontenot had brought him to the previous day. He came off the gas, coasted for a safe distance so he wouldn't get wiped out when the tail came around the bend, then swung the car hard left. Stopped in a cloud of billowing dust broadside across the narrow gravel road, blocking it, the trees dense and impenetrable on either side.

He hadn't seen a single car since he left the Interstate, either today or the previous day. It would be a particularly perverse twist of fate if one came along before the tail. If and when it did, he'd deal with it then.

He spent a minute preparing himself before he got out of the car. Not for the potential killer tracking him. For the millions of little, if not actual killers, airborne biters that called this unspoiled place home. As on the previous day, he rolled down and buttoned his sleeves, fastened his collar up tight and slathered any remaining exposed skin with insect repellent—preparations he'd failed to mention to Landry, *ha, ha*. Completed the ensemble with his newly-acquired camo baseball cap and a pair of thin cotton gloves—although they had more to do with dealing with the man following.

He fetched the hickory axe handle he'd bought from the trunk, then threaded his way into the roadside trees to wait. Thirty seconds out of the car and already sweat trickled down his back and out of his hairline making his head itch. His skin crawled as he imagined a new strain of DEET-resistant little monsters feasting on him, sucking his blood greedily up their long probing proboscises.

He heard the car before he saw it. Driving slowly, a

combination of the poorly-maintained gravel road and a growing wariness in his pursuer's mind.

The car came around the right-hand bend, Evan's car twenty-five yards in front of it blocking the road. The driver stomped the brakes, skidded a short distance on the loose gravel and came to a halt.

Evan stayed in the darkness of the trees watching as the dust settled and the silence returned, heart racing, his breathing slow and measured.

The car door opened. Then a tall rangy man in a lightweight khaki safari jacket stepped cautiously out. Evan gripped the axe handle tighter as the guy scanned the trees, eyes straining at the ever-changing pattern of movement of sunlight and shade. Looking directly at where Evan hid. Then he cocked his head.

Evan heard it at the same time.

A car approaching way faster than the one that had been tailing him. Safari Jacket leaned back into his car. For a brief moment Evan thought he was going to attempt to get past or even shunt his car out of the way. Except he wasn't getting in. He was getting something out.

Hiding in the trees with a piece of hickory in his hand, Evan was very grateful Landry had made a detour to see a man in Lafayette about a gun when Safari Jacket stood up out of the car again, a 9mm Glock in his hand.

Then he was gone in the blink of an eye. Disappeared into the trees without a sound as if he'd never been there at all.

Landry's car came careening around the bend a second later. No time to stop. Slamming on the brakes too little too late. Shunting the car immediately in front, a jerking bunny hop forwards, the trunk on the now-sandwiched car popping open with the impact.

Landry's door flew open as if the car was about to explode.

Evan stepped partially out of the trees, yelled at him.

'*Landry!* In the trees on your right. He's armed.'

Landry dived as a shot rang out proving it, hit the ground hard and rolled. Evan threw himself backwards as the shooter brought his gun arm around and fired at where he'd been a heartbeat before.

Then another shot, different than the other two, louder. The sound of Landry's .357 Colt Python.

A howl of pain bounced off the trees as Landry's bullet tore through the meaty part of the pursuer's left shoulder. Sent him spinning, the gun flying from his right hand.

Evan was moving before it hit the ground. Closing the gap in seconds, scooping the Glock up as Landry clambered to his feet, blood leaking from gravel-studded grazes on his forehead and cheek.

They advanced on the injured man, one from each side. A pincer movement. He had nowhere to go. Behind him, nothing but an endless expanse of trees and waterways. He raised his right hand. Showed them his palm as if taking a solemn oath. Left arm hanging limply down, blood soaking through his safari jacket sleeve, dripping off his fingertips into the dirt.

Landry raised the big revolver, pointed it at the middle of the guy's face.

'Get down. Then throw him your wallet and phone.'

Safari Jacket did as instructed. Lowered himself carefully to his knees on the ground.

Landry tracked him with his gun arm, the Colt never leaving the kneeling man's sweating face. He swiped angrily at his neck as a mosquito dive-bombed him, fingers smeared with his own blood, mounting irritation in his voice.

'Wallet and phone,' he growled again. '*Slowly.*'

Evan mirrored Landry's stance, two guns pointing at the prisoner's head.

'Okay, okay. Give me a goddamn chance.'

Safari Jacket put his right hand in his left inside jacket pocket, slowly brought out his phone. Threw it gently to land at Evan's feet. His wallet was more of a problem. 'My wallet's in my right inside pocket. I can't get to it with my right hand.' He showed them how, unsuccessfully trying to twist his hand into his pocket.

Landry barked at him, the pragmatism of a man who doesn't give a shit in his voice.

'Use your left.'

'You shot it—'

He bit the end of the sentence off. Everybody knew what he'd almost appended.

Asshole.

'Do I look like someone who gives a damn?' Landry spat. Then, to Evan when the kneeling man didn't make a move, 'Hit him with the gun butt and get it out of his pocket.'

Evan gave him a look as he bent to pick up the phone.

'You hit him. I'll shoot him if he tries anything.'

Landry looked at him like he didn't believe he had it in him. An accurate assessment, as it happened. Shooting an unarmed already injured man on his knees in cold blood wasn't one of Evan's strong points. Nor was it a skill he planned to acquire.

Landry shrugged, fair enough. Reversed the big revolver and took a step closer.

Safari Jacket screamed at him.

'Okay, okay. *Jesus.*'

He gritted his teeth, inched his left hand up his body like a dying spider, blood trailing behind his fingertips, then burrowing into his pocket. Flipped the wallet out with his fingers onto the ground at his knees, his arm immediately dropping again, an involuntary hiss escaping through gritted teeth.

Evan stepped in and flicked the wallet away with the axe

handle, pocketed the Glock and scooped it up. He rested the axe handle against his leg, started with the wallet, an expensive alligator skin affair.

A second later his head came up. Staring uncomprehendingly at the kneeling man.

And wondering how big a mistake they might have made.

28

'What is it?' Landry said.

Evan ignored him, studying the police ID in his hand in the name of Detective John Rawlings of the Baton Rouge PD. He glanced from the picture to the kneeling man and back again. It was the same man without a doubt.

He went quickly through the rest of the wallet's contents, breathing again as his panic of a moment ago subsided. The driver's license, the credit cards, were all in a different name.

John Ritter.

'Who is he?' Landry said, not hiding the impatience in his voice.

'His name's John Ritter. But he's got a fake ID identifying him as Detective John Rawlings of the Baton Rouge PD.'

Landry gave a non-committal twitch of his shoulders—*doesn't everybody?*—as Evan stuffed the wallet into his own pocket.

'*Hey!*' Ritter yelled as the wallet disappeared from sight.

Landry raised his arm, the gun still reversed. To a man on his knees the butt looked very big and very hard. Ritter leaned away, kept his eyes on the gun as Evan started with the questions.

'You're not a cop. What are you? A PI?'

'Not exactly.'

Evan understood then that Ritter knew who he was, what he was. The ill-concealed contempt in his voice made that very clear. He was tempted to let Landry take a free shot at Ritter's head with the gun butt. Teach him some manners.

It didn't actually matter what Ritter was, beyond the fact that he wasn't a cop. Evan asked the more important question.

'Who do you work for?'

Ritter glanced at Landry briefly, then back to Evan, the same contemptuous note in his voice as before.

'You wouldn't have heard of him.'

'Try me.'

'Esteban Aguilar.'

Landry looked at Evan, a frown on his face.

'You heard of him?'

'Uh-huh. He traffics narcotics, drugs, people. Anything illegal that makes money.' Studying Ritter as he said it, seeing the confirmation register in his eyes.

'What are you doing following me around?'

Ritter pointed off into the trees with his good arm.

'You're investigating the plane that went down over there, right?'

Evan was still looking at Ritter. But he was aware of his ears burning as Landry stared at the side of his head, the frown on his face hardening into anger.

This is all news to me. And to the man who's paying you.

Evan ignored him. Concentrated on Ritter who couldn't fail to see that the two men standing over him, working together on the face of it, were not on the same page.

'What's Aguilar's interest?'

'It was his plane. A lot of money that belonged to him disappeared when it went down. He wants it back.'

Evan thought back to the case file he'd read. There'd been no mention of money. It wasn't surprising. The file would be a foot thick if the investigating officer had to list everything that wasn't on board.

It fit with the story as he currently understood it. The unidentified man who'd been handcuffed in the back, and who had subsequently shot and killed the pilot and Justin Sanders, had also made off with the money. Some of that money would have filtered down to the people who made the forensic evidence identifying that passenger disappear.

'Who was the man handcuffed in the back of the plane?'

Landry was staring at him now as if he was thinking about pistol whipping Evan, not Ritter. Evan felt Landry's anger growing commensurately with the additional revelations about the things he and Stan Fraser hadn't been told. It didn't help when Ritter laughed at the question.

'You think I'd be following you around if I already knew that?'

Something didn't make sense.

'It was Aguilar's plane. There was a man handcuffed to the seat in the back. You're telling me Aguilar didn't know anything about it?'

Ritter stared at him like he was thinking he'd gotten things the wrong way around. He'd been thinking Evan was the top dog, Landry the brain-dead muscle—now he was revising that opinion.

'The guy was using a false name. Juan Pérez. Señor Aguilar caught him skimming. That's why he was handcuffed in the back.' He slapped at a mosquito on his neck with his good hand, then extended it towards Landry. 'On his way to see a man like your friend here. Someone who likes to torture people. Find out who else was involved. You can imagine how pissed off Señor Aguilar was when the guy ended up with a lot more than the few bucks he'd been skimming. And got to retire down to the Caribbean with a couple of pretty señoritas instead of ending up with his greasy head on a spike in some Mexican shithole.'

It all sounded so plausible. But was it true? It fit with everything Evan had read in the file. Against that, the best lies contain the most truth. Would Ritter tell him the whole truth so readily? On his knees at the mercy of two armed men or not, he didn't look like a man scared of being summarily executed and dumped in the endless wilderness of the Atchafalaya basin.

For the moment, Evan had no option but to plow on with what felt like increasingly pointless questions.

'What was the money for?'

A supercilious smirk crept onto Ritter's face despite his obvious distress at his shoulder wound.

'Cars, boats, houses, women, what do you think?'

Again, Evan was tempted to nod at Landry, give him the go ahead. Let the lesson in manners and an appropriate way for a man on his knees to answer begin.

'I meant why was it being transported?'

'I'm the hired help, for Christ's sake. The money went missing. Señor Aguilar asked me to find it. End of. He didn't share with me what he'd been planning on doing with it before it was stolen. Like he valued my opinion on whether he should invest it in art or fine wine or play safe and stick it in T-bonds.'

The answer was overly full as well as being facetious. More than anything it advertised that Ritter was other than he seemed —and therefore someone to be wary of.

Evan took things in a different direction.

'Why you? We've got Señor Aguilar and Juan Pérez. Why go to John Ritter, an Anglo? Why not use one of his own people?'

Ritter tried to shrug and immediately regretted the gesture, a sharp hiss of pain leading into his answer.

'Maybe he trusts me more than his own people. Or he thinks

I've got more chance of success than a guy with a Mexican bandito mustache and pointy cowboy boots asking questions. *Eh, gringo, you seena da money?*'

It was clear to Evan that he wasn't going to get a sensible answer. He turned his attention to Ritter's phone in the hope that it contained the answers its owner was unprepared to give. It was obviously a burner. The guy had an alligator hide wallet. In contrast to the casual appropriateness of his safari jacket for their current location, he was wearing expensive leather city shoes. An ostentatious chronometer watch that might have helped the plane's pilot avoid the crash was poking out of the blood-soaked sleeve. No way was the piece-of-shit phone currently in Evan's hand his regular phone.

The home screen was virtually devoid of apps. A situation that would have a young person hanging their head in shame, if not booking a session on the couch with a shrink. The only one beyond the defaults was for the tracker. No surprises there. He didn't bother opening it. He knew where he'd been today.

He brought up the call list.

The last two calls were to the same number. An outgoing call made by Ritter first thing this morning, then a return call a few hours later. He shoved the phone in Ritter's face.

'Who are the top two calls?'

Ritter answered immediately, no hesitation or pointless time wasting.

'A guy called Marvin Fleck.' He flicked his eyes at Landry, scorn in his voice. 'He's in the same line of business as your silent friend here.'

'Why'd you call him?'

'To see if he was available, what do you think?'

'For what?'

Stupid question, but hey-ho.

'To help avoid this situation occurring,' Ritter said. He

cocked his head theatrically towards his car and Landry's behind it, the empty road beyond that. 'You're a PI. Go ahead and deduce from the lack of anyone approaching that he wasn't available.'

The next three numbers in the call list were the same. One outgoing followed by two incoming.

'Who's this?' Evan said.

A sour smile twisted Ritter's mouth at the question, no humor in his voice despite the answer.

'Deputy Dawg.' He stretched the word *dawg* out, then raised his good hand before Evan thought about taking a swing at his head with the axe handle. 'That's what I call him. The badge on his uniform says Dixon. He's a deputy with the St. Martinville sheriff's office.'

Again, it made sense. Something had alerted Ritter to the renewed interest in the plane crash. That something was Deputy Dawg.

'When did he get in touch?'

'Day before yesterday. If you're wondering about the timeline, the file relating to the crash was pulled a week ago, which you already know seeing as you've spoken to Fontenot and Mercer. Dixon didn't get in touch until two days ago. You can appreciate why I call him Deputy Dawg.'

Evan would've sworn he saw genuine anger on Ritter's face, hard as it was to tell with the pain from his shoulder wound etched into it. The guy was pissed at being a week behind the curve because of another man's laziness and incompetence.

If that were true, it had one important implication. It meant Ritter didn't have anything to do with Arlo's disappearance.

He went back to the call list. There were no other calls made or received. He said so.

'I'm not a popular guy,' Ritter said.

Evan had no problem believing it. Landry's face suggested there was at least one thing they were agreed on.

'No calls to Señor Aguilar?'

'Nothing to report. He wants his money back. He doesn't much care how that's achieved. Like I said, he trusts me.'

Like you can trust a scorpion sleeping in your shoe to sting you, Evan thought and very nearly said, although Ritter would most likely have taken it as a compliment.

He closed the call list, opened the photo gallery.

There was only one photo in it. It looked a lot like a business card lying face down on a table with two addresses handwritten on the back.

Evan recognized the first address. He'd been there with Fontenot only yesterday. It was Mercer's house.

It, too, made sense. Deputy Dawg told Ritter, albeit a week late, that Mercer had pulled the file. Ritter then went to watch Mercer's house, see what happened next.

Evan confirmed with Ritter what he guessed had happened.

'That's where you picked us up? At Mercer's house?'

'Yeah. If you search my car which I'm sure you're planning on doing you'll find my camera. There are some nice shots on it of you and Fontenot turning up and going inside. Then I followed you back to that big old Creole house where you're staying. I flashed my Detective Rawlings badge at the woman there when you went out for dinner. She was happy to give me your name.'

It seemed to Evan that Ritter was volunteering far too much information. None of it really mattered. Where he'd picked them up. How he'd learned Evan's name. It didn't give anything away that couldn't be guessed at, or that Evan didn't already know.

He got the impression Ritter was talking for the sake of it.

Because he didn't want the time for Evan's next question to arrive. Evan was forced to disappoint him.

'Who's the second address for?'

'Dixon said there were two addresses on file for Mercer. He doesn't know the guy personally. He thought the first one was current, gave me the other one just in case.'

'Not so incompetent, after all?'

'More a case of the exception that proves the rule, you ask me.'

Evan didn't know whether to believe him or not. Either way, there wasn't a lot he could do about it. Not unless he wanted to give Landry free rein to ask in a different, more persuasive way like he had with Arlo's friend Aiden.

He'd look the second address up later when they got back to civilization.

Except Landry had other ideas. Less commonplace and nastier, spawned by his own expertise and experience.

'That's crap. Small town like this, everybody knows everything about everybody else down to who's screwing whose wife and how they like it. The other address has something to do with Mercer, but it's not where he used to live. It's someone he knows. Family, whatever. Something he'—jabbing his gun at Ritter—'can use against him. He looks like the sort of douchebag who'd use a guy's family against him.'

And you'd be the sort of guy to know, Evan thought and didn't share with bug-bitten Landry looking to vent his anger.

It had the unpleasant ring of the ugly truth about it. Landry was right. Ritter wasn't an out-and-out thug. He'd use other means that were far more effective than the threat of violence against a person's own body. Their flesh and blood in the figurative sense were a much better lever. Evan prodded Ritter on the chest with the axe handle, wasted his breath.

'Is he right?'

Landry didn't give Ritter a chance to answer one way or the other.

'Of course I'm right. You can see it in his eyes.'

Evan prodded a second time. Closer to Ritter's torn and bloody shoulder.

'Well?'

Ritter grunted in pain, spat the words out.

'What's the point of me saying anything? You've already made up your minds. Especially him.'

They were at an impasse. And they were wasting time. It didn't actually matter at this point. Nothing had happened to Mercer's family or Evan would have heard about it when he talked to him outside the sheriff's office that morning. He'd check it out when they got back. Warn him if necessary.

The more immediate problem was what to do with Ritter.

He went to search Ritter's car before deciding. The camera was in the glove compartment. Evan checked it and confirmed what Ritter had told them. There was nothing on it other than the shots of himself and Fontenot at Mercer's house, along with one of Mercer's license plate. Ritter clearly had access to someone who could run it for him. No big deal.

Apart from that, the car's interior was empty. A quick search of the similarly spotless and clue-free trunk was facilitated by Landry having tailgated Ritter's car, popping it open. It wouldn't stay shut again when Evan tried to close it.

He went back to where Landry stood guard over Ritter. Both men looked increasingly irritable at the persistence of the kamikaze biting insects, slapping at every exposed expanse of flesh in the vain hope of evening the score.

'What are we gonna do with him?' Landry said. He took a step closer, pushed the barrel of his gun hard into the side of Ritter's head. Answered his own question. 'I say we kill him, piece of shit like him who'd go after a man's family. Dump him in the bayou. Nobody will ever find him.'

Ritter's face made it clear he took the threat more seriously coming from Landry than he would have Evan, leaning away sideways as Landry screwed the gun harder into his flesh.

A nod from Evan was all it would take for Landry to pull the trigger. Except it wasn't going to happen. Not while Evan stood and watched.

'No.'

He may as well have said *blue* or *potato* for all the notice Landry took. He put his foot on Ritter's chest. Pushed him over sideways as if he was a rotten tree stump. Ritter landed on his injured shoulder and howled in pain. Landry squatted down, put the barrel of the Colt in Ritter's eye to stem the stream of abuse that followed.

Evan touched him on the arm with the end of the axe handle.

'Leave him.'

'What's your suggestion?' Sounding as if he expected to hear, *give him a bandage and let him go*.

'I've got rope in the car.'

He took Landry's resentful silence as acquiescence. A minute later he was back with a hundred-foot hank of braided-nylon paracord that he'd picked up at the camping store.

Landry rolled Ritter onto his front, pulled his wrists roughly together. Ritter hissed and cursed him through gritted teeth as the blood pumped afresh from his shoulder.

'Turn him back,' Evan said.

Grudgingly, Landry did so. Tied his wrists in front, then secured his ankles. Together, they dumped him in the trunk of his car.

Then Evan let Landry have his spiteful fun. Ritter had tried to kill them, after all.

Landry pushed the barrel of his Colt hard into the side of Ritter's head again. Cocking the hammer this time, the sound like breaking knuckles, a question on his lips.

'Yes? No?'

Evan didn't hesitate.

'Do it.'

Ritter screamed.

'*No!*'

Landry fired twice. Two quick shots, raising the gun at the last moment punching a pair of clean holes upwards through the trunk lid.

'He's pissed himself,' Landry said sounding like it was the outcome he'd been hoping for.

Evan didn't bother checking. Happy that he hadn't soiled himself as he leaned in and threaded the paracord up through the holes from the inside, then slammed the lid on Ritter's desperate protestations about needing to get to the hospital before he bled out or roasted alive in the trunk.

He fed the rope under the car, tied it off around the rear axle. Got his fingers under the trunk lid and lifted. It opened an inch or two at most as the paracord stretched. An uninjured man not trussed up like a turkey at Thanksgiving might kick his way out given enough time. It was a task too far for Ritter in his present condition.

They'd call it in when they got clear. Whatever Landry might be thinking, Evan didn't want Ritter's death on his conscience.

They took his wallet, phone and camera, left the Glock. A tied-up man suffering from a gunshot wound with a gun of his own that has recently been fired twice has more explaining to do than a man without. The thin cotton gloves Evan had worn throughout the incident ensured that it was free from his own fingerprints.

He left a couple of other things on the passenger seat to keep the cops guessing. The first was a brief note scrawled on a piece of scrap paper.

This man works for Esteban Aguilar.

The second item was the fake police ID in the name of Detective John Rawlings.

Ritter was going to have one hell of a lot of explaining to do.

In a perfect world Evan would also have seen the grim smile on Ritter's face despite his pain and predicament, taken something from that gesture. As it was, he threw the tracker far out into the trees and drove away leaving Landry to back up all the way down Bayou Manuel Road with the front end of his car caved in.

With any luck he'd given himself a bit of breathing space before his admittedly-useful partner caught up with him again.

29

Evan crossed Alabama Bayou and followed the road for a mile and a half to where it joined Whiskey Bay Highway. There, he made a left heading south back towards the Interstate. He pulled off the so-called highway a quarter mile before Bayou Manuel Road and made his way on foot to where he could see the junction. A hundred yards short of it, he slipped into the roadside trees, hunkered down and waited.

Landry had somehow managed to turn the car around rather than back up all the way. He shot out of the mouth of Bayou Manuel Road without slowing and kept on going towards I-10 and civilization—and what he believed was Evan ahead of him.

Evan followed him five minutes later, but didn't join the Interstate. He pulled onto the shoulder right underneath it. Checked Ritter's burner for a signal. It was good to go. He opened all of the windows, let the roar of the traffic overhead fill the car—the same ploy he'd used when he called Fontenot pretending to be Arlo. Then he called the most recent number in the call list. The one Ritter had said belonged to Marvin

Fleck, a man supposedly in the same unsavory line of business as Landry.

The man who answered was clearly having a bad day. Didn't even give him a chance to imitate Ritter's voice and say, *Fleck?*

'Jesus, Ritter, I told you. The guy ain't around. Nobody's seen him for a couple days. I'm in the middle of something. I'll call you if anything changes.'

The line went dead in Evan's ear.

He'd gotten more than he expected but less than he'd have liked.

Ritter had told him he'd called Fleck for assistance. To help him tail Evan and deal with wherever that led. *Deal with* in the Landry sense of the expression.

That was a lie. He'd asked Fleck to find somebody. It would be useful to know who. Trouble was, Evan couldn't call him back, ask him who they were talking about. Whoever it was, he figured Ritter wanted him dealt with—again Landry-style.

He called the other number in the call list, the one supposedly for Deputy Dixon aka Dawg.

It went to voicemail. The guy was obviously busy pulling files for people who had no right to see them. Evan listened to the recorded message. The phone's owner duly identified himself as Deputy George Dixon of the St. Martinville sheriff's office and invited the caller to leave a message.

Evan declined the offer.

That only left Ritter to deal with.

After learning that the guy had lied to him about Fleck—which made him question everything else that had come out of his mouth—Evan was feeling like Ritter didn't deserve to be rescued. Except he really didn't want his death on his conscience. Or to have to deal with the potential repercussions.

He thought about how he hoped things might pan out going forward. Given what he'd learned about Esteban Aguilar's involvement and the business Aguilar was in, there was a good chance he'd be speaking to vice squad detectives in the future if he was going to get anywhere.

Accordingly, he made a rudimentary attempt to disguise his voice by sticking his first two fingers up his nose—Guillory would've said better than up his ass where his thumb normally resided.

Then he used Ritter's burner to call the Baton Rouge PD, asked to be put through to the vice squad. The detective picking up was as brusque as Evan expected him to be.

'Vice. Detective Gauthier speaking.'

Evan let the phone's microphone slip down his chin to further muffle his voice, the roar of the Interstate overhead making things worse still.

'There's a man tied up in the trunk of his car in the Atchafalaya National Wildlife Refuge.'

'That's not us. Call the St. Martinville sheriff's office, tell them. Give them something to do.'

'I thought you might be interested—'

'I'm interested to know how come you know about it.'

'That's not important. The guy says he works for Esteban Aguilar.' He paused to let the name register. 'I'm assuming I've got your attention now?'

'Who are you?'

'Doesn't matter. Have you got a Detective John Rawlings there?'

Gauthier didn't respond immediately, the sudden change of direction throwing him.

'Not that I know of. Why?'

'Because the guy in the trunk has got ID on him that says that's who he is. If you can be bothered to go out there, I suggest you don't believe a word that comes out of his mouth.'

'I'm not sure I'm believing anything that's coming out of yours.'

'Only one way to find out. Bayou Manuel Road right before it crosses Alabama Bayou. You can't miss him. Gotta go.'

'Wait—'

Too late. Gauthier was talking to a dial tone.

Evan had made a point of not mentioning all the things Gauthier would have been most interested to know. Ritter's real name. The fact that he'd been shot in the shoulder with a gun that wouldn't be found at the scene. The fact that his own gun had been fired twice. All those things plus a stay in Baton Rouge General Hospital meant he wasn't going to be in Evan's hair for a good long while.

Which couldn't be said for Evan's other problem.

His own phone had rung three times in his pocket while he'd been busy checking Ritter's story and muddying the waters. He didn't need to look at the screen to know who it was. Landry. He'd have to talk to him sooner or later, but for now he switched his phone off.

Then he called Guillory on the burner. As expected, her greeting was even more curt than Gauthier's.

'Guillory.'

He didn't say anything. Put the phone right up close to his mouth. Cupped his hand over it to amplify the sound. Breathing heavily down the line like an excited dog.

An explosion of laughter hit him in the ear.

'Idiot. You think I don't recognize the sound of your heavy breathing?'

'I thought I'd try to brighten your day.'

She laughed again, a gentler sound this time.

'Really? And you read on the internet that's the way to do it?'

'Twelve hundred miles puts a bit of an obstacle in the way of some other things I might have thought of.'

'It's very kind of you to think of me, but I can probably wait until you get back. I hope you didn't buy a burner phone just for this.'

'No. It belongs to Ritter. He's the guy who was following me.'

A knowing silence ensued. One that suggested a person who had just identified the point at which they should end the call. Except she couldn't help herself.

'I believe I heard the past tense there.'

'Yep. He's taking a nap in his trunk at the moment. He's not feeling well.'

'I'm not sure I want to hear how that came to happen. I'm assuming you hooked up with Landry?'

'Uh-huh. He says, *hi*.'

There wasn't so much of the gentle laughter in her voice now. More like a small boy who'd pulled all the legs off one side of a cockroach and was watching it go around and around in circles before he did the other side. He knew the tone well.

'Ask him how his balls are. In fact, put him on. I'll ask him.'

'He's not here at the moment. But he's been calling me a lot to try to remedy that situation.'

She sucked the air in through her teeth.

'He won't be happy when he finds you. Or is that the point? Get him good and riled up then point him at some other unlucky schmuck?'

He worked an approving note into his voice. One that reflected the fact that she, as the proper badge-carrying detective, knew how it should be done.

'Now that's what I call a good idea. So, you want a second chance to see if you can find out anything about this guy Ritter?'

'How can I refuse when you put it like that?'

He gave her all the details off Ritter's driver's license as well as those from a number of the credit cards. Told her it was best if she called him back with anything she found on the burner. She asked for clarification.

'You want the heavy breathing as well?'

He pretended to think about it, but not for long.

'Nah. I know that's yours and Ryder's thing when it gets quiet in the car. I don't want to spoil that.'

Unsurprisingly, he was now the one talking to a dial tone.

30

He thought carefully about his next move before getting back on the Interstate, aware that he needed to make the most of his Landry-free time.

He was faced with the same decision as Arlo had been faced with a week previously. Talk to Justin Sander's widow, Fleur, or to the detective on the case who'd had his investigation brought to a premature end, Lou Bordelon.

He figured Arlo had opted for Fleur on the basis that Bordelon was unlikely to give him the time of day. He made the same decision, for a different reason. The interview with Fleur would go a lot better without Landry's intimidating presence. Bordelon would take it in his stride if he agreed to talk to him at all.

Added to that, Fleur Sanders' address had been in the case file that Arlo had copied. It was five years old, but it was somewhere to start. He didn't have anything for Bordelon beyond his name.

He put the address into Google maps on the burner phone, relieved to see that it wasn't in the list of recent search suggestions that popped up. At least she hadn't had to suffer a visit from Ritter.

It took him forty minutes to drive the thirty miles to where Fleur Sanders lived in Whittington Oaks, three miles south west of downtown Lafayette. There was a blue Ford Escape parked in the driveway when he drove up, as well as a Subaru Forester, also blue but darker, parked on the street immediately outside the house. Somebody was home, at least. Unfortunately, it looked as if they had a visitor already.

To wait, or not to wait?

Conscious of wanting to get as much done as possible before Landry caught up with him, he decided not to waste any time. He didn't want to wait until the visitor left, only to find that Fleur Sanders had moved away immediately after her husband was killed because she couldn't stand to be in a house full of memories.

A woman in her mid-thirties answered the door to his knock, looking like she was already having the worst day of her life. At least nobody could blame him for that. Yet.

'Mrs. Sanders?'

'Yes.' Glancing around him as she said it, as if there was somebody else coming up the path behind him.

He resisted the urge to turn around, find out what she was looking at. Started to introduce himself and explain his presence on her front step.

'My name's Evan Buckley. I'm a private investigator.'

That was as far as he got before another, similarly-aged woman dressed in a crisp white blouse and a dark-grey business skirt appeared behind her. From her sensible, no-nonsense attire, she looked as if she owned the Subaru Forester parked at the curb.

From her face, she looked as if she wanted to hug him.

Not because he was so huggable, but because he'd never

seen a person who looked so desperate to get away, so grateful to the person providing the excuse.

'It's okay, Fleur,' she said. 'I really do have to go.' She put her hand on Fleur's arm, squeezed. 'You're going to be fine.' Then she raised a finger, a strange gesture following the arm-squeeze —until she came out with a parting admonishment. 'I know things are bad at the moment, but don't forget what I said about the dosage.'

Evan stepped back as the woman came around Fleur. She looked him up and down briefly in a way that would've earned him a slapped cheek if he'd done the same to her, a hint of a smile at the corners of her mouth.

'I don't think I've ever met a private investigator before. I have to say I'd have expected you to look more . . . sleazy.' She smiled at him, perfect teeth on show, a predatory light in her eyes. 'I wouldn't mind being investigated, myself. Have you got a card?'

It wasn't worth pointing out that people don't hire a PI to investigate themselves. That missed the point. She was flirting with him. He wasn't sure what Fleur thought about the fact that the woman who'd nearly knocked her over in her haste to get out of the house because she was so pressed for time, now found the time to flirt with him.

She wasn't going on her way, either. Seemed she was waiting for a card. He had to make something up.

'I'm from out of town. I don't usually travel this far.'

'Give me one anyway.'

He didn't have a choice, not unless he wanted to offend her. All she'd done was make it clear she'd like to devour him, after all. And in different, Guillory-free circumstances, he wouldn't have objected to being devoured. Or reciprocating.

He got out his wallet, extracted a card. Handed it over. Very glad her crisp white blouse was buttoned all the way to her very nice neck. He got the impression she'd have tucked it inside her bra if it didn't mean undoing the blouse buttons.

'I'm Laura Hunt, by the way,' she said as she dropped it into her bag. 'I'm a doctor. It's not as exciting as being a private investigator'—making it sound like a man who rips women's clothes off for a living—'although I suppose it depends on who the patient is.' She had a way of making the word *patient* sound like *prey*, too. 'Fleur can give you my number if you're feeling unwell and need someone to give you a thorough examination.'

Neither he nor Fleur quite knew what to say as Laura sashayed down the path to her shiny Subaru.

Fleur recovered first, Evan trying hard not to think about a *thorough examination* at the hands of the woman who'd just driven off with a cheery wave for them both.

'Sorry about that. She isn't normally like that.'

He saw when the realization registered on her face that he wasn't at her house in order to potentially satisfy Dr. Laura Hunt's sexual appetite. That he'd come to see her. She was immediately back to looking as if it was five hours since her husband had been shot to death by an unknown assailant, not five years.

'Can we talk inside?' he said.

'If you like.'

He heard: *if we must*.

She led him through the house to a sitting room overlooking the back yard. He wanted to ask her where Laura had been sitting so he could sit somewhere else rather than try to have the difficult conversation ahead with the residual warmth of the good doctor's shapely butt coming through the seat of his pants.

'Can I get you something to drink?' Fleur said.

He said coffee or water would be fine even though he wanted neither. He guessed it would be coffee. She needed time to get herself together after he'd turned up unexpectedly on her front step, the longer, the better. Another time he might have followed her into the kitchen, but despite being aware of Landry out there somewhere searching for him, he let her go alone. He was about to drop into the chair with the plumpest, most un-sat-in cushion when he saw what could only be described as a shrine to her late husband against the far wall.

He went over to it, ran his eye over the multitude of photographs that covered every inch of every horizontal surface of the display cabinet. Not so much because he wanted to see a photograph of her husband. He'd already seen the most recent ones, those taken by the Medical Examiner, in the police file. Nor did he particularly need to see any of him in better times minus the two bullet holes in his chest. His presence in front of the shrine would tell Fleur why he was here, if the pills that Dr. Laura Hunt had prescribed had addled her brains to the point where she didn't already know.

After a length of time that suggested she'd made a special trip to Colombia to personally collect the beans, Fleur came back into the sitting room carrying two cups of coffee, as predicted.

She saw him standing at the shrine, a sad smile pushing away some of the apprehension on her face.

He took the cup she offered him, jumped right in with as concise an explanation as he could muster. He remained standing as he did so. As did she, it being a standing-up sort of conversation.

'I'm trying to locate a young man called Arlo Fraser. He went missing while looking into the plane crash following which your husband was killed.'

'Murdered.' Spat out with a venom that surprised him. Her too, from the way she dropped her eyes to her coffee cup.

'Murdered, yes. Your obvious distress suggests Arlo came to see you as part of what he was doing. His visit brought it all back just when you'd reached a place where you thought you could move on.'

'You have no idea.'

Actually, I do, he thought, deciding nothing would be gained by explaining.

She picked up one of the photographs, held it against her body. The gesture was easy to interpret.

Do I look like a woman who's ready to move on?

He'd be forced to say *no*, had he been asked. Something else was going on. Despite the horrors of her past being unceremoniously dumped on her as a result of Arlo's—as yet unconfirmed—visit, he'd have expected her to get over it by now. Five years is a long time for time itself to do its healing work.

That would have to wait. She still hadn't answered his question.

'Did Arlo come to see you?'

She nodded, still holding the photograph to her bird-like body.

'And did you talk to him?'

She nodded again. Sighed heavily.

'I wouldn't have, if he'd been a real reporter. He started out trying to be so professional, but it was obvious he didn't know what he was doing. I challenged him.' She looked at the photograph she'd been clutching to her body as if her dead husband could help with what she wanted to say. Then she replaced it on the display cabinet, straightened it until it was just-so. Looked him in the eye. 'Challenge is the wrong word. I was horrible to him. I accused him of being a ghoul. A pervert who got off on other people's pain.'

She lapsed into silence. Took a sip of coffee in an attempt to hide her embarrassment. He made an easy guess based on what Fontenot had told him.

'That's when he told you the truth? That his girlfriend's

father is the editor of *The Daily Acadian*, and how he gave him the job to prove himself.'

'Yeah.' She held up her left hand, finger and thumb pinched half an inch apart. 'I felt about this tall. Then he got up and said he was sorry to trouble me and upset me and he'd be on his way. I ended up practically dragging him back into the house begging him to stay and listen to what I could tell him.'

She smiled suddenly at the memory of the farcical situation brought about by two people's guilt and good nature fighting it out. Then it was gone, as if it had never existed. Nor would it ever try something so stupid as to settle on her face again.

'Now I feel even worse. I thought he'd gotten what he needed out of me and that was the last I'd ever hear of him. Now you're telling me he's disappeared and it's all my fault.'

A blatant lie was called for.

'It's not your fault. We'd all have to walk around mute if we had to worry about the possible consequences of everything we say.'

It crossed his mind as the words rode out that it didn't sound such a bad state of affairs.

She nodded, an automatic and appropriate response to a person saying something for the sole reason that it was what the person listening wanted to hear.

She glanced towards the front of the house. As if somebody had unexpectedly come through the door. A man carrying a long list of reasons why it was most definitely her fault as well as a graphic photograph of Arlo's mutilated body from the look on her face.

It reminded him of the way she'd looked past him when she first opened the door to him. Those two things added to the feeling that there was more than the unwelcome reminder about her husband's death behind her distress made him say what he did next. They needed to get it out of the way if he was to have a chance of getting any useful information out of her.

'I get the impression that you're not only upset. You seem scared, too.'

She glanced towards the front of the house again, swallowed nervously.

'There's a man watching the house.'

She led him cautiously into the front room like they were a pair of burglars. The lights were off and with the sun on the back of the house the room was in semi-darkness. Nobody outside would be able to see in. Despite that, she stood at the side of the window to peek out. He did the same on the other side, for no other reason than not to alarm her further.

'See that car over there?' she said, not even daring to point.

He did. A couple of hours ago, he'd have said it was Ritter. Except it wasn't Ritter's car and Ritter was tied up in his trunk in the middle of nowhere. He'd noticed the car when he drove up, hadn't thought anything of it. It wasn't possible to see who was inside.

'He was there all day yesterday,' she said. 'That's why Laura was here today. She was supposed to bring me sleeping pills last night, but she forgot them. I'm too scared to go out with him sitting there. That's why she came again today. I wouldn't have answered the door to you if she hadn't been here with me.'

Evan hadn't missed Dr. Hunt's stature as she eyed him up and down. An inch under six foot, and with shoulders that would put a lot of men in the gym to shame. She'd reminded him of Guillory in a way. Not a match for a large, strong man but still a reassuring comfort to the diminutive Fleur.

'Have you called the police?' he said.

'No.'

'Why not?'

'Because they wouldn't be interested. They'd think I'm a stupid hysterical woman who's scared of her own shadow. I keep telling myself that if he's still there in an hour's time I'll call them. I never do. I just want him to go away. Can we go in the other room again?'

She didn't actually sidle around the room with her back pressed into the wall, although it wasn't far off. He did the same, not wanting to be the one responsible for the sudden unprovoked attack that she was expecting any minute.

'I can have a word with him, if you like,' he said once they were back in the safety of the back sitting room. 'Ask him what he's doing?'

She looked at him as if he'd produced her husband, alive and well after all, out of his pocket.

'Would you? He might be armed.'

He worked hard at not smiling at her paranoia, a grim determination on his face as befits a man who delivers scared women from fear. Her own personal guardian angel. It wasn't altruism all the way, of course. Saint Evan wanted to know who the guy was for his own purposes. It was too much of a coincidence to think that his presence signified anything other than another interested party—in addition to Ritter and himself—following in Arlo's footsteps.

He thought about how to play it. He could go out the back door and try to work his way through the neighboring back yards to further down the street, then sneak up on the car as he'd tried to do with Ritter the previous night.

Except it was likely to be similarly unsuccessful. Ignoring fences and dogs and irate homeowners with shotguns, the guy no doubt had all his doors locked. All he'd achieve would be a wrenched shoulder as the car drove off with him hanging onto the door handle. He wasn't ever going to get a chance to talk to the guy.

A direct approach was called for. Get the license plate and take it from there.

That didn't mean he couldn't make the guy regret he ever thought about scaring a vulnerable woman living on her own.

'Have you got a hammer?'

She looked at him as if he'd said, *change of plan, you do it instead.*

He glanced out the window, saw a small shed at the bottom of the well-maintained yard.

'Are there any tools in there?'

'Some garden tools. There might be a hammer in there.'

She found the shed key, unlocked the back door and let him out. It didn't take him long to find what he wanted. Not a hammer, but a wrecking bar. Much better. Back inside the house, he showed it to her, asked her for a bag big enough to put it in. She disappeared upstairs, came down a minute later with a black sports duffel bag.

'It was my husband's. It's been sitting in the closet ever since he died. I don't go to the gym.'

He let himself out the front door and headed down the path towards his car, the wrecking bar hidden in the unzipped bag. The man in the car opposite would be wondering what he'd collected from the woman he was watching.

He'd find out soon enough.

His car was parked with the passenger side nearest the curb. He walked around to the driver's side. Went to the rear door as if he was about to open it and throw the duffel bag on the back seat. Nothing to arouse suspicion so far.

Without warning, he about-faced. Marched directly towards the parked car. Memorizing the license plate as he took hold of the wrecking bar inside the bag. No overt indication of violence or aggression yet, conversation theoretically still an option.

Except everybody knew it wasn't going to happen.

The man in the car started the engine, stomped the gas, a screech of rubber on the blacktop as the car rocketed away from the curb. Evan quickened his pace, the wrecking bar out of the bag now, put himself directly in front of the oncoming vehicle.

A challenge.

One thing becoming clearer by the second.

No way was the guy going to back down, swerve around him or brake.

At the last moment he leapt up and out of the way. Back arched and butt pulled in standing erect like an arrogant matador sidestepping the lethal charge of a pain-maddened bull. On the driver's side of the car now. Swinging the wrecking bar in a vicious backhand arc scything through the air, an explosion of glittering glass shattering, showering the driver, the impact juddering the length of Evan's arm from fingertip to shoulder, recoil like an electric shock ejecting the bar from his hand bouncing on the hood and off into the gutter.

Then the car was gone, burning rubber down the quiet suburban street.

Evan caught his breath, head down and hands on his knees as the thundering of his heart subsided. He retrieved the wrecking bar and dropped it back into the duffel bag. Threw it all onto the back seat of his car for real this time. Fleur wouldn't want it back. And it would make a useful backup should he break the axe handle he already had in the trunk on somebody's head—a situation that felt as if it was drawing closer by the minute.

Fleur looked as if she wasn't sure who she should be letting back into the house when she opened the door to him. Peering around the edge of it like a frightened child watching a scary movie from behind the sofa. Her voice was a mix of relief and surprised awe.

'I thought you said you were going to talk to him.'

He shook his head as he came inside and shut the door behind him.

'That would only ever have happened if you'd been wrong and he wasn't watching your house.'

'Do you think he'll come back?'

'Probably not. I don't think he ever planned to approach you. He's been alerted to the renewed interest in the case somehow. He doesn't want to advertise his own interest, so he was watching you to see who might turn up.' He opened his hands wide, palms up as if accepting manna from heaven. 'And here I am. If anyone's going to have a problem with him going forward, it's me.'

He didn't point out that even though the man watching would have taken his license plate number, it wasn't going to do him any good when it led back to the car rental company. He was happy to let her believe that he'd diverted the danger away from her onto him, her guardian angel.

Something else he didn't say—the unknown man currently covered in broken glass was most likely the man Ritter had asked Marvin Fleck to find and dispose of.

Those were all details Fleur was better off not knowing. Not unless she wanted to down a whole bottle of her friend Laura's sleeping pills every night in her quest for elusive sleep.

Time to get back to why he came in the first place.

'You think we can get back to what you told Arlo, now?'

31

'You look like you need a drink,' Fleur said. 'I know I do. I don't mean another cup of coffee, either.'

They were in the kitchen. She pulled a bottle of red wine from a well-stocked wine rack sitting on top of the fridge without giving him time to answer. Then looked at him, a question on her face. Shook her head immediately.

'Nope. You don't look like a red wine man to me.'

He couldn't disagree. After being shot at by Ritter and everything that had followed, there was only one thing that hit the spot.

'You got a cold beer?'

'I have, actually.'

She dropped her eyes as she said it, embarrassed at something. As if he'd asked about sex toys. She turned away. Took her time selecting a wine glass and a beer glass from the wall cabinet before clearing her throat.

'I was dating a guy for a while. I bought the beers for him.' She brandished the bottle of red wine, holding it by the neck as if she was going to drink it from the bottle as soon as she'd opened it. 'Lucky for you I drink this and don't touch white wine or I'd have thrown them out to make room in the fridge. It didn't work out, in case you're wondering.' She glanced at the door leading to the sitting room. He knew what she was about to say. 'What Laura calls the *shrine* put him off. I'll have to get rid of it before I try again. Why don't you go sit outside in the sun while I get the drinks ready?'

He did as he was told, got himself settled in a white molded-plastic chair that was so sparklingly clean it hurt his eyes. He took the opportunity to rest them as he waited for refreshments to arrive.

But not for long.

Without warning, something heavy landed on his legs. He startled, opened his eyes. A white cat with tabby markings on its head and tail stared back at him. It turned around a couple of times, then settled down on his lap. Stuck one back leg in the air and started cleaning with big long licks. He stroked the back of its neck as it worked, the cat purring contentedly in response.

A minute later Fleur came out of the house carrying a tray loaded with glasses, the now-open bottle of Pinot Noir, and a bottle of beer in a bright pink neoprene cooler sleeve with the tagline on the back, *Start your crawl at zero Duval*.

She rolled her eyes at the cat that had stopped cleaning, pink nose in the air sniffing at the tray to see if it contained anything of interest.

'I see you've met Leonard already. He obviously likes you. I don't know how I'd have made it through the past five years without him. He was only a kitten when Justin died.'

She put the tray containing the other item that had helped her through her grief on a matching, equally-spotless molded-plastic table. Smiled to herself. It seemed to him that it was more than simply in anticipation of sitting in the late afternoon sun, drink in hand, a mellow alcoholic buzz easing her troubles, if only temporarily.

'What?'

Again, she looked embarrassed, although less so than before.

'You're having a relaxing effect on me already.'

'Not many people say that, I can assure you.'

'I'm sure that's not true. I don't just mean chasing that man in the car off, either. Laura is so disapproving. I suppose it's her job to be. Whenever she's here, I feel guilty about how much I drink.' She flicked her head backwards at the house behind them. 'I always leave the bottle in the kitchen, as if that makes any difference. You don't strike me as a man who disapproves of very much at all.'

He admitted it had been said before, poured his beer and they clinked glasses. He took in the yard with a broad sweep of this hand. Thinking he'd relax her further talking about what was clearly her passion. 'The yard looks amazing. I feel like I should take my shoes off.'

'Thank you. It's the only thing that keeps me sane. Apart from this.' Raising her glass to him as she said it. 'It's lucky really. My husband didn't take any interest, except for the birds. I used to say to him, how many birds do you think will come if you concrete over the whole yard and paint it green? He spent all his time in the gym. The catharsis of physical exercise, he called it. I called it posing in front of the mirror. He said it helped get rid of all the images in his head of what he had to deal with all day every day. He was a paramedic.' She swept her hand around the yard as he had. 'I get my catharsis out here. There's no posing involved. Just me and Leonard. No one can see us, which is how I like it.'

He groaned inwardly. He'd complimented her on her gardening skills in order to relax her. It had done the job so well he'd been worried she might get carried away. Point out each individual plant and test him on their Latin names at the end. Give him a cutting of each one he got right. Now she'd brought them full-circle to her being watched.

There wasn't any way to avoid it.

'Did you see anybody watching the house around the time Arlo came to see you?'

It had the anticipated effect, deflating her. Now it was a case of the man out front's compadres hiding in the bushes. Trampling all the plants flat when they made their murderous assault on the house.

She shook her head, like wouldn't it be nice to go back to those heady days.

'Definitely not.'

He felt himself deflate with her. Despite what Ritter had said, he'd still harbored suspicions that Ritter could be behind Arlo's disappearance. His gripe that it took Deputy Dixon-Dawg a week to let him know about the file being pulled could have been a lie. He'd lied about Fleck. Why should everything he said about Dixon be true? He'd looked genuinely angry, but that could be faked easily enough by the sort of man Evan guessed Ritter was.

One thing was for sure. If he'd known that Ritter had lied about Fleck before they left him in the trunk, he would never have walked away. He'd have let Landry take him somewhere private for a more in-depth aka painful conversation. And if he hadn't alerted Detective Gauthier to Ritter's whereabouts, he'd go back there now himself.

Fleur didn't miss the effect her negative response had on him.

'I can ask the neighbors, if you think it's important. I might have missed something, although I can't imagine how.'

He shook his head, not wanting to put the idea in her mind

that there might have been two people watching her house. Her friend Laura wouldn't be able to dispense the sleeping pills fast enough.

'No. I've got his license plate.'

He hadn't noticed in the mirror that morning, but it seemed he'd taken on the appearance of a particularly stubborn, deep-rooted weed. Fleur was determined to not let go until she'd dug him out.

'Do you think that's what happened to Arlo? Someone was watching the house and they saw him and followed him and...'

He couldn't lie to her, despite her increasing distress.

'It's possible. Although if you didn't see anyone watching, it's unlikely. Why don't you tell me what you told Arlo?'

It was lucky that Fleur's back yard was pleasant and green, the molded-plastic chair surprisingly comfortable, if a little harsh on the eyes, the sun warm and the beer cold, because what followed added very little to what he'd already learned from the interview transcripts.

She looked a little put out when he asked a question that made it clear he'd heard it all before.

'One of the detectives asked you if there was anything unusual about that day. Whether your husband was upset or depressed. You said not that you knew of. Did anything come to mind subsequently?'

'No, nothing. I didn't like the way he was suggesting that we'd had an argument which is why he went hiking on his own. I feel bad enough as it is. I can't imagine what it would be like if we'd had a fight and he stormed out, and then I never saw him again.'

She took a large gulp of wine as if to wash the awful thought away, then refilled her glass. He declined the offer of another beer, thinking you can't beat self-medication.

Leonard the cat saw the movement around the tray as an

invitation to stand up on Evan's legs, stretch indulgently with his tail and butt in Evan's face, then climb onto the table to sniff the tray's contents. Finding nothing of interest, he jumped down onto Fleur's lap and immediately got settled. Fleur stroked him absentmindedly, drawing comfort from the simple pleasure it gave them both as Evan worked hard at doing the opposite, continuing to probe the worst times of her life.

'Did your husband's phone ever turn up?'

'Not here, it didn't. If the police found it, they didn't give it back to me. Whoever killed him must have taken it, although I can't think why. It wasn't as if it was a brand-new iPhone or anything like that.'

He could've made a few suggestions, none of which she'd want to hear. Instead, he moved on, something else from the interview transcript coming back to him.

'Did you get all of your husband's personal effects back?'

'Most of them. His wallet. His watch. His wedding ring.' She reached inside her blouse, hooked her finger under a gold chain around her neck to show him the simple gold band hanging from it. Then laughed, a bitter, self-deprecating sound. 'This didn't do anything to help make the guy I was dating stick around, either.'

'Was there anything you didn't get back?'

She nodded as she dropped the wedding ring back between her breasts.

'A gold cross he wore around his neck. It was only a cheap thing. I don't know if the person who killed him took it. They were pretty stupid as well as a cold-blooded killer if they did. His watch was worth ten times as much. Maybe he was in a struggle to get the gun and the chain snapped and it got lost.'

Neither of those things had happened as far as Evan was concerned. According to Ritter, there'd been a ton of money on board which had gone missing. The killer wouldn't have hung around in a plane where he'd just killed two men for the sake of a cheap cross—not even if he didn't already have the money. Neither had there been any mention in the file of the deceased having been involved in a fight before he was shot twice in the chest.

'Did Arlo tell you what he planned to do next?'

'He said he was going to talk to Kevin. He didn't think Detective Bordelon would agree to talk to him, even though he knew that's where he'd get the most information.'

'Do you know if he actually managed to talk to Kevin? Do you still keep in touch?'

'We never did. Kevin's single. Or at least he was back then. He was Justin's friend. It never really worked, the three of us going out. The woman he brought along the one time we went to dinner as a foursome ... well, let's just say she wasn't my kind of person. There was never any contact after Justin died. Kevin didn't even come to the funeral. He sent flowers but he didn't turn up.'

'Did you think that was odd?'

She took a mouthful of wine, looking out across the lawn, adrift in a place that only she could see.

'Not really. He couldn't face me, I suppose. He felt guilty. If he hadn't injured his knee and he'd been there Justin might still be alive, that sort of thing. He was probably right to stay away. Back then I was looking for somebody to blame. He'd have seen that I was thinking exactly the same thing as he was. It was his fault. Now, I realize that the most likely outcome would've been an extra dead body found in the plane. I suppose I could call him, tell him I don't blame him.' She shrugged, a helpless gesture. 'What's the point? All it would do is bring it all back for him, too.'

No, that's my job, he thought.

Seemed they were on the same page, her words condemning him.

'I don't envy you your job. Making people re-live the worst times of their lives.' She raised her glass to him, but not in a toast. 'I bet you do plenty of self-medicating yourself.'

He tipped his glass at her in response, words redundant.

32

'CALL FRASER,' GUILLORY SAID

Evan had just come out of the shower in preparation for going out to get something to eat. It had washed away the dust and sweat and residual DEET from the trip out to the Atchafalaya wildlife refuge, but hadn't provided any deeper cleansing of his mind or soul.

He still hadn't switched his own phone back on, enjoying a few more hours in a Landry-free zone. Then Ritter's burner rang.

His pulse quickened as, momentarily, he thought it might be Marvin Fleck calling back with an update for Ritter that he might inadvertently let slip.

It wasn't. It was Guillory.

Naturally, his pulse remained heightened, but for different reasons. Her opening remark put an end to that.

It also confused him.

'How come—'

She didn't give him a chance to finish, a tide of annoyance flooding down the line at him.

'Your new best friend Stan sent a messenger to the Jerusalem to tell Kieran to tell me to tell you to call him. And to turn your damn phone back on. Except he used a different word than *damn*. Do it as soon as I get off the line.'

'Or you'll give him the burner's number?'

'I hadn't thought of that, but yeah, good idea. I am not, repeat *not*, going to be Stan Fraser's go-to means of contacting you because you want to avoid him and Landry.'

Refreshed from his recent shower, he immediately identified that a quick *bad day, dear?* was not the way to go. Nor was inquiring whether she'd found out anything about Ritter in the few hours since he'd asked her to be advised.

Seemed he'd waited too long to reply—a length of time so short that it can only be measured by very expensive scientific instruments.

'I'm not hearing immediate and enthusiastic agreement, Evan.'

'Absolutely.'

'Absolutely what? Absolutely I'm not hearing it? Or absolutely you're going to call him the minute you finish talking to me?'

Once more, he correctly identified that pointing out that he wasn't getting much of a look in as far as talking went was a bad idea.

'The latter.'

'I need to hear the words, Evan.'

'I'll call Stan as soon as you stop chewing my ear.'

'At the moment, that feels like some time next week. Or do I mean year?'

Maintaining his unbroken run of knowing when not to open his mouth and let the wind blow his tongue around, he didn't mention what had just gone through his head. Make a joke of how Dr. Laura Hunt had looked as if she wanted to swallow all of him whole. Forget about his ear and the chewing.

However, it didn't feel right to end the conversation right there, on a tetchy note.

A quick update was called for.

'I found out Ritter lied to me.'

She laughed out loud, a sudden spontaneous bark. It seemed a little off to him, coming as it did from a person who had to deal with people in her job lying to her all day long. Except it wasn't that at all.

'I believe I've just been hit with the Evan Buckley patented method of introducing a topic into the conversation that he's too scared to come straight out and ask about.'

'Can't blame me for being scared.'

'And no, I haven't had a chance to run your latest errand and look into Ritter.'

It hadn't been the reason he'd said it. There was no point trying to convince her of that. At least he knew the answer now to the question he hadn't dared ask.

Not only that, he'd aroused her curiosity.

'What did he lie about?' she said. 'And don't say everything.'

'That's what I'm starting to think...'

He then took her through what Marvin Fleck had let slip. That Ritter wanted a person, as yet unidentified, found and killed, given Fleck's line of work.

'Who do you think it is?' she said.

No idea was halfway out of his mouth before he bit it back. Went in a different, very sly, direction.

'I'm scared to say.'

Without having access to the inner workings—or not—of his mind—and to be fair, few people did—she jumped to the wrong conclusion.

'Not Stan Fraser's son, Arlo?' Then another one before he

could reply. 'That's why you're keeping your phone switched off. So you don't have to tell Stan.'

'No. And no.'

'That's a relief, I suppose. Who, then?'

He'd wandered over to the French doors in front of which he'd sat and read the case file the previous night, opening them as they talked. Thinking how he'd looked out into the night oblivious to Ritter sneaking in and attaching the tracker to his car. It made him wonder about the unidentified man watching Fleur Sanders' house. Whether he was out there watching him now.

'I think it's a guy whose windshield I busted with a wrecking bar who was watching Fleur Sanders' house.'

The bark of laughter echoed in his ear again. This time there was an undercurrent of admiration in her voice as she summarized what she'd just heard.

'The Buckley method becomes subtler still. I'm impressed. Dump a ton of intriguing information on me that naturally leads to a question from me about whether you got the guy's license plate and, voilà, we've got what you're too scared to ask because you think I'm in a bad mood.'

'Think?'

'Okay. Was.'

'So, you want to hear what happened?'

'Give me the license plate first.'

'Don't tease.'

'Just give it to me.'

He obliged, then took her through the whole thing—apart from his encounter with Dr. Laura Hunt, that is. He didn't see what that would add to her understanding of the situation. It almost made him feel guilty. As if he was keeping quiet about her because they were having dinner later that night.

'You probably don't want to hear this,' she said when he'd

finished, 'but it sounds as if you're going to have bad news for your friend Stan.'

She was right. He didn't want to hear it. Nor was it anything he didn't already know. Hearing it out loud simply made it that little bit more real. She hadn't finished, either.

'If it turns out Arlo's dead and you have to give Stan the bad news, don't even think about telling me to tell Kieran to tell Stan's messenger to tell Stan. That's a strictly one-way street.'

'I thought it was closed.'

'That too. Speak to you tomorrow.'

AS PROMISED, HE SWITCHED ON HIS OWN PHONE AFTER THEY ended the call. He waited with it in his hand for a minute to see if it would ring, then dialed Stan Fraser's number when it didn't.

Things didn't start well. Stan laid into him without even saying, *hello*.

'What part of keep in touch with Landry don't you understand?'

Evan followed his lead. Skipped the pleasantries and came right back at him.

'What part of stay away from Kate Guillory don't you understand?'

He couldn't remember if he'd actually said that, but hey-ho.

'Keep your phone switched on and it won't be necessary.'

'What's your problem? I'm sure Landry's already updated you.'

'With all the things you should've updated me with earlier, yeah.'

'You want to come down here and do it yourself, find out even earlier still?'

'You want to watch your mouth.'

Evan didn't miss that there was no question mark at the end of that one. Fraser wasn't finished, either.

'I heard you were pig-headed. I never realized it would be this bad. *Jeez*. Answer me this—could you have done what you did today without Landry?'

'Maybe not.'

'Bullshit. There's no maybe about it. Tell me about this guy, Ritter. You think he had anything to do with what's happened to Arlo?'

Evan thought about taking him all the way through it. Telling him the conflicting thoughts he had about Ritter. Let Stan flounder in a sea of doubt and then try to complain he wasn't being given enough information. Instead, he kept it a lot simpler.

'What does Landry think?'

'Don't get smart with me.'

Evan had wandered out onto his balcony to get some fresh air as they talked. Or argued. Thinking again about the unidentified man who'd been watching Fleur Sanders. Who might be watching him at this very second. Landry might well be useful again in the future, but for now Evan decided not to mention the incident outside Fleur's house. Nor did he give the license plate to Stan, a man with a greater sense of urgency in tracing it than Guillory having to fit doing him yet another favor into her already busy day. It might come to it, but not yet.

Stan had been right to a certain degree. He *was* being smart asking what Landry thought. That didn't mean the remark was completely facetious.

'Landry and Ritter are a lot alike. They do unpleasant jobs for men who don't much care how it gets done. I'd say his thoughts on Ritter are worth hearing.'

Despite the implied insult to him, Stan didn't immediately

come back at him with either a countering insult or another warning to watch his mouth.

Evan was aware of a sudden movement on the periphery of his vision. His head snapped right, feeling as if some of Fleur's paranoia had rubbed off on him. He half-expected to see the man last seen burning rubber down Fleur's street with a busted windshield staring at him.

Instead, he saw a middle-aged man who'd come out onto his balcony to get some air—and pollute it for everybody else, a packet of Marlboros in his hand. He looked surprised to see Evan a few feet away from him, despite the fact that he couldn't have missed Evan's acrimonious exchange with Fraser. Some of that bad blood must still have been in the air. The guy turned on his heel and went back inside, closing the door pointedly behind him.

Evan went back to Stan, kept his voice down.

'I don't know what to make of Ritter. That's the truth. You can believe me or not. It makes no difference to me.'

'No need to get so touchy.'

'I get the feeling we'll hear from him again. Maybe with backup.'

'You let me know if you need any more guys.'

Evan wanted to laugh in his face, as much as you can from the other end of a phone line.

'If you're thinking of starting a gang war, I'm out.'

'Nobody said anything about that. Landry told me about this beaner, Aguilar. I'm gonna make inquiries about him. Ritter, too. Take a picture of his driver's license and send it to me.'

'Anything else before I switch the phone off?'

'Ha fucking ha. Not funny, Buckley. Tell you what. You keep your phone switched on and I won't break your legs.'

'Ha fucking ha. Not funny, Fraser.'

'You started it. Keep your phone on and I'll tell Landry he's not there to follow you around like a puppy dog.'

'Hell of an ugly puppy.'

'I'll tell him you said that, too. One last thing. You tell Detective Guillory I'm very impressed with the message relay system. I'll be using that again, for sure.'

Tell her yourself felt like a provocation too far. He liked his legs the way they were.

33

Jack Bray as good as soiled himself when he saw the email. It wasn't from the same email address as the original threat five years ago, but the address itself was enough to chill the blood in his veins.

last-chance-Bray666@gmail.com

The subject line was hard to disregard, too.

Ignore this and kiss your career goodbye.

Bray almost felt as if the message itself would be a letdown. Except the way his hand shook as he prepared to click on it told him otherwise. He closed his eyes. Breathed deeply as if that would do anything to slow the racing of his heart banging away like a triphammer in his chest.

He couldn't do it. Not without help.

He got up from his desk, went to the drinks cabinet. Poured himself two fingers of Macallan single malt Scotch—if you've got fingers like a Sumo wrestler, that is. Straight down his throat. Another two fingers. *Whoosh*. Down it goes.

It might as well have been iced tea. Apart from the fact that he felt even more sick than he had a moment ago, a feeling that a moment ago he wouldn't have believed possible.

He went back to his desk, feet dragging like he was a giant blow fly and the carpet flypaper. His desk seemed to change appearance as he approached it. Not so much the place where he composed bullshit memos, as the console from which a stony-faced prison guard flicked the switch on a lethal injection machine to serve up a cocktail of sodium thiopental, pancuronium bromide and potassium chloride.

He dropped into his chair, too soft to be the electric variety, even if the high headrest that he'd paid extra for had an unnerving similarity to Old Sparky.

He couldn't put it off any longer.

He clicked the evil message that laughed open-facedly at his downfall, his disgrace.

I have the video. I have kept quiet about it for five years even though I believe a man like you deserves to burn in hell. I am not a blackmailer. I am not going to threaten to upload it to YouTube or social media, but now I feel under threat myself. People are asking questions. I don't need to remind you that if they find me, they also find the video. You have two choices. Do the world a favor and take your own worthless life. Or do something about the people asking questions. You can start with a private investigator called Evan Buckley.

Bray slumped in his chair, drained. He'd read half a dozen sentences, felt as if he climbed the six highest peaks in the Himalayas.

He didn't know whether he felt relieved or not.

He gripped the edge of his desk to stop himself from replying immediately, knuckles white like he was in a jet aircraft and the windows had just blown out.

What the hell do you think I'm already doing, asshole?

He didn't know what to do.

Offering money wouldn't help. If they'd wanted money, they'd have been in touch years ago. That had always surprised him. Turned his hair gray and his stomach inside-out as he waited for an email such as this one to arrive.

He figured there had been money on the plane, as well. Whoever had the video also had that. They didn't need any more. They were sensible, not greedy. Intelligent enough to realize that changing the game, becoming a blackmailer for a few dollars more until they'd bled him dry wasn't worth the risk.

And they were right to feel under threat.

Aguilar would want his money back. He'd send people after it. People like Ritter. Worse than Ritter.

Where the hell was the incompetent prick, anyway? Why hadn't he heard from him?

He got up from his desk again, resisted detouring to the drinks cabinet for another stiff one—an unfortunate turn of phrase in the circumstances—then veered off towards his private safe.

He got out the burner phone. Checked it for messages.

Nothing.

He couldn't sit around waiting forever.

He dialed Ritter's number, didn't care if he interrupted him humping some syphilitic whore down in Lafayette.

EVAN HAD JUST LEFT HIS ROOM AFTER THE ACRIMONIOUS conversation with Stan Fraser. Thinking he'd grab a quick beer to help him wind down before finding somewhere to eat when Ritter's burner rang in his pocket.

Forget winding down.

Guillory and Fraser both knew his own phone was back on. If they needed to speak to him again, which was unlikely, they'd call on that.

Was this Marvin Fleck calling back with an update about the man Ritter wanted found?

He answered it, feeling as if he'd been caught out before he started.

'Yeah?'

He needn't have worried. The guy on the other end immediately ripped into him.

'For Christ's sake, Ritter, where the hell have you been?'

Evan froze, mouth suddenly dry.

It wasn't Marvin Fleck. The tone of voice, the accusation in the words themselves, suggested it was whoever Ritter worked for.

Ritter had said he was working for Esteban Aguilar. Clearly, he'd lied about that, too. The chances of the man on the other end of the line being Mexican were precisely zero.

But what to say so the guy didn't realize he wasn't Ritter?

He smiled to himself as it came to him. The guy was angry. Incandescent with rage. Impatient with the man who worked for him who wasn't updating him. A lot like Stan Fraser, in fact. It was a no-brainer.

He laughed. A mocking derisive sound like he couldn't give a shit.

Got the reaction he was expecting. And some.

'Don't you fucking laugh at me, you lazy piece of shit. I got another email while you're down there with your finger stuck up your lazy ass. Threatening me.'

Evan said nothing.

It only infuriated the guy more, his voice rising.

'Say something for Christ's sake. Have you achieved a single damn thing since you've been there? Did you even talk to the cop who pulled the file yet? Jesus Christ, Ritter, what the hell have you been doing?'

Evan felt his time slipping away. The guy was going to catch on any minute. He couldn't risk saying anything.

So he acted like any employee who's had enough of his boss

yelling abuse at him might. He ended the call. The dialogue was still open, so to speak, ignoring the temporary interruption.

The phone rang again. Obviously.

He ignored it. Let it ring out. Dropped it back in his pocket. If the guy had any sense, he'd wait, cool down. Call back later. Maybe tomorrow. There was also the chance of a text message.

That put an idea in his head.

Out came the phone again. He took a minute to think about it, then composed a message.

I'm not talking to you when you're like this. I shouldn't have laughed, sorry, but I've had a bitch of a day. Who was the email from? What did it say exactly? Call me tomorrow when we've both cooled off. Hopefully I'll have some answers by then.

He hit *send* feeling like he'd bought himself a little time—time that might well work in his favor in the background if the guy swallowed the bait and texted back with details.

It would be even better to know who he was. That would have to wait. He felt like calling Detective Gauthier in the Baton Rouge PD vice squad, asking him for a heads-up if and when they let Ritter go. Give him and Landry a chance to pick him up again themselves. As of right now, he wasn't believing a single word that had come out of the guy's lying mouth.

That was all for tomorrow.

Or so he thought.

He'd just got himself settled up at the bar in The Greenroom on Jefferson Street, a cold beer in front of him, when his own phone rang. He pulled it out thinking that at this time of night it would normally be Guillory—apart from the fact that it wasn't the distinctive ring tone he'd assigned to her.

It wasn't a number in his contacts, either. He hit the green button as his pulse picked up speed, wondering where his evening was about to take him next.

34

Laura Hunt thought long and hard about making the call. Phone in one hand, the investigator's business card in the other. It would make a change from drinking alone at home or with Fleur which always felt like work more than socializing—which it was, she supposed.

Besides, who knows what might result from a drink with the investigator? He hadn't been wearing a wedding ring, after all. Unless he took it off when he was away on business like all the other douchebags she'd met in bars over the years.

She hesitated, nonetheless.

Fear of rejection? Or flying too close to the flame?

She made the call. Liked the sound of his voice when he answered.

'Hello?'

She nearly backed out then and there. Told herself to get a grip. Carried on in the same lighthearted vein as earlier.

'There's something I need investigated.'

There was a short pause. Then he laughed, an infectious sound that put a smile on her own face.

'Is that Dr. Hunt by any chance?'

'Laura, please.'

'Well, Laura, were you thinking of a thorough investigation?'

She felt a warm rush in her belly at the word *thorough*, something that had been absent for too many years.

'Is there any other kind?'

'It depends on who and what is being investigated.'

If that wasn't an invitation, she didn't know what was.

'How about an initial consultation over a drink? I'm sure you don't want to sit alone in your hotel room watching TV.'

'As it happens, I'm already in The Greenroom.'

She heard the background sounds then. Laughter, men and women's voices, something she couldn't identify on the jukebox that sounded good, made her wish she was there already.

'Of course you are. I don't want to sound disapproving, but my professional antennae have just twitched. As a doctor, I don't advise self-medicating alone.'

'We're going to have a joint consultation, are we? I'll investigate and you examine.'

She cleared her throat, croaked out a reply.

'Sounds like fun. I can be there in fifteen minutes if you're sure I'm not intruding.'

'Some intrusions are more welcome than others.'

He couldn't simply have said, *not at all*, she thought as they ended the call, the warm rush intensifying.

EVAN WASN'T SURE WHAT HAD JUST HAPPENED.

He'd been asked out for a drink by a predatory single woman he'd met for two minutes earlier, obviously.

And he'd responded, matching her flirt for flirt. Nobody could deny there was something about the word *thorough*. He supposed it was the context, too. A thorough interrogation—like the one he'd subject Ritter to if he got the chance—didn't sound as much fun.

They'd have to dial it down when she arrived. That would happen naturally, the comfortable and anonymous distance provided by the phone no longer protecting them.

She turned up exactly fifteen minutes later, as promised. It offered an easy way into the conversation. He glanced at his watch.

'I wish my doctor was as punctual keeping to appointments.'

She smiled, the gripe about her professional colleagues in general washing over her.

'No, I keep patients waiting for ten minutes, as well. We lose our license otherwise.'

She'd changed since he saw her earlier. The crisp white blouse and severe gray skirt had been replaced by a pale-blue casual shirt and faded jeans that fit very nicely in all the right places. She ordered a beer when the bartender came over, feeling the need to explain herself for some reason.

'Fleur always pushes red wine onto me. She doesn't keep beer in the house.'

'She gave me one. Said she bought them for a guy she was dating.'

Laura threw her eyes, the tone of her voice suggesting that she'd suspected as much.

'She wouldn't tell me that. She thinks I'd give her a hard time for ruining her chances keeping that shrine to Justin in her living room.'

'Would you?'

She smiled softly, an admission that he'd got her.

'Probably. And for wearing his wedding ring around her neck. If I'd been married, I wouldn't be advertising that I hadn't moved on like that.'

'Have you been married?'

She shook her head, a resigned acceptance at the way her life had panned out.

'Only to my job. No time. At least that's what I tell myself.'

He gave an admiring dip of his head, his voice equally so.

'Psychiatrist, too.'

She raised an eyebrow at him.

'There's not much hope for you if you don't know yourself. What about you?'

'Everybody tells me I haven't got the first idea about myself. I tend to agree.'

She laughed, a throaty sound that was too reminiscent of Guillory. Then she leaned away, studied him.

'If I *were* a psychiatrist, I'd say that you choose to make a joke when you're faced with a difficult question or a situation you want to avoid. What I meant, and what you understood perfectly well, was, have you been married?'

'A long time ago.'

'Didn't work out?'

'No.'

She caught the unintended sharpness of his tone, misinterpreted it. Assumed he'd gone through a messy, bitter divorce where everybody came away feeling grubby, disappointed with themselves at their failure to rise above the petty squabbles over money and possessions they never liked to begin with.

Except it hadn't been like that at all . . .

In front of him the woman who used to be his wife. Six years since he saw her last. A stranger to him, her face all but unrecognizable. Flushed red and cheeks wet with tears from CS gas. Eyes glassy and bloodshot. Makeup streaked across her face from clawing frantically at the burning pain.

Her front a sea of wetly glistening blood.

He couldn't see the wound for the stinging, the sweat and tears in his eyes.

Slumped in her seat. Not moving. Mouth open, head lolling onto her shoulder like a little girl who's dozed off in the back of the car at the end of a long journey.

He felt for a pulse. Not an easy thing to do. His own heartbeat rocked the whole damn car on its suspension. Fingers throbbing with it. Thump. Thump. Thump. A hundred and twenty to the minute. Slick with blood. His blood. Sarah's blood. The blood of every person he'd ever known and held dear.

And over it all the pure clear voices of all those he'd wronged joining as one in their condemnation.

This is on you.

The misunderstanding did the trick, nonetheless. Stopped Laura from prying. It didn't stop her from continuing to study him like he was a new patient who'd walked into her office with symptoms she'd never seen before.

And she was still firmly in shrink mode.

'But you're in a long-term relationship, aren't you?'

'Uh-huh. How did you know?'

'Well, if you're fishing for compliments along the lines of you're too good-looking to be available, you're going to be disappointed. Women can tell, is all. I don't think a real shrink could tell you how. So, what does your partner do? She's not your secretary, is she?'

His mouth became a perfect O, a look of horror on his face.

'If I really didn't like you, I'd tell her you said that. Sit back and watch the show. You're a little taller than she is, and you look like you work out—'

'Not these days, I don't. I used to go to the gym a couple times a week. Not anymore.'

She pinched an inch around her midriff. What he saw as an

invitation to him to say how there was nothing to pinch, how trim she was.

'I've seen more fat on a butcher's pencil. That's something else the two of you have got in common. You'd be a good match for each other in a fight.'

She narrowed her eyes at him as if the new patient had just described a set of symptoms at odds with the first ones.

'C'mon, then, what does she do?'

'She's a detective. A proper badge-carrying one. And don't let me forget it.'

A look flashed across her face. It was a lot like the mock horror on his only a moment ago, immediately replaced by the man-eating grin he figured was second nature to her.

'Really? That must be fun.'

'I believe the phrase is, it has its moments.'

'I'll bet. Especially when the handcuffs come out.'

'No more so than when you get the rubber gloves out.'

Now it was her turn to dip her head at him.

'Touché. And before you ask, no, I don't currently have anyone to use them on. Except for genuine patients, that is.'

It was too good an opportunity to pass on. Not only to stop the innuendo from getting out of hand—despite his declared unavailability—but also to attempt to get something out of the evening beyond the thrill of narrowly avoiding being eaten alive.

'Like Fleur, you mean?'

She rocked her hand, the mischief still in her eyes.

'Not quite. Fleur's more pills than rubber gloves.'

'Were you her doctor when her husband was killed?'

'I was, yes. It's how we know each other. I hadn't seen her or Justin on a regular professional basis before he was killed. You don't see the younger patients very often. Unfortunately, it tends to be something bad when you do. She came to me for anti-depressants and sleeping pills. It was strictly professional to start with. Gradually we became friends. Then it was more about the red wine than the pills.'

'Same effect.'

She wagged her finger at him.

'I can't possibly agree with you. They'd take away my white coat for that, too.'

It was time to make a decision.

Take it to the next stage or not? Not in terms of saying to her, forget what I said about a long-term partner and get your rubber gloves out, but whether to discuss Fleur in more detail.

'I noticed she's back on the pills with a vengeance.'

Laura didn't actually throw her eyes, although it was close.

'I know. Did she tell you—'

'About the man watching the house? Yeah. Had you noticed him?'

'Not before Fleur mentioned him. I saw him as I was leaving. I told her she should call the police. I knew she wouldn't. I would have called them myself on her behalf if she didn't already think I interfere too much, nagging her about her drinking. I suppose that's why she called you . . .' Her brow compacted as her words registered in her own mind. 'That can't be right. You said you're not from around here. Where do you fit in?'

He was surprised it had taken as long as it had to get to this point. Admittedly, there'd been a lot of flirting to get past, then the joking about Guillory and handcuffs, not to mention her and rubber gloves and nobody to use them on.

Despite how well they'd gotten along, he drew the line now. Kept things vague and bent the truth a little out of shape.

'The case regarding the plane crash hasn't been re-opened officially, but there's been renewed interest. I can't say more than that. You know all about client confidentiality.'

She raised a hand, say no more.

'And the man watching Fleur is connected to that? I was sure there would be an innocent explanation.'

He got a sudden vivid picture in his mind. The car accelerating towards him. Leaping out of the way at the last minute, the fender kissing his butt. Swinging the wrecking bar into the windshield, glass exploding.

'I don't think so.'

'You sound very sure.'

'That's because I am . . .' He told her the rest of the story, got a nervous laugh back as if she was wishing she'd never asked.

'As I said earlier, your job's a lot more exciting than mine. The guy really was watching her house? I can't believe it. Do you have any idea who he is?'

'None whatsoever.'

'Do you think it could be the man who killed Justin? Tidying up the loose ends.' The nervous laugh made a reappearance before he could answer. 'That sounds so stupid. Like we're in a movie.'

'It happens in real life, too.'

'I suppose. Hopefully not in your own back yard. Certainly not in Fleur's. Not unless the killer took their shoes off first.'

He smiled with her, the memory of Fleur's immaculate yard fresh in his mind.

'She said her husband wanted to concrete over it, paint it green.'

'I'm with him on that. Who wants to mow the grass just for it to grow again? Dig up weeds for twice as many to come back overnight? Not me.'

The talk of, not exactly rampant but recalcitrant, plant growth brought to mind the Atchafalaya wildlife refuge. Made him think of Justin Sanders fighting his way through the undergrowth to get to the aircraft he'd seen come down and where his untimely death awaited him. It prompted what he asked Laura next.

'Did you know Justin's friend, Kevin Clark?'

'No. Why should I?'

'No particular reason. I thought he might be one of your patients, too.'

She shook her head, a slight frown creasing her brow.

'You're never off duty, are you? To answer the question, no, he wasn't a patient of mine.'

It seemed a strange way to phrase it. They were talking about events five years in the past, but to his ear it sounded as if Kevin was also dead. He didn't mention it. She appeared to be getting bored with the conversation already. He couldn't blame her. What might in her mind have been a drink leading to a quick noncommittal romp between the sheets with a man from out of town had turned into, not so much the investigation they'd joked about, but an interrogation. Hence the pointed remark about never being off duty.

That's when Ritter's burner phone came to the rescue, beeping in his pocket as a message arrived. He didn't make a move to get it out.

The man-eating grin was immediately back on Laura's face, what had felt like an uncomfortable moment over Kevin Clark a thing of the past.

'I bet that's your lady detective checking up on you. Aren't you going to see what it says? I need to go to the ladies' room, anyway.'

She slipped off her stool and sashayed away, much as she had going down Fleur's path to her car earlier. The swing in her hips advertised a message that had been getting men in trouble since time began.

Yours for the asking...

He waited until she was out of sight, pulled out Ritter's

phone. The unidentified man he was assuming was Ritter's boss had taken the bait, replied to his message.

It's a made-up email address. He's got the video. He's not asking for money. But if you don't stop people asking questions, the cops will find the video when they find him. You need to deal with an investigator called Evan Buckley.

Seeing his own name without any warning was like a slap across the face to Evan. As if he was reading his own death sentence—which he was if the sender's message had actually reached Ritter.

He composed a reply, kept it brief.

Leave it to me. Don't call me, I'll call you.

He ordered another beer as he digested the new information.

The man who had killed Justin Sanders and the plane's pilot had escaped not only with Esteban Aguilar's money, but with a compromising video of the man who'd sent Ritter. Given Aguilar's business interests—drugs, arms and people trafficking—that video could be very compromising indeed.

It explained why that man was still unaware of Ritter's current predicament, why he was continuing the exchange with Evan.

Ritter would have been rescued from his trunk hours ago. Evan would have expected him to immediately call the man employing him, get him to do something about getting him out of the mess he was in.

Except he was doing his job. A loyal foot soldier protecting the—presumably rich and important—man who had something to hide by not dragging him into the mess he was in with the Baton Rouge PD vice squad.

He was missing something.

Ritter admitted he'd first seen Evan with Fontenot at the part-time deputy, Mercer's house. He'd then used his fake police

ID to learn who Evan was at his bed and breakfast. But how had his boss known about him when Ritter clearly wasn't updating him?

He startled as Laura suddenly appeared beside him.

'That bad, huh? You've got a face like your dog just died. And you needed another beer.' The grin was immediately back, her eyes alive. 'Don't tell me she's dumped you?'

'It wasn't her. But yeah, it wasn't good news.'

She put her hand on his arm. It was warm and comforting, but lacking in any intimacy or sexual intent.

'I'm going to go. I shouldn't have called you.'

The man-eater was safely back in its cage. He felt sorry for her. In other circumstances he'd have been happy to see where things led. She was attractive and her humor matched his, the earlier flirting proof enough of that.

'Have one more drink.'

'Okay. But no more talking shop.'

He raised his glass to that, *agreed*. Wished it was as easy to stop thinking about it.

They talked about this and that, kept it light with a lot of laughter. At one point right before they were leaving, she asked him where he was staying without any outward sign of regret that she wouldn't be going back there with him. She raised an appreciative eyebrow when he told her—an innocent question and answer that would have far from innocent repercussions.

35

LAURA HUNT HAD BEEN RIGHT TO QUESTION THE WISDOM OF calling Evan. She just didn't know it yet as she walked back to her car after they'd parted on the sidewalk with a chaste peck on the cheek.

In contrast, Innocent Lejeune was feeling like maybe Jesus did love him after all. He hadn't been feeling that way a few hours ago. Not after the madman attacked his car and smashed the windshield with a wrecking bar. Things had gone downhill from there when his contact with DMV access had informed him that the guy's car was a rental. So, a berserker from out of town.

Great.

It hadn't left him with many options.

He'd already identified Fleur Sanders' female visitor from the previous night. Dr. Laura Hunt. With nothing else to follow up, he'd paid a fortune to a bunch of emergency windshield repair cowboys, then driven to her office. He'd then followed her home. He was thinking about how best to get to her, when she came out again almost immediately—barely enough time for a quick shower and change of clothes. He'd then followed her to a bar called The Greenroom.

That was when Jesus decided to make it up to him.

He'd waited for ten minutes after she'd gone inside, then he'd gone in himself. Immediately about-faced and left again as if he'd inadvertently walked into the wrong bar.

Five seconds, but it had been enough.

She was sitting up at the bar having a drink with the out-of-town berserker.

Were they working together? From the quick look he'd gotten it looked more like they were about to jump into the sack together. Except it was too much of a coincidence. Combining work with pleasure, then. Although he hoped not. Prayed to the currently amenable Jesus they weren't going to leave together.

He had a feeling the madman might know more, but it would be a much harder job getting it out of him. Innocent preferred the path of least resistance whenever possible. In this case, that was Dr. Laura Hunt.

He smiled to himself when they came out a short while later and she pecked him on the cheek. *Ha, ha*, no rumpy-pumpy for the madman. Serve him right for busting people's windshields, the bastard.

He watched them as they went their separate ways. Dr. Hunt turned to look behind her after a dozen or so paces. The madman kept on going without a second look. Perhaps it was the doctor who had the hots for him and not the other way around. Innocent figured the guy should see a doctor—*ha, ha*—if that was the case. Something seriously wrong with him. She was hot. Innocent could make a lot of money out of a woman like that.

Maybe not after he'd finished with her tonight . . .

He didn't wait until she got to her shiny Subaru to follow her home. He already knew where she lived. He pulled away, hit the gas, tempted to toot as he blew past her.

See you later.

He parked half a block from her house and jogged the rest of the way, a black ski mask and a roll of duct tape he always kept in the glove compartment stuffed into his pocket.

At the house, Jesus proved his love once more. The garage and driveway were on the left-hand side, a line of dense bushes running down the property line to the sidewalk. When she drove up and got out, she'd be in the narrow gap between her car and the bushes with nowhere to run. Not out in the open in front of her house illuminated by the security light.

And if the garage wasn't full of junk and she put the car away for the night, even better. He wouldn't have to worry about manhandling her into the house.

He ran up the driveway, wormed his way into the bushes, invisible in the blackness of the night.

Not a moment too soon.

On went the ski mask, head dipped as she drove in to preserve his night vision. Sent up a second prayer—of thanks this time—when she stopped with the engine still running. The garage door lifted smoothly up in front of the car like a giant metal mouth opening to receive its dinner-cum-prey.

He pulled his switchblade from his pocket, kept it closed. He wasn't worried about the glint of metal flashing in the darkness of the bushes. He knew from long experience that the snick of the blade springing open was as frightening as the cold touch of metal against a woman's neck that followed it.

And he needed every advantage. She was a tall, fit-looking woman. Not at all like the scrawny widow Sanders.

Panic gripped him momentarily as a thought flashed across his mind. What if she closed the garage door before getting out?

Then the car door opened and she climbed out, the garage door still fully up.

She was a doctor, after all. Wouldn't lock all those noxious exhaust fumes in the garage, then step out into them. Let the night air come in, dissipate them.

And with it, his good self. Sneaking up like a darker patch of shadow as the garage door started its descent with a footstep-muffling whine.

Then he was on her.

Left hand over her mouth, wrenching her head upwards and back to expose the defenselessness of her throat.

Snick.

The blade pushed up into the soft flesh under her jaw. Flesh that she'd hoped the madman would be nuzzling. Hustling her around the front of the car as the door closed behind them. Just the two of them now, safe from prying eyes. He pushed her violently forwards, snatching her bag as she staggered into the side door to the house and fell to her knees.

'Move and I'll cut your eyes out.'

He up-ended the bag, dumped the contents onto the hood of the Subaru. Her keys tumbled out with all the other unnecessary crap women carry around. A can of pepper spray, too. He threw the keys onto the ground beside her, the pepper spray in his hand.

'Stay on your knees. Reach up and open the door. Is there an alarm?'

'No.'

'You'll be sorry if there is.'

She fumbled with the keys, hands shaking. Found the one she wanted. Reached up and slipped it in the lock. Pushed the door open.

He breathed again when nothing but still air greeted them.

'Crawl in on your hands and knees.'

She did as he said. He followed her in, thinking what a nice view it was. A quick slash with his blade across the tightly-stretched denim and it'd be even nicer.

Except there was no time.

He barked orders at her when she was halfway across the kitchen floor.

'Stop there. Lie on your front. Put your hands behind your back. Don't try anything stupid.' He gave the pepper spray a quick squirt into the air. 'Unless you want me to empty this into your eyes and we'll try again.'

Once more, she did as she was told. Pressed her wrists together in her desperate need to comply. He put one knee on the firmness of her butt, squeezed a guttural grunt out of her. Taped her wrists together then stood up and back.

She twisted her head to the side, cheek squashed against the cold tile floor.

'There's nothing valuable in the house. Go ahead and look around. Take the car if you want.'

'I don't want your money. Or your car.'

'What do you—'

He knew then that she'd figured out exactly what he wanted. She immediately proved it, her voice filled with horror.

'You're the man who's been watching Fleur Sanders' house.'

He didn't need to confirm it. Started in with his own questions.

'Who's the man you had a drink with? The one who smashed my windshield. He's driving a rental, so I know he's from out of town. Don't make the mistake of sacrificing that pretty face of yours for someone you don't even know. Someone you'll never see again. You won't have any patients left if your own face looks like a badly-stitched patchwork quilt. Nobody wants to be examined by Freddy Krueger.'

He nudged her in the ribs with his toe when she didn't immediately answer.

'Don't think. Talk.' Without warning he dropped onto both knees in the middle of her back. Punched all the air out of her lungs like it wasn't ever coming back. Crouched over her like a predator protecting its prey from hungry rivals as she wheezed and heaved in her fight to breathe. He put aside the pepper spray, laid his left hand on the side of her head as if to stroke her hair. Pressed the tip of his blade into the corner of her gasping mouth. 'Unless you want to talk for the rest of your life with a mouth from here to here.' Drawing a line lightly across her cheek to her earlobe as he said it.

She shuddered under him. Trying to pull her head away from the knife, her words coming between stuttering gasps.

'He's a private investigator. Evan Buckley. His card's in my bag. He said the case into Fleur's husband's death has been re-opened. He didn't tell me who he's working for. That's all I know.'

He straightened up, still on his knees on her back. The movement expelled what little air she'd managed to reclaim. Then he stood, leaned his butt against the counter studying her.

He had a lifetime's experience holding a knife or a razor close to the precious parts of a woman's face. Her eyes, her lips, even her tongue. Enough to recognize the truth when he heard it. They knew him for what he was. A man who did not make idle threats. He was good with a blade, prepared to use it. People understood that instinctively. Apart from a few individuals—the investigator Buckley was most likely one of them—the truth and fear often go hand-in-hand.

He had a good idea what Buckley would do next. Talk to the detective, Bordelon. It's what he'd do himself, if he thought Bordelon would talk to him. Buckley had a better chance. At least he was on the same side of the law.

'Where's he staying? Don't lie to me.'

'A big old Creole house on North Sterling Street. At the intersection with Mudd Avenue.'

That sounded about right to Innocent. Fit with the guy's style. He'd be back to see the doctor if it wasn't. He nudged her with his toe again.

'Get up.'

He was surprised at how easily she managed it with her hands tied behind her back. Raised her butt towards him like she was offering herself to him, made herself look like a giant caterpillar. Then up onto her knees and from there onto her feet all in one fluid movement. He could make a lot of money out of a fit energetic woman like her, no two ways about it. Except the whine in her voice let her down. Made him want to slap her.

'What are you going to do to me?' she said.

'Relax. Gonna get you comfortable, is all. Upstairs. Now.' Then, when she stayed put. 'I can leave you lying on the cold hard kitchen floor instead, if that's what you want. You're gonna be here for a couple of days before this is done.'

'Before what is done?'

He thought about saying, *none of your damn business*. Changed his mind. It helped to say the words out loud. Keep the anger at a steady rolling boil.

'Before the cocksucker who killed my brother gets what's coming to him, that's what.'

She recoiled at the force, the venom he put into the words. As if he'd said he'd changed his mind. He was going to kill her, not leave her tied up. He leaned in, made her recoil even more as he yelled in her face.

'*Move!* I haven't got all night.'

She spun around as if he'd bitch-slapped her. Led the way upstairs.

'You need to pee first?' he said when they got to the landing.

'What are you? A pervert?'

He smiled at her, eye teeth on show.

'Yes, ma'am, I am. Whenever I get the opportunity. Yes or no?'

'No, thank you. I'd rather pee in my pants.'

'Your choice. Your sheets.'

Jesus came through for him once again with her choice of bed. An old-fashioned brass bedstead just made for tying people to—willing or otherwise.

It took him a while, and took a little violence that he couldn't see any way of avoiding. He punched her on the jaw, a straight right hard enough to make her eyes go out of focus and her head spin. Slit the tape securing her wrists together as she wobbled, dazed. Then threw her on her back on the bed. Sat astride her as she moaned softly and taped one and then the other wrist to the bed frame, BDSM-style. Thinking he could charge extra for that.

He glanced around the bedroom before leaving. Saw a laptop sitting on the dresser. It made him think. Would there be blank prescription forms on there? Handy for when she made house calls? He took it, sat on the edge of the bed beside her. Opened it.

'Password? If you make me get the knife out again it won't go back dry.'

She hesitated momentarily, saw the truth in the coldness of his dead eyes. He tapped it in when she told him, gave her cheek an encouraging caress that made him wish he had more time when the laptop let him in.

Then he pulled the drapes closed, turned out the light and bid her good night.

36

Detective Gauthier of the Baton Rouge PD vice squad was an impatient prick, Ritter decided. Didn't even have the decency to let him have one night's sleep after being locked in the trunk of his car for half the day where it was hotter than the devil's ass crack *and* with half his shoulder blown away *and* every biting insect in southern Louisiana sucking what little blood he had left.

Not that he was surprised, coming from a man who appeared to have cornered the market in polyester clothing. He laid his head on the pillow, closed his eyes. Tried to pretend Gauthier wasn't there. Ignore him like he was an over-sized mosquito.

Except Gauthier wasn't having any of it.

'The guy who called it in said you're working for Esteban Aguilar.'

Ritter opened his eyes for the sole reason of letting Gauthier see in them exactly how much of a moron he thought he was.

'You know who Aguilar is?'

The question made Gauthier's mouth turn down even more.

Something Ritter would not have believed, had he not seen it with his own eyes.

'My life would be a whole lot easier if I didn't.'

'So, tell me. Can you think of a single occasion when Aguilar has employed someone whose family hasn't lived in the same shithole barrio for the last five hundred years as his own family? No? I didn't think so. Next question. Or even better, see you tomorrow.'

'If not Aguilar, who?'

'I can't tell you that.'

Gauthier looked as if he wanted to spit, hospital or not.

'Yeah, yeah, yeah. Client confidentiality. We'll come back to that. Tell me again how you ended up in your trunk with a bullet wound in your shoulder.'

Ritter had had more than enough time while in that very trunk to think about how to play it if and when he was let out.

He'd considered constructing a story loosely based on the truth to attempt to drop Buckley in the shit. Trouble was, he didn't know how Buckley would react if the cops hauled him in. *Loose cannon* was the phrase that popped into his head when he pictured the guy's face in his mind. Best to leave his name out of it altogether.

'The story's not going to change however many times you ask me.'

'Tell me again, anyway. I like bedtime stories.'

His face and voice suggested that like other bedtime stories featuring wicked witches and wizards and brave children helped by talking woodland animals with big brown eyes there would be very little truth in it. His job obliged him to keep on plugging away, nonetheless.

'I was driving on I-10—'

'Going where?'

'You asked that before. I thought my answer made it clear—'

'That the client confidentiality bullshit covered that, too? I thought I'd try again, anyway. You thought those mosquitos were persistent, you just watch me.' He extended a large hand towards Ritter that they both knew he'd rather be using to slap the truth out of him. 'You were saying...'

'There'd been a car behind me for some time. I thought it might be tailing me. Exit 127 was coming up. You know as well as I do that it doesn't go anywhere any normal person would want to go. It's for people who like hugging trees and getting eaten alive by 'gators. So I came off. The car came with me. I thought to myself, maybe he's going to a fish camp on the Atchafalaya River. I kept going. Then I made a right onto Bayou Shithole Road. *Away* from the river. And he's still there. That's when I knew for sure. Then when we're absolutely in the middle of nowhere he shunted me. I'm thinking, there's a bridge with a paper guardrail up ahead. He's gonna push me off it into the bayou. I can't swim. I thought I'd take my chances on dry land. With all the dust kicking up I didn't see there were two of them. I didn't think they'd start shooting the minute I got out the car, either. I shot back at them to defend myself as is my right'—raising his voice to emphasize the point—'then I took one in the shoulder and that was the end of it. They interrogated me, swallowed the bullshit story I fed them—'

'Was it the same bullshit story you're feeding me?'

'Actually, no. I said I thought they were dirty cops after me. That's why they found it so easy to believe. Then they tied me up and left me to die in my trunk.'

'Except they called it in.'

'I could've bled out by then.'

'Lucky for you that you didn't.' His face said the rest of it.

Not so lucky for the rest of us.

Then Gauthier threw something down onto the bed covers. Ritter didn't need to look at it to know what it was. Gauthier's voice took a patronizing turn, the tone of a man who expects that what he is about to hear will barely be on nodding terms with reality.

'Care to explain how a fake police ID in the name of Detective John Rawlings stacks up with the idea of you being the innocent victim? And telling us that your name's Ritter? Or does the client confidentiality bullshit cover that, too?'

Ritter had known it would be a sticking point.

'Doesn't matter what I say. You're gonna book me for it just the same.'

'Damn right, I am. How about the fact that the car you were driving has got plates that belong to a man in Baton Rouge called Thomas Nieves? Who also happens to be eighty-four years old. You look like shit—'

'So would you with half your shoulder blown off.'

'—but you don't look eighty-four.'

'The longer you're here, the closer I feel I'm getting to it.'

'Is that so? The longer I'm here, the more I feel you won't make it through the night.'

'Are you threatening me, Detective?'

Gauthier gave up then, the tide of bullshit overwhelming him. He picked up the fake ID, got to his feet.

'We've only just started. Get a good night's sleep—'

'What's left of it.'

'—because you're gonna need it tomorrow. I'm leaving a couple of guys on the door in case you're feeling lonely and talkative.'

Ritter sank back into the pillows feeling drained. Every inch of his body itched. His shoulder hurt like hell despite the drugs they'd pumped him full of. It wouldn't have surprised him if Gauthier had told the doctor to only give him half strength—supposedly so he didn't fall asleep while being questioned and not just because he was a vindictive prick as well as an impatient prick.

To think that one call to Bray and he'd be laughing in Gauthier's face as he waltzed out.

Except he wouldn't do that.

He was good at keeping his mouth shut to protect the interests of Jackass Bray.

The guy had no idea. No idea about what went on in the background to protect him that he didn't even know about.

He only hoped Bray didn't call the burner, announce himself to Buckley.

This is Jack Bray speaking...

He wouldn't put it past the guy.

He hated to think what kind of a state Bray would be in now if he knew that Mercer pulling the file wasn't the first time he, Ritter, had to step in, clear up somebody else's mess.

Sanders' hiking buddy Kevin Clark four years ago, for instance.

Jesus. What a clusterfuck that had been. At least it wasn't a problem anymore.

Jackass Bray didn't have the first idea anything had even happened.

Ungrateful bastard.

37

Part-time-Deputy Mercer laughed out loud when Evan called him first thing the next morning.

'So, you wait a day after apologizing before asking a favor?'

Evan worked a contrite note into his voice.

'Sometimes two, depending on how big the favor is. But yeah, you got me.'

'Don't worry about it. Let me guess. You need help getting in touch with Lou Bordelon?'

'You're the one should've been the detective.'

'No way.'

There was something about the way he said it made the hairs on the back of Evan's neck stand up. He could put a lot of feeling into two words when he wanted to—a phrase ending with *off* came to mind—but Mercer had him beat hands-down.

He figured it was to do with whatever made Bordelon quit.

'I don't know where he lives,' Mercer said, 'but I know he got a job as head of security for some big corporation in Baton Rouge. I figure quitting was the best thing he ever did. Even if he didn't think so at the time. I can't remember the name of the company. Hang on.' The background sounds muted as Mercer put his hand over the microphone. He was back a minute later. 'It's called Wright Industries. They're on United Plaza Boulevard. I'm guessing he sits in an office all day with his feet on the desk. Talking to you will give him something to do. Say *hi* to him from me, if you get to speak to him. You made any progress so far?'

Evan felt exhausted just thinking about the previous day. The argument with Stan Fraser before he'd even finished breakfast, being shot at by Ritter, questioning him after Landry shot him back, going to Fleur's house and chasing off an unidentified man with a wrecking bar, then narrowly avoiding being eaten alive by Dr. Laura Hunt.

'There's been plenty going on. Whether you'd call any of it progress is another matter.'

He was reminded of the things Ritter had told them as he said it. That a deputy called Dixon had alerted Ritter when Mercer pulled the file. He figured Mercer had a lot of guilt over Arlo he wanted to work out. But was pointing him at Dixon the way to do it? Pulling the file hadn't exactly been official sheriff's office business.

He kept it to himself for now. Decided to do the same about Ritter. But Mercer was clearly waiting for something back in exchange for Bordelon's place of work.

'I went to see Fleur Sanders, ended up chasing off a guy who'd been watching her house. I got his license plate if you wanted to run it.' Thinking he'd already asked Guillory, but it would make Mercer feel like he was doing something.

Mercer didn't exactly bite his hand off. It was the unofficial nature of the whole business again.

'I can run it for you, if you want. But I can't get involved myself.'

'I understand. Do it, anyway. I'll text you the details.'

. . .

Evan found Wright Industries on Google as soon as he'd finished with Mercer, called them and asked to be put through to Bordelon.

That's when things started to go wrong. He was put through to a woman who identified herself as Bordelon's secretary. She made it sound like *gatekeeper* which is exactly what she turned out to be.

'Mr. Bordelon isn't in the office today. He called in sick. Is there anything I can do to help?' Giving the impression that putting the phone down immediately would be her suggestion.

Evan huffed a weary sigh down the line. A tired over-worked man just trying to get his job done.

'No. I really needed to talk to Lou. My name's Evan Buckley. I'm a deputy with the St. Martinville Parish Sheriff's Office. I used to work with Lou back before he left us to go to the big city and make his fortune.'

The secretary laughed politely.

'I'm not sure anyone who works here would call it that. Can I take a message? He said he expects to be back in tomorrow.'

'It's actually quite urgent. Something's come up on an old case he worked. All I need is a quick word. I wouldn't dream of going to the house, dragging him out of his sick bed. The cell phone number we have on file isn't in service any longer.'

'I'm afraid it's against company policy to give out personal cell phone numbers.'

Evan took a deep breath as he pictured the self-satisfied smile on the woman's face as she hid behind gatekeeper excuse #1.

'I understand.' Keeping the rest of it to himself. *That you're an awkward cuss.* 'I'd appreciate it if you would call him, ask him to call me on this number. Tell him it's to do with the Justin Sanders case. I guarantee he'll want to speak to me once you tell him that. As I said, it's urgent. The Justin Sanders case.'

'I heard you the first time, Deputy Buckley. I'll see what I can do.'

He ended the call not knowing what to expect. The name Justin Sanders would make Bordelon sit up and take notice. If his secretary remembered the whole conversation and said that he was a deputy called Buckley, who Bordelon had worked with, that'd get his attention, too—in a different way. Whether he was sufficiently intrigued to call was another matter.

He called Guillory while he waited.

Like Mercer before her, she started the conversation with a laugh.

'What?' he said. He was used to her laughing after he'd said something, but this was a first.

'I ran the plate of the guy you attacked—'

'I didn't attack him. I chased him away.'

'Whatever. I think you'll find he believes he's innocent.'

That set her off laughing again. Made him wonder what she'd been up to with Donut in the car. Smoking confiscated weed, perhaps?

'Okay. You ran the plate . . .'

'Uh-huh. The car's registered to a guy called Lejeune.'

'Makes sense. Sounds like a very Cajun sort of name. I can hear the accordion already.'

'You want to guess what his first name is?'

He didn't. He wanted her to spit it out, get off the line in case Bordelon called back. He played along, nonetheless.

'Remy?'

'Close. It's Innocent.'

'*Innocent?*'

'Yep. Innocent Lejeune.'

'Is that even a real name?'

'Apparently so. Obviously, it doesn't mean anything to you.

It's not a name you'd forget. And before you ask, no, I haven't had a chance to look into the other guy. The one you shot—'

'Landry shot him.'

'—Ritter. Anyway, gotta go.'

He sat and thought about what he had after the connection went dead in his ear. There were a number of players in the game now:

Esteban Aguilar, the ruiner of lives in so many different ways.

Ritter and his murderous sidekick, Marvin Fleck.

And now Innocent Lejeune.

In addition, he had a number of not-necessarily mutually-exclusive motivations.

Aguilar had lost a ton of money and wanted it back. Had he sent the strangely-named Innocent Lejeune to look for it?

A compromising video of Ritter's unidentified boss was out there somewhere and Ritter was tasked with recovering it, whatever the cost.

Ritter had employed Marvin Fleck to find and presumably kill *someone*, as yet unspecified. Was that someone Lejeune? Find and kill him before he found the money and the video along with it?

As usual, every additional piece of information or new name threw up more questions than answers.

It was unfortunate that he hadn't been able to speak to Lejeune the previous day, that the guy had driven off. He had a feeling he couldn't explain that they might be working towards the same goal. Ritter was looking to clear the decks. Destroy everything he found to protect a guilty man. Lejeune felt different. He might be wrong. The guy might be a cold-blooded killer like Ritter. But he wanted the option to find out, not have Ritter kill him first. Because the more he thought about it, the more convinced he became that Lejeune was the man Marvin Fleck was tasked with hunting down.

He pulled out Ritter's burner, composed a message to Fleck. Aware that it could backfire if he was wrong.

Change of plan. Lejeune's here in Lafayette. I'll deal with the situation.

He hit *send*, surprised when a reply bounced back within a minute. He opened it. Half expecting a confused, *who the hell's Lejeune?*

Instead, the reply made him laugh out loud. A single thumbs-up emoji. It seemed so incongruous coming from a man who killed people for a living.

That's when his own phone rang.

He checked his watch. Ten minutes since he'd spoken to Bordelon's rottweiler of a secretary.

Something told him he wouldn't be laughing so much when he answered this one.

38

He was right, the barely-suppressed anger he sensed on the other end of the line warning him that he was dealing with a man who didn't like to be messed with. A man who appreciated being deceived even less. His words were short sharp barks that felt to Evan like slaps across the face.

'This is Lou Bordelon. Two questions. Who are you really? And why should I talk to you?'

'Evan Buckley is my real name. But I'm not a deputy with the St. Martinville Parish Sheriff's Office.'

'No shit.'

'I'm a PI.'

'Better than a reporter.' His tone of voice suggesting it was almost too close to call. A similar contest to the one between dying of cancer and dying of AIDS.

'Have you heard of Arlo Fraser?' Evan said.

'No.' Immediately, he backtracked. 'That's not strictly true. The name sounds familiar.'

Evan didn't prompt him. Bordelon was sufficiently interested to try to make the connection himself.

'That's it. My secretary told me someone claiming to be from

The Daily Acadian in Lafayette called and asked to speak to me. I'm sure that was his name. I didn't speak to him. What about him?'

'He's disappeared. He was working freelance for the paper looking into the Justin Sanders case. I'm working for his father. I don't know whether you not talking to him made it more or less likely that he went missing, but he hasn't been heard from for a week.'

He almost felt guilty for saying it. Putting the idea out there that Arlo might not have gone missing at all if Bordelon had given him two minutes of his time, busy head of security for Wright Industries or not. Given the way his law enforcement background would've worn down his humanity over the years, he doubted Bordelon was susceptible to emotional pressurizing.

A lengthy pause stretched out where it could have gone either way. Evan got the impression of a man struggling with his conscience as something he'd worked hard to put behind him was dumped without warning in his lap.

There was less of the aggression in his voice when Bordelon spoke again.

'Come to the house. I'll text you the address. Don't worry, I'm not contagious. Damn back's gone, is all. I can barely move.'

Bordelon's house was smaller than Evan would've expected. More in line with the salary of a detective in a small sheriff's office than that of the head of security in a big corporate organization. Most likely the guy hadn't moved since leaving the sheriff's office—something that would shortly be proved. It meant a lengthy commute each day to Baton Rouge, but that was his choice.

Bordelon took an age to answer the door. Walking like he was strapped to a leftover plank of the lumber it was made from. Evan followed him slowly down the hallway to the sitting room.

'My wife's out,' Bordelon said over his shoulder, 'or she

would've let you in. I sent her out for more painkillers.'

Strange way to put it, Evan thought. He wondered if Mrs. Bordelon was happy with the idea of being *sent out* to get them rather than being asked to pick some up for her husband. But Bordelon struck him as a gruff sort of guy, his mood not improved by relentless nagging back pain.

That too would become clear with time.

'What did you do to your back?' Evan said as he watched Bordelon using both hands to carefully lower himself into his chair.

Bordelon didn't immediately answer. Waited until he had a free hand so that he could wave the question away.

'You didn't come here to talk about my back. Tell me about the guy who's gone missing.'

Evan took him through it. Explained how the editor Ralph Fontenot had been pressured by his daughter to give Arlo a chance, how Arlo had then read Bordelon's original file and from there gone to see Fleur Sanders.

'That's as far as he got as far as I know. Ignoring the attempt to speak to you. I don't know yet if he talked to Justin Sanders' hiking buddy, Kevin Clark, before he disappeared.'

A small brown dog of indeterminate parentage had wandered into the room as Evan talked. Unlike Fleur Sanders' cat, it ignored Evan, went directly to Bordelon. Looked up at him hopefully for an ear scratch, tail wagging, then lay down at his feet when Bordelon's condition stopped him from leaning down and obliging.

'Who let him see the file?' Bordelon said.

'Mercer.'

Bordelon shook his head like he'd suspected as much.

'He was always a soft touch. I take it you've read it?'

'Uh-huh. Arlo took copies, saved them on the cloud.'

'Whatever that is,' Bordelon said, his face suggesting it

sounded like a shorter way of saying hidden up a horse's ass.

'His girlfriend let me take copies.'

Bordelon made a show of looking around the room, albeit slowly and painfully, disgust on his face. Raised his voice as if addressing a crowd.

'Anybody else like a copy?'

Evan figured it wasn't a good time to mention that Mercer wasn't the only one guilty of professional misconduct. Deputy Dixon-Dawg was on the take, too.

He waited for Bordelon's tone to change, as if he was now talking to the dog at his feet. Which it did soon enough, the age-old disdain with which the badge-carrying professionals view the interfering amateurs coming through in a challenge.

'Tell me what you think.'

'A number of things. The location where Sanders' car was found doesn't make sense. His cell phone was missing and never found. Most importantly, there's no DNA report on the man who was handcuffed in the back of the plane. His blood and skin tissue would've been all over the handcuff around his wrist. As a result, he was never identified. Nothing that might be expected to be on a plane owned by a man like Esteban Aguilar was recovered from the wreckage. I think that's about it.'

Bordelon smiled at him, a knowing, pitying look in his eyes.

'And you choose to stick your nose into a mess like that? It was my job.'

'It's mine, too.'

Bordelon nodded. Acceptance that he'd failed to acknowledge that fact. Even if he felt that he had to have the last word.

'Except you get to choose which jobs you take on.'

'True. But not in this case. I owe Arlo Fraser's old man.'

'That must be one hell of a debt.'

'Big enough.'

Bordelon studied him a minute longer until it became clear Evan wasn't about to volunteer what the debt entailed.

'Ask your questions.'

'Start with the cell phone. You got the call logs from the cellular carrier?'

'Uh-huh. Everything you'd expect to see. Wife, work, friends. Including a call received from Kevin Clark on the day in question which confirmed Clark's story that he'd begged off at the last minute due to a knee injury.'

'Or he could have been altering the time they'd agreed to meet.'

'He could. We got the impression he was telling the truth, that he cancelled.'

Evan accepted it. If he'd wanted to bring the interview to an early conclusion, he could've pointed out that Kevin Clark might have lied—in effect questioning Bordelon's professional judgment.

'I get the impression there were other calls you might not have expected.'

Bordelon gave a long, slow nod.

'Yep. He'd made and received a number of calls, including on the day he was killed, to and from a number which later turned out to be a burner.'

'Was the call on the day before or after Kevin Clark's?'

'After.'

'Meaning he made an arrangement with the burner's owner after Clark cancelled. The fact that it was a burner suggests it wasn't another male friend. He was having an affair and called her. They met in the Texaco gas station and drove to the Atchafalaya wildlife refuge in her car.'

Bordelon nodded again.

'That was the conclusion I came to, yeah.'

'But you never said anything to his widow?'

'No.' It was only one short word. But the way he said it implied a lot of thought had gone into making the decision. 'We might have, if the investigation hadn't been shut down prematurely. The fact that the other party felt the need to use a burner and Sanders didn't suggests that his wife was the trusting kind. Not the sort of woman to go through her husband's phone. At the time, we thought we'd spare the recently bereaved widow a grilling over whether she had any suspicions about her husband's infidelity in the weeks or months preceding his death until it became unavoidable.'

Evan agreed that when he put it like that, he'd have done the same.

'Have you been to her house?'

'Not in the past five years,' Bordelon said.

'There's a shrine to him in her living room. And she keeps his wedding ring on a chain around her neck.'

'Then I'm glad one good thing came out of the investigation being shut down. Getting back on track, it looked like Sanders arranged to meet his lover at the gas station and she drove them to the Atchafalaya wildlife refuge. Then what?'

'They set off hiking together, obviously. Whatever they might have done in the car or on a blanket on the ground when they got there, she wouldn't have waited in the car while he went hiking. That means they were together when the plane came down. They went to investigate—'

'Or he went to investigate while she went back to the car to drive to where she had a signal to call it in.'

'And then left him there?'

Bordelon shrugged, as much as his fused spine allowed him.

'Just sayin'.'

'Okay. Let's talk it through my way first. They go to investigate together. He says *wait there* while he goes in the plane. He's the paramedic, after all. And he's worried the plane might explode. He goes in, uncuffs the passenger-prisoner who then shoots him and the pilot. She hears three shots and runs for her life.'

Bordelon held up a hand, clearly enjoying his role as devil's advocate.

'She doesn't hide in the bushes? Wait for the killer to come out and get the hell out of there, then go to see what's happened to lover boy? He might not be dead, after all.'

'That's some cojones. Especially for a woman.'

'Unless she was a man. What if Sanders discovered he bats for the other side, trapped in a marriage to a woman he no longer loves? He's having an affair with another fruit until he decides to come out.'

Evan almost laughed. Came out with Bordelon's next line for him.

'You're just sayin'.'

'I am. Carry on.'

'She runs for her life, gets back to the car and escapes. Doesn't call it in because she wants to keep the affair secret. Most likely because she's also married. That fits with the secret burner phone. Not only that, what's she going to tell you? I heard three shots and ran for my life. I didn't see anyone. Sorry.'

Bordelon held up his hand again.

'We're doing exactly what we were doing back then. Talking around and around in circles. What if, what if, what if? The mystery lover was a dead end. Apart from grilling his wife about it, that is. We asked his buddy Kevin about it. He said as far as he knew, his friend Justin was blissfully married to the woman of his dreams. Was it true? Was he just being a good friend? Wanted to protect the wife? You tell me.'

Bordelon went to push himself up, grimaced. Settled back again.

'You mind getting me a glass of water and some painkillers?

They're on the kitchen counter.'

Evan hopped to it, found them easily enough. There was at least a dozen still left in the packet. It was better to send his wife out to get more before they ran out completely, but even so. He got an uncomfortable feeling Bordelon had used it as an excuse to get his wife out of the house. To ensure that she wasn't there when they discussed the case.

He carried the water and pills back into the living room, handed them to Bordelon. Went to sit down again himself.

'Before you sit down,' Bordelon said, pointing at a display cabinet against the wall. 'Fetch me the photograph in the frame over there. The one on the left.'

Evan did so. It showed a very similar-looking dog to the one at Bordelon's feet. In the back yard that Evan could currently see through the window. Looking like it was ready to play. Tongue lolling out, a drool-soaked tennis ball on the ground in front of it. The sort of unfair game dogs like to play. See who can get to it first when they're already twice as close.

Bordelon took a minute to look at the photograph, his eyes out of focus.

'She was this little guy's mother,' he said, nudging the dog at his feet with his foot. 'We couldn't have children. Decided we didn't want to adopt. Friends of ours did, and it was an absolute nightmare. We have dogs instead.' He held the photograph out to Evan. 'You hold onto that for a minute.'

Evan took it, not liking the feel of the way things were moving.

'Let's move on from the phone and the mystery lover, male or female,' Bordelon said. 'Concentrate on the missing DNA report. You feel like asking me something stupid and insulting?'

Evan was happy to oblige.

'You did collect samples from the handcuffs and send them off to the lab, didn't you?'

'Absolutely. You don't often get blood and skin tissue left so conveniently for you. So, what happened?'

Evan made an easy guess. Pointed upwards.

'Someone further up the food chain took it?'

'Yep. We sent it off. Nothing came back. We called them. We know you're busy, but hey, how long is the backlog? And they said no backlog, we sent it back to some big swinging dick in Baton Rouge weeks ago. We followed it up. Got told that we'd wandered into the realms of an investigation that was way above our pay grade. We had one unidentified missing person who might be responsible for two homicides. They had the whole of southern Louisiana's organized crime network to worry about. Thanks for calling.'

He downed what was left of the water after he'd taken the painkillers, put the glass carefully on the table beside his seat.

'You've gotten this far, I figure it says something about you. You're the sort of man who won't have a problem telling me what sort of a man I am.'

'You don't like to be told, *no*.'

'Exactly.' He took a deep breath as if he needed to calm himself just at the memory of it. 'We were told to drop it. The burner phone mystery lover thing wasn't going anywhere. The only thing that was, the missing passenger's DNA, was now officially not our problem. I thought, okay, I'll come at it from a different angle.'

'Different as in unofficial?'

Bordelon rocked his hand.

'More like unsanctioned. Seeing as we had Señor Aguilar in the mix, I talked to a guy I know in the Baton Rouge PD vice squad. Word obviously got around. That's when the shit hit the fan.'

He put his hands on the arms of his chair, pushed himself painfully to his feet. Evan felt a coldness settle in his stomach that whatever it was that was coming, it wasn't a simple task like fetching pills that he could ask Evan to do for him.

'Come with me. And bring the photograph with you.'

Evan followed him down the hall towards the front door. When he'd answered the door, Bordelon had looked as if he was strapped to a piece of lumber. Now he looked as if that lumber had been broken in two.

Bordelon opened the door and they both stepped out onto the front step. Unlike Fleur Sanders' house, Bordelon's got the sun on the front of the house. It was a beautiful morning. Warm, not too hot, not too sticky.

Evan got an uneasy premonition it wasn't going to stay beautiful for much longer.

'I was a good detective,' Bordelon said, jabbing his breastbone with his middle finger. 'Even if I do say so myself. I was meticulous. Never cut corners. Not ever.' He reached out, ran his fingertips down the front door's paintwork. 'But I'm the world's worst at painting. The exact opposite of what I'm like at work. I haven't got the patience for the prep. I can't be bothered with sanding down the old paint, filling all the cracks and holes. I just slap it on.' He mimicked running a paintbrush up and down the door in big long strokes. 'Give me your hand and stick out your finger.'

Evan did so, liking the way things were going even less, the knot in his stomach tightening. He let his arm go limp so that Bordelon had control of his movements, the photograph still in his other hand.

'Feel that?' Bordelon said, holding Evan's index finger over a hole that had been painted but not filled beforehand. 'Now you tell me what connects what you've got in your two hands.'

Evan bit down and swallowed hard. He did not want to say the words that refused to come.

Bordelon was staring at him like he was the man who'd done

it, the rage in him shaking both their arms.

'Some sick bastard nailed your dog to the door,' Evan said, his voice tainted with something beyond horror, beyond revulsion.

Bordelon was no longer with him. Forever lost in a place where he lived alone with his rage and his memories and his dreams of vengeance. Still holding Evan's finger to the hole in the door, he put his own finger in the hollow between his collar bones, his words striking at Evan like a blade.

'A six-inch nail through her neck. My wife found her. Had to leave her there until I got home as her blood ran down the door. Now you know why I sent her on a bullshit errand to replace the pills I flushed down the toilet after I spoke to you on the phone.'

He let go of Evan's hand. Took the photograph from him. Didn't, couldn't look at it. Evan trailed after him back into the house. Bordelon threw himself into his chair as if he was trying to maximize his pain. The spasm that twisted his face suggested he'd achieved his aim.

Evan waited for him to continue—if there was anything left to say.

When at last he spoke again, Bordelon sounded as if he was ready to meet his maker, forget about a bad back.

'The story about compromising a bigger case was bullshit. Someone didn't want the identity of the passenger becoming known. That person, who necessarily has some considerable clout, pulled strings and effectively buried the DNA results. Somehow, word also got back to that person that I wasn't playing ball. A message was sent. I heard it loud and clear. A friend had been bugging me for a long time to get out like he had, make some proper money in the private sector. And I thought, fuck it, I don't need this shit in my life. I got out. And apart from every time I walk through my own front door, I never gave it another thought.'

39

Bordelon suddenly cocked his ear towards the front of the house, a look on his face as if his back had gone into spasm.

'*Shit!* My wife's back.'

He looked around, eyes darting here and there. As if he was looking for somewhere to hide Evan. Failing that, about to tell him to run out the back door.

'Let me handle this,' Bordelon said as they heard the sound of a key in the front-door lock.

Evan shrugged his agreement. They waited together in silence feeling like a pair of naughty schoolchildren outside the principal's office.

'Nurse Kathleen is home with the patient's medication,' rang out as the door opened, a happy, playful note to the voice—one which both men knew would change all too soon.

The next words weren't quite so cheerful.

'Some idiot's parked right outside the house. Almost blocking the driveway.'

She appeared in the doorway then. Startled at the sight of Evan getting up out of his chair. Then smiled—something else that would soon be absent.

'*Oh!* Sorry. That must be you.'

She came into the room, couldn't fail to pick up on the atmosphere. In line with what they'd been discussing, it didn't feel like two guys talking about football—or even women.

'Kathleen, this is Evan Buckley,' Bordelon said.

Evan didn't miss how incomplete the introduction was. The lack of a qualifier along the lines of *he's an old friend* advertising that the full facts were being deliberately withheld.

Kathleen picked up on it immediately. Now looking at Evan as if he was from the bank and was in their house to foreclose on them. Despite that, her tone remained politely neutral as they shook hands.

'I'm sorry, I can't remember Lou ever mentioning your name. How do you know each other?'

'Evan joined the company recently,' Bordelon chipped in before Evan could think of what to say. 'Something's come up at work.'

Kathleen immediately took on the demeanor of a woman who was sick to the back teeth of her husband's work intruding on their home life.

'Really? It must be important if it couldn't wait until tomorrow. Or be dealt with over the phone. I hope old Mr. Wright hasn't been kidnapped.'

Evan glanced at Bordelon for help. Wondering exactly how deep a hole the guy was going to dig.

Didn't matter. It was already too late.

Kathleen turned to him as if Bordelon had just handed him the shovel. Except she didn't put him on the spot, ask him what the problem was.

She had a secret to share with him.

'I probably shouldn't be telling you this because it wouldn't look good if it got spread all around the company. My husband thinks I'm stupid. We've been married twenty-six years and yet he acts like you live here with him and I'm the one who he's just met for the first time in his life. He thinks I can't see the look on his face.' She spun around to face Bordelon looking very uncomfortable in his chair. 'Yes, *that* look. You think I don't know what that look means?' She drew back her arm, hurled the packet of painkillers at his head. Bordelon didn't move, let the packet bounce off and onto the floor. '*Jesus Christ, Lou!* What do you think you're doing? Wasn't that enough for you?' Her arm rigid, quivering, pointing towards the front door.

The small brown dog had run to greet her when she came into the room. Up on his hind legs, front paws on her thighs. Tail wagging like he was attempting to lift off and lick her face.

He backed away now as her voice rose. Hiding behind Bordelon's legs as she pointed at him like he'd eaten their dinner she'd left on the kitchen counter.

'You want him nailed to the front door, too? Do you? I can't believe this is happening.'

Evan wished Bordelon had managed to dig a bigger hole. One that he could jump into now, pull the dirt in on top of him. Sadly, there was no escaping his duty.

'It's my fault, Mrs. Bordelon.'

She turned on him, tears in her eyes.

'No, it's not. It's *his* fault. You're just doing your job. *He* should have told you to get lost when you called or turned up at the door.'

He saw the realization dawn in her eyes then. That it was actually worse than she'd imagined. She went back to her husband, anger taking a bigger role in her voice.

'You sent me out of the house because you knew he was coming to talk about this. I can't believe you did that. Not only are you bringing all this down on our heads again, you were going to hide it from me.' She pointed at the cowering dog again. 'What were you going to say when I came home and found him nailed to the front door? Sorry, I forgot to mention it.'

Evan had been wondering if Bordelon would ever speak again. His wife, he knew best. He made an attempt now and even Evan knew it was going to be something stupid.

'I was trying—'

'Don't you dare. Don't you dare say you were trying to protect me. I fail to see how you doing anything other than telling this man and anybody else who comes looking to just leave us alone is in any way protecting me.'

The word *protecting* came out as a scream. Sent the dog high-tailing it out of the room. It left her drained, visibly slumping. All the anger and disbelief and fear was gone from her voice, only a resigned bone-deep sadness left behind.

'I'm going out. I can't stay here in the house while you discuss this. I know I'm wasting my breath, but I don't have to sit here and listen to it. I'm certainly not going to play at being the dutiful wife and serve you coffee and cookies while you discuss the quickest way to ruin our lives.'

She stared at her husband for a long while. Challenging him to say something in his defense before heading for the door. Her parting words were for Evan.

'Don't be here when I get back, Mr. . . . whatever your name is.'

Harbinger of doom? he thought, and kept to himself.

Neither man said anything as they waited for the sound of the front door closing. Except it didn't happen. Kathleen came back into the room, what she had to say for Evan's benefit once more—even if she was looking at Bordelon as she said it.

'I don't suppose you'll be surprised by this, but he's still got the nail that was used to . . .' She waved vaguely towards the front door. 'I won't have it in the house. But I know he's still got it somewhere. I don't know what that says about my husband. In fact, I don't think I understand men at all.'

And I don't want to drifted back before the front door banged shut a minute later, hard enough to rattle the windows.

Evan was the first to recover.

'Sorry. I shouldn't have come.'

Bordelon waved it off.

'It's not your fault. I made the decision to talk to you. If it hadn't been for my back and I could drive, I'd have met you somewhere else. Except I wanted you to see the front door, so maybe this was always going to happen. You can't run or hide forever. I plan to use that nail. I've filed it and sharpened it and polished it. I think about where I'm gonna put it when I catch up with the sick bastard every single day. There are lots of choices.'

'And you don't need to limit yourself to one.'

'I surely don't. Anything I can do to help, just say the word.'

To that end, Bordelon pushed himself out of his chair, went to get the key to the shed at the bottom of the back yard. It looked to Evan like he was moving a lot easier. The promise of approaching payback can do that to a person, forget about anti-inflammatory pills and painkillers.

In the shed-cum-man cave, Bordelon showed him the nail first. Told him to go ahead and test the point with his finger. It was as sharp as it was shiny.

Bordelon lifted down an old shoe box from a high shelf as Evan pricked his thumb, wondering how long it would take Bordelon to make another one like it for him. He wasn't surprised to see copies of the original file inside the box. Bordelon gave him the name of his vice squad contact—the same detective, Gauthier, that Evan had spoken to when calling about Ritter, as he'd known it would be.

'You look as if the name means something to you,' Bordelon said.

Evan forced out a laugh he was sure sounded as strained and false to Bordelon as it did in his own head.

'I'd be a lot further forward than I feel like I am if it did.'

There was no way he wanted to tell Bordelon that he'd had Ritter—one of the top contenders for the sicko who'd nailed Bordelon's dog to his front door—at his mercy and had let him go.

Bordelon didn't need that, not right now.

That wasn't all.

If he told Bordelon about it, the guy would immediately call Gauthier. They likely still had Ritter in custody or under guard at the hospital. All Bordelon could tell Gauthier was that he suspected Ritter of killing his dog in a sadistic cruel way. No proof. No witnesses. All it would achieve would be to alert Ritter to the fact that Bordelon was onto him. Nor would Bordelon approaching Gauthier through the official channels help him any when something bad and definitely cruel and sadistic happened to Ritter shortly thereafter.

In addition to Gauthier's private cell phone number, Bordelon gave Evan the contact details for Kevin Clark. Evan had already made a note of them after finding them for himself in his copy of the file. It was more to give Bordelon the opportunity to reiterate what he'd said earlier.

'We thought he was telling the truth at the time. He cancelled due to a genuine knee injury. Was he lying and he fooled us? Was the work colleague who vouched for him lying? I was a good detective, but I'm not infallible.'

Evan glanced at the address Bordelon had given him as Bordelon spoke. He was sure it wasn't the same address he'd copied from the file earlier. Bordelon saw the confusion on his face.

'You noticed that, huh? Clark moved about three months after we first spoke to him. The case had already been shut down by then and the file wasn't updated. But the guys knew I was still interested. They gave me a call, asked me if I wanted the new address. I took it. I doubt it means anything to you, but it's a much nicer neighborhood than he was living in. The place he was living at the time Sanders was killed was a real shithole. Perhaps he got a pay raise. Or he came into money some other way.' He opened his hands wide. 'Is it suspicious? Who knows. Like I said, everything was shut down by then and I wasn't in the right place'—tapping his temple with his middle finger a couple times—'to think about doing something about it myself.'

The talk of addresses reminded Evan of the second address he'd found in Ritter's phone that he hadn't yet identified—and the reason Landry accused Ritter for having it on him.

'Do you know Deputy Mercer well?'

The change in direction put a temporary crease in Bordelon's brow, swiftly pushed aside by a scowl as he remembered Evan telling him it was Mercer who'd pulled the file for Arlo.

'Not as well as I used to before I quit.'

'Has he got any family?'

'A son. Luke. Married with a couple of kids. Why?'

Evan pulled out his wallet. Found the slip of paper he'd copied the address onto the previous evening mindful that he didn't want to show anyone Ritter's phone.

'Is that his address?'

Bordelon studied the slip of paper briefly, a small crease in his brow.

'I think so. Why?'

Standing shoulder to shoulder with Bordelon in his small shed having recently admired the sharpened nail with Ritter's name on it, Evan felt bad for deceiving him now. But Ritter was no longer an immediate threat. And he was determined not to mention him at this point, jeopardize the chances of a more satisfying outcome later.

He fell back on the excuse Ritter himself had used.

'I found it when I was trying to trace Mercer. Then Ralph Fontenot took me to a different address.'

He shrugged, mystery solved.

For the life of him he couldn't have said whether Bordelon believed him or not. The guy walked him back to his car either way—and it wasn't parked across the driveway at all.

'I can't tell you how much I wish I could get involved with you.' Fists clenching and unclenching at his sides as he said it. Then he put his hand on Evan's shoulder. 'Don't feel bad about the way my wife reacted. Shit happens and sometimes it's nobody's fault.'

Just not this time Evan thought as he got in and drove away. Good detective or not, the guy didn't know jack shit about guilt.

40

Due to the potential awkwardness that might result when he met Detective Gauthier—awkwardness that could extend to him ending up in jail on suspicion of shooting Ritter—Evan decided to talk to Kevin Clark first.

The address Bordelon had given him was also closer.

As Bordelon had implied, Clark had moved to an obviously affluent neighborhood. River Ranch was what realtors liked to call a *village* lying south of the Vermilion River. The house itself was a brick and stucco single family home with a steeply pitched gable and turquoise shutters. There were neatly-clipped bushes in the front yard and a large two-car garage on the side, all set behind a quaint picket fence. A shithole it was not, and nobody could be faulted for questioning Clark's sudden change in circumstances.

Evan didn't know if the woman who answered the door was the same woman Kevin Clark had brought along to the night out with Justin and Fleur Sanders—the woman Fleur had described as *not being her sort of person*.

If she was, he could understand the comment. He wasn't

sure if she was his kind of person, although she was obviously somebody's.

She was mid-thirties, tall with long jet-black hair and piercings in places he could see that made him not want to think about the piercings she no doubt had in the places he couldn't see—even if the tight white T-shirt she was wearing tucked into her even-tighter jeans meant he could almost see them. And tattoos. Lots of them, again in places he could see and no doubt in those he couldn't. It made his eyes water.

He imagined mouse-like Fleur's horror at being introduced to her. Somehow, he couldn't picture them having an animated heads-together chat about favorite plants and the best way of dealing with troublesome weeds.

Enough being judgmental.

He introduced himself and got straight to it.

'I was hoping to talk to Kevin Clark. This is the last address I've got for him.'

That's what he thought he said. She looked at him as if he'd told her that scientific research had proven conclusively that every piercing knocked a year off your life.

He tried again when she failed to say anything.

'Does he still live here?'

She cleared her throat. Made an effort to pull herself together.

'He's dead. He died four years ago.'

Evan couldn't stop himself from doing the math—one year after Justin Sanders had been shot to death. On the face of it, a time span too long to link the two deaths—but that's exactly what he'd been thinking as soon as he heard the word *dead*. He wasn't sure if that said something about him or the world he lived in.

'Were you his girlfriend?' Congratulating himself for remembering that Fleur had told him Kevin had been single.

'Yeah. We'd only been together about nine months when he was killed.'

Two conflicting emotions immediately registered in Evan's mind.

His interest peaked as the word *died* changed to *killed*. Then it slumped again as he subconsciously did the math a second time. They'd met three months after Justin Sanders was killed. Kevin hadn't been with this woman at the time.

'What did you want to talk to him about?' she said.

He'd been about to apologize for disturbing her, ask her a quick question about whether she'd been approached by Arlo—which currently seemed very unlikely—then think about calling Detective Gauthier for a hopefully more productive meeting. Her question stopped him from doing so. Because he got the feeling she already knew.

First, he needed to confirm his suspicions about Arlo.

'Before I get into that, did a young guy called Arlo Fraser come looking for Kevin?'

'No. You're the first.'

'Did he call you at all? Make any contact?'

'No, nothing. I've never heard the name before.'

It made sense. Arlo only had Kevin Clark's old address, the one he'd found in the police file. There was no way he could have found his own way to Kevin's girlfriend's door. Bordelon hadn't given him the updated address, the only reason Evan was here now.

It meant Arlo had disappeared at some point after talking to Fleur Sanders.

'What did you want to talk to Kev about?' the girlfriend repeated, sounding as if the door would be shutting in Evan's face any time now if he didn't give her an answer. He kept it vague to test his suspicion that she already knew.

'About an incident that happened five years ago.'

'You mean his friend Justin being killed?'

'Uh-huh. You know about that?'

She laughed like it was the stupidest question she'd ever heard.

'Of course. It was only three months before we met. He was still a bit shell-shocked. It's not everybody who has a good friend who gets shot twice in the chest and nobody's ever caught. It tends to come out in the conversation when you've finished talking about favorite movies and where you like to go on vacation.'

Again, it made sense. Particularly what she said about being shell-shocked. He figured Kevin had played the *what-if* game a thousand times, alone and with her.

What if my knee hadn't been injured? Would I be dead, too?

'Do you want to come in?' she said, already moving to one side to let him past. 'My name's Jane, by the way.'

Plain's one thing you're not, he thought as he went past her, then followed her directions to the right and into a large sitting room full of old-fashioned furniture very much at odds with its owner.

Seemed she read his mind, or people who knew her better had commented before.

'My parents gave the house to me when dad retired and they moved to Florida. I've never bothered to change the furniture. So long as it's comfortable I don't really care what it looks like.'

He could only think she didn't apply the same logic to her appearance, kept the thought to himself. It was time to say something with a strong sexist bias behind it.

'So the house was always yours? Kevin lived here with you.'

She grinned at him. At least she didn't have pierced or tattooed teeth.

'Disgraceful, isn't it? A kept man. Against the natural order of the world.'

'It didn't take him long to move in.'

'You didn't see the shithole he was living in. I only saw it once. That was enough. He was renting. I suggested he move in with me.'

'Big risk with someone you've only just met.'

'Not necessarily. Things felt right. And they were, until he was killed.' She smiled again. This time there was more sadness behind it. 'I can see you're not convinced. The thing is, Kev had money problems. He had no problem earning it. It was keeping ahold of it. You know the Evangeline Downs Racetrack & Casino in Opelousas?'

'I know of it.' He didn't, but it was better than telling her that he was from out of town and potentially getting into a discussion about his involvement.

She nodded approvingly.

'That's the best way to keep it. I figure Kev kept them afloat single-handedly. He should've had his salary paid directly into their bank account. Save himself the time and gas driving twenty-something miles there and back to achieve the same result. The thing is, he had a *system*.'

If there was a way to work more contempt into a word, Evan would've liked to know what it was. She then surpassed herself with what came next.

'It was *foolproof*.' Throwing her hands in the air as she said it. Then a mock admiring dip of her head. 'And it was. Kev had a one-hundred-percent-foolproof system for losing money hand over fist. He was about to be thrown out on the street when I said he could move in with me.'

Just as she'd escalated the bitterness in the words *system* and *foolproof*, she took the sadness behind her smile to a new level.

'I thought I could help change him. But you can't. It's an addiction like any other. He even went to Gamblers Anonymous for a while although I think that was only to get me off his case.'

She waved the remark away immediately. 'No, that's not fair. There was a woman there who he said was very helpful. I ought to be able to remember her name, but I can't. Not that it matters. It was only temporary. The only thing moving in with me achieved in the long run was to allow him to gamble with what little money he used for rent beforehand.'

On the subject of gambling, Evan would've liked the ability to read the future as accurately when it came to doing the lottery as he did now, knowing what was coming. She knew that he knew, too.

'You won't be surprised when I tell you that it wasn't only Evangeline Downs where he threw his money away betting on three-legged horses and rigged roulette wheels.'

'Places owned by the sort of people who take your unpaid debts in body parts?'

'That's them. He was in deep shit with some really nasty people. I don't know whether it's a good or a bad thing that he was killed before they got a chance to start chopping off fingers.'

The random choice of body part she chose to illustrate her point made him glance involuntarily at his left hand. At the empty space where the top section of his little finger ought to be. She caught the glance, fast as it was, looked herself.

'Looks like you've come across people like them yourself,' she said.

'A lot worse, I'm afraid. You want to tell me what happened to Kev?'

From her face, it was clear what she wanted was for him to explain the remark. She sighed when it became obvious he wasn't about to.

'You mind if we go for a walk while we talk? I feel like I need some fresh air.'

He waited while she fetched a faded denim jacket and tied her hair in a loose ponytail at the nape of her neck. They left the house, and despite knowing he was still in the hospital or the police station, Evan couldn't stop himself from scanning the street, half-expecting to see Ritter watching them from a parked car. Or if not him, Innocent Lejeune.

She set off at a brisk pace, sufficient to make him wonder if she'd be able to talk and walk for any length of time.

'He was found dead in a sleazy motel room in Lafayette,' she said. 'Cause of death was autoerotic asphyxia. I know the definition by heart. Accidental death occurring during individual, usually solitary, sexual activity that results from a failure of devices, or an unexpected effect of tools that are used to enhance the sexual experience.'

It crossed his mind as she talked that she'd wanted to come outside in order for them to walk side by side. Not facing each other across her sitting room, having to look at the floor if things got too embarrassing.

She raised a finger as they kept going, an important point to be made.

'There are two types. There are *typical* autoerotic fatalities. Want to guess what they are? And it's not typical because it's the sort of thing your average housewife would do?'

'That's what I was going to suggest.'

'Liar. Typical means it involves mechanical compression of the neck, chest or abdomen. The other kind is *atypical*. That doesn't mean it's the sort of thing supposed freaks like Kev liked to do. It involves using other things to enhance your orgasm. Normally gas and chemical substances.'

Had it not been such a raw nerve, her words so bitter and sarcastic, he might have asked if there was going to be a test at the end.

'Kev was typical,' she said, increasing her pace as she said it, her breath coming faster as if she wanted to replicate what she said next. 'He was wearing a used gas mask and a plastic bag over his head. The opening of the bag was loosely secured around his neck with his belt. Gay porn mags and DVDs and adult toys were found in the room. There were pictures of freaks wearing gas masks and rubber suits on a burner phone. Cause of death was suffocation caused by the plastic bag covering the mask's ventilation. The coroner's verdict said it was an accident.'

She stopped abruptly, turned to face him. Breathing heavily, hands on her hips as if they were having a heated domestic argument in the street.

'I can tell you, Kev did *not* go to a shitty motel room in Lafayette, put on a gas mask and plastic bag and then suffocate while jerking off to gay porn. But that's what the police said happened. Case closed. Do you want the gas mask and the plastic bag when we've finished with them, madam?'

She started walking again, at a more leisurely pace this time. He could feel that there was more, waited for her to continue.

'I told them their story was crap. They wanted it both ways. What they actually said was that I was refusing to accept the truth that my boyfriend was a sexual deviant. Except the way they were looking at me suggested what they really thought was that someone looking like me with piercings and tattoos would be into all that shit and ought to understand how it happened. Like I forgot to warn him to be careful when I gave him the money to buy the gas mask and pay for the motel room.'

She lapsed into an uncomfortable seething silence. He waited until they'd walked on for a short while and he felt her relax slightly before he asked the obvious question.

'What do you think happened?'

'Someone else was there with him. Traces of the date rape drug GHB were found in his system. Their answer to that was that Kev took it voluntarily because it increases your sex drive. They said there was no evidence of anyone else being in the room with him.' She gave him a look like he was saying it to her now. 'That has got to be the stupidest thing ever to say about a no-tell motel that charges by the hour. At least be honest. Admit they haven't got a chance of tracing the five hundred different people's DNA that would've been on the sheets since they last washed them. According to them, if there had been another person, it was most likely another deviant who picked him up. They showed me a grainy CCTV image of a man who they thought might have been in the room. Like they're expecting me to say, yeah, that's Kev's friend Pete the pervert. Then they said that even if he was in the room, it was consensual and it was still a tragic accident. Except they didn't say *tragic*, of course. More like one dead deviant isn't as many as we'd like, but it's a start.'

The more she talked, the more Evan felt sorry for the investigating officers. He was talking to her four years after the event. He couldn't imagine what she'd been like back then. He couldn't blame her, either. What he was more interested in was whether it was linked in any way to Justin Sanders' death.

'If we assume Kev was murdered, who by, and why?'

The questions warranted another stop. Or she was getting tired. Again, she faced him, but without the hands on the hips this time.

'By the person his friend Justin was having an affair with.' She paused, dropped her eyes momentarily. 'Kev wasn't a deviant sex freak. But he wasn't an angel, either. He had a gambling problem. I know he stole money from my purse at least once. I think he tried to blackmail the person and they killed him.'

Evan didn't miss the use of the non-gender-specific *they*. He was immediately reminded of what Bordelon had said, albeit while playing devil's advocate.

Unless she was a man. What if Sanders discovered he bats for the other side, trapped in a marriage to a woman he no longer loves?

'You're suggesting it could be a man or a woman?'

She nodded, why not?

'It's possible. I read up on all this stuff after it happened. It's almost exclusively men who are into all that autoerotic shit. It's possible that a woman bought the gas mask and the mags and the DVDs and all the rest of it, but I don't think you should rule out the chance that it was a man. It wouldn't even cross my mind to think of it. I think most women would be the same.'

'Whereas it's the first thing most men think of?'

She laughed, a sound full of genuine amusement, lacking the bitter irony behind so much of what she'd said.

'You tell me.'

He wagged a finger at her instead, about to move on when he stopped. There was something about her conviction that the person she believed Kevin had tried to blackmail could have been a man—and it wasn't only that men participated in autoerotic rituals more than women.

'I get the feeling there's more to you thinking it could be a man.'

Her smile was more wistful when it came again, thinking about her own imperfect man.

'Kev wasn't the most politically-correct person on the planet. And he had a warped sense of humor at times. He told me that getting shot twice in the chest wasn't the worst thing he knew about Justin. He thought he might also be gay. He said as far as he was concerned, it would be worse to be gay than dead. I never knew if he really meant it.'

'What made him think it?'

'They were talking one time . . .'

Evan stopped her immediately.

'No man tells another man he thinks he might be gay.'

She raised a finger, cocked her ear.

'Was that a dinosaur roaring I just heard? Besides, I didn't say that. They were talking, and Justin told him how a guy tried to pick him up in a bar one time. Justin claimed he told the guy to get lost before he kicked his queer ass all the way down the street. Kev thought he was being too aggressive to cover up the fact that he'd been tempted to try it.'

It was too dependent on Kevin Clark's supposed homophobic attitudes for Evan to take it seriously. He backed up.

'How do you know Justin was having an affair at all?'

'Kev told me.'

'Okay. How did he know?'

Her mouth turned down at the question. The way she looked at him made him feel guilty for being a man.

'Because he covered for Justin. A lot of the times when Justin told his wife he was with Kev, he was with his lover. Kev knew that as soon as he cancelled because of his knee, Justin would be on the phone to them.'

He held up a hand to stop her, the ambiguity irritating him.

'Did Kev know if this person was male or female?'

'He must have. But we were both drunk and a bit high when he told me all this. He didn't mention any names. Or if he did, I didn't remember in the morning. To tell you the truth, I thought I might have dreamed it. I didn't ask him about it. He had a hangover and was in a filthy mood. Like he'd get when he lost a ton of money. I knew when not to ask a bunch of questions. I figured he was regretting saying as much as he did. It didn't exactly say anything good about him or his cheating friend, Justin.'

'What exactly did he tell you?'

'That this person was with Justin when he found the plane. The fact that Justin was shot to death suggested something illegal was going on. Most likely drugs. Kev figured the lover hid until the guy who shot Justin escaped, then went back to the plane and found something. He didn't come right out and say he was going to blackmail them. It was more like he'd suddenly found the answer to all his money problems. Kev hadn't said anything to the police about Justin's lover at the time because he was trying to protect his wife. Not make it worse for her than it already was. I think he was genuine about that. But fear concentrates the mind. Later, when he was in debt to the gangsters, he realized he had this big secret he could use to make money. He was a good man, but money does things to people.'

Neither of them needed to say what was hanging in the air between them.

And he paid the price for his mistake.

'Did you say anything about Justin's affair to the cops when Kev was killed?'

She shook her head, a weary sigh on her lips that spoke of a lesson already learned about trying to tell cops how to do their jobs.

'No. What was the point?'

Evan couldn't disagree with her. It was easy to imagine the exchange.

You believe Justin Sanders was having an affair, do you madam?
That's right.
With a man or a woman?
Either.
Do you have a name? First or last?
Neither.
And how did you learn of the alleged affair?
Kev told me.
In what circumstances?
When we were both drunk.
Just drunk?
No. High as well.
And you believe Kevin was killed to protect the identity of the

unidentified man or woman allegedly having an affair with the now-deceased Justin Sanders?

And because he wanted a share of the drug money.

Drug money?

That's right.

Are you drunk or high on drugs at the moment, madam?

If he hadn't spent the last few days unearthing information that supported her theory, he'd have sided with the cops.

HE THOUGHT ABOUT WHAT HE'D LEARNED—OR NOT—FROM HIS visit to Jane as he drove away. She clearly believed her story, and reserved a special, caustic loathing for anyone—the cops, basically—who did not.

It was also plausible.

The biggest weakness was that the prisoner-passenger had escaped and left the money or drugs behind. How likely was that? He would've been injured in the crash. It was a case of how badly. His cuffed wrist or arm might have been broken on impact. Perhaps the bag was too heavy to carry and he didn't want to slow himself down as he ran from the scene of the double murder he'd just committed. None of it actually mattered. All that was needed was that Kevin Clark believed the guy left it behind and Justin Sanders' lover found it.

Jane so desperately wanted to believe it. That the man she'd taken pity on and taken into her home when he was at rock bottom wasn't a sexual deviant. He was simply a regular guy driven by fear into becoming a blackmailer, extorting a person who had no more right than he did to the illegal cash or drugs they'd found.

Jane wasn't aware of Ritter's existence, either.

Lucky Jane.

Evan figured there was a good chance Ritter was behind

Kevin Clark's death. He could imagine a man who was able to nail a living dog to a wooden door suffocating a man with a plastic bag while he watched him die. Whatever the video contained that Ritter was trying to find, it implied more than a passing acquaintance with the seedier side of life. A staged autoerotic asphyxiation accident might well be the first thing to cross the twisted mind of such a loathsome man.

That didn't mean he should ignore the lover angle. The question was what to do about it. He had nothing to go on.

Or did he?

He glanced over his shoulder at the back seat. Justin Sanders' sports duffel bag was still where he'd thrown it after smashing Innocent Lejeune's windshield, the wrecking bar inside it. The bag Justin took with him to the gym three, four, five times a week while his wife tended her garden. The gym where he may well have met the person who became his lover. He pulled to the curb, reached around and grabbed it, dumped it on his lap.

He could hear the answer calling to him from inside.

I'm in here.

He could almost taste it, the truth tingling on his tongue.

Then Stan Fraser called him.

41

'I've found someone in Baton Rouge who's agreed to talk to you about the beaner, Aguilar,' Fraser said. 'With any luck he knows something about the other guy, Ritter, too. Pick up Landry and get your ass over there.'

'Don't you trust me?'

'Of course I trust you. But you don't know where to go.'

'You can tell me now.'

Fraser laughed, a mirthless sound without humor.

'Nice try. Trouble is, I don't want your psychotic friend Guillory kicking me in the balls if the big bad criminals I send you to talk to hurt you or make you cry.'

'He's babysitting me?'

Fraser laughed again, more humor in it this time at Evan's displeasure.

'Call it backup, if it makes you feel better. Now call him. He's got the location.'

Evan ended the call, not sure how he felt about Landry babysitting him. He called the guy anyway, threw the sports bag on the back seat again as he waited for Landry to pick up. The exchange was short and not at all sweet when he did. The name and address of the motel where Landry was staying and nothing more.

'You want to tell me who we're going to see, and where?' Evan said for the fun of it, a dial tone in his ear the reward for his trouble.

He picked Landry up fifteen minutes later. The guy was outside his room, leaning his butt against the caved-in fender of his car, ankles crossed. Smoking, as usual.

Evan bibbed the horn a couple times to make him jump, even though Landry had clearly seen him arrive. Pay him back in advance for the reek of cigarettes he brought with him into the car.

'What's the address?' Evan said as they set off heading towards I-10.

'Baton Rouge.'

'It's a big place.'

Landry tapped his temple with his middle finger.

'That's why I've got the rest of it in here.'

Neither of them said anything after that until they were approaching exit 127 where Evan had come off to lead Ritter into the middle of the Atchafalaya refuge the previous day.

'Shouldn't have let Ritter go,' Evan said as they cruised past.

Landry stopped staring out the window long enough to grunt a reply. Pointing at himself to make sure there was no room for misunderstanding.

'*I* didn't. That's on you, whatever's happened.'

'Nothing so far. But I found out a few things about him.'

'Yeah? Like what?'

'He likes to nail dogs to doors, for one.'

Landry looked at him as if Evan had told him Ritter liked doing jigsaw puzzles. Then he grinned, eye teeth on show.

'Then it'll be your fault if he does it again.'

Anybody else and Evan would've said, *you think I don't know that?* Seeing as it was Landry he waved it off like it was no big deal.

But if he thought that was the end of it, he was more stupid than some people said. Landry took great pleasure in what he said next.

'Better hope for your sake it doesn't turn out Ritter did something to Arlo, eh?'

Funny how that thought had crossed Evan's mind, too.

Normally he wouldn't deliver a man to someone like Fraser knowing what was likely to happen. The remembered feel of the painted-over nail hole in Bordelon's front door, the memory of the horror and fear on his wife's face, made him think he could be flexible, make an exception in Ritter's case.

Landry pulled out his phone as they approached the Mississippi River ten minutes later. Told him to get off at the first exit after they crossed its wide brown expanse. They looped around and headed north on Nicholson Drive, under the Interstate then first left which took them back down to the river. They parked in a dirt and grass lot at the top of a jetty leading down to a dock where a number of barges were moored. Despite the constant roar of the traffic thundering past on the Interstate overhead, somebody had put a wooden picnic table with benches on the grass overlooking the river.

It was currently unoccupied. Landry sat down facing the river. Evan remained standing looking out over the water, the distance and traffic noise stopping them from feeling obliged to make conversation while they waited.

Five minutes later a black, tricked-out Ford Super Duty F-450 pickup rolled into the lot. Two Hispanic guys climbed out and swaggered towards them kicking up dust with the Cuban heels of their boots as they came. Landry got to his feet as they approached, hands clasped loosely in front of him.

And Evan heard the haunting melody of Ennio Morricone's Spaghetti Western soundtrack running through his head.

Landry and the man in front greeted each other. He was Áxel. Then Landry introduced Evan. They all sat down like two teams opposing each other. Evan and Landry as guests on the best side facing the river, Áxel and his nameless sidekick who looked like he'd cut out your liver for the price of a couple of beers on the landward side. Landry traded evil looks with him. He'd do it for a single beer—and a warm one, at that.

'You wanted to know about Esteban Aguilar?' Áxel said to Evan, his English heavily accented.

'Him, and hopefully some other people you might know.'

'Why?'

Evan figured Áxel must already know, went along with it for an easy life.

'I'm working for Stan Fraser, same as Landry here. His son's gone missing. We think it's connected to Señor Aguilar's plane crashing five years ago. Some background information would be useful to avoid stepping on anyone's toes or offending anyone.'

Bit late for that went through his head, Guillory's voice giving it life.

Landry was looking at him like he agreed with her.

'Fair enough,' Áxel said. He then spent the next five minutes telling Evan everything he already knew. How Aguilar was into trafficking anything it was illegal to traffic and ruined lives at the same time—drugs, arms and people in particular.

Landry pulled out his cigarettes as Áxel talked, offered them around. Everybody declined. He lit up with a *suit yourselves* shrug, the wind blowing the smoke over everybody at the table except for himself.

Evan nodded along and said *uh-huh* a couple times, his mind working in the background as Áxel waxed lyrical about a man he clearly admired.

Thinking about the video that Ritter was searching for. It was unlikely to show his boss doing anything as commonplace as snorting coke or puffing on a big fat joint. With a man like Ritter working for him, he had no need for illegal guns himself. It was sex. That conclusion prompted his first question.

'How does the people trafficking work?'

Áxel laughed, a harsh sound that combined an unsympathetic attitude towards the victims coupled with admiration for the criminal gangs who'd devised a way to double their profits.

'The migrants think they pay the money, hide in a truck to get across the border, then they will be set free. Welcome to America, *mis amigos*. Except they are not set free. They are taken to stash houses. The gang hold them there. They contact the migrant's family already living in the US and demand more money before they release them.' He raised his hand. Extended his thumb and little finger, the other fingers tucked into his palm, in the universal symbol for a telephone. Put it to his ear. 'They call the family. Make them listen as they torture the migrants. Break their fingers. Burn them with cigarettes. Anything to make them scream. The family pay, if they can. It is different for pretty young girls.' He smiled again in a way that suggested that *different* was not a good thing. Not if you were one of the pretty girls. 'They are sold to pimps who force them into prostitution. After Aguilar's men have tested the quality of the merchandise, of course.' He rubbed his groin provocatively. Looking as if he'd like to take his turn as one of those test purchasers.

Evan bit his tongue, made a point of not asking questions. What happens to the migrants who are not young and pretty and whose family are unable to pay? How old are the young, pretty girls sold into sexual slavery? Should I be sick right here at the table or shall I throw up in the river? He told himself he was not here to single-handedly resolve the growing problem of human trafficking across the US-Mexican border fueled by unscrupulous US employers' demand for cheap, easily-abused and readily-deportable labor and facilitated by poorly-enforced laws and corrupt border officials, both American and Mexican.

Instead, he asked a question that he was aware would get a reaction from Landry if nobody else as he introduced a name that he hadn't shared with Stan Fraser.

'Do you know a man called Innocent Lejeune?'

Áxel nodded like they'd been best friends since high school, their first crimes committed together when they were ninth graders.

'He is one of the men who buys girls from Aguilar. Him and his brother put them to work in their whorehouses.'

Evan was aware of Landry staring at him. At any other time, he'd expect him to let out an incredulous laugh, *is that even a real name?* Like Evan had when Guillory told him. Except appearances had to be maintained. Landry did not want to give Áxel and his sidekick the impression that he was nothing more than a glorified taxi driver. That the man he'd brought along to talk to them hadn't even brought him up to speed beforehand on what he'd be talking about.

Not that Evan cared. Everything had just fallen into place.

Aguilar supplied the young girls. Lejeune put them to work in his brothels. If somebody important or rich turned up to get his rocks off with a potentially under-age migrant forced into prostitution against her will, they videoed it, then blackmailed the guy. Ritter's boss was one such guy. The video had been on the plane and had gone missing with the cash when it crashed. Either taken by the prisoner-passenger, or, if you believed Kevin Clark's girlfriend, Jane, Justin Sanders' mystery lover-cum-hiking buddy.

The only thing that didn't make sense was why the video

hadn't been used to blackmail Ritter's boss. It clearly hadn't if they were still searching for it. Unless it was at the bottom of the bayou and everybody was chasing their tails.

'Where are the whorehouses?' Evan said.

Áxel gave a small shake of his head.

'Here in Baton Rouge. But you do not want to go to them. They are bad places. A man like you would not be welcome there.'

Evan didn't ask for clarification. Whether he meant a man asking questions or a man who clearly wasn't their typical customer. It struck him that if the brothels were that bad, Ritter's boss wouldn't be welcome there, either.

'Do Lejeune's girls work out of hotels?'

'Sometimes. The more expensive ones. He saves the best ones for his best customers.'

All Evan needed to know now was who that best customer was. He threw out another name. One that at least had the possibility of leading to him.

'Have you heard of a guy called John Ritter?'

Áxel shook his head. Looked at his sidekick. The guy shook his head back.

'Never heard of him,' Áxel said. 'Who is he?'

'That's what we're trying to find out. He said he works for Aguilar.'

'Ritter is an Anglo?'

'Uh-huh.' Thinking, *and a lot of other things I don't want to think about besides.*

He got a solid headshake back from Áxel.

'No way. Aguilar does business with Anglos, but he doesn't trust them enough to employ them. Like Lejeune.'

For the second time in under a minute Evan felt that he'd have liked clarification, but didn't feel comfortable asking for it.

Did Áxel mean that Aguilar was happy to do business with Lejeune, or that he didn't trust him? And if not, why not?

So far, all Áxel had done was to sing Aguilar's praises. Clearly in awe as he explained all the criminal enterprises Aguilar was involved in, adding a few unsavory details about the mechanics of people smuggling, as well as a passing reference to supplying Lejeune with illegal girls. In effect, a quick summary of how they all worked together so that everybody made a ton of money and forget about the lives ruined.

A question about a potential problem of trust between Aguilar and Lejeune was a very different matter, akin to asking about those ruined lives.

The meeting also had the feeling of drawing to a natural close. Landry felt it, too.

'I think we're done here.'

Everybody stood up together. Evan made sure he stuck out his hand first, shook with Áxel.

'Thanks for your time. I appreciate it.'

'My pleasure. I hope it's been helpful in finding Señor Fraser's son.'

Nobody else shook hands. A curt nod or two, and a minute later the tricked-out pickup blew out of the dirt parking lot in a cloud of dust.

Evan was already thinking about his next move. Best to meet things head-on. Not wait for Landry to lay into him with the accusations. It meant massaging the timeline since Guillory had given him Lejeune's details at eight-thirty that morning, but Landry would never know.

'Before you get in a hissy fit about everything you haven't been told, it's only two hours since I talked to Detective Guillory. You remember her?' Wishing he'd phrased it better—*do your balls remember her?* 'That's when she gave me the name Lejeune. Two hours ago. I've been busy. Maybe if you and Stan hadn't kept me in the dark about who and where we were meeting, I'd have been more talkative myself.'

Landry dropped heavily onto the bench like he'd been worn down by a man who always had an answer.

'Whatever. Just tell me how come you were asking about Lejeune.'

'I've got something in the car that I need to show you. Did you see the sports duffel bag on the back seat?'

'Vaguely.' Shaking out a cigarette from the packet he'd left on the table as he said it.

'Let me get it.'

Landry was sitting staring out over the river when Evan got to the car and looked back. Ignoring the roar of the traffic overhead it wasn't such a bad place to sit and enjoy a cigarette.

Which was lucky. Because he got in the car and left him there.

42

She felt the heavy coldness of the gun in her hand, the power it promised flowing into her.

It felt so good. More than that. It felt *right*.

But she didn't know how it had gotten there, in her shaking hand like that. She didn't own a gun.

In front of her a man face-down on the ground. Head turned sideways, cheek in the dirt.

She couldn't see who it was, his face covered by a black ski mask.

Crawling away from her.

A rage like no other burning inside her.

How dare you?

He had something in his hand, dragging it along the ground.

Her laptop? No, it was something else. Something she couldn't make out.

She stalked behind him. Long slow strides as he struggled in his pain, her anger growing.

How dare you? I'm a doctor. I'll put a syringe in your eye.

The gun in her hand called to her so insistently, so sweetly

—*shoot him*. You're within your rights. Everybody will understand.

She could see them now, the jury. Shaking their solemn heads. Unanimous.

She had no choice.

Her finger tightened on the trigger, her pulse racing as an intoxicating warmth flooded her belly.

On the ground, the bastard moaned.

Please.

Pathetic. Not so big and tough now, are you? Not when the boot's on the other foot.

Again, the gun called to her. Like a petulant child stamping their foot. Demanding that she act, put right the wrong.

Shoot the bastard. He doesn't deserve to live.

She squeezed the trigger, the gun kicking violently in her hand, the noise deafening.

But oh-so satisfying, so addictive.

Squeezing again, her arm jolting with the recoil in time to his dying body jerking on the ground. A perverted dance to the tune of an insane choreographer.

And her mind screamed at her, a crazy unhinged song.

Again. Again. Again.

But no. Enough. He was dead.

Good riddance.

She looked at him a long time, wondering what to do next.

Drift away, perhaps?

Then it came to her as the world came back into focus, the deafening silence receding as the harsh glare of uncompromising reality intruded on this private moment.

She leaned forward, grabbed the ski mask. Hesitated for a heartbeat. Then ripped it right off like it was his face itself torn from his flesh.

Ha!

No surprises there.

Investigate that, why dontcha?

She poked him gently with her toe. He was as cute now as he'd been in life.

What's your lady detective friend going to do with her handcuffs now, eh?

Laura Hunt jerked awake at the sound of the front door opening. Tried to sit up. Her shoulders twisted painfully in their sockets as the duct tape binding her wrists to the bedstead stopped her short.

She flopped back on the bed, exhausted.

How the hell had she fallen asleep?

No matter. Thank God for her cleaning lady, Mrs. Ortega.

Let's hear it for her. God bless Mrs. Ortega. Long may she scrub and clean and rescue grateful employers in distress.

Just so long as the old bat didn't have a heart attack when she saw her lying tied to the bed.

Laura swallowed drily, her throat like sandpaper. Called as loudly as she could. Almost wet herself with the effort.

'Mrs. Ortega. I'm upstairs. I need help.'

Laura heard the old woman come bustling up the stairs, then stop on the landing on the other side of the closed bedroom door. As if she suspected her ageing ears were playing tricks on her.

'In here,' Laura yelled.

Then the door opened and Mrs. Ortega's face peeked around the edge, as if scared she might interrupt her employer in the midst of some bizarre sex act. Her scrubbing hand flew to her toothless mouth, a stifled prayer on her lips.

'*Madre de Dios!*'

Fat lot of good she's done me, Laura thought. *Just get the goddamn scissors.*

. . .

It took forever to get rid of the fussing Mrs. Ortega after she'd cut her loose. Persuade her that all she wanted to do was lie down and sleep forever—without being tied to the bed.

If that wasn't too damn much to ask!

'Call the police,' Mrs. Ortega pleaded as Laura hustled her towards the door with double her usual money clutched in her hand.

'I will. I promise. As soon as I get some rest.'

'Let me do it for you.' Already digging in her bag for a cell phone that belonged in a museum.

'I can't handle their questions right now. My head's coming apart.'

'Then let me make you something to eat.'

Laura took a deep breath. To stop herself from yelling in Mrs. Ortega's face more than anything else.

Get out of the damn house before I tie you to the bed and set fire to it, you stupid old woman.

Instead, she put her hand on Mrs. Ortega's elbow. Reluctantly the old woman allowed herself to be steered through the now-open door.

But she wasn't ready to give up yet.

'I'll come tomorrow.'

Laura nodded. Anything to get rid of her.

'Yes. Do that.'

'Are you sure there's nothing I can do?'

Too late. The door was already closed.

Maybe let's not hear it for Mrs. Ortega, God bless her, after all, Laura thought as she leaned her back heavily against the door until she heard the noisy exhaust of Mrs. Ortega's ancient car fade to nothing as she drove away.

She pulled herself together. Went into the kitchen to make herself a sandwich.

Because, yes, she was absolutely starving. And no, refried beans wouldn't hit the spot, thank you anyway, Mrs. Ortega.

She thought about what to do as she hunted through the sparsely-stocked fridge.

First up, log into her laptop tracking account on her phone. Find where the bastard who'd stolen her laptop was. She figured it was already too late to activate the remote file encryption feature. At least she could track him.

Call the police? She didn't think so.

But she'd call the investigator, Evan Buckley. The man who'd featured so prominently and vividly in her nightmare. Warn him that the lunatic who'd held her at knife point and threatened to cut out her eyes was after him. It had been the purpose of the attack, the theft of the laptop an opportunistic afterthought.

Except it was more of an opportunistic shitstorm as far as she was concerned.

43

Evan wasn't looking forward to talking to Detective Gauthier of the Baton Rouge PD vice squad—with or without a personal recommendation from Lou Bordelon.

He had to assume Gauthier wasn't stupid.

He wanted to ask him about a plane that had gone down in the Atchafalaya refuge five years previously. The request for information came exactly twenty-four hours after persons unknown had left an injured man in a car trunk not more than a hundred yards as the crow flies from the scene of that crash. And had then called it in anonymously.

He could only hope Gauthier wasn't feeling on top of his game today.

It was one reason he left Landry behind. Although the guy didn't look like an archetypal thug, he gave off a vibe that would wrinkle the nose of an experienced cop like Gauthier as readily as if he had dogshit on his shoe.

That wasn't all. Ritter would have told them he'd been attacked by two men—and here were two men, one of whom looked very capable of shooting a man in the shoulder at the drop of a hat. One man on his own wasn't a whole lot better, but his options were limited.

It was why he'd have preferred to get all of the information from Áxel.

As it was, there'd be hell to pay with Stan Fraser. Still, it was better than Gauthier wheeling in Ritter to take a look at them, and then everybody winding up in jail.

He parked in Independence Park, a mile from the police precinct. Then he called Gauthier on the personal cell phone number Bordelon had given him—using his own phone this time, not Ritter's burner.

Gauthier was wary when he answered the unknown number.

'Lou Bordelon gave me your number,' Evan said, hopefully putting him at ease. 'He said you're the man to talk to about a case that might be connected to what I'm working on. I'm a PI looking for a missing kid.'

Kid was stretching it. But it didn't hurt to imply it was someone young and vulnerable. He might as well have said *missing hamster* for all the difference it made to Gauthier.

'Uh-huh.' Sounding like, *so what?* 'What case?' Sounding like he already knew.

'The plane owned by Esteban Aguilar that crashed in the Atchafalaya refuge five years ago.'

He knew it was only guilt, made him picture Gauthier smiling to himself, punching the air.

Gotcha.

'Where are you?'

'Independence Park.'

'Wait there. What are you driving?'

'Silver Ford Fusion.'

Gauthier arrived ten minutes later. Alone. Despite the space beside Evan being empty, he parked two spaces over. Evan got out, waited while Gauthier walked slowly around his car. Checking for damage. The back of Ritter's car had been caved in when Landry drove into it.

'You mind if I look in the trunk?' Gauthier said.

Evan told him to go ahead, relieved that he'd used the whole length of paracord to secure Ritter's broken trunk lid when they locked him in.

That's where the relief ended. Gauthier leaned in, came out with the axe handle in his hand. His face said it for him.

You like cutting down trees?

'I mentioned Aguilar's name in the first two minutes of speaking to you,' Evan said. 'You can appreciate how I might feel the need for some protection.'

'You're not carrying a gun?' The incredulity in his voice reflecting what he thought of a man who went up against Aguilar's thugs with a piece of hickory.

'Nope.'

Gauthier slammed the trunk shut, peered through the back window.

'What's in the bag on the back seat?' Already reaching for the door handle. He paused, mock politeness in his voice. 'You mind?'

One hundred percent, Evan thought as he told him to go ahead again.

Gauthier already had the door open. He leaned in, unzipped the bag.

'More protection?' he said pulling out the wrecking bar. 'Or do you help out on demolition sites when the PI business is slow?'

'A bit of both. Can I ask what this is about?'

'You can ask.' Looking as if he wouldn't care if Evan held his breath waiting for an answer.

'I feel as if I'm going to be told to assume the position any minute,' Evan said when he didn't get one.

'I'm not ruling that out. Let's get in and talk first.'

If he'd wanted to be a pedant, Evan would've pointed out that *answering* was a better word for describing his part in the conversation.

Gauthier threw the wrecking bar on top of the bag, closed the rear door and climbed in the front.

'Let me see the rental papers,' he said once Evan had joined him.

Evan opened the glove compartment, didn't miss the way Gauthier peered in. He passed the papers to him, knowing why he'd asked. To determine whether Evan had changed cars after shunting Ritter's vehicle the previous day.

The guy was going to be disappointed. That didn't mean it put an end to his awkward questions.

'You get paid by the hour?'

The question threw Evan momentarily.

'By the day or for the job, normally. Why?'

'I'm glad I'm not your client. You've been here three days and you're only talking to me now. Looks to me like you've been stretching the job out. What have you been doing? Apart from chopping down trees and helping out on demolition sites, that is.'

'Talking to people.' He started to count them off on his fingers. 'Ralph Fontenot, the editor of *The Daily Acadian*. He took me to the crash site.'

Suddenly Gauthier lost the bored look that suggested that whatever Evan might say or do, he'd seen and heard it all before.

'In the Atchafalaya refuge?'

'Uh-huh. Where else?'

'What for? You think there'd be some clues there that we missed five years ago?'

'To get a feel for the place. You want to call Fontenot?' Reaching for his phone as he said it.

'Nah. I hate that place. Damn mosquitos eat you alive.'

Evan was aware of Gauthier studying the exposed areas of skin on his hands and face.

'Yeah. Lucky I was with Fontenot. He brought along some DEET spray.'

'Who else?' Gauthier said.

'Just the two of us.'

He knew what Gauthier meant. Who else have you been talking to? But his guilt was making him play it too straight. Any other time he'd have deliberately misunderstood to get a laugh.

He didn't get one from Gauthier.

'I meant—'

'Who I've been talking to? Right.' He went back to counting them off on his fingers. 'Fontenot's daughter, Elise. She's the girlfriend of the kid who's gone missing. A sheriff's deputy called Mercer. Justin Sanders' widow Fleur and her doctor.'

Gauthier's head snapped sideways, a deep crease in his brow. 'Her doctor?'

'She's a friend, too. She was at the house when I turned up. Then I talked to Lou.' He paused. Waited until Gauthier looked him in the eye. 'He showed me his front door. Put my finger in the nail hole, in fact.'

Gauthier held his gaze for a couple of beats. *Understood.*

'Then I talked to Kevin Clark's girlfriend—'

'You didn't talk to Clark himself?'

'He's dead.'

The look that crossed Gauthier's face suggested someone had told him an interesting but irrelevant fact—something about the way dung beetles maneuver large balls of dung with their back legs, for instance.

'I didn't know that. He wasn't very old. What was it? An accident?'

'Autoerotic asphyxiation.'

Gauthier nodded, the tired cough of a laugh on his lips of a man who long ago stopped being surprised at how people choose to live and end their lives.

'Takes all sorts, I suppose. Anyone else?'

Evan hesitated. Looked down at his lap. Still holding a finger as if he really didn't want to move onto the next one.

Gauthier was right on it, the *gotcha* gleam in his eyes. Like he'd pushed Evan into a corner having to admit he'd spoken to Ritter.

'What? You run out of fingers?'

Evan cleared his throat a couple times as if the admission just wouldn't come.

'A guy called Áxel. He's—'

'I know who Áxel is.' The *gotcha* gleam was gone, but what replaced it wasn't much better. 'What interests me is how you know to talk to him. It suggests to me that you might not be what you seem. Or claim to be.'

Evan couldn't see how he could get around telling the truth —or at least an edited version of it. Then hope Gauthier dropped it.

'The guy I'm working for, the guy whose son is missing, gave me the name. He's not the sort of man you ask questions about how he knows what he knows. You say, *thank you* and get on with it asap.'

Gauthier looked at him. Considering whether to push it. Was he making more connections? A man who could get in touch with the local criminal network would have people working for him who were happy to shoot a man and leave him in his car trunk.

In the end he moved on. But it hadn't done anything to improve the trust between them.

'Why did you speak to Áxel?' Gauthier said.

'Background info on Aguilar.'

'You could've asked me.'

Evan laughed, genuine amusement that Gauthier would appreciate.

'That doesn't seem to be the way this is going. Seems to me you're doing all the asking.'

'Fair enough. Sounds like you've been busy, anyway. Talk me through how it all connects to the missing kid.'

'He was trying to do what I'm doing now . . .' He told him the whole story. How Fontenot had given Arlo the chance to prove himself, how he himself had been re-tracing Arlo's footsteps. And that Arlo had gone missing at some point after talking to Fleur Sanders.

'He didn't get far, did he?' Gauthier said when he'd finished, then corrected himself. 'Or maybe he got too far.'

Evan opened his hands wide. *That's why I'm here.* He felt bad about deceiving Gauthier, but there was no good way telling him what he believed had happened could end.

He wanted to say to him, hold onto Ritter, you've got the nastiest piece of work in this whole sorry tale right there.

'What do you want to know?' Gauthier said eventually.

Evan started with a long shot, even though he knew it wasn't going anywhere.

'Do you know what happened to the DNA report on the plane's passenger?'

Gauthier shook his head, the look on his face suggesting he hadn't expected to be asked about it.

'No.' He looked as if he was about to say more, then stopped himself.

Evan tried again.

'So the bigger-picture investigation that was supposedly the reason for it being kept away from Bordelon didn't have anything to do with you?'

'Uh-uh.' He immediately added a caveat indicative of a man who'd been in the job a long time. 'Not that I'm aware of.'

'And you would be?'

'That's how it's meant to work. But we're getting off-track here. I'm assuming you're not here to expand your investigation into wider issues of potential police corruption?'

'I don't plan to move down here permanently, no.'

Gauthier laughed out loud at that. It made Evan feel even worse for deceiving the guy.

'Let me save us some time,' Gauthier said. 'I'll tell you how it relates to us in vice rather than you keep asking—'

'Stupid questions?'

Gauthier rocked his hand, working hard at keeping a straight face.

'I assume you know all about Aguilar now?'

'Drugs, guns, people trafficking.'

'Yeah. All-round scumbag. This relates to the people trafficking. Did your friend Áxel tell you how that works?'

'Aguilar brings them in, sells the young pretty girls to a pimp called Innocent Lejeune.'

'Yeah. There are two brothers, Innocent and Thibaud. A pair of bedbugs on the ass of humanity. They own the whorehouses. Not all of the women are illegals, and not all of them are working against their will. The high-class ones can make a lot of money. A lot more than you or me, that's for sure. But prostitution is illegal in Louisiana. Period. We'd had our eye on the Lejeune operation for some time, had some people inside the organization. We were at the point where we were ready to raid the brothels, close them down. If we could've made it stick .

. .' He raised a cautionary finger. 'And it's a big *if*, the Lejeune brothers would've been in deep shit. Not only garden-variety prostitution. Active involvement in human trafficking and sexual slavery, as well.'

Evan's phone rang in his pocket at that point.

Suddenly cooperative Gauthier took a back seat, his suspicious alter ego coming to the fore once again.

'Aren't you going to answer that?'

Evan didn't have a choice. Not unless he wanted to wave goodbye to cooperative Gauthier for good. He pulled it out, expecting to see Landry's name on the display.

Gauthier didn't miss the small double-take when he saw who it actually was.

'Not somebody you're expecting?' Gauthier said.

Evan showed him the screen.

Gauthier's brow furrowed.

'Laura Hunt?'

'She's Fleur Sanders' doctor that I told you I met. I've no idea why she's calling. It'll wait.'

Gauthier seemed satisfied. Didn't demand he answer it so that he could listen in.

'I'll text her,' Evan said, then pecked out a quick message.

In the middle of something. I'll call asap.

He meant it, too. He had a premonition it was more than a second sexual foray by the predatory Dr. Hunt.

'This is all conjecture,' Gauthier said, 'but we think Aguilar got wind of the upcoming raid. He's where he is today because he's a careful man, as well as an immoral vicious one. He thinks ahead. He pictured a scenario where we raid the brothels and pick up the Lejeune brothers—'

'Who immediately do a deal giving up Aguilar as the supplier of the illegals you find chained in the basement, so to speak.'

'Exactly. Aguilar then kidnapped Thibaud Lejeune as a way of ensuring that Innocent kept his mouth shut. He could've killed them both, except they had a good thing going. All they had to do was get over this little hiccup and then they could get back to ruining lives and making themselves a ton of money.'

'Meaning Thibaud Lejeune was the handcuffed passenger on the plane?'

'That's what we think. Aguilar was flying him down to Mexico. You remember how both names on the manifest turned out to be false?'

'Uh-huh.'

'Taking him to Mexico helped concentrate Innocent Lejeune's mind. You cut off a person's head and put it on a spike on US soil and the shit's gonna hit the fan, big time. It's an everyday occurrence in Mexico. Aguilar's the sort of guy who'd have shipped the head back to Innocent afterwards.

'So we raided the whorehouses, rounded everybody up and notice that Thibaud's missing and supposedly nobody knows where he was. Which happens to be true, as far as Innocent Lejeune's concerned. He knows Aguilar's got him, but that's it.'

'Then the plane went down and the passenger and Aguilar's money go missing.'

'Yeah. Whatever happened on that plane with Sanders getting killed and all the rest of it, we were thinking Thibaud got away with Aguilar's cash and went to ground. He's not exactly going to make his way back to his brother for Aguilar to grab him again. Or decide maybe he will kill everybody in sight after all. I don't suppose I need to tell you, but the case fell apart. These people are scum, but they're not stupid scum. Innocent is a stupid name, especially for a guy like him, but if he wants a stupid name, Teflon would be better.

'Everything settled down. You'd expect Thibaud to pop up again. Sorry I shot your pilot, Señor Aguilar. At least I saved all your money from the crash investigators, here it is. Then it's back to business as usual. The thing is, we've watched Innocent Lejeune for the last five years. The view is that he doesn't know where the hell his brother is. Except he probably is *in* hell, which is where they both belong.'

'You think Thibaud might have kept on running and left Innocent to deal with Aguilar? And now he's on a beach in the south of France somewhere?'

Again, Gauthier rocked his hand, moving his whole body with it.

'It's possible. Thibaud might have decided he didn't like the idea of being Aguilar's go-to bargaining tool every time something went wrong with the business. But the brothers were close, so who knows?'

The thoughts that went through Evan's mind made him feel guilty all over again for not sharing them with Gauthier.

The reason for the cover-up, for burying Thibaud Lejeune's DNA report, now became clear. Identification of Thibaud in the plane would lead to difficult questions for his brother, Innocent. Aguilar had successfully stopped Innocent from dragging him into the unholy mess. That didn't mean Innocent wouldn't do a deal by implicating the man Ritter worked for, the man in the compromising video.

It was clear that Gauthier was not aware of the video's existence. Much as it troubled Evan's conscience—a small shriveled thing according to Guillory—to keep him in the dark, there were other motivations at work.

He could still feel the indentation in Lou Bordelon's front door under his finger. Still hear the fear and anger and despair in his wife's voice. See it on her face accusing him for resurrecting the worst days of their lives. And for putting sweet temptation in her husband's path. But despite her wishes to be left alone, it was already too late. He was determined to give

Bordelon a shot at justice first. As Gauthier had bitterly remarked, all those who should be held to account were Teflon-coated, any attempt at a legal form of justice doomed to failure.

He'd never be able to look himself in the mirror if he passed on the opportunity to put right such a travesty.

44

Evan waited until Gauthier had driven away before he called Laura Hunt back. There was no joking with the associated innuendo about *thorough investigations* that had characterized their previous phone call and meeting.

She sounded as if she'd been holding her breath since he texted to say that he'd call her back, the words bursting out of her in a rush.

'The man who was watching Fleur's house was waiting for me when I got home last night. He attacked me.'

'Are you okay?'

A thought crossed his mind as the words rolled out of his mouth. Did the intruder, Innocent Lejeune, have a gun to her head now? Forcing her to trick him into supposedly meeting her again only to find Lejeune waiting for him? Except why wait until now?

'I'm fine,' she said, her voice calmer after the initial outburst. 'At least I am now. He didn't hurt me. Not much, anyway. The bastard punched me before he tied me to the bed and left me there overnight. I'd still be there now if my cleaning lady hadn't come in.'

'You want me to come over?'

'No, really, I'm okay. It's not me he's interested in. It's you.'

It was hardly surprising after what had happened the previous day. Lejeune would've hit a dead end tracing his license plate. After that, Laura was the obvious route to him.

'What did you tell him?'

She hesitated momentarily, her voice apologetic when she answered.

'Who you are. What you do. I didn't have any choice. He put a knife in my face, threatened to cut my eyes out.' Her voice broke as saying the words made the horror of her ordeal come flooding back.

'It's okay.'

'I had to tell him where you're staying. I was too scared to lie. He knows where I live. He would've come back. Blinded me. I know he would.'

'Don't worry about it.'

He glanced around the parking lot as he said it. There were too many cars to identify whether one of them contained a man watching him with only a cursory look. Had Lejeune been following him all day? From the B&B to Bordelon to Kevin Clark's girlfriend to Axel to Gauthier? He didn't think so. But if not, what was the guy waiting for?

'Did he say what his interest in me is?'

'No. But he said something odd. He told me he was going to leave me tied to the bed until something was done. I asked him until what was done. I thought he was going to tell me to mind my own business. Instead, he said, *until the cocksucker who killed my brother gets what's coming to him*. I don't know what he was talking about.'

He could've told her.

Because part of what Gauthier had told him they were guessing at had just firmed up. Innocent Lejeune's brother

Thibaud, the handcuffed passenger on the plane who'd shot Justin Sanders, hadn't been seen for the past five years because he was every bit as dead as Sanders was. And Innocent was determined to find and kill the man who'd killed him.

Laura didn't need to know any of that. The confident predatory femme fatale of the day before was long gone, replaced by a frightened woman wondering how the hell her life went down the toilet so fast.

'Did anything else happen?'

'He stole my laptop. It was more of an afterthought because it was sitting there right under his nose.'

'Anything important on it?'

'That doesn't matter. The thing is, I've got tracking software on it. I know where it is.'

He wasn't sure he knew how he wanted her to answer when he asked the obvious question.

'Have you contacted the police?'

A guilty silence came down the line before he heard a different note in her voice. A harder edge to accompany the conspiracy implied in the words themselves.

'I thought I'd tell you first.'

He wasn't stupid. He knew what she was saying. But he needed to hear her say it. Because the implications were serious, a first step down a road where turning back is never an option.

'Why?'

'Because it must be connected to what happened to Fleur's husband, Justin, five years ago. Nobody was ever caught and punished for cold-bloodedly killing him when all he did was go to see if he could help. Why would things be any different now? If telling the police about this man—'

'His name's Innocent Lejeune.'

'Are you serious?'

'Uh-huh.'

She laughed, a cynical sound prompted by the irony contained in the name she'd just been told.

'If I tell the police where to find this man, Innocent, who isn't innocent at all, they'll probably end up letting him go again as if he was innocent. With a small i, that is.'

He took a moment to get his head around all the Innocents or innocence floating around. Thinking how well her cynicism and paranoia fit with what Gauthier had said about all the bigger players in the sorry sordid game being Teflon-coated.

Except Innocent Lejeune hadn't killed Justin Sanders in pursuit of the man who killed his brother. He hadn't staged Kevin Clark's death. Nor was he behind Arlo Fraser's disappearance. He was watching and waiting for someone, anyone, to lead him to his brother's killer. He wasn't clearing the decks in an attempt to bury the truth like Ritter was. He wanted the killer caught—preferably by himself.

To Evan, that sounded a lot like a potential ally.

'Give me the location,' he said, not caring if Laura misinterpreted his intentions.

If it meant difficulties further down the road trying to contain Lejeune's murderous desire for Old Testament-style revenge, he'd deal with that if and when it happened.

'What are you going to do now?' he said. 'Lejeune might come back.'

'I know. Talking about it makes me realize this has spooked me more than I thought. I'm going to check into a motel. Don't be offended if I don't tell you where.'

'I'm not.'

She didn't need to spell it out. That if he confronted Lejeune and Lejeune got the upper hand, she didn't want him to be able to give Lejeune her location, risk Lejeune coming after her for setting Evan on him. It implied a direct trade-off between her safety and his pain. He didn't hold it against her. The world continues to turn because people look after number one first and foremost.

After they ended the call, he sat for a while thinking about how best to approach Lejeune. Turning up unexpectedly and unannounced at the location Laura had given him wasn't a good idea—not after their last encounter ended with him shattering Lejeune's windshield. Lejeune's attitude might be shoot first, let him apologize later. Just because he'd decided Lejeune could be an ally, didn't mean Lejeune thought the same way.

That's when his phone rang.

He smiled to himself as he pulled it out and saw the unidentified number. Was fate having fun? Working with him for once, not against him. Was this Lejeune calling now to suggest they work together?

He answered, tempted to start with a cheery, *hey, Innocent, how's it going?*

It was lucky he didn't. Because he was wrong. Hadn't been more wrong in his whole life, difficult as people—Guillory came to mind—might find that to believe.

And when he heard the voice on the other end of the line he felt as if it was him Guillory had kicked in the balls.

GAUTHIER DIDN'T GO FAR AFTER LEAVING EVAN. NOT EVEN AS FAR as the police precinct a mile away. Instead, he pulled to the curb and got out his phone. Opened the browser and typed *Evan Buckley* into the search box. Didn't hit *enter*, not yet. Thinking about adding *lying bastard* to the search string. Probably get him way too many hits to wade through. Put on his sensible head, typed in *private investigator*, instead.

Buckley's face stared back at him from the little screen a split-second later courtesy of the miracle that is Google. He browsed a few of the top news articles, grudgingly impressed by most of what he read. Then he tapped the images tab.

Whoa!

That'd give a lesser man and small children nightmares. Dozens of little images of Buckley filling the screen. He scrolled until he found the best—meaning clearest—one, opened it.

Then he drove to the hospital to see the other lying bastard, the one who'd been locked in his trunk. He wasn't sure if he wanted to buy whoever did it a beer—or punch them for only shooting the pain in the ass in the shoulder.

Lou Bordelon wasn't surprised when he took a call from Gauthier. *Nosir*, not after he'd aimed Buckley in his direction. He was only surprised that it took as long as it did.

Surprised too that Gauthier didn't shout at him from the get-go.

What the hell d'you think you're doing giving him my number?

No, Gauthier sounded thoughtful.

They spent a few minutes catching up, then Gauthier got to it.

'I talked to that guy Buckley you gave my number.'

'Uh-huh.'

Gauthier laughed, happy that they were still in tune even if they hadn't spoken for a while.

'*Uh-huh?* That tells me everything I need to know. He's an interesting guy.'

'One way of putting it.'

'But you trusted him enough to tell him . . . about what happened?'

Bordelon's voice took on a harder edge, the words themselves blunt.

'About some sicko nailing my dog to the door? Yeah. I

thought Buckley was going to ask me to sharpen another nail just for him.'

'Nail?' There was an embarrassed pause as Gauthier realized his faux-pas. '*That* nail. Yeah, right. I don't think you better tell me about that while I'm on duty. The thing is, I was about to give you a call right before you—'

'Sicced?'

'Good word. Sicced Buckley on me.'

'Yeah? What about?'

'Got a phone call yesterday afternoon. Sounded like a guy with his fingers up his nose trying to disguise his voice. He tells me there's a man tied up in the trunk of his car with a bullet wound in his shoulder. Want to guess where the car was? Or do you need me to tell you?'

'Jeez, you must think my brains have atrophied in the private sector. In the Atchafalaya wildlife refuge.'

'Yep. Then the very next day I get a call from Mr. Evan Buckley PI wanting to talk about events that transpired in that same wildlife refuge five years ago.'

'Spooky.'

'Is that a corporate term?'

'I believe so. You want me to check with one of my secretaries?'

'You have more than one?'

'Uh-huh. One for the typing and the filing, one for...'

'I bet the pay's good, too.'

'Yep.'

'But you don't get to arrest people.'

Gauthier knew he'd made a mis-step as soon as the words were out, the amusement in Bordelon's voice proving it.

'Neither do you, from the sound of this conversation.'

Gauthier moved swiftly on.

'I asked Buckley what he'd been doing. He's been a busy guy.

Talked to half the population of Lafayette and Baton Rouge by the sound of it. About the only thing he didn't tell me he'd done was shoot a guy in the shoulder and leave him tied up in his trunk in the middle of—'

'The Atchafalaya wildlife refuge.'

'Exactly.'

'What about the guy who got shot and left in his trunk? What does he say?'

'He tells a lot of lies, is what he does. He's also got a fake police ID. A good one, too. You'd think it was real apart from the fact that *Detective John Rawlings* doesn't exist. Or at least I haven't been introduced to him yet.'

'So he's connected to someone with the clout to acquire—'

'Another good word.'

'—a genuine ID.'

'Looks like it. I won't bore you with the horseshit that came out of his mouth when I asked him how it happened. However, when I talked to Buckley I was so impressed I felt the need to look him up on the internet.'

'You're only human, after all.'

'I am. Found some nice photos of him. And seeing as I was on my way to see the other lying bastard—you're not getting confused here with which lying bastard is which, are you?'

'There are a lot of them around.'

'There surely are. Anyway, I showed the picture of Buckley to the one in the hospital.'

'And he said, *never seen him in my life*?'

'He did indeed. Looks like you're not getting as rusty as everyone says.'

'But he was lying?'

'I'd bet your life on it.'

'From the sound of things, I'd be happy to let you do it.'

'Just thought you should know there's more to Mr. Evan

Buckley PI than he lets on, a lot more. I also get the feeling what he does let us see are all the best bits.'

'*Best* being a relative term.'

'You got it. I figure there'd be a job here for you if you wanted it.'

Bordelon coughed like he'd swallowed a fly.

'Sorry, there seems to be a problem on the line. I missed that.'

'Good to talk to you, Lou. We'll have to grab a beer once I've got all of these jokers safely in jail.'

Amen to that, Bordelon thought as he headed out to his shed to make sure his nail was good and ready.

He had a feeling he'd be using it sooner than he'd thought.

45

'Arlo?' Evan said, then felt the need to say something stupid. Blame it on the shock. 'You're not dead?'

Arlo laughed nervously. The sound suggested he'd gotten a lot closer than he'd ever wanted to be.

'No. I've been keeping my head down. Can we meet?'

Call him paranoid, but Evan was immediately on his guard. Was this Lejeune? Laura would have told him he was looking for Arlo. Except the voice on the other end didn't have a southern accent, although that wasn't conclusive.

'Tell me something about your old man.'

The fact that Arlo didn't ask him why suggested that what had sent him into hiding had scared him sufficiently that he understood Evan's wariness.

'His name's Stan. He's had a throat operation that makes his voice croaky. He does business out of a shithole bar called The Backroom...'

'Okay, that's enough. You want me to come to wherever you are?'

Arlo hesitated, Evan's wariness contagious.

'Or we can meet somewhere else,' Evan said.

'No. It's okay. Come here. I'm staying with a friend...'

Evan took down the address, then immediately set off—by a very circuitous route. He made four consecutive right turns on a couple of occasions, as well as making a wide U-turn in the middle of the street that nearly caused a crash and got him an earful of abuse from an irate trucker leaning out of his cab.

Watching for two possible tails, not one. Lejeune and Detective Gauthier. He was confident neither of them was behind him by the time he parked a block away from the address Arlo had given him and took an equally indirect route on foot to the house.

A young man who wasn't Arlo answered the door, his phone in his hand. He held it at arm's length towards Evan's face then nodded to himself. Showed Evan the screen. An image of himself stared back at him.

'We looked you up on the internet,' the guy said, standing aside. 'I'm Liam. Arlo's in the back. Door on the right at the end.'

He stayed by the door as Evan went down the hall. Evan glanced back when he became aware that Liam wasn't following him, saw a baseball bat leaning against the wall. He felt like offering to lend him the wrecking bar for all the good either of those things would do against an armed man.

Arlo was pacing the floor as Evan entered. Looking like he was already regretting having made the call. Not looking so handsome as in the photo his friend Aiden had shown Evan. Stress is never a good look. Can't beat it for getting rid of a few excess pounds, not so good for the dark bags under the eyes.

Arlo stuck out his hand, a strangely formal gesture. Like he'd read you should always shake the hand of the man you've called to save your bacon.

Evan started easy.

'Where did you get my number?'

'Elise gave it to me.'

That answered half of his next question.

'Has she known where you were the whole time?'

Arlo shook his head, his expression reflecting the memory of a very difficult conversation. One that the lack of bruises on his face suggested had been conducted over the phone.

'I don't think she's ever going to speak to me again.'

'You can't blame her. What about her old man? Does he know?'

'No. I suppose Elise might have told him even though I asked her not to. She wasn't really listening to a lot of what I was saying after she found out that I hadn't been held prisoner by a psychopath for the past week. Too busy screaming at me about me sitting around on my ass watching TV and drinking beer with Liam while she was sick with worry.'

Evan nearly told him not to worry about it, that she'd get over it. Then again, she might not.

Seemed the mention of Elise's father prompted what had clearly been playing on Arlo's mind.

'How come you work for my dad? You don't look like one of his leg-breakers.'

It wasn't the time to say that one of them was only a phone call away. He tried to keep it simple.

'I owed him a favor.'

Arlo looked at him as if the wisdom of calling him was again at the forefront of his mind.

'I don't think I want to ask what it was. Does he want you to drag me back home?'

Evan didn't know how many lies he might end up telling, but it was time for the first one.

'He just wants to know that you're safe. Was it you who called him?'

'Yeah. It was stupid. I shouldn't have done it. I hung up as soon as I heard his voice and all the shit came flooding back.'

They were getting ahead of themselves.

'Let's back up,' Evan said. 'The last I heard was that Deputy Mercer let you read the file and you'd spoken to Fleur Sanders. It seemed to me you disappeared after that. You didn't get as far as talking to a detective called Bordelon or Kevin Clark.' Not mentioning for the moment that Clark was dead—a fact that would only increase Arlo's agitation if he didn't already know.

Apart from stopping momentarily to shake hands, Arlo hadn't stood still for more than a second or two. Now, he dropped heavily onto a low couch opposite a massive TV on the wall as if all the pacing had exhausted him. Evan perched on the other end.

'What did you do after talking to Fleur?'

Arlo ran his hand through hair badly in need of a wash, blew the air from his cheeks.

'I went to the address in the file for Kevin Clark.'

'But he'd moved.'

'Yeah. I asked the neighbors but nobody had even heard of him. I've lived in some shitholes over the years after I ran away, but this place was the pits. Nobody in their right mind would stay there five weeks, let alone five years. I got the landlord's details from one of the tenants.'

Thirty seconds flopped on the sofa seemed to be Arlo's limit for sitting still, his nervous agitation propelling him to his feet once more. He headed for the door and the kitchen beyond.

'You want a beer?'

'Yeah, why not?'

Evan went with him into the kitchen expecting to feel as if he was entering a war zone. It wasn't in too bad a state considering two young men were living alone there, at least one of them under a lot of stress. Evan figured if he checked the trash he'd find nothing except fast food containers and crumpled beer cans. At least they weren't covering every horizontal surface, the floor included.

Arlo grabbed a couple of cans of Heineken from a fridge that contained little else, then took a seat at the breakfast counter. Evan remained standing, the small breakfast bar too intimate for both of them to sit at.

'I don't know what I feel saying this, given what my dad is,' Arlo said. 'The landlord was obviously a criminal. I got the impression he bought the shitty apartment block where Clark had been living using drug money or whatever. Like he was using it to launder the cash. At first, I was really surprised when he agreed to talk to me. It became obvious why when I met him.'

Evan made an easy guess based on his discussion with Clark's ex-girlfriend, Jane of the many piercings.

'Clark had left owing him rent.'

'Yeah. He hadn't left a forwarding address, obviously. The landlord had put the word out that he wanted him found. I thought that's why he spoke to me. He was going to offer me money. Like a commission on the rent, if I found Clark. As if I'm gonna give a thug like him the address of a man whose legs he's going to break in order to earn myself a few bucks. I felt like I was back in my dad's world.'

He took a long swallow of beer as if to wash away the reference to his father, the sour look on his face suggesting someone had pissed in it while he wasn't looking.

'But it wasn't that at all?' Evan said to move him on from dwelling on Stan Fraser and everything he'd run away from.

'No. It was like he was bragging. This is what happens to people who cheat me. He told me how after he put the word out somebody got back to him, told him how Clark had died under suspicious circumstances. Apparently, he—'

'I know all about that.'

Arlo gave him a look. *Then what are you doing talking to me?*

'I'll tell you in a minute,' Evan said.

Arlo took another swallow of beer, resumed his story.

'I did a search on the web, found the details. I got the impression the landlord was taking the credit for it. He thinks that if he tells me, word will get around. Don't mess with this guy. Pay your rent or else. Except I don't actually think he did it.'

'Why not?'

Arlo scrunched his face, tried to find the right words. And failed.

'I don't know. The guy was full of shit, is all. He's a low-life criminal, no doubt about it, but sticking a knife in someone's gut is as sophisticated as he gets. No way a moron like him staged Kevin Clark's death.'

'So you'd hit a dead end.'

'Yeah. Except now I was starting to ask myself what I'd gotten into. You've read the file?'

'Uh-huh.'

'So you know how things weren't right. Things were missing. Then the lead detective quit.'

Evan nodded. Not saying anything. He saw in Arlo's eyes that he already knew exactly how wrong things had gotten.

Arlo glanced around the room, a mixture of guilt and shame on his face.

'Before I moved in with Liam, Elise told me how she overhead her dad and Mercer talking. Arguing, really. Both blaming each other for getting me started on this thing. She heard them talking about what made the lead detective quit.'

'His dog was nailed to his front door.'

Arlo swallowed nervously.

'Yeah. And I'm thinking, *shit*. I don't have a dog. What are they going to do to me? Is somebody going to find me dead in a crappy motel wearing a gas mask and with a plastic bag over my head?'

Evan might have suggested that was when Arlo decided to go to ground. Except there was no feeling of, *so here I am* to end his story. There was more to come—and when things are already going badly, more is always worse.

'I was thinking about telling Elise's dad that I'd hit a dead end. Making something up about contacting the lead detective and how he wouldn't talk to me on account of what had happened to his dog. Blaming him for getting scared, basically. So it didn't look like it was me deciding I'd bitten off more than I could chew. Then I'm thinking, what if Elise's dad knows Bordelon from back when it happened and contacts him? He'll know I lied and never trust me again. I know it was only me feeling guilty about quitting that was making me think that way. The end result was that I didn't know what the hell to do. Then I got a phone call.'

'From Dr. Laura Hunt?'

Arlo gawked at him as if he'd gone to the fridge to get another beer, opened it and found Laura asleep inside.

'How did you know?'

'The only person you'd spoken to was Fleur Sanders. She's big buddies with Laura Hunt. Fleur would've told her about your visit. I know you can't help blaming yourself, but it shook Fleur up to have all this raked over. Dr. Hunt can't prescribe the pills fast enough. What did she say?'

'That she had information and she wanted to meet. She said she hadn't said anything to the cops because she knew there'd been a cover up. She was worried that if she went to them it would be buried and all she would've done was to identify herself as another loose end to be dealt with. Like Kevin Clark.'

'Did she actually mention his name?'

'No, that's just me saying.'

'Did you meet with her?'

'Yeah. She sounded nice. Like she was really worried about Fleur.'

Evan bit back the smile trying to break through at how a friendly voice on the phone had Arlo doing an immediate about-face. He couldn't help wondering how often he'd done the same.

Nor could he stop the thought that went through his mind.

Who or what might be waiting for him at the location where Lejeune was supposedly holed up with Laura's laptop?

He couldn't remember whether he'd ever specifically asked her whether she'd met Arlo? Even if he hadn't, it was a hell of an omission for her not to mention it voluntarily.

'What happened when you met her?'

He held off from saying more, from prompting him. Did she come on to you? Did you come away feeling lucky you hadn't been eaten alive? Did she try to lure you somewhere remote or secluded?

That last question was immediately answered by Arlo's reply.

'We met for a drink in a noisy bar called The Tap Room. It was as if she didn't want to meet somewhere private. She told me about this friend of hers who she trained with as a doctor who became a psychiatrist. She'd been treating a patient for depression. The only reason the friend was telling her about it was because the patient had killed herself. She had a history of mental illness, but what pushed her over the edge was when the man she'd been seeing was shot to death. He was married and had promised to leave his wife, but then he was killed. The time frame fit with what happened to Justin Sanders. Apparently, the woman felt guilty. She never actually came out and admitted it, but from things she said, the psychiatrist got the impression she'd been there at the time when her lover was killed but she'd run away or hid.'

'Survivor's guilt.'

'Yeah. There was a lot of psychobabble bullshit about how she needed to admit it and face up to it before she could get over it and move on. In the end, she killed herself instead.'

'Were the circumstances suspicious?'

'No idea. I think Dr. Hunt would've said if they were. Unless she didn't know.'

'Did she give you any names?'

Arlo scrunched his face, looking as if it had never crossed his mind to ask.

'She'd already told me her friend the psychiatrist wouldn't talk to me. That she'd only release her case notes with a court order.'

'Another dead end, basically.'

Leaving out one important word—*convenient*.

'Yeah.'

'So what happened? You meet Laura. She tells you about this woman whose existence explains a lot of the unanswered questions. Why Justin Sanders' car was found thirteen miles away. The reason his phone was taken to protect the woman's identity. His gold cross taken as a memento. It all makes sense.' He took in the room with a sweep of his hand. 'But the next thing, you're hiding out here in Liam's place. Sufficiently scared to let everyone think you're dead and put up with the guilt you must have felt knowing how worried they all were.'

'You sound like Elise.'

'So, why?'

Arlo shook his head. A helpless gesture at his inability to justify his actions.

'I don't know. It felt wrong. It was too convenient. Like you say, I've just been handed this big dead end on a plate. I couldn't help wondering if it was all a big lie and I'm sitting having a drink with the woman who was actually having the affair with

Justin Sanders. And I can't help thinking, what happens if I don't swallow the story? I needed to get away. Get my head straight.'

'That's when you called your old man?'

'Yeah. I don't know what I was thinking.' He held up his beer can, a knowing, self-aware curl to his lip. 'Too many of these. As soon as I heard his voice I snapped out of it, killed the call. All that would've happened is that he thinks I'm a pussy for calling him when I'm scared. Not only that, I've set in motion a Stan Fraser standard operating procedure. Break every leg in sight to get the information you need, then kill the poor bastard who's responsible. I don't want any part of that. Forget survivor's guilt, I'd have . . . I don't know what you'd call it.'

'A shitload of guilt? Although I don't think that's an actual medical term.'

Arlo squeezed out a reluctant laugh.

'It ought to be.'

'What made you call Elise, and then me?'

Arlo glanced around the kitchen, relatively clean and tidy as it was.

'I can't hide forever. I've spent my life drifting, being outside. I felt like the walls in here were closing in on me. I had no idea you existed. It never crossed my mind that my dad would do something about the phone call. After all these years I didn't think he gave a shit. But it wasn't fair to Elise. I had to call her.'

'And take your punishment like a man.'

Arlo smiled at the memory of it, more humor than regret behind it this time.

'You got that right. What happens now?'

Evan heard something very different.

Can we turn the clock back, please?

That wasn't an option. But walking away was—for Arlo, at any rate.

'I can tell Stan you're safe and leave it at that. Or I can take you back to him for a tearful reunion.'

'Yeah, right.'

'What do you want to do? Drop it? Get used to the feel of your tail between your legs?'

A spasm of anger rippled across Arlo's face. Gave Evan the first inkling that maybe some of Stan's genes were in there, after all.

'That's not fair.'

'I know. I also know it's something you've thought about a lot.'

The anger turned to disdain, the look on his face of a man who's sick of other people telling him what's going on inside his own head.

'What are you? Another psychiatrist?'

'No. But I figure I could get a job as one. What's it gonna be?'

'What would you do?'

'Depends on how bothered I am about looking myself in the eye in the mirror every morning.'

Arlo looked at him a long while. Except he wasn't seeing him. Replaying the last ten years of his life. Weighing up the options of hitting the road again or staying put. Trying to make things right, make a life with Elise.

'I'm not going back home, that's for sure. The last week has been a nightmare, but at least it reminded me what I ran away from and why.'

It was as good a time as any to get to the bottom of something that Evan had been told way back in the beginning.

'I heard that one of the reasons you ran away was because you thought your dad killed your mom.'

Arlo gawked at him. Evan saw the realization slowly filter onto his face, his mouth turning down along with it.

'Who told you that? It was Eleanor, wasn't it?'

'Uh-huh.'

Arlo coughed out a dismissive laugh. At life, at how fate likes to pick on some little thing, blow it out of all proportion. He held up his beer can again. The root of, if not all, a lot of evil.

'I never said that, but I know what makes her think I did. We were both drunk one time. Things were really bad at the time. I was looking for someone to blame for the way I'd screwed up my life. So I blamed my dad. He did this, he did that, sort of thing. I didn't say he killed my mom. I might have said he killed the man she left him for.'

Evan knew exactly what he was talking about. The parable from the gospel according to Guillory that she'd told him on their way to his sister's house for dinner. About the heartless criminal who took pity on his cheating wife and took her back and cared for her in her final days after she got ill and the man she'd left him for dumped her. That man, Tony Christensen, had subsequently been found floating in the river after having been beaten to death.

'I never knew if it was really true or not,' Arlo said, 'but it sounded like the sort of thing my dad would do. Eleanor was more drunk than I was that night. That's why she got things mixed up. I don't know how she ever remembered me saying anything at all.'

Evan watched his face change as he talked about his past life, what he'd left behind. Saw the anger growing that life had dealt him a shitty hand and just when he thought he'd turned a corner, here was another great lake of it waiting for him to fall face first into.

It was a good time to tell him what he planned to do.

'Text Dr. Hunt. Tell her you've spent the last few days researching on the internet and you think you've found the suicide of her friend's patient. Then say you want to meet to clarify something.'

Evan's phone rang before Arlo had a chance to get his own phone out, the bring-it-on ballsy approach in Evan's suggestion paralyzing him momentarily. Evan held up a finger to stop Arlo from going ahead as he pulled it out.

He wasn't surprised by the name he saw on the screen. Couldn't help smiling at fate's timing.

'It's your dad. I left one of his men he sent to babysit me stranded in Baton Rouge. If this guy finds you, he will take you back, no question about it. Hog-tied, if necessary.' He held the phone towards Arlo looking at it as if his father was already materializing out of the speaker as a noxious gas, taking shape in front of him. 'You want to speak to him? Tell him you're not coming home any time soon so he might as well call the other guy off. I don't think he'll give up until he hears it from you.'

Arlo took the phone from him, recognition of the truth in Evan's words in his eyes.

He hit the green button. A torrent of abuse poured out of the phone before he had a chance to put it to his ear.

What the fuck do you think you're playing at, Buckley?

Evan grinned at him, shrugged. Arlo grinned back, bit the bullet.

'Hi, Dad. You sound pissed. Some things never change . . .'

Evan sidled out of the room, left them to it. Went down the hall to where Liam was still standing guard, Arlo's receding voice measured and calm behind him. He went outside to get some fresh air, wondering how long it would last.

He spent the time as he waited thinking about Dr. Laura Hunt. It seemed so obvious now. Maybe too obvious. It was easy to construct a narrative that fit.

She was Justin Sanders' lover—perhaps meeting him as a result of being the family doctor, or at the gym.

She was with him on the day Sanders died after Kevin Clark cancelled.

They saw the plane go down together.

Justin went inside while she waited outside.

Justin released Thibaud Lejeune and was promptly shot twice in the chest by him.

Thibaud then left the plane, presumably injured from the crash, presumably also carrying Aguilar's money and the video of Ritter's boss.

Spurred on by fear and rage, did Laura attack him, overpower him and subsequently kill him and dispose of his body? She was a big, fit woman, after all.

Did she then make off with the money, having taken Justin's phone and the cross he wore beforehand?

Kevin Clark was aware of the affair and had previously covered for his friend Justin. Did he figure it out and try to blackmail her for a share of the money to settle his gambling debts?

Did she then kill him and stage his death to look like an accident making use of the date rape drug, GHB, to subdue him? Her good looks and provocative behavior would have made such a setup easy to engineer.

Did she then get close to Fleur Sanders by abusing her role as Fleur's doctor? Cynically nurturing that supposed friendship so as to be in a position to hear if and when somebody took an interest in the case?

It could all be made to fit perfectly.

But could he see her doing it? The rage at the callous and brutal murder of her lover would lend her the courage and blind determination to kill Thibaud Lejeune. But what about Kevin Clark? He couldn't say.

His thoughts were interrupted by Arlo coming out of the house, Evan's phone in his hand. He was red in the face, the dominant emotion on it impossible to gauge. A slight tremor was in his voice.

'It's for you.'

Evan mouthed *Stan* back at him.

Arlo shook his head.

'We were arguing. I hung up on him. The phone rang immediately. I thought it was him calling back so I answered it. It wasn't. It's somebody who says he's innocent...'

46

'You the cocksucker who busted my windshield?' Innocent Lejeune said. 'Evan Buckley?'

'Two out of three,' Evan said.

'Huh?'

Evan didn't waste his breath trying to explain.

'What can I do for you, Lejeune?'

'You got that the wrong way around, my man. It's what I can do for you. I got something here I think you should see. Suggests to me, you and me are on the same side. Even if you did bust my windshield.'

Evan could've been a pedant. Pointed out that it was more a case of being after the same result—broadly speaking. It was unlikely they would ever be on the same side. Not while Lejeune was happy to put underage migrant girls to work in his brothels against their will. It was a good thought to bear in mind going forward should they end up working together.

'You want to tell me what it is? I'm not inclined to meet you somewhere, not after what you did to Laura Hunt.'

Lejeune laughed the laugh of a man talking to an idiot, a man who could not get with the program.

'She's the one you need to worry about, not me. You'll be grateful I paid her a visit when you see what I've got. I'm telling you, she's one lucky bitch. I went back there today after I saw it myself. Bitch is gone. You ever hear of a cocksucker called Jack Bray?'

Evan was getting the impression that in Innocent Lejeune's book, most people were cocksuckers, certainly until they'd proven otherwise. It wasn't an unreasonable stance, one that he might adopt himself. He answered the question honestly.

'I don't think so.'

'Look him up. See what you've stirred up here. Then call me back on this number if you're interested in me saving your sorry ass.'

The phone went dead in his ear.

Arlo had been watching him throughout the exchange, a crease in his brow as he listened to the one-sided conversation.

'What was that about? And what's he innocent of doing?'

'No, that's his name. Innocent Lejeune. He's the brother of the prisoner who was handcuffed in the back of the plane...'

He took Arlo through the rest of the story courtesy of what Detective Gauthier had told him. Arlo's face fell progressively as Evan talked, the realization that his fears had been justified growing ever stronger.

'This isn't an old, dead case, is it?'

'They never are. Especially when there's a compromising video still out there somewhere featuring a very important cocksucker, to borrow Lejeune's description. He mentioned a man called Jack Bray. I think he's the guy in the video. He sent a man called Ritter to find it. He's the sicko who nailed Bordelon's dog to his front door. We had him—'

'We?'

'I told you. Your dad sent another guy down here to babysit

me. Landry.' Arlo shook his head at the name. 'We had Ritter and we left him tied up in his trunk because we didn't know any of this at the time. Now he's in police custody or under guard in the hospital so we can't get to him.'

Arlo picked up on what Evan had left unspoken immediately.

'In the hospital? Because this other guy my dad sent put him there?'

Evan couldn't lie to him, even though the truth only confirmed what he saw in Arlo's eyes—*plus ça change*. Every story involving his father or men who worked for him ended the same way.

'Landry shot him in the shoulder. But Ritter shot at us first. He was following me at the time thinking he was going to get rid of me in the middle of the Atchafalaya wildlife refuge. So, I don't feel too bad about it. Apart from letting him go, that is.'

Arlo didn't look convinced, moved on anyway.

'Are you going to meet this guy, Lejeune?'

'Uh-huh. I just need to think of a way to make sure it's on my terms.'

Arlo held up his phone still in his hand.

'You want me to send the message to Dr. Hunt now?'

Evan looked him up and down. Thinking about the maneater Dr. Laura Hunt, the hunger in her eyes. About how Arlo looked like a tasty bite-sized piece of bait.

'Send it.'

He did a search on the web for Jack Bray while they waited for a reply to Arlo's text. What he found didn't surprise him.

Bray was a member of the Louisiana House of Representatives. Even the two-dimensional nature of his photograph couldn't stop an oily sycophantic insincerity from coming through, a barely-concealed hypocrisy that made Evan go to wipe his hand on his pants leg as if in the aftermath of a warm limp handshake. The impression was of a man who'd done well for himself, thank you very much. A man who'd filled his own pockets first and then trod the well-worn path to power as is the way of rich egotistical men whose wealth leads them to believe that they exist on a higher plane than other, lesser men, that they are among the chosen few. Evan didn't need to read his manifesto to know that foremost amongst his political convictions was an ardent belief that the answer to the country's problems was to make the wealthy wealthier.

He did a second search for *Jack Bray + Ritter*. It didn't throw up anything new. Pretty much the same results as the first search for Bray alone. It didn't change anything. It was too much of a coincidence for Bray not to be Ritter's boss. Given the sort of jobs he performed for him, Ritter would be careful to minimize the public connections.

He thought not very long and not very hard about what he did next, a spiteful flame of retribution burning in his gut making the decision for him. Despite what a lot of people said about him—act first, think later—he was able to plan ahead when he needed to.

He pocketed his own phone, pulled out Ritter's burner. Composed a message to the man he now knew to be Jack Bray.

I'm in trouble with the cops. I might need help. I'll get back to you if I can't deal with it myself.

Thinking that should get him nicely primed for what he had in mind for later.

Then he thought about what to do about Innocent Lejeune.

There were two issues. The first was that despite his first name, Lejeune was a military-grade douchebag who exploited underage illegal migrants by forcing them to work as prostitutes in his brothels. In a perfect world, he'd find a way to put an end to it and Lejeune behind bars at the same time. Sadly, Lejeune was only a small part of a far-reaching bigger problem that was beyond Evan's remit or capabilities. A more pressing problem concerned Lejeune's immediate plans. One thing was for certain. He was hell-bent on killing whoever turned out to be responsible for his brother's death. At the moment that was looking like Dr. Laura Hunt, the person on whose call or text back they were waiting.

As it turned out, it was a text. And it surprised the hell out of Evan when it arrived. Arlo opened it, read it, passed the phone to Evan.

Meet me at the same bar as last time. 8 p.m.

What Arlo had called a noisy bar, *ergo* full of people. Not a dark alley or a deserted factory or a parking lot in the middle of the woods. Was the doctor about to prescribe GHB once again à la Kevin Clark? Except things wouldn't get that far this time.

It was time to call Lejeune.

'I looked up Jack Bray. You're right. He looks like a grade A cocksucker.'

'Told ya. You interested in seeing what I've got to show you, now?'

'You bet. There are some things I need to do first—'

'Like what?' The voice instantly suspicious as Evan introduced an element outside of Lejeune's control.

'You heard of a guy called Ritter?'

'Uh-huh. Works for Bray. Cleans up his shit. That's all I know 'bout him. Why?'

'I heard a rumor he's sniffing around. I want to check it out.'

'You need help?' He pronounced it *hep*.

'Uh-uh. I've got a guy working with me. Is it okay if I bring him along when we meet?'

Lejeune chuckled, a good-natured sound on the face of it at odds with what he said.

'Sure thing. You're gonna need him after you see what I've got.'

Evan took down the address Lejeune gave him—the same one Laura had given him earlier as being the location of her stolen laptop—and ended the call. Then, much as it pained him to do so, he called Landry.

47

SITTING IN HIS CAR IN THE DEEPER SHADOWS ON THE FAR SIDE OF the parking lot, Evan watched Laura Hunt's Subaru Forester drive in at a few minutes before eight. She parked as close to the bar as she could get. As if she expected she might have to make a quick exit. That suited him fine on the other side of the lot. It was dark, but not that dark.

Arlo was already inside with strict instructions that if he needed a drink to calm his nerves, to only drink beer out of a bottle—even if he wasn't going to be alone with Laura for more than a minute or two.

Evan gave it five minutes, then went inside. Arlo hadn't exaggerated. The noise hit him like a wall of sound, the excited chatter of people winding down at the end of a long day, something indistinguishable beyond an insistent bass beat playing overhead. If you were up to no good, it ticked the box as far as hiding in plain sight was concerned. As instructed, Arlo had chosen a booth at the back of the bar—tailor-made for boxing a person in. Laura had already joined him there, a glass of white wine on the table in front of her.

Evan felt the atmosphere between them from across the

room. He guessed Arlo hadn't perfected his lying technique yet, and Laura was already wise to him.

She startled as he materialized at the table, then slid in beside her. He wagged his finger at her.

'Cheating on me, huh? With a younger guy, too.'

There was no laughing, no joining in with the, admittedly not very funny, joke. She looked at Evan, then at Arlo and back to Evan again, surprise giving way to anger at the way she was trapped between them.

'What's going on?' This to Evan.

'That's what I want to know.'

Arlo was watching them, gripping his beer bottle like his life depended on it. Evan was only surprised he didn't have his thumb over the open top.

Evan pulled out Ritter's burner phone. Found the reply he'd received from the man he now knew was Jack Bray.

'I want to show you something.'

He handed her the phone, sat back to watch her read the message.

It's a made-up email address. He's got the video. He's not asking for money. But if you don't stop people asking questions, the cops will find the video when they find him. You need to deal with an investigator called Evan Buckley.

He didn't give her a chance to say anything when she looked up after she'd finished reading.

'You know anything about that? Ignoring that it says *he* all the way through. It could just as easily be *she*. The guy sending it is a member of the Louisiana House of Representatives called Jack Bray.' He took the phone back from her unresisting hand. 'This belongs to the guy who cleans up after him, Ritter. Bray doesn't know I've got Ritter's phone, which is why he inadvertently gave me the heads up.'

She didn't answer. Moving her wine glass around on the

table top in a big looping circle. He gave her a minute then pushed harder.

'You've got two choices, Laura. Talk to me. Or talk to Detective Gauthier of the Baton Rouge PD. I'm meeting with Lejeune after we're finished here. He says he's got something to show me. I'm guessing it's something he's found on your laptop. I bet Detective Gauthier would be interested in seeing that, too.'

She continued to say nothing. Eyes down not looking at either of them, her glass still occupying all of her attention—on the outside. He pushed harder again.

'You had a very lucky escape last night. Lejeune's brother disappeared five years ago. He thinks somebody killed him after he shot Justin Sanders. Unfortunately for you, Lejeune's found something on your laptop that makes him think that somebody is you. And he doesn't believe in an eye for an eye. Hey, Arlo. What does Lejeune believe in?'

Arlo startled at the way Evan brought him into the conversation unexpectedly, a crease in his brow as he thought about it. Then a nod, *got it*, as it clicked.

'An eye for an eye for an eye.'

'Exactly. And Laura here is the third eye. But she knows that already.' He remained looking at Arlo, asked him another question as if Laura wasn't there between them. Holding up Ritter's phone as he did so. 'What do you think *deal with an investigator called Evan Buckley* means? Sorry for bringing it up, but think about your dad's world before you answer.'

Arlo didn't need to think for long, his voice reflecting the disgust he felt at the answer.

'Kill you.'

'That's what I thought, too. You think I'd be within my rights to retaliate against the person who set that in motion? Laura here threatened Bray who told Ritter to deal with me. I think I'd be justified in calling Lejeune. Telling him we've got Laura if he's interested in joining us.'

'*No!*' It came out as a scream. Made a lot of people turn around to see what was happening even above the noise of the bar. Laura raised a hand and shook her head until people reluctantly looked away again as the promise of excitement, of other people's problems played out in public, faded. She dropped her voice to an insistent hiss. 'I didn't mean that. I only wanted them to scare you off. All I want is for this to end.'

'That starts with telling me the truth about exactly what happened after the crash.'

He felt like laughing at himself, it sounded so pompous. She nodded, nonetheless, a weary resigned gesture as the last of the fight went out of her.

It seemed to him that the noisy sounds of the bar receded as she began to talk, the hot mass of sweating humanity that filled the room metamorphosing imperceptibly into the sticky steamy heat of the Atchafalaya wildlife refuge, the weaving to-and-fro of people on the periphery of his vision and consciousness slowing, their indistinct chatter merging into the primeval sounds of the ancient swamp.

The gunshot sounded impossibly loud from outside the aircraft. Recently-settled birds exploded into the air once again, a maelstrom of beating wings and startled cries as if today was the day the men came with their saws and bulldozers to desecrate this paradise on earth as every creature living in it knew they always would.

What the hell? she thought, *Justin doesn't have a gun.*

Then two more shots. A quick double-tap she felt in the pit of her stomach.

Silence now. Deep and full of the promise of more violence to come.

Panic gripped her, the urge to run overwhelming. And then

what? Be shot in the back by a maniac? Her eyes darted frantically looking for somewhere to hide.

Ha! Trees. Millions of them.

She pressed her back tightly up against a big one. Sweat trickling. In her hair. Down between her shoulder blades sticking her shirt to her itching skin, and then onwards, downwards, an impudent trickle between the cheeks of her ass. Her palms slick, humidity or fear, who knew or cared. Mosquitos buzzing incessantly, biting hungrily oblivious to the insect repellent.

On the ground, a large irregular-shaped rock called to her. A quick dart forward and it was in her hands, its weight comforting, its edges sharp.

Not daring to breath, ears straining.

The forest silent. Every living creature with survival instincts intact a mile away by now. The same couldn't be said for their two-legged cousins.

Then the sound of metal creaking and a soft *whumph* as a man landed on the ground, a sharp hiss of pain cutting through the still forest air.

Footsteps and the sound of trampled undergrowth. Coming her way.

Pressing her prickling back harder into the tree now, heightened senses feeling every ridge and groove in its bark.

Still not daring to breathe.

Then a man lumbered past dragging one leg. A small man. Heavy duffel bag in one hand, gun in the other looking like the arm that held it was broken.

Oblivious to the impending retribution, his time on Earth at an end so very soon.

A fast step out from behind the tree, no time for the guy to react. The heavy rock scything through the air, gym-toned arms and shoulders powering it towards its righteous target, the soft wet thud of the impact sending him staggering forward, stumbling, on his knees now, then another murderous blow to the bloody mess that a second ago was the back of his head.

On his face in the dirt, the gun on the ground two feet away. Not moving. But still breathing, you bastard.

She snatched up the gun. Wanting to use it so badly. See how he liked it. Finger twitching on the trigger.

No time. Because when the time came, the moment was to be savored.

She ran for the plane. Knowing it was already too late.

Like a slaughterhouse inside.

The pilot with half his head blown away, blood and gray brain matter spattering the window.

And Justin, eyes wide with shock and fear, two gaping bullet wounds in his chest. Sitting in his own blood, the floor awash with it.

Above the gore, the cheap gold cross he wore around his neck sparkling in the dappled light of this hell on earth.

How much good did that do you, you poor dead Good Samaritan?

She lifted it carefully over his head, held it tightly in her hand.

Not a memento. A reminder. Of how quickly life can turn to shit. Because the man with his face in the dirt twenty yards away would not be the only one to kill today.

Feeling sick, she felt inside Justin's pocket until she found his phone. The cops would be all over the place soon. No need to make their jobs too easy, the lazy pricks.

She pressed her lips to his brow, the taste of his sweat on her tongue, hot tears pricking the backs of her eyes behind closed lids.

Then it was time to go.

Back to the man on the ground pathetically trying to crawl away like the sub-human creature he was.

His gun felt so good in her hand. So right. Poetic justice fashioned into metal and polymer to put right a grievous and unforgiveable wrong.

It didn't take a rocket scientist to figure the bag he was dragging was stuffed full of illegal cash.

Not a fair exchange, more one spawned in hell.

A conscience forsaken for the sake of a few ill-gotten dollars.

The satisfaction, too. Let's not forget that as the gun kicked and the murdering bastard's body jerked. Two shots—an eye for an eye—and it's done.

Her only regret that it hadn't lasted longer. That the guy hadn't cried out as she took his life from him.

God was sure as hell smiling on the wicked today. The dead man was only a small murdering bastard. The bag of money weighed almost as much as he did, dead weight or not.

Up on her shoulder, fireman's-carry style, all those tedious workouts in the gym rewarded at long last. Not too far to the bayou.

Looked like the 'gators were going to get a free lunch today, after all.

The noise of the bar came back with a sucking rush and a bang as Laura stopped talking. A sudden cacophony of sound as all around them people came alive laughing and talking excitedly.

'What did you do with the money?' Evan said.

'Used most of it to set up my doctor's practice. I like to think that some good came out of Justin dying.'

She held his eyes. Daring him to contradict her. He had no intention of doing so. Thibaud Lejeune had deserved to die. She could've blown the money on booze and drugs for all he cared.

'There's only one thing I regret,' she said, then immediately corrected herself, a spiteful edge entering her voice. 'No, two. I wish his death hadn't been so easy. But more than that, I hate myself for the way I've abused Fleur's friendship.'

He'd have been hard pressed to say which of those conflicting sentiments contained more vitriol. He moved her on before she sank deeper into a trough of self-loathing.

'I'm assuming the video was in with the cash?'

She nodded, the hard light remaining in her eyes at the mention of something from which no good had, or ever could, come. Then she snorted, a sudden sharp bark filled with disgust tempered by an amused incredulity at the stupidity of men.

'I knew who was in it. The idiots named the file *Bray*.'

'I'll need it.'

'What for?'

'Call it a consolation prize for Lejeune when I don't give him you. *If* I don't give him you, I mean.'

She laughed, a hollow rattle without humor as befits a person who feels the lifeline they were thrown a moment ago has been pulled away, that it was only ever meant to tease. And as the laughter faded, it left a sneer on her face.

'And why would he accept that instead of me?'

'Because I'm going to make sure it's in his best interests to do so.'

Arlo shifted in his seat. Looking at him as if he was slowly turning into his father before his eyes. Evan ignored the look thinking the kid needed to get real. His old man took things to an extreme, but you didn't want to go too far the other way, either.

'Is the video at your house?' he said to Laura, then, when she nodded, 'Give Arlo your key and tell him where it's hidden.'

She hefted her bag onto the table as if it contained all the money she'd stolen from the plane. Dug around and came out with a ring of keys, threw them on the table in front of Arlo. Pointed.

'It's that one. You'll have to go up into the crawl space in the roof...'

Evan tuned them out as she ran through detailed instructions about where to find the thumb drive she'd hidden five years previously. Thinking so far, so good. Lejeune wouldn't be so easy. Before that, there was Laura's other story to listen to. And weigh up. Because for the life of him he couldn't see how she could convince him that he shouldn't hand her over to the badge-carrying grown-ups for the murder of Kevin Clark. However justified the killing of Thibaud Lejeune might have been in the heat of the moment, murdering Clark amounted to nothing more than callously covering her ass, shapely or otherwise.

They sat in silence watching Arlo all the way to the door. He turned around before going out as if he expected to catch them necking as soon as he was out of the way. Evan raised a hand and Arlo disappeared from sight.

Then Laura had him all to herself. Just not in the sort of way she might have hoped the previous evening.

'Tell me about Kevin Clark.'

And half an hour later when Arlo came back with a satisfied gleam in his eye and a thumb drive in his hand, Evan had a very different opinion of Dr. Laura Hunt MD.

48

It was a little after nine when Evan and Landry turned up at Lejeune's motel. The short journey from The Tap Room where Evan had left Laura with Arlo had been characterized by a brooding resentment on Landry's part. Evan figured Stan had told him how things were going to be after he'd talked to Arlo. Landry would not be dragging Arlo home against his will. What he would be doing is exactly what Evan told him.

Landry waited in the car while Evan went inside. Lejeune looked past him at Landry as he let Evan in.

'He ain't coming in?'

'He wants a cigarette. He'll join us later. Sorry about your windshield, by the way.'

Lejeune waved it off, the promise of the bigger prize looming endowing him with an all-encompassing largesse. The room and Lejeune's breath smelled as if he'd been celebrating in advance. A half-empty pint of whiskey and an all-the-way-empty glass sat beside an open laptop on the small desk pushed up against the wall.

Lejeune went over to the desk, ran his finger lightly over the laptop's touchpad to bring it to life. Refilled his glass while he was there. He didn't immediately offer to let Evan see what he'd found. Evan had to prove his bona fides first.

'What's your interest?' Lejeune said.

Evan couldn't see any reason why the truth wouldn't work—at least an out-of-date version of it.

'My client's son has gone missing. It's looking like the person who killed your brother is responsible.'

It was exactly what Lejeune wanted to hear. He pulled out the chair in front of the desk, offered it to Evan with a sweep of his hand.

'Take a look at that. You want a drink?'

'Not for me.'

He didn't bother sitting down. Leaned in and read the email that was open on the screen. It had been sent to Jack Bray the previous day.

I have the video. I have kept quiet about it for five years even though I believe a man like you deserves to burn in hell. I am not a blackmailer. I am not going to threaten to upload it to YouTube or social media, but now I feel under threat myself. People are asking questions. I don't need to remind you that if they find me, they also find the video. You have two choices. Do the world a favor and take your own worthless life. Or do something about the people asking questions. You can start with a private investigator called Evan Buckley.

It was exactly what he was expecting. It was still a shock to see his name in the same sentence as the threat. Even if the threat was vague—*do something*. Laura could still claim that she only meant gentle persuasion.

'Whatcha think of that?' Lejeune said. 'Bitch wants you out the way and she don't much care how.'

Evan couldn't disagree it was the other way of interpreting it.

Lejeune didn't give him a chance to answer the question, rhetorical or not.

'That ain't all.' He put his whiskey glass down, went back to the laptop. Came out of the *sent* folder and into the *inbox*. Then scrolled back years—literally. 'I was looking to see if there was anything from back when the bitch killed my brother.' He kept on scrolling, a mumbled *c'mon, c'mon* on his lips, the smell of whiskey on him strong in Evan's nose in the small airless room. He stopped at an email from five years ago, opened the attachment. '*Ha!* Look at that.'

Evan looked. It showed Laura Hunt entering a motel room that could have been the same one they were in now. She was carrying a sports duffel bag. Even a glass eye in a duck's ass could see she looked guilty as sin. She might as well have had a placard around her neck: *Up to no good. Arrest on sight*.

Lejeune spelled it out in case Evan was blind.

'She ain't just checking in. No way. She's up to something. I know that motel. Used to use it all the time for business. Until some guy was found dead there. All kinds of freaky shit going on. They cleaned their act up after that.'

Two thoughts went through Evan's mind as Lejeune talked. There was a good chance it was where the video of Jack Bray had been filmed. There was an even better chance the man who'd died there after getting up to *all kinds of freaky shit* had been Kevin Clark.

Seemed Lejeune was waiting for him to say something. He obliged with a complete waste of breath.

'It's definitely her.'

Lejeune wasn't listening, beyond wanting to hear confirmation of his own cleverness at having found it.

'Just wait. This gets better.'

He went back to the inbox. Evan stopped him before he moved on.

'Wait. Let me see who it's from.'

Lejeune ignored him, already scrolling.

'It's a bullshit email address. Mickey mouse at Gmail, whatever. There ain't no message. Only the picture.'

Lejeune was right. It was a waste of time. Evan didn't bother insisting he go back. Lejeune was hopping with excitement now as he found the next email he was looking for. The file extension of the attachment indicated that it was a video clip.

'You ready for this? Get yourself nice and comfortable before the movie starts. Sorry I ain't got no popcorn.'

He hit *play*. And by the time Evan leaned over and hit *pause* a minute later, his mind was made up, the way forward clear.

'That's who you're dealing with.' Lejeune said, jabbing his finger at the screen. 'Bitch killed my brother and now she wants to kill you. We need to find where she's at.'

He downed the remainder of his drink, poured himself another two fingers. This time Evan nodded when Lejeune offered the bottle to him. He fetched a plastic cup from the bathroom and let Lejeune pour. Then they silently toasted to an unspoken supposed common aim.

'She's not at home,' Evan said after taking the smallest sip.

'I just told you that.'

'I know, but I went there before coming here.'

Lejeune was instantly suspicious, animal cunning in his eyes as he remembered something he'd forgotten in his excitement to show Evan what he'd found on the laptop.

'You said you were checking out Ritter?'

Evan rocked his hand like maybe there was room for some misunderstanding—he'd said Laura Hunt and Lejeune had heard Ritter. Worked an apologetic note into his voice at being caught out.

'I already had my suspicions about her. I was going to call you from her house if she was there.'

Lejeune looked at him as if his mother had just told him the Tooth Fairy had announced a fifty percent increase in the money left for each tooth. But there was no anger. As if he accepted that all's fair in love and getting to the woman you want to kill first.

Evan patted his pocket before Lejeune had a chance to put his disbelief into words. Words that would very probably include *cocksucker*.

'You'll be glad I did.' He pulled out the thumb drive Arlo had recovered from Laura's house. 'I broke in and found this. It was on the floor in the kitchen. She must be really spooked if she dropped it and didn't even notice.'

He handed it to Lejeune. Waited while Lejeune turned it over in his fingers a couple times looking at it like his mother's long-lost wedding ring had been returned to him.

'You look like you recognize it.'

Lejeune's face hardened as the evidence against Laura Hunt grew ever more damning.

'Uh-huh.'

'I looked up Bray like you said.'

Lejeune wasn't listening, too intent on inserting the thumb drive into the laptop's USB port, then navigating to the file it contained.

Evan pointed at the screen as Lejeune clicked on the video.

'I've watched it. Bray's on it. How did you know?'

Lejeune had half his concentration on the video that had started to play, half on Evan's question. It left nothing to notice Evan pull his phone out of his pocket. He answered with the bragging confidence of a man comfortable in the company of a like-minded individual. One who shared his murderous desire for revenge.

'Because we made it, Thibaud and me. We were going to blackmail the cocksucker. Then Aguilar grabbed Thibaud. Thibaud had the video with him.'

Evan flicked his hand at the laptop again.

'You can turn that off. I don't need to watch it again.'

Lejeune did as he asked, his attention elsewhere as he stated the obvious.

'The video was on the plane. If the bitch had the video, she was at the plane. She killed my brother.'

'What are you going to do?'

Lejeune looked at him as if he'd suggested forgiveness was the way to go in the interests of Lejeune's immortal soul.

'Are you serious?'

'Uh-huh. Your brother killed her lover. She killed your brother. Sounds fair to me.'

Lejeune gawked at him.

'Fair my ass. Bitch is gonna get what's coming to her. I ain't thought about nothin' else for five years. I'm gonna kill her, nice and slow. Have a little fun first, good looking woman like that.' He jabbed his chest with his middle finger a couple times. 'That's what I call fair. You got a problem with that?'

Evan showed him his palms, went over to the door. Opened it. Landry was still where he'd left him in the car.

'Must have smoked a whole damn packet by now,' Lejeune said.

Evan ignored him, waved until he caught Landry's eye. He left the door open and came back into the room. Landry came in a minute later, closed the door behind him.

Evan made the introductions. Neither man said, *pleased to meet you*. Despite that, Lejeune seemed encouraged by the extra help in the task ahead.

'Now all we gotta do is find the bitch.'

Evan stopped him there.

'It's not going to happen, Lejeune.'

Lejeune had been in the middle of ejecting the thumb drive. His head came up as if he'd heard Landry cock the hammer on a gun behind him.

'What you talking about?'

'You've got the video,' Evan said. 'Do what you like with it. Blackmail Bray, post it on YouTube, it's up to you. But you're not getting Laura Hunt.'

Lejeune misunderstood him.

'No way. She killed my brother. She ain't done nothing to you except threaten you. And you don't have to worry about that after I'm finished with her.'

'Nobody's going to do anything to her.'

Lejeune still didn't get it.

'What? We gonna forgive her murdering ass, are we? Because you got the hots for her? Give her six *Hail Marys* and don't do it again? You a priest or something? Fuck that.'

Evan pulled out his phone, the voice recorder app still on the screen. He hit *play*. The phone's small speaker faithfully reproduced the anger and hatred in Lejeune's voice as it filled the room.

Bitch is gonna get what's coming to her. I ain't thought about nothin' else for five years. I'm gonna kill her, nice and slow.

Evan hit *pause*.

There was silence for a split second. Then Lejeune roared, a savage subhuman sound filled with rage and frustration. He charged at Evan and Landry standing side by side in front of the door. Until he saw the Colt Python now in Landry's hand pointing at his chest, that is. He stopped short like he'd run into a door, held up his hands.

'*Whoa!* No need for that. We can work something out here.'

Evan waved his phone at Lejeune.

'Anything happens to her and this goes to Detective Gauthier.'

Lejeune stared at him, lost for words.

'Why you doing this, man? She's gonna kill you. Get Ritter to kill you if she don't do it herself. You let her go and you'll be jumpin' at your shadow for the rest of your life. You won't never be safe.'

An irritating whining note had entered Lejeune's voice to go with what he saw as a compelling argument. Kill them before they kill you. A variation on do unto others as you would have them do unto you.

Except it was more than that for Evan. It was a wake-up call.

It highlighted the world of difference between the killings of Justin Sanders and Thibaud Lejeune. Made him feel stupid and naive for thinking it was as simple as an eye for an eye. Filled him with a blood lust that threatened to consume him.

'Face down on the floor. *Now!*'

Lejeune stared at him, realization entering his eyes that he'd misjudged the man he'd thought of as an ally in his murderous quest. He looked from Evan to Landry with his gun and back again, no room for argument or bargaining on their faces. He lowered himself to his knees without further complaint or pleading, then down onto his belly, face pressed into the none-too-clean carpet.

Landry needed no instruction. He stood over Lejeune, his gun aimed at the back of his head.

Then Evan spelled it out for Lejeune, the anger vibrating in his voice.

'Your brother killed a man in cold blood who did nothing more than risk his own life by going into a crashed plane to see if he could help. You're right, I think anyone who killed a murdering piece of shit like that deserves to get what's coming to them. A medal. And I think somebody needs to finish the job Laura Hunt started. Put an end to every last Lejeune to make sure that particular mis-step of nature doesn't go any further. You want to give me one good reason why I shouldn't walk out that door and wait in the car while Landry does the world a favor?'

Lejeune shook his head, defiance in his words despite his situation.

'Do what you want, cocksucker.'

Evan felt all the anger drain out of him, a weariness left behind. There was no dealing with a man like Lejeune. Not while evil men recognized the goodness in their adversary. Even if the adversary has someone like Landry to actually pull the trigger.

The truth in his own words sank in now that the anger had fallen away. Made him realize how close he'd come to embracing the world of men like Lejeune and Landry and Ritter. How it would be a grievous sin to walk away and leave a man like Lejeune free to persecute a man like Bray, himself as bad in different ways, for his own personal gain using an obscene video that condemned them both.

Lejeune's car keys were on the table along with the laptop and whiskey bottle. Evan took them and searched Lejeune's car, came back five minutes later with a roll of duct tape—the same roll that Lejeune had used to tie Laura Hunt to her bed. They taped his wrists and ankles, then strapped him to the bed with what remained of it, the final piece stuck over his mouth. Evan spent a minute with the laptop, made a copy of the video file before sending an email to Bray using the same email address Laura Hunt had used.

Ritter is in police custody in Baton Rouge. Detective Gauthier is the investigating officer. If you pull enough strings and get him out, he'll find Innocent Lejeune tied up in room 23 at the Super 6 Inn on I49. The original thumb drive is there with him. I have a copy. As I told you before, I'm not a blackmailer. I just want to be left alone.

True to his word, he left the thumb drive on the table, but took the laptop away with him, as well as the door key. He switched on the bedside radio to mask Lejeune's desperate protestations behind the tape, then dropped Landry back at his motel.

Feeling a lightness of spirit that he hadn't experienced since he arrived in Lafayette, he drove to Lou Bordelon's house to bring a ray of righteous sunshine into a good man's life.

49

Evan sent up a silent prayer of thanks for the lateness of the hour when he got to Bordelon's house. It minimized the chances of Bordelon's wife answering the door. She would see the reason for his visit in his eyes, reinforcing her view that she didn't understand men at all, nor did she want to. In the process, she'd make him feel ashamed that he should provoke such a feeling in another person, male or female. Seemed Bordelon was thinking the same thing. He didn't appear surprised and immediately stepped outside when he saw who it was. Evan led him to the car to get more privacy still.

He let Bordelon go first once they were settled inside. The guy wouldn't be able to concentrate until he got what he had to say off his chest—nor could Evan blame him.

'Detective Gauthier called me not long after you came to see me. Filled me in on a few of the details you forgot to mention.' His brow creased in mock concentration as if those details eluded him. 'Something about an anonymous tip-off concerning a guy called Ritter who'd been left in his car trunk with a bullet wound in the shoulder?'

Evan worked hard at looking suitably penitent, not sure whether he pulled it off.

'Yeah, that was me . . .' He took Bordelon through it, how Ritter had followed him using the tracker he'd fixed to Evan's car, how they'd ambushed him—not mentioning Landry by name—and how Ritter came off second despite shooting at them first.

'Should I ask who the other guy with you was?' Bordelon said.

'Probably not.'

A wide, knowing smile broke out on Bordelon's face when Evan then updated him with the news that Arlo had been found, alive and well. And it had nothing to do with him liking a happy ever after ending.

'Your job here is done. Your client's missing son has been found. Time to go home. And yet here you still are at my house in the middle of the night. Looks to me like you're a man after my own heart. I hope for your sake you haven't got a dog.'

Evan didn't reply immediately. He let the raw bitterness behind Bordelon's remark—the purpose of which seemed more to punish himself than for any other reason—subside for a moment or two. He then updated Bordelon on what he'd learned as a result of speaking to Kevin Clark's girlfriend, attributing a lot of the credit to Bordelon for having supplied a current address. He finished by telling him that the missing passenger-cum-prisoner on the plane had been identified as Thibaud Lejeune, brother of Innocent.

Bordelon became progressively quieter as Evan laid it all out for him. He didn't ask questions or comment on the suspicious death of Kevin Clark. Nor did he ask for an explanation about how Evan had found out everything that he had, whose help he'd enlisted.

Because it was becoming increasingly clear that this wasn't simply a late-night courtesy call to update Bordelon on the case that had ruined his law enforcement career.

There was a point to it. And Bordelon could taste it, didn't want to waste time with questions.

'Innocent Lejeune is tied to the bed in room twenty-three at the Super 6 Inn at Carencro,' Evan said. 'He has a compromising video of a member of the Louisiana House of Representatives called Jack Bray with him. Ritter works for Bray. He's the sick bastard who killed your dog in order to protect Bray. I've set things in motion that make me think your friend Detective Gauthier is about to get an unwelcome call from above telling him to let Ritter go immediately. When he does, Ritter will be heading directly to room twenty-three at the Super 6 Inn.' He lifted his butt off the seat, dug into his jeans' pocket. Offered the motel key to Bordelon. 'I thought you might like to be there waiting for him when he arrives.'

Bordelon took the key, looked to Evan as if he might kiss it— better that than kiss him, he supposed. He expected Bordelon to get out of the car with a curt man-to-man nod, no further words required. *A man's gotta do*, and all that stuff his wife didn't understand. Bordelon put his hand on the door handle. Then changed his mind, settled back into his seat again.

Evan knew what was coming.

'Seems to me you've done a damn good job, here,' Bordelon said, his voice filled with an admiration that masked the sting in the tail coming. 'We know who the prisoner on the plane was. We know what was on board with him. We know who sent who to keep a lid on it all. About the only thing we don't appear'— putting a lot of emphasis on the word—'to know is who actually killed Thibaud Lejeune after he shot Justin Sanders to death.' He raised a finger, a point of clarification on its way. 'Of course, when I say *we*, that doesn't necessarily include you.' He stopped short of jabbing Evan in the chest, even if Evan felt as if he'd used a cattle prod to do so.

'Are you asking if I know who it was?'

'I am.'

'The answer's yes. And the answer to the next question is no.' Bordelon shook his head.

'I wasn't going to ask you to tell me. But I'd be interested to know how you arrived at the decision to let them, or to be more accurate, let *her* walk.'

Evan pointed at the key in Bordelon's hand.

'Will you be taking your nail when you go to wait in that motel room?'

Bordelon held his gaze. No hesitation in his answer, no self-doubt in his voice.

'And a sixteen-ounce claw hammer.' He massaged his bicep, strong fingers working the muscle. Fingers Evan would've sworn looked excited at the prospect. 'I can feel my arm aching already.'

Evan felt something else every bit as vividly. The impression of the nail hole in Bordelon's front door under his fingertip. He wished he could be there with him in room twenty-three. And since he couldn't, he had no problem with telling Bordelon exactly what put him in the unenviable position of having to decide the fate of each man or woman.

'I'd never have guessed it,' Bordelon said as finally he went to get out of the car.

Evan stopped him, handed him Ritter's burner phone.

'Take this, as well.'

He watched Bordelon as he stalked up the path, no sign of a bad back in his purposeful stride, then buzzed the window down.

'Send me a picture when you're done,' he called, adding an unnecessary parting slur on Bordelon's intelligence. 'Not from that phone, of course.'

50

'You better not be here to kick me in the balls this time,' Stan Fraser said

Guillory gave him a tight smile. Evan didn't know about Fraser, but his own cojones contracted at the vitriol behind it—and in her voice.

'Then you better not give me a reason to, Mr. Fraser.'

Fraser smiled back as if she'd wished him *Happy Birthday*. He got up from his usual table, led them to a booth that offered more privacy. Evan sat in the middle. As if he was keeping two squabbling children apart.

Guillory hadn't been happy at the choice of venue. But Evan said Fraser deserved to hear what had happened seeing as his son had set it in motion. The alternative was the Jerusalem Tavern.

So here they all were in the den of iniquity that was The Backroom.

At least Evan didn't have to give Fraser the bad news. Arlo wasn't coming home. Not ever. Arlo had made that very clear himself on the phone. Evan didn't mention that Arlo had told him in private that the events of the past week had made him twice as determined to keep a minimum of half of the continent between himself and not-so-dear old dad.

Evan started by explaining how Ralph Fontenot had given Arlo the assignment as a means of proving himself.

Immediately, Fraser interrupted.

'Did Arlo get the job?' Sounding like the prognosis for Fontenot's legs wasn't good if not.

'He doesn't want it.'

Fraser shrugged, *it's only a job*, unaware of what was coming. Unlike Guillory. She was almost bursting at what was soon to follow. It was the only reason she'd agreed to tag along. Evan extended his hand towards her. *The table's all yours.*

'The thing is,' she said, 'he enjoyed the challenge and the excitement. What he didn't like was the idea of getting into dangerous situations without a gun, a legal one, that is, and some kind of official standing.'

She did a great job of making *official standing* sound like *badge*.

Fraser caught on immediately, dismay draining the color from his face.

'You're telling me—'

'Yep. He wants to be a police officer.'

Evan wanted to congratulate her for remaining seated. Not climbing onto the table, calling for everybody's attention.

Fraser was looking as if he'd have preferred it if she'd kicked him in the balls.

'You're kidding me.'

Guillory smiled again, real pleasure in it.

'Nope. There's a chance he might not be accepted. But a lot of people down there are going to back his application. He has good instincts.'

They all heard the longer version.

Living with you for the formative years of his life has given him the ability to spot a criminal a mile off.

Then a wistful note entered her voice, sadness at an opportunity missed.

'I only wish it was here and not down in Lafayette. I could take him under my wing. Just think, we could arrest you together.'

Evan jumped in before she got carried away—although he couldn't imagine what she might say next.

'Shall I continue with the story?'

Fraser told him to go ahead. Trying to pretend Guillory didn't exist. He didn't interrupt again, whether because he had nothing to ask or because he hadn't liked where the first interruption had led was impossible to say. Until Evan got to the part about the situation he'd set up with Bordelon.

'You know if Ritter turned up at the motel?' Fraser said.

'If he did, Bordelon hasn't told me about it.'

Guillory gave him a questioning look, one that Fraser missed. It suggested he'd be hearing more about it.

He'd saved Laura Hunt's story until last. He took them through it now, told them how she'd been Justin Sanders' lover, how she'd killed Thibaud Lejeune as he tried to flee the scene after shooting Sanders and the pilot. They both looked more disgusted at the calculated way she'd abused Fleur Sanders' trust and friendship than they did at the killing of a bottom-feeder like Thibaud Lejeune.

Stan put into words the question that was on his and Guillory's minds. He put it differently than she would, sounding as if he was looking for pointers.

'How come you get to play God and decide who walks and who doesn't?'

Guillory nodded, good point.

'I'll get to that,' Evan said and got a scowl back from them both. 'Kevin Clark owed a bunch of Baton Rouge gangsters a ton of money for gambling debts. They're the sort of people who accept body parts when you can't pay in cash. He told them he knew where he could get the money. Except they didn't trust him. They thought he'd run. This is what happened next.'

He got out his phone, found the video clip that had been emailed to Dr. Hunt that Lejeune had found on her laptop. They all leaned in as he hit *play*.

A cheap motel room came into view. Then the focus settled on a man tied to a wooden chair. It wasn't possible to see his face. Not only because his body was slumped forwards and his head hanging down. A clear plastic bag covered his head, condensation from his breath misting it. Without warning, a hand appeared from off-screen, whipped the bag off, then grabbed a big handful of the man's hair. Pulled his head back. They all knew they were looking at Kevin Clark's oxygen-starved face.

A man's bottom half appeared behind Clark before he'd heaved two gasps. A fast blur of movement, and the plastic bag was over Clark's head once more. He kicked and thrashed and bucked sucking in air that wasn't there, the plastic drawn tighter and tighter across his gaping mouth, distorting his features, the whole sickening episode made surreal by the lack of sound, like some cult 1920s snuff movie.

Evan hit *pause*, froze the horrific scene mid-gasp.

'That was emailed to Laura Hunt. If you watch to the end, you'll see that they don't kill him.'

'They will.' This from Stan, a man it could be argued who ought to know.

Evan ignored the interruption, carried on.

'Then Laura got a call demanding the money Kevin Clark owed, plus extra for their trouble.'

Stan nodded approvingly. Good to hear that standards weren't slipping in Baton Rouge.

'Laura paid what they asked,' Evan said. 'Compared to what she'd stolen it was chicken feed. She was told to drop it off at a motel. She went there, made the drop, didn't see anyone. The next day she received another email with a photograph attached.'

He scrolled to the date-stamped picture that Innocent Lejeune had found showing her entering the motel room, a sports duffel bag in her hand, the guilt-ridden expression on her face underscoring the general air of furtiveness about her.

Stan smiled broadly at the further proof that the men down in Louisiana knew their onions.

'That's the same motel where the video was taken and where Kevin Clark was subsequently found dead,' Evan said. 'The bag Laura was carrying could easily have contained the gas mask and all the other paraphernalia that was found. You can see she's a big, strong woman. She fits most people's pre-conceived idea of what a dominatrix should look like.'

Stan was looking as if his day had just improved, a new avenue of business that hadn't occurred to him before presenting itself.

'And they've been blackmailing her ever since?'

'Nope. She never heard from them again.'

Stan gawked at him. As if he'd said Jesus had appeared to them as they'd been driving out of the motel lot, persuading them to renounce the evil of their ways, donate the cash they'd extorted from Laura to the church, then go forth to spread the word.

'Never heard from them?'

'Nope. She figured Clark told them she was a doctor and made good money, but that was all. He didn't tell them his suspicions about what she'd stolen or they'd definitely have come back for more.'

Stan scratched his jaw like he'd heard some strange things, but this was the strangest.

'And he ends up dying to protect her. Stupid prick.'

'You've got that wrong,' Guillory cut in. 'He didn't think they would kill him. People like that hurt you, hurt your family. They don't kill you. Not if they think they'll make money out of you in the future.' She paused, the sole purpose being to let the unspoken words sink in—*you should know*. 'Clark thought they'd let him go. The reason he didn't mention the cash she'd taken from the plane was because he was planning on extorting her himself as soon as they did.'

Stan looked at Evan, got a nod of confirmation back.

'Clark was right to believe they were going to let him go. His problem was that he didn't take account of Ritter. I remembered Clark's girlfriend telling me how the cops showed her a grainy CCTV image of a man hanging around. I called her, asked her if there was anything she remembered about him. All she could say was that he was tall and wearing a light-colored safari jacket. She remembered it because she bought one like it for her father. That's what Ritter was wearing when we caught him.

'I figure Ritter was suspicious of Clark. He thought he was either at the plane with Sanders despite what he claimed, or he knew who was. Then Clark moved into a much better neighborhood and Ritter's thinking, *I was right*. He didn't know Clark's girlfriend owns the property. I figure Ritter was watching him when the guys he owed money grabbed him. Suddenly Ritter's scared he'll lead them to the video. Except Laura Hunt came up with the cash Clark owed and they left him in the motel room still alive. That's when Ritter went in and finished him off. Set it up to look like an autoerotic accident.'

Stan was shaking his head, the confusion of a man who doesn't leave loose ends on his face.

'It doesn't make sense. If Ritter saw them take Clark to the motel, he must've seen Laura Hunt go there, too. How come she got a free pass?'

'Ritter was aware of Kevin Clark from the police file, but not Laura Hunt. She wasn't in it. When she turned up at the motel, he assumed she was part of the gang's setup. He couldn't see what was in the bag, after all. Then, when he killed Clark and they didn't hear anything more from the blackmailers, he's thinking *job done*. As Innocent Lejeune said, she was one lucky bitch.'

Evan and Guillory left The Backroom shortly after. Stan was looking like he couldn't wait to get rid of them, anyway. Give him a chance to call some people in Louisiana, see if he couldn't buy a piece of their action.

Guillory linked her arm through Evan's as they walked. He got the impression it was less about affection and more about making sure he couldn't run away when she started with the difficult questions.

'Did you tell Fleur Sanders about Laura Hunt?'

He gave her a pained look. Flicked out the fingers on his left hand to start counting off.

'By my reckoning, Fleur's got her back yard, her cat, her memories and one friend, Dr. Laura Hunt. You want to know if I took fifty percent of that away from her in my relentless pursuit of the truth? Took all of Laura's considerable guilt and turned it into fresh pain for Fleur?'

She pulled her head back as if she'd scorched her eyebrows opening the oven door.

'Sorry I asked. You want to tell me the truth about Bordelon now?'

He didn't bother denying the earlier lie, already reaching for his phone.

'Tell? Or show?'

'Show, definitely.' A throatiness creeping into her voice, sworn police officer or not.

He found the image Bordelon had sent him from his personal cell phone taken in room twenty-three.

'That's Ritter, is it?' she said as she took the phone from him.

'Yep.'

'Looks painful.'

'No more so than childbirth, I'm led to believe.'

He got a sharp hiss back at his reckless words.

'I wouldn't let your sister hear you telling me that or you'll be the one with both hands nailed to the floor. I don't suppose you know how Ritter ended up that way, do you?'

'Funny you should ask. Bordelon called me . . .'

Lou Bordelon slipped quietly into the motel room, tool bag in his gloved hand. On the bed Innocent Lejeune struggled against the duct tape binding him. Sweat beading his face and eyes wide with fear, the muffled nngh, nngh, nngh coming from behind the tape across his mouth competing with the radio playing softly on the nightstand.

Bordelon ignored him, scouted around the small room. The thumb drive with the compromising video of Jack Bray was sitting on a cheap desk up against the wall, a half-empty bottle of whiskey and an empty glass beside it.

He fetched a plastic cup from the bathroom, poured a couple of inches for himself and a couple more into the glass, then emptied the contents of a small vial into it, gave it a quick stir with his finger.

Back in the bathroom, he opened and closed the door a couple of times, satisfied that the radio masked any sound. Gun in hand, he switched out the light, pulled the door to. Lejeune was visible on the bed through a two-inch crack, the exterior door beyond him.

Time passed. Too fast and too slow in equal measure as images both good and bad raced through his mind, helped bolster his resolve.

He came alert at the sound of the outside door opening cautiously. Then a man in a blood-stained safari jacket stepped quickly into the room locking the door behind him.

Ritter.

Exactly as Evan had described him.

Staring at Lejeune helpless and writhing on the bed like Christmas had come early, the desperate nngh, nngh, nngh louder now as Lejeune saw the news of his death in Ritter's eyes.

Bordelon bit down, forced himself to remain still, remain silent. Be patient. Ignore the overwhelming urge to burst into the room, jam the gun down the sicko's throat and break every tooth in his filthy mouth as he emptied the clip, forget about the nail.

Ritter went to the nightstand, turned up the volume until Bordelon could no longer hear Lejeune's muffled cries. With the tape over Lejeune's mouth Ritter's job was already half done. He pulled the pillow sharply out from under Lejeune's head, clamped it over his face. Hand squashing his nose, his whole weight bearing down as Lejeune thrashed beneath him.

For his part, Lou Bordelon thanked the Lord that he no longer carried a badge with the obligations it entailed. Thinking about underage migrant girls in search of a better life. On their backs in cheap motels such as this one while sweating married men humped and grunted on top of them. Much as the man who enslaved them for his own profit was grunting now as he fought for his final breaths.

So it was that Lou Bordelon reached an accommodation with his conscience as he watched one evil man kill another for the benefit of a third.

When the last limp kick had petered out, and Ritter straightened up, his back to him, Bordelon stepped silently from his hiding place into the room. Gun in one hand, Ritter's burner phone in the other.

Like the Angel of Death with the twin harbingers of Ritter's doom in his hands.

'Hey!'

Ritter spun around, stared slack-jawed at him. Pillow clasped in both hands like a child from hell clutching a favorite teddy bear, Lejeune's lifeless body below him as Bordelon caught the scene on Ritter's burner phone.

Bordelon moved quickly now, put himself between Ritter and the door. Forced him at gunpoint face-down onto the floor in the middle of the room. He placed the whiskey glass on the floor beside him, stepped away. Took the hammer from his tool bag, felt its honest weight in his hand. Pointing with it at the glass.

'Drink it or I'll beat you senseless and pour it down your throat.'

Ritter took the glass, downed the contents in one, his eyes never leaving the hammer. He knew who Bordelon was. And the rattle of the glass against his teeth made it clear he knew why he'd brought the hammer.

Then Bordelon watched and waited. Sipping from the plastic cup of whiskey in his hand as the ketamine did its work, Ritter's muscle function deserting him as he slipped deeper into the detached, hallucinogenic state drug abusers call the k-hole. Still conscious and with a dream-like awareness of what was happening as Bordelon took a pair of matching six-inch nails from his bag then stretched the helpless man out on the floor like Christ on the cross.

And when it was done, the blood pooling under Ritter's splayed hands soaking into the cheap carpet, he sealed the burner phone and the thumb drive in a plastic evidence bag, stuffed it all in Ritter's silently screaming mouth.

Guillory stopped abruptly as Evan finished talking. Searching the ground at her feet as if she'd dropped something. He stopped with her, a good idea of what was coming in his mind.

'Lost something?'

'Uh-uh. Looking to see if there are any loose ends that haven't been tidied up.'

He rocked his hand doing a very poor job of keeping the self-satisfied smile off his face.

'Gauthier called Bordelon, told him about the unexplained scene the local cops found in the motel room. How a man had somehow nailed himself to the floor.'

'Because he was feeling guilty for murdering an asswipe who forced underage illegal migrant girls into prostitution?'

'Exactly. Then Gauthier told him how he'd been in the hardware store and saw something that made everything fall into place. It was a product called *Buckley*. Apparently, it was advertised as the best way to remove the Teflon coating from criminals or other lowlifes who deserve to be dead or in jail.'

'Really? Is it still available? We could do with some of that around here.'

He shook his head sadly.

'It was withdrawn from the market. Too dangerous in untrained hands.'

She looked down at her own capable hands. Resignation in her voice at even their failure to control this dangerous substance.

'I don't think God had anything like that in mind when he was designing hands.'

'Maybe next time, huh?'

She hoped not.

BOOKS BY JAMES HARPER

The Evan Buckley Thrillers

BAD TO THE BONES

When Evan Buckley's latest client ends up swinging on a rope, he's ready to call it a day. But he's an awkward cuss with a soft spot for a sad story and he takes on one last job—a child and husband who disappeared ten years ago. It's a long-dead investigation that everybody wants to stay that way, but he vows to uncover the truth—and in the process, kick into touch the demons who come to torment him every night.

KENTUCKY VICE

Maverick private investigator Evan Buckley is no stranger to self-induced mayhem—but even he's mystified by the jam college buddy Jesse Springer has got himself into. When Jesse shows up with a wad of explicit photographs that arrived in the mail, Evan finds himself caught up in the most bizarre case of blackmail he's ever encountered—Jesse swears blind he can't remember a thing about it.

SINS OF THE FATHER

Fifty years ago, Frank Hanna made a mistake. He's never forgiven himself. Nor has anybody else for that matter. Now the time has come to atone for his sins, and he hires maverick PI Evan Buckley to peel back fifty years of lies and deceit to uncover the tragic story hidden underneath. Trouble is, not everybody likes a happy ending and some very nasty people are out to make sure he doesn't succeed.

NO REST FOR THE WICKED

When an armed gang on the run from a botched robbery that left a man dead invade an exclusive luxury hotel buried in the mountains of upstate New York, maverick P.I. Evan Buckley has got his work cut out. He just won a trip for two and was hoping for a well-earned rest. But when the gang takes Evan's partner Gina hostage along with the other guests and their spirited seven-year-old daughter, he can forget any kind of rest.

RESURRECTION BLUES

After Levi Stone shows private-eye Evan Buckley a picture of his wife Lauren in the arms of another man, Evan quickly finds himself caught up in Lauren's shadowy past. The things he unearths force Levi to face the bitter truth—that he never knew his wife at all—or any of the dark secrets that surround her mother's death and the disappearance of her father, and soon Evan's caught in the middle of a lethal vendetta.

HUNTING DIXIE

Haunted by the unsolved disappearance of his wife Sarah, PI Evan Buckley loses himself in other people's problems. But when Sarah's scheming and treacherous friend Carly shows up promising new information, the past and present collide violently for Evan. He knows he can't trust her, but he hasn't got a choice when she confesses what she's done, leaving Sarah prey to a vicious gang with Old Testament ideas about crime and punishment.

THE ROAD TO DELIVERANCE

Evan Buckley's wife Sarah went to work one day and didn't come home. He's been looking for her ever since. As he digs deeper into the unsolved death of a man killed by the side of the road, the last known person to see Sarah alive, he's forced to re-trace the footsteps of her torturous journey, unearthing a dark secret from her past that drove her desperate attempts to make amends for the guilt she can never leave behind.

SACRIFICE

When PI Evan Buckley's mentor asks him to check up on an old friend, neither of them are prepared for the litany of death and destruction that he unearths down in the Florida Keys. Meanwhile Kate Guillory battles with her own demons in her search for salvation and sanity. As their paths converge, each of them must make an impossible choice that stretches conscience and tests courage, and in the end demands sacrifice—what would you give to get what you want?

ROUGH JUSTICE

After a woman last seen alive twenty years ago turns up dead, PI Evan Buckley heads off to a small town on the Maine coast where he unearths a series of brutal unsolved murders. The more he digs, lifting the lid on old grievances and buried injustices that have festered for half a lifetime, the more the evidence points to a far worse crime, leaving him facing an impossible dilemma – disclose the terrible secrets he's uncovered or assume the role of hanging judge and dispense a rough justice of his own.

TOUCHING DARKNESS

When PI Evan Buckley stops for a young girl huddled at the side of the road on a deserted stretch of highway, it's clear she's running away from someone or something—however vehemently she denies it. At times angry and hostile, at others scared and vulnerable, he's almost relieved when she runs out on him in the middle of the night. Except he has a nasty premonition that he hasn't heard the last of her. Nor does it take long before he's proved horribly right, the consequences dire for himself and Detective Kate Guillory.

A LONG TIME COMING

Five years ago, PI Evan Buckley's wife Sarah committed suicide in a mental asylum. Or so they told him. Now there's a different woman in her grave and he's got a stolen psychiatric report in his hand and a tormented scream running through his head. Someone is lying to him. With his own sanity at stake, he joins forces with a disgraced ex-CIA agent on a journey to confront the past that leads him to the jungles of Central America and the aftermath of a forgotten war, where memories are long and grievances still raw.

LEGACY OF LIES

Twenty years ago, Detective Kate Guillory's father committed suicide. Nobody has ever told her why. Now a man is stalking her. When PI Evan Buckley takes on the case, his search takes him to the coal mining mountains of West Virginia and the hostile aftermath of a malignant cult abandoned decades earlier. As he digs deeper into the unsolved crimes committed there and discovers the stalker's bitter grudge against Kate, one thing becomes horrifyingly clear – what started back then isn't over yet.

DIG TWO GRAVES

Boston heiress Arabella Carlson has been in hiding for thirty years. Now she's trying to make it back home. But after PI Evan Buckley saves her from being stabbed to death, she disappears again. Hired by her dying father to find her and bring her home safe before the killers hunting her get lucky, he finds there's more than money at stake as he opens up old wounds, peeling back a lifetime of lies and deceit. Someone's about to learn a painful lesson the hard way: Before you embark on a journey of revenge, dig two graves.

ATONEMENT

When PI Evan Buckley delves into an unsolved bank robbery from forty years ago that everyone wants to forget, he soon learns it's anything but what it seems to be. From the otherworldly beauty of Caddo Lake and the East Texas swamps to the bright lights and cheap thrills of Rehoboth Beach, he follows the trail of a nameless killer. Always one step behind, he discovers that there are no limits to the horrific crimes men's greed drives them to commit, not constrained by law or human decency.

THE JUDAS GATE

When a young boy's remains are found in a shallow grave on land belonging to PI Evan Buckley's avowed enemy, the monster Carl Hendricks, the police are desperate for Evan's help in solving a case that's been dead in the water for the past thirteen years. Hendricks is dying, and Evan is the only person he'll share his deathbed confession with. Except Evan knows Hendricks of old. Did he really kill the boy? And if so, why does he want to confess to Evan?

OLD SCORES

When upcoming country music star Taylor Harris hires a private investigator to catch her cheating husband, she gets a lot more than she bargained for. He's found a secret in her past that even she's not aware of - a curse on her life, a blood feud hanging over her for thirty years. But when he disappears, it's down to PI Evan Buckley to pick up the pieces. Was the threat real? And if so, did it disappear along with the crooked investigator? Or did it just get worse?

ONCE BITTEN

When PI Evan Buckley's mentor, Elwood Crow, asks a simple favor of him – to review a twenty-year-old autopsy report – there's only one thing Evan can be sure of: simple is the one thing it won't be. As he heads off to Cape Ann on the Massachusetts coast Evan soon finds himself on the trail of a female serial killer, and the more he digs, the more two questions align themselves. Why has the connection not been made before? And is Crow's interest in finding the truth or in saving his own skin?

NEVER GO BACK

When the heir to a billion-dollar business empire goes missing in the medieval city of Cambridge in England, PI Evan Buckley heads across the Atlantic on what promises to be a routine assignment. But as Evan tracks Barrett Bradlee from the narrow cobbled streets of the city to the windswept watery expanses of the East Anglian fens, it soon becomes clear that the secretive family who hired him to find the missing heir haven't told him the whole truth.

SEE NO EVIL

When Ava Hart's boyfriend, Daryl Pierce, is shot to death in his home on the same night he witnessed a man being abducted, the police are quick to write it off as a case of wrong place, wrong time. Ava disagrees. She's convinced they killed him. And she's hired PI Evan Buckley to unearth the truth. Trouble is, as Evan discovers all too soon, Ava wouldn't recognize the truth if it jumped up and bit her on the ass.

DO UNTO OTHERS

Five years ago, a light aircraft owned by Mexican drug baron and people trafficker Esteban Aguilar went down in the middle of the Louisiana swamps. The pilot and another man were found dead inside, both shot to death. The prisoner who'd been handcuffed in the back was nowhere to be found. And now it's down to PI Evan Buckley to find crime boss Stan Fraser's son Arlo who's gone missing trying to get to the bottom of what the hell happened.

Exclusive books for my Readers' Group
FALLEN ANGEL

When Jessica Henderson falls to her death from the window of her fifteenth-floor apartment, the police are quick to write it off as an open and shut case of suicide. The room was locked from the inside, after all. But Jessica's sister doesn't buy it and hires

Evan Buckley to investigate. The deeper Evan digs, the more he discovers the dead girl had fallen in more ways than one.

A ROCK AND A HARD PLACE

Private-eye Evan Buckley's not used to getting something for nothing. So when an unexpected windfall lands in his lap, he's intrigued. Not least because he can't think what he's done to deserve it. Written off by the police as one more sad example of mindless street crime, Evan feels honor-bound to investigate, driven by his need to give satisfaction to a murdered woman he never knew.

Join my mailing list at www.jamesharperbooks.com and get your FREE copies of Fallen Angel and A Rock And A Hard Place.

For Leonard

Printed in Great Britain
by Amazon